Sawyer and I ran through the parking lot and hopped into my car like we were skipping school, only much better than that one time I tried it by walking across the football field during morning announcements like I was under a cloak of invisibility. I floored it—you know, in case the scooter guy was after us on his fifteen-mile-an-hour hot wheels—and headed straight for Starbucks.

We were in a fit of giggles when my phone rang Duran Duran's "Union of the Snake."

"Hey, Kim, what's up?"

Kim didn't ask me what was so funny. Her voice was tight and had an echo like she was cupping the mouthpiece with her hand. "You need to get down here right now and help me with this disaster. One of the tour guests is dead. . . ."

Books by Libby Klein

CLASS REUNIONS ARE MURDER

MIDNIGHT SNACKS ARE MURDER

RESTAURANT WEEKS ARE MURDER

THEATER WEEKS ARE MURDER

WINE TASTINGS ARE MURDER

Published by Kensington Publishing Corp.

Wine Tastings
Are
MURDER

LIBBY KLEIN

KENSINGTON BOOKS
www.kensingtonbooks.com

KENSINGTON BOOKS are published by

Kensington Publishing Corp.
119 West 40th Street
New York, NY 10018

All Kensington titles, imprints, and distributed lines are available at special quantity discounts for bulk purchases for sales promotion, premiums, fund-raising, and educational or institutional use.

Special book excerpts or customized printings can also be created to fit specific needs. For details, write or phone the office of the Kensington Sales Manager: Kensington Publishing Corp., 119 West 40th Street, New York, NY 10018. Attn. Sales Department. Phone: 1-800-221-2647.

Kensington and the K logo Reg. U.S. Pat. & TM Off.

First Kensington Books Mass Market Paperback Printing: December 2020

ISBN-13: 978-1-4967-2339-0
ISBN-10: 1-4967-2339-2

ISBN-13: 978-1-4967-2340-6 (ebook)
ISBN-10: 1-4967-2340-6 (ebook)

10 9 8 7 6 5 4 3 2 1

Printed in the United States of America

For
Carol and Vicki
Laverne and Shirley
Lucy and Ethel
In a world full of rock stars, you're mine.

And for Sawyer. Every girl needs a ride or die.

Chapter One

Kale frittata is proof that I'll eat anything if it has enough cheese in it. I'd read on the Internet that a famous celebrity lost fifty pounds on the kale diet, so I thought it was foolproof. It was like eating an omelet full of yard clippings. I'd lost nothing in the nine days of my sentence, and I was starting to think the secret to celebrity weight loss was starvation, because right now I'd rather eat nothing than another forkful of misery.

I should have been further along with my workout this morning, but I was dragging. The sun was already bobbing in the Atlantic like an abandoned pink beach ball. I'd been seeing a crunchy doctor of Alternative Wellness since returning to Cape May six months ago. She was convinced I was sick because my body was under stress, and she wanted me only doing yoga. She would not approve of my six a.m. tromp down the boardwalk on very little sleep any more than my current Hollywood crackpot nutrition plan. But then Dr. Melinda wasn't overweight and didn't have two men wooing her for a romantic commitment. At least not that I knew of. Maybe she did. The topic never came up when she was lecturing me about sleeping more and trying to get healthy instead of trying to get skinny. All advice that I was currently ignoring in my desperate push to look good in lingerie without investing in blackout drapes. Not that anything was happening, mind you. But if the opportunity were to arise, I wanted to be prepared.

I made a hundred-and-eighty-degree turn where the cement promenade smacked into the beach grass and started the mile-and-a-half trudge back toward home. The salt air stung my eyes but not my resolve. Recent amorous declarations had given me a burst of nervous energy to fight through the wind rolling in on the crashing surf. Gia and Tim had both said they loved me, and I was sure that I loved them. Choosing was like cutting my heart in half, but it had to be done. I'd tried stalling over Valentine's Day, but that just made me feel icky, like I was stringing one of them along. If only I could figure out which one. You only get to fall in love so many times in your life. Why did I have to lump mine together? I wasn't made for drama.

"On your left!" I took a step to the right of the path and an elderly couple out power walking lapped me in a swish of nylon from their matching yellow tracksuits. I picked up my pace—not because my pride was poked but because I was interval training. Starting now.

The houses across from the ocean on the other side of

Beach Drive were getting ready for the tourist season. Flower boxes were being filled with pansies. Red, white, and blue bunting was being draped across awnings, and Keep Out—Private Property signs were being repositioned at the edges of driveways by those residents who were less enthusiastic about the hordes destined to descend on Cape May for our sand, surf, and seafood. As a plus-size redhead, my teen years on the island had been more of the study, shame, and sunburn variety. It was twenty-five years later, and I was back, launching the debut season of the Butterfly Wings Bed and Breakfast in Aunt Ginny's three-story Victorian. I had to store our own Keep Out sign in the garage next to Aunt Ginny's statue of a garden gnome mooning the neighbors.

A tiny little twentysomething in a coast guard T-shirt jogged past me, her brunette ponytail swishing side to side with the rhythm of her steps. Self-pity made its customary move to squeeze my heart, but I dodged it with the positive affirmations I'd been practicing: *I'm good enough just the way I am. I am beautiful, strong, intelligent, and amazing. I don't have to be skinny to be loved. Any man would be lucky to have me.* That last bit wasn't supposed to derail me into a different obsession, but my mind was like the teacup ride on Morey's Pier and I spun around to the soap opera that was playing on channel two.

I just wanted a life full of passion. Was that so much to ask? I had twenty years with an amazing husband who was the best friend I could ever want. John was everything a husband should be—patient, kind, generous—but we skipped over all the fun stuff at the beginning. Where you can't eat, can't sleep, and your heart speeds up and your stomach bottoms out when he's near. The total infatuation when you first fall for someone and you fall hard. We missed it entirely. We went from friendship to peach schnapps to pregnancy test to blue-light special bridal registry at Kmart. If he wasn't so amazing our next step after miscarriage would have been Divorce Court. What a life we had until. . . . At least he's not suffering anymore. He hung on until his mother said she was moving in with us to take care of him. I think that's all he needed to let go.

Tim and I, however, had the fun stuff; we just never had anything else. We were high school sweethearts—all passion and plans for the future with none of the bills or taxes or fights over who took out the trash last. My relationship with Tim ended . . . abruptly. I reference you to the aforementioned peach schnapps. Could we start life over as if college had never happened? Now was our chance to recapture that passion and see if it had wings. But once again, fate had sabotaged our plans. This time, his name was Giampaolo.

Gia was passion in pinstripes. Just being near him made me all giggly. When he brings me coffee and calls me Bella it's all I can do to remember Tim's name. I had no doubt that the honeymoon phase with Gia would be fantastic, but was there enough there to get us through the sick, poor, cranky side of life? What will happen when Gia finds out I snore? Or that I don't wake up with this makeup on? How could I hold his attention when gorgeous young girls threw themselves at him every day?

I didn't want a comfortable life. I'd had that. I wanted electricity. I wanted to be swept off my feet. Just once I'd like a fairy-tale romance. Everyone says trust your instincts and choose, but my instincts had always been wrong. Again—schnapps. I knew this decision would change everything. I was about to set fire to some bridges, and I'd have to live with the consequences. As much as I'd like to, I couldn't stall any longer. It was time to light the match.

Chapter Two

I heard the tango music from around the corner. I thought maybe Mr. Winston was watching *Master-piece Mystery!* with his morning Danish. He loved his British mysteries. The whole street knew when PBS was running a *Midsomer Murders* marathon. Mr. Winston vowed not to get a hearing aid until he couldn't adjust the TV volume any higher. When I passed the Butterfly Wings B&B shingle in the yard, I was surprised that the music got louder. It wasn't coming from Mr. Winston's. It was coming from inside my house.

"What in the world are you two doing?"

Aunt Ginny was in the peach and copper kitchen wearing a floor-length black dress with a red rose running down the side into three rows of ruffles. Her Sharon Osbourne red hair was slicked back, and she had dark eyeliner sketched in crooked lines past the corners of her eyelids. She was holding Figaro against her face, his whiskers to her cheek, his orange eyes aflame with alarm. He was clearly not so much into this plan.

Aunt Ginny dipped Fig and he slid panicked eyes to mine. "We're celebrating!"

I reached the boom box and turned the knob down until the stemware stopped shaking. "Both of you?"

"Of course."

Figaro flicked his tail toward me like he was reaching for a lifeline.

"How'd you convince him to wear the bow tie?"

Aunt Ginny held his paw out and they did a few steps toward the sink. She grabbed a cat treat and popped it into Fig's mouth, spun around and led him back toward me. "It was his idea."

Of course it was. "And just what are you celebrating?"

Aunt Ginny slid her leg out to the side and did a low lunge. Figaro reached his free paw and swatted at the second pile of cat treats on the island. When Aunt Ginny dipped him for the finale, she pulled a paper from her cleavage. "Dingdong the bat is gone."

I took the letter from Aunt Ginny's hands and unfolded it. "Dear Ms. McAllister, I regret to inform you," yada yada yada. Mrs. Galbraith had formally tendered her resignation.

Aunt Ginny let Figaro down and opened a can of minced crab. "I found it next to the coffeepot with her key to the side door when I had breakfast this morning."

"This says she's not just quitting our house; she's leaving the cleaning service permanently."

Aunt Ginny grinned showing two rows of pearly white dentures.

"She says stress and high anxiety have forced her into

early retirement." I dealt Aunt Ginny a *you know what you did* look, and she raised me with a prim shrug.

"No matter how breezy you're acting, I know you know you caused this."

"Now Figaro will have the freedom to run the house again."

Figaro looked from Aunt Ginny to me while open-mouth chomping on a piece of crabmeat.

I sighed and folded the letter back up and put it in the mail basket to file later. "Now I have to hire a new chambermaid before Wednesday. That newlywed couple is arriving in three days for the South Jersey Wine Tour and we have a few weekend bookings leading up to Memorial Day."

Aunt Ginny got the coffee beans down and handed them to me, her idea of a subtle hint. "Try to find someone with a better temperament this time. Someone who won't act like we're crazy for every little request."

I filled the kettle with water and forced myself not to roll my eyes."I don't think we'll find anyone willing to curtsy and call you mum."

"I said 'the Dowager Frankowski' was close enough. I'm not unreasonable. And while we're on the subject of dying old and alone."

"No."

"Oh, come on."

"Nope."

"Just tell me who you're going to pick."

"I'm not talking to you about this."

"If I find out from those busybodies at the Senior Center, I'll never forgive you."

"If they're such terrible busybodies then why do you hang out with them?"

"They're my best friends."

I raised an eyebrow at *the Dowager* and hit the button on the coffee grinder. After thirty seconds it made the high-pitched whirring sound of finishing its task. I flicked my eyes to her "Addicted to Love" hairstyle. "Is that my new anti-frizz gel?"

Aunt Ginny grabbed two coffee mugs and set them on the counter. "No. . . . It's Vaseline."

"Have fun washing that out."

"I don't have to, smarty-pants. I'm getting my hair dyed today. This will be Yolanda's problem in about an hour."

"I hope you're a good tipper."

"That reminds me. While I'm gone, will you set up my new doohickey?"

"You're going to have to be more specific."

Aunt Ginny pointed with two stevia packets to a box sitting by the cookie jar. "Royce bought me something called a *Zalexa* to make my life easier."

I almost dropped the kettle. The last thing Aunt Ginny needed was more free time. Her high school boyfriend had returned a few weeks ago and he'd been turning our lives upside down from the moment Broadway spit him out in Cape May. I was all for eighty-year-olds going "a-courting," but Royce Hansen had the short-term memory of a fruit fly and Aunt Ginny could do crazy all on her own. "I'll do what I can, but I'll be at Maxine's making desserts for Tim most of the day."

"So, it's Tim then?"

I set the time for the coffee press. "I didn't say that.Tomorrow I'll be at Gia's to do the gluten-free baking."

Aunt Ginny handed me her cup and gave me a dubious

eyebrow raise. "How do you think the loser will react when you tell him?"

I wanted to ask if the loser was the one who gets me or the one who dodges this crazy train, but the whole concept of there being a winner and a loser seemed ridiculous, and I blinked it away. "We're all adults. I'm sure everyone will carry on with their lives no matter what happens. . . . Right?"

"Oh, honey." Aunt Ginny snickered and shook her head. "I've been married five times and never once did any man whose heart I had to break carry on like nothing happened. You mark my words; this will be a spectacular train wreck."

Chapter Three

I wound my little Toyota through streets packed with rows of gingerbread cottages and Victorian mansions over to the harbor. The first few days of March had been cold and rainy, but today the sun was glittering off the water like fairy lights. Squalls were common here being set off the southern tip of New Jersey in the Atlantic, and the rainbow horizon of windsocks shot out like soldiers at full salute warning would-be sailors of dangerous gusts.

Maxine's was a tiny little cottage nestled in the heart of the harbor flanked by million-dollar condos and Cape May Yacht Tours. Tim was out front hanging a giant red wooden crab on the white clapboard in between the blue awnings. The wind was whipping his black T-shirt up exposing a flat stomach with just the beginning pouf of love handles. He tossed me a cheesy grin matching the one on

the crab when my tires crunched onto the crushed clam-
shells of the parking lot.

I parked and he waved me over to inspect his handi-
work. "What do you think?"

"It's a giant crab wearing a pearl necklace."

"It's the new Maxine." He gave me an excited smile.
"Isn't she a doll?"

"Maxine" was the size of a radial tire, with blue eyes
and blond curly hair. She had a coy smile that was both
eerily familiar and unsettling at the same time. "Uh-huh.
Well, she's got your eyes, but I thought Maxine was an
invisible classy French lady."

Tim shrugged. "The Lobster House has its topless
mermaid, the Crab House has its one-legged sea captain,
and Urie's has its palm trees. It's Cape May kitsch.
Tourists are gonna love her."

I took one more look at the perky crab and icy fingers
tickled up my spine. *Well, she's creeping me out.*

Tim was oblivious to my wariness and pulled me in for
a proper kiss. "Hello, gorgeous. Are you here to make my
dreams come true?"

"Are your dreams about Nutella Crème Brûlée and
Piña Colada Cake?"

Tim pulled back in mock horror. "How did you know?"

"That French rolling pin I left here is bugged."

Tim grabbed his chest. "Mon Dieu!" He led me in the
front door, and we passed through the blue and white dining room that still smelled like rosemary from last night's
lamb roast.

The front-end manager was setting new vases of apri-
cot roses on every table and checking the silverware for
spots. "Hey, Poppy."

"Hey, Linda."

A kerfuffle was in full swing in the kitchen, as Chuck was in a very heated hockey debate. "Chef! Tell the new guy here that there's no way the Penguins are going to knock out the Flyers in the play-offs. Giroux is hot right now!"

A shaggy blond in chef whites shook his head. "The Penguins are having a better season. I'm telling you, brah, they're gonna take it."

Tim pointed toward the door. "Tyler. You're fired."

Tyler threw his arms out dramatically and protested while Chuck threw an apron at him. "Told you."

The kitchen was prepping for the day's lunch and dinner services. Juan was hauling trays of shellfish from the walk-in to the sink, Tyler got back to his station of chopping vegetables, and Tim checked on what smelled like scallop stock he had simmering for the soup of the day.

I reached for my apron and Chuck hustled back in to hand me a double espresso. "Here you go, Chef Poppy."

I gratefully took the demitasse cup from him. "You don't have to call me Chef, Chuck."

Chuck grinned. "Are you making those Peanut Butter Mousse pies today?"

"I thought I'd make a couple, yes."

"Then you get to be called Chef."

"Chuck!" Tim called from around the corner. "Stop flirting with Poppy and get back to work."

Chuck, who was about twenty years younger than me, grinned again and blushed up to his eyebrows. "I better go. You know how he is."

"Oh yeah."

Tim came around the corner holding something behind his back. "I've got something for you."

"Ooh, a present?"

He held his arm out and handed me a pink chef coat with my name embroidered over the breast pocket.

"It's beautiful. Thank you!"

"You're part of the team now. Go put it on."

My heart started beating a familiar dirge—*it's gonna be too small; it's gonna be too small.* "Uh . . . okay."

"You can use my office."

Tim's office was a jumbled mess of logbooks, invoices, and a mostly empty bag of Doritos. There was a whiteboard with Maxine's hours of operation and employees' names with notes about who wanted off when scribbled in the margins. I looked at the tag inside the uniform. The jacket was a size smaller than what I usually wore, and I thought about staging an emergency evacuation. Tim seemed to have absolutely no idea that I had gained weight since high school. I think his image of me was cached like the chef supply website he visited daily. I pulled off my long-sleeved blouse down to my tank top. If I was going to fit into this chef coat, I needed every millimeter of space I could make. I promised God I'd never eat ice cream again if he made this miraculously fit. I prayed the pink jacket over my head and shoulders, then begged it down to my waist. It was a bit snug in the northern hemisphere. *I don't care what Dr. Melinda thinks. I've got to turn up the workouts if I'm going to get this weight off fast.* I considered taking the padding out of my bra to make space but decided my push-ups just gave me a little tent action over the breadbasket. Whoever designed chef uniforms must have used SpongeBob as their prototype. Everyone looks like a box.

Tim was waiting for me in the hall. "That looks good on you."

Those aren't the words I would use. That looks like you've stuffed yourself in a pink legwarmer feels more realistic. I cocked my elbow and gave a little runway strut. "You don't think it's a little small?"

"Oh no. It's tight in all the right places." His eyes bored into where Chef Poppy was being stretched out and my face went all warm and prickly. "I don't know if I want you wearing that in front of the line. Chuck has already asked if this is serious, and I think Juan's looking for a new green card."

I giggled in spite of myself. "You're being ridiculous."

Tim pulled me against him. "Am I? How am I supposed to get any work done looking at you across the room in this?"

I giggled. "I don't know. I guess you'll have to realize that I'm middle-aged and that this uniform is probably two sizes too small."

Tim nuzzled my neck. "Now who's being ridiculous. I can't wait until you're here every day working for me."

That dropped like a rock in my belly. "Tim, I would love to be here every day working with you, but you know the bed and breakfast is about to get very busy. I've had a PR company working on fixing the damage from last month's attack with all those bogus bad reviews. And we just started working with a tour company that does custom theme weekends. I'm going to be stretched too thin." *At least my time will be.*

Tim didn't so much as pause. "We'll work it out. Don't worry."

But I did worry. I worried about paying my bills and taking care of Aunt Ginny. I worried about hurting Tim and leaving him in the lurch. I worried my way through four hours of crafting cakes, custards, and mousse. I worried through Chuck stealing my spatula so he could get an early sample of peanut butter pie. And I worried myself all the way home to conduct the new chambermaid interviews where I discovered my worry was not in vain.

Chapter Four

While I was gone, Aunt Ginny had scheduled six applicants all to arrive at the same time and was currently interrogating them en masse. It had all the earmarks of a hostage situation.

"I will not tolerate any shenanigans on those hickey-doos! Do you understand?"

Aunt Ginny had the six young ladies tightly packed on a four-person sofa in the wood-paneled library. She had changed into khaki pants, a white T-shirt, and a faded olive army jacket that I was pretty sure I'd seen in the attic yesterday next to her fox stole and three of her wedding dresses. She was pacing back and forth in front of the sofa with her hands clasped behind her back like General Sherman. Figaro, always willing to be the menacing backup, sat on the coffee table grilling the ladies and flicking his tail like a switchblade.

"If I catch you playing on your phone, I will confiscate it and you will show me how to play the game. You will not get it back until the end of the day after I have beaten your high score."

The ladies were all from parts of Eastern Europe who came to Cape May every year on work visas. I had no doubt their English lessons had not prepared them for shenanigans or hickey-doos.

One of them was cowering into the throw pillows biting a hangnail. Another was hugging herself and gently rocking back and forth. One of the girls in the middle was watching Figaro like she thought he would sprout horns and strike at any minute; her eyes were the size of quarters behind her thick glasses.

"You are not to chat with anyone named Keith. Keith is a stupid name."

The brunette on the other end of the couch was shaking her head and muttering to herself.

"You are never to turn the television off when I am in the room. I am not sleeping; I am just resting my eyes. If you turn off my program, I'll take a switch to you."

Uh-oh. The girl with the hangnails just crossed herself.

Aunt Ginny stopped pacing and pointed her finger at the girls. "And above all, if you find a jar of peanut butter hidden anywhere in this house you are to bring it to me at once. I've hidden one and I can't remember where it is. And don't let Poppy know where you found it. I may want to use that spot again."

The girls all looked around Aunt Ginny to where I was standing in the archway, still in my pink chef bustier.

Aunt Ginny followed their eyes and jumped when she saw me. "Oh, Poppy. When did you get here?"

Figaro flopped over and accidentally slid off the coffee table and landed on the floor. The nervous girl in the middle of the sofa let out a little squeak and pulled her knees up to her chest hugging them tight against her.

I stepped into the library and scanned the girls' faces before looking back at Staff Sergeant Frankowski. Her green coat had a patch with the name Wyatt sewn over the breast pocket. Her second husband. "What's going on?"

Aunt Ginny gave me a toothy smile. "I was just doing some preliminary interviews." She turned her head away from the girls and gritted her teeth. "To weed out the weak ones."

"Uh-huh. And just how does that work?"

Aunt Ginny turned to the girls again. "Okay, anyone no longer interested in the position may go."

The girls fought each other to get off the couch, through the library, and out the door like hikers running from a hatchet-wielding bear. Only one girl remained on the sofa. She was pale and thin and had long straight black hair and large blue eyes over high cheekbones. She gave me a timid smile.

"What's your name?"

The girl held out a delicate hand and spoke in a clipped, lilting voice. "Victoryna Rostyslavivna Yevtushenko."

Aunt Ginny flicked her eyes to mine. "Did you get that?"

The girl shook my hand like she was shaking up a Yoo-hoo. "You may call me Victory."

"Well, Victory," I said, pulling my hand gently from hers. "It looks like you've got the job."

Victory did a fist pump. "Yes. And what ees job?"

I narrowed my eyes at Aunt Ginny. "What did you tell the service when you called?"

Aunt Ginny shrugged. "I said send me some foreign girls who like to work."

I sucked in some air and let it out to the count of five. "We are looking for a chambermaid to clean the rooms and do laundry. Are you interested in doing that, Victory?"

"Yes, yes. I can do thees. I have J-1 visa."

A beeping started from somewhere down the hall. I stuck my head out of the library and looked toward the kitchen. "What's that noise?"

Aunt Ginny tossed her head. "I don't know. I was talking to it earlier, but I didn't tell it to beep like we were under attack."

The three of us and Figaro followed the sound to the kitchen where Aunt Ginny's new Alexa device was flashing.

Aunt Ginny looked at me. "Why is it doing that?"

"I don't know. Alexa, what are you doing?"

The device paused the alarm to answer me. "I'm waiting to answer your questions." The alarm sounded again.

"Alexa, what's that noise?"

"*What's That Noise?* is the first album from Coldcut."

Alexa continued her long-winded answer and I finally cut in and said, "Alexa, stop."

The alarm stopped and Victory pointed to the device. "Ees theis going off all of time?"

Since the Alexa personal assistant had only been installed for seven hours, I had no idea. "I'm sure it's just a fluke."

Aunt Ginny shook her head. "It probably won't happen again."

Chapter Five

I jumped around my bedroom trying to shove my foot into my UGGs. Figaro darted back and forth with his ears pinned like he was playing defense. I was running terribly late this morning, having overslept my alarm. Of all the days for Figaro to fall down on his nuisance duties, why did it have to be the day the newlyweds were checking in for their romantic weekend? I had spent the last two days training Victory how to clean and make up the rooms and run the washer and dryer. She was officially hired as my summer chambermaid because she passed my strict vetting process. One, she was available. Two, she had a valid work visa. And most important, three, she wasn't spooked away by Aunt Ginny and Figaro. That last qualification was harder to achieve than you would think.

Now I was stuck inside my shirt having made the bold

move to not unbutton it before yanking it over my head. I heard a loud complaint of the feline variety and Figaro bolted from the bedroom. *I did say watch out.*

The Bakers were coming in around one this afternoon, and I had to set up for the Wine and Cheese Happy Hour at four. Lily Snow was the tour guide who arranged the theme week and she'd asked me to host one of the wineries in a little "get to know you" mixer for the group. Of course I agreed, and I immediately called Kim at the Laughing Gull Winery to work out the details. Kim was part of my squad in high school. We were a squad of nerds, but that's what the kids call it today. Squads gotta stick together into middle age. It was a world of millennials, and we needed people we could talk to without texting.

I ran down the stairs and hopped over Figaro, who was strategically placed on the bottom step to teach me a lesson about stepping on his paw. Aunt Ginny came down the hall from the kitchen wiping her hands on a dish towel. "Where you goin'?"

"I'm late. I promised Gia I'd be there by now to make some stuff and I have to be back by one. I didn't even get to work out today."

"You've worked out enough over the last two weeks; you can sleep in till seven once in a while."

I kissed Aunt Ginny on the cheek. "I gotta go."

"Bring me some stuff home."

Five minutes later, I rushed in the back door of the La Dolce Vita espresso bar ready to give Gia a flirty apology and make some blueberry scones, but he wasn't in the back room waiting for me as usual. I put my things in the office and grabbed my apron off the hook, shook out yesterday's flour, and was in the process of pulling the apron over my unruly baking braid when I heard a giggle. I yanked the apron down and peeked around the corner. There was a miss young thing behind the bar with my sexy Gia. *What the . . . ?* She was about twenty years old, five-foot-seven–ish, with a tiny little waist, birthday boobs, and strawberry blond hair. Gia was showing her how to pull a shot of espresso.

"Hello?" I croaked through the cloud that I'd set free. I attempted to clear the panic from my throat and tried again. "Hi."

Gia gave me his usual megasexy smile. "Bella, you are here." He motioned to Miss Thing in her pink belly shirt and booty shorts. "We were going to wait for you to do the training, but you are running late."

Miss Thing mooned a grin at Gia like he was the last piece of chocolate cake on a PMS cruise.

Gia motioned to me. "Sierra, this is Poppy."

Sierra tore her eyes away from Gia and gave me what I can only describe as a *keep your enemies closer* smile. She threw her hand out like a karate chop and her belly button ring reflected off the pendant lights. "Hi, Poppy. Gia told me you're the baker who will be responsible for my gaining twenty pounds with this job."

I shook her hand and looked from her to Gia back to her. *We can only hope so.* Of course, what I said was, "Nice to meet you."

She sized me up and I sized her up. *Another redhead.*

Gia clapped his hands. "Okay. Sierra is learning the bar. Why don't I teach her to make your latte and we'll bring it back to you in a bit?"

I swallowed hard. "Sure. Sounds good." *I'll just go*

back to my cave and make some scones. Don't worry about me; I'll swing from the bell tower if I need anything.

I stomped back to my lair in a recently acquired sourness, laid out my ingredients for Paleo blueberry scones, and listened to Sierra learning how to work the espresso machine. I had no idea making coffee was so funny, but from the giggling going on in the next room it was the unsung comedy routine of the Jersey Shore.

I mauled my scone dough into the shape of a cannonball. Or a cake pan; it was open to interpretation. By the time I'd slammed the oven shut, Gia came back with a smile on his face and a perfect latte.

"This is going to take some work. In the meantime, I made your latte so you wouldn't have to wait all day."

I gave him a stony look as I took my coffee.

His eyes took on a familiar teasing sparkle. He leaned into me. "Bella." He kissed me and looked at me some more. The front doorbell chimed, and I inwardly vowed that if it was Sawyer, I would kill her after work. Gia grinned. "I better see to that." He stopped and turned around. "I told her to wear pants down to the knees and a shirt that covers her stomach from now on." He winked at me before heading back into the dining room.

I had a lot of nervous energy for some reason. I felt like kneading bread, but you don't knead gluten-free bread because there's no gluten to develop. So, I took a clean chef knife down from the magnet on the wall and stared at it. What could I chop? More giggling from the dining room gave me a couple of ideas. I opened a bag of macadamia nuts and went to town. I had to stop myself from turning them into powder. If I was going to make cookies, I'd need them to have some substance left. I had some dried pineapple from Morrow's Nut House and shredded coconut, so I decided on piña colada macaroons. Shaped like skulls and crossbones.

Look, don't judge me. I realize I was being ridiculous. This could have been my easy out. All I had to do was drive over to Tim's and tell him I was ready to commit. Gia would clearly rebound. Maybe before I got out of the parking lot. So why was I letting this get to me? Maybe I was just feeling sorry for myself because despite all my efforts I hadn't lost weight and Sierra was so thin you could see her hip bones through her satin shorts. Maybe I was feeling threatened because a new woman was in my domain. Gia had never asked me to work the espresso bar. I could have put in extra hours if he needed summer help. *When exactly I would have had time to do that I don't know, but I would have made the time, so he didn't have to hire anyone young and pretty.*

I heard Gia laugh at something Birthday Boobs said and slammed the cookie sheet into the oven. I didn't let myself think about why I was feeling what I was feeling, but I knew instinctively that I was at war. I slipped into the bathroom and took off my apron. I washed the flour off my face and put on fresh makeup. Then I fixed my hair and put it back into my baking braid, but this time I fancied it up and frenched it down one side. I unbuttoned my top button, then the second. This was all I could do today. I'd be better prepared the next time. I had a long morning ahead of me. I had to be home at one when the newlyweds arrived, so I planned to bake cookies and muffins within earshot of the espresso machine from now until exactly 12:58.

Chapter Six

I had stomped halfway home before I remembered I'd driven my car today. I had to turn around and go back to get it. On my way I texted Sawyer: **Gia hired a slinky young girl.** Three frowny face emojis. I got into my car and raced the two and a half blocks on autopilot. I swerved into the driveway and cut the engine, then stomped into the house. Sawyer texted me back with a video of Nicki Minaj shaking her head no in exasperation.

The lady of the manor was ready to receive guests in her vintage June Cleaver getup, complete with pumps and pearls.

"Shouldn't you have a lace apron on?"

"That's only for dinnertime so I look like I've been cooking all day."

"I'm going to go change."

"Why are you in such a snit?"

"Gia hired a little college girl named Sierra."

Aunt Ginny tried to hold in a snicker, but she was so obviously amused it made me even more crabby and I'd come home pre-cranked, so that was saying something.

I threw some things around in my room and changed into more presentable clothes appropriate for the happy hour event. I was just spraying my perfume and walking through it when I heard the slam of a car door out front. The newlyweds had arrived.

Aunt Ginny, Figaro, and I lined up in the foyer like the staff at Buckingham Palace ready to meet the French Ambassador. I was expecting a set of fresh-faced twenty-year-olds, pink with the bloom of love, but Vince Baker was pushing fifty if he was a day. He wasn't bad looking for a man in middle age, but he had salt-and-pepper hair and a middle-aged paunch that said he had stopped trying to impress anyone.

Hanging off his arm was a much younger beauty who could have been his daughter. Hanging off *her* arm was a diamond tennis bracelet. She looked to have a big enough self-care routine for the both of them. Everything was lifted, toned, tanned, lacquered, and plucked. Her golden hair was piled up on top of her head in a mass of curls. She wore a cute little white jumper with accents of bubble gum pink on her lips, fingernails, toenails, purse, belt, and shoes. She gave me a big smile and reached out a hand. "Hi, I'm Sunny Baker and this is my husband, Vince."

"Welcome." I reached out my hand to say hello and snatched it back when her purse growled. "What was that?"

Sunny put the carrier on the floor and unzipped the top. "That's just my baby."

A yellow nose poked out the top of the bag and yapped. Sunny reached in and pulled out a round ball of fluff that could have passed for a tribble with a snout. The tribble pranced in a circle, then stood with all four paws on the toe of Vince's boot and yipped again.

Figaro hissed and jumped straight in the air without bending his legs.

Aunt Ginny stared at the pouf with her mouth open.

I was stunned beyond my ability to be canny. "You brought a dog."

Sunny picked up the fluff and nuzzled it. "Yes, I hope that's okay. The Innkeeper website said you were pet friendly."

Aunt Ginny breathed out a quiet, "Oh no."

"Huh. I don't remember adding that yet." *Right now we're only friendly to our naughty pet.*

Aunt Ginny cleared her throat. "I may have done it."

I slid my eyes to Aunt Ginny.

"I used your login and told the person inside the website to add it because of Figaro."

I gave Aunt Ginny an *I will deal with you later* look, then gave Sunny a tight but friendly smile. *Weren't people supposed to ask before they showed up with extra guests?*

Figaro was glaring at me from behind the coatrack. Only one eye was visible, but his meaning was clear. I'd have a present left for me tonight and wouldn't find it until I was walking around with bare feet.

Vince looked around the foyer like he was adding up the cost of the valuables while Sunny held up the ball of fur. "This is Tammy Faye. She's a teacup Pom and she'll be two years old on Saturday. Won't you, baby?"

Tammy Faye licked Sunny's chin.

Aunt Ginny snickered. "Your dog's name is Tammy Faye Baker?"

Sunny nodded eagerly, but she had that glassy look to her eyes that let you know she had no idea what you were talking about.

"With the mascara?" Aunt Ginny made finger fans under her eyes.

Sunny cocked her head and blinked.

Vince nudged her. "I'll explain it later."

Figaro stretched high up on the coatrack making himself as big as possible, his tail bristling, never taking his eyes off Tammy Faye. He was plotting either her demise or mine; time would tell.

"Why don't you come on in and get comfortable. I'll go get your bags for you." I led the Bakers into the sitting room where Aunt Ginny had set out a pitcher of strawberry rose lemonade and some iced lemon cookies.

"Can I have a little bowl of water for Tammy Faye, please? She prefers bottled water in a crystal bowl if you have it."

"Of course. Aunt Ginny?"

Aunt Ginny gave me a peeved eye roll behind their backs before she went to the kitchen. I gave her an *I'm sorry; who added it to the website that we're pet friendly?* look in return.

When I came in with the first round of bags, Tammy Faye was drinking spring water from Waterford crystal that I really hoped was a candy dish and not an old ashtray and Figaro was in the bay window scowling over the back of the couch. Vince was in a wingback chair with Sunny perched on his lap.

"The house is beautiful. We've never stayed anywhere with antiques before, have we, Boo?"

Vince smiled up at his young wife.

"So how long have the two of you been married?"

Sunny gave Vince a dreamy smile. "Almost six months. This weekend is to celebrate our half anniversary. It's like a mini honeymoon, right, Boo?"

Vince ran his finger down the side of Sunny's face. "Whatever you want, baby."

Aunt Ginny had to leave the room.

Vince tickled Sunny and she giggled until she snorted.

I went out and fetched another round of bags. Sunny had packed for a six-month cruise on a ship with no gift shop. When I returned, Tammy Faye was barking at the top shelf of Aunt Ginny's curio hutch and Figaro was about to push a Japanese statue over the edge. I rescued the Geisha and gave Figaro the evil eye. "You know you're not allowed up there."

He moved to the back corner out of my reach and demurely wrapped his tail around his feet to taunt me.

I needed a minute to catch my breath, so I tried another round of small talk. "How did you two meet?"

Sunny launched into her meet-cute story the way a starving writer pitches a sitcom in Hollywood. I had to sit down halfway through to conserve my energy for taking the suitcase collection up to their room later.

"I was right out of my second year of college with my associate's degree and had a summer internship with BakerCom. That's Vince's company. They're a PR firm. They'd be on the Fortune Five Hundred if it went to Seven

Fifty. Anyway, Vince came in to greet the interns dressed for the red carpet and looking just like George Clooney."

Aunt Ginny peeked around the dining room archway and narrowed her eyes at Vince, who looked exactly like George Clooney if you were terribly nearsighted and had a really good imagination. She shook her head and slowly melted back around the corner.

Sunny was regaling me with all the ways Vince flirted with her and how many times he asked her out before she said yes. "He would not take no for an answer." She giggled. "And I'm so glad he wouldn't." She leaned back against his chest and put her hand on his cheek, showing off a two-carat yellow diamond. "I don't know what I would do without my handsome hero."

Figaro knocked Aunt Ginny's Japanese fan off the shelf, and it landed on Tammy Faye, who yelped, then started another round of yapping. I could hear Aunt Ginny snicker from the dining room.

I snatched Figaro off the shelf and glared at him. "I am so sorry; is Tammy Faye hurt?"

Tammy Faye launched herself into Sunny's lap. "Are you okay, Precious? Let Mommy see your paw."

She made whimpering sounds and held her paw up, but I couldn't help but feel her eyes were boring into Figaro's with a message of approaching retribution.

Figaro responded by swishing his tail in a way that said, *Bring it!*

I tried to apologize. "Figaro is normally such a good kitty." *Shut up, Aunt Ginny. They can hear you laughing.* "I'm sure he and Tammy Faye will be able to get along great."

Vince looked at Fig in my arms, his orange eyes boring into Tammy Faye's. "I hope so. Our little angel comes from a champion bloodline."

Sunny smiled warmly. "I'm sure they will be just fine together. Tammy Faye will win him over." She leaned down and gave Vince a kiss. "Right, Boo?"

I wasn't so sure. Tammy Faye spun in a circle twice and plopped down on Sunny's lap. She laid her head down on her front paws and bared her teeth at Figaro.

I put Figaro down in the foyer and went out for the last round of bags calculating how much it would cost to hire a bellboy and what utility I would have to turn off to afford it. When I returned, I could see that I needed to show Sunny and Vinnyboo to their room as quickly as possible.

I cleared my throat. "Lily, your tour guide, has arranged a little get-together event today at four, in the library. Why don't I show you to your room so you can get settled?"

Vince somehow managed to stand with Sunny still sitting on his lap. "I could use a little nap before five. What about you, baby?"

Sunny growled in a seductive way and Tammy Faye yapped for them both to knock it off.

Just then, Aunt Ginny's Alexa went off in the kitchen: "A gold digger is usually defined as a person who digs for gold in a goldfield."

I don't know if you can scientifically feel colors, but I'm pretty sure I felt myself go white. I grabbed three of the bags and said a little too loudly, "Come on, your room is this way!"

I prayed that the Bakers were too busy canoodling to hear the offensive device and rushed them up to the Purple Emperor butterfly suite chattering like an imbecile. "You're gonna love happy hour. I've got some yummy cheese; you like cheese, don't you? Everybody likes cheese. And grapes. I've got so many grapes—both green and red. I love the red ones. No seeds. Don't worry, I know how to put together a real fancy cheese plate. You're going to have a great time. Look, you're in a suite."

I showed them the champagne in their room and how to work the air conditioner and the TV remote and made a hasty retreat. It wasn't until I was back downstairs that I realized Tammy Faye had not gone to the room with us. She wasn't in the sitting room either. "Here, doggie. Tammy Faye, where are you?" I whistled and looked under the couch and behind the hutch.

Aunt Ginny caught me on the floor with my butt in the air. "What in the world are you doing?"

I looked toward the steps and whispered, "The dog is gone."

Chapter Seven

I followed Figaro's hisses to the kitchen where Tammy Faye had a snootful of top-shelf Persian cat food. Fig's bowl of gourmet chicken-flavored pebbles was now empty and Tammy Faye's tail was creating a gale force wind of gloating. Fig arched his back for reinforcement when I scolded the teacup Pom who had just eaten twice her weight in kibble. "Tammy Faye, no!"

Aunt Ginny handed me a pink satin leash from Tammy Faye's Louis Vuitton travel bag. "You know what they do after they eat. And she just ate enough to explode."

"What? No. We don't offer pet-sitting services."

Aunt Ginny arched an eyebrow. "Are you going to interrupt their 'nap' to usher Tammy Faye into their room?"

"You're the one who said we were pet friendly. Why don't you do it?"

"I'm old and frail. I could catch my death of cold out there."

I let out a sigh and snatched the leash. *I saw Aunt Ginny try wakeboarding in January. Suddenly she's old and frail.* "Come on, Tammy. Let's get this over with." I attached the leash while thinking about all the rules I'd have to add to our reservation contract. Rules about pet sitting, feeding, pet Baggies, and where to deposit said Baggies after deposits were made in my yard.

Tammy Faye did not feel the same level of urgency that Aunt Ginny was concerned about. She also did not like to get her paws dirty. She gave me a panicked and confused look at the threshold of the grass like she'd never seen it before. Once I'd trotted her out to the back corner, she immediately hopped up on my foot to get as far away from the ground as possible. I looked back at the house. Aunt Ginny and Figaro were laughing at me from the mud room door. Figaro had a holier-than-thou *this is why cats are better than dogs* smirk to his whiskers. After ten minutes I was ready to give up and head back into the house.

Aunt Ginny shook her head and locked the door. "We just had the rugs cleaned."

This is your fault, old woman! I dragged Tammy back into the yard. Three false starts later, she finally did what we came out here to do. She pranced back into the house and posed, ready for a reward. I dug around until I found a gourmet dog cookie in her satchel. She made sure Fig got a good look at it before she gobbled it down.

Fig flattened his ears, and Aunt Ginny opened the fridge and took out a piece of prosciutto for him that was waiting to be wrapped around asparagus spears for tonight's canapés.

"Can you take Tammy Faye into the sitting room?" I took the bundle of asparagus and rinsed it in the sink. "I've got to start on these hors d'oeuvres so they're ready for happy hour."

The Alexa started its alarm again and Tammy Faye shot from the kitchen with Figaro galloping behind her.

Aunt Ginny took the grapes and cheese out and put them on the island. "Well, that problem solved itself."

"Alexa, stop that." Alexa ignored me. "Alexa, cancel alarm." The alarm continued.

Aunt Ginny leaned down and hollered into the black cylinder, "A-lex-a, stooop!"

The device silenced.

"What did you do to set that alarm again?"

Aunt Ginny shrugged. "I have no idea."

"Where's the owner's manual?"

"Threw it away."

"Why would you do that?"

"I don't like books that tell me what to do." Aunt Ginny popped a grape into her mouth.

I took my frustrations out slicing a baguette into rounds and brushed the slices with orange-infused olive oil. Then I topped each slice with half a fig, a pinch of goat cheese, and a drizzle of more olive oil. I set the cookie sheet aside and started working on the blue cheese–stuffed bacon-wrapped dates when the doorbell rang followed by a cacophony of Tammy Faye. "Are you expecting someone?"

Aunt Ginny shook her head and mumbled through a mouthful of sneaked canapés, "No. But I'll go see who it is."

She left the kitchen, and I replaced three of the fig and goat cheese tops that she'd pinched off their baguette rafts.

The front door opened, and all hell broke loose in the foyer. Tammy Faye was going to do some serious damage to someone's ankles. I wiped my hands on a towel and ran into Aunt Ginny on my way to the hall. "What's going on?"

"This couple has just turned up and said they want a room for the night."

"Without a reservation?"

"They said they're joining the Bakers."

"Why is this the first I'm hearing about it? And why'd you leave the dog out there?"

"They said they know her."

I came around the corner and slammed into an argument. A young man in his early thirties was dressed in black jeans that were applied with an airbrush. He also wore a short-sleeved paisley shirt and a Kangol hat over spiky dark bangs and round pink sunglasses. He was holding Tammy Faye at arm's length like a baby with a stinky diaper, and Tammy Faye was growling at him and his companion.

She had all the sex appeal of a bowl of Cream of Wheat. She wore slacks the color of a cedar pond that were a size too large and a tight mustard-colored silk blouse that made her complexion look like she had liver disease. She had on no makeup, which was a shame because her eyes were set really close together and some well-placed eyeliner could have helped. Her limp hair was the color of a horseshoe crab that had washed up from the bay. Her appearance could have improved greatly if she lost the condescending expression. "He's not going to like this."

The man answered her, "We're too close to back out now. For once, just do what I'm telling you. We have to stop her before she ruins everything."

As soon as we made eye contact they stopped talking. He put Tammy Faye back on the floor and gave her head a little pat.

She immediately turned into a professional attack dog. Not with the K9 team, she was too small to be a drug-sniffing dog with the police, but maybe one of those illegal fruit–sniffing dogs with Hawaii TSA. The man pulled his hand back when Tammy nipped him.

Figaro didn't want to be left out, so he was lurking from the console table in the hall behind the potted spider plant, his eyes glued to the Pom.

I reached down and grabbed Tammy around the middle. Although to be fair, she was all middle. She was still biting at the air when I introduced myself. "I'm Poppy. The owner of the Butterfly Wings B and B. What can I do for you?"

"Ryan Finch. This is my wife, Alyce. We'd like a room please. Your sign out front says you have rooms available. We're with the wine tour."

"You're on the tour?"

Alyce nodded and looked at the floor. "We forgot to make a reservation for lodging ahead of time."

Ryan muttered through gritted teeth, "*We* didn't forget."

Alyce blushed. "I'm Vince's daughter. We're joining my father on his vacation."

Aunt Ginny had snuck up behind me as was her custom. "You're joining him on his mini honeymoon?"

Alyce's cheek twitched, but she didn't break her smile. "It's not really a honeymoon. They went to the Azure coast six months ago . . . we're on the wine tour. We set it up with Lily Snow."

I glanced at Aunt Ginny and she made a grimace so imperceptible only I could see her exasperation. "I do have a couple of rooms available."

Ryan put his hand in my face. "Do you have a suite?"

"Yes."

"Is it as nice as Vince's?"

Alyce blushed again. "Ryan . . ."

"It's very nice. It has a lovely view of the rose garden next door." *That isn't in bloom right now.*

"I bet it's not as big as Vince's, though, is it?"

What the . . . I had to keep myself from sighing. "Mr. Baker booked the largest suite in advance, but the other rooms are just lovely if you're interested in seeing them. They're all butterfly themed."

Aunt Ginny made an offer of her own. "Or if you want, I can get you my old tent out of the garage."

I tried to cover my alarm with a laugh and gave her a gentle side kick. "She's kidding. Aunt Ginny is a riot once you get to know her." *And you're slightly hammered.* I leaned down to Aunt Ginny. "Could you please finish wrapping the asparagus so I can get them in the oven? I'm running short on time here."

She pursed her lips together and scooted back to the kitchen. "Fig! Treat!"

Figaro hopped off the console table with a fly-by swatting of Tammy Faye, who never saw it coming, and cantered after Aunt Ginny.

Tammy Faye jumped back, glanced at Ryan and Alyce, and growled one more time to make her point, then begrudgingly trotted sideways behind Figaro to the kitchen.

I didn't want to create a problem where one didn't have to be made, so I agreed to give the Finches the best room that I had left and charged their credit card.

Ryan handed Alyce the check-in documents. "Here. You're the secretary."

While she was filling out the registration card, Sunny came down the stairs. "Ryan, is that you? What are you guys doing here?"

Ryan suddenly turned on all the charm of Bill Clinton meeting the Swedish Bikini Team. "Hello, darling, don't you look beautiful. We wanted to surprise you. We booked the same wine tour."

Sunny looked from Ryan to Alyce and her shoulders drooped. "Oh, that's nice. I'm sure Vince will be happy you could come."

Alyce found her voice and tapped into her inner teenager. "Daddy is always happy to see me."

Sunny took a step toward Alyce. "Of course he is, Alyce. I didn't mean—"

Ryan jumped in and derailed the apology. "Where is Vince? I thought we could go play a round before dinner."

"He's resting. We're having happy hour with the tour group in a little while."

"Daddy drinks too much. You're going to make him an alcoholic."

Sunny's eyes were pleading with Alyce. "He's just freshening up from the long drive."

I was standing awkwardly in the middle and wanted to be anywhere but here, but Ryan still hadn't taken his credit card back. And Alyce was making a project out of the check-in papers.

Tammy Faye finally broke away from whatever bribe Aunt Ginny was plying her with to keep her and Figaro quiet so she could eavesdrop on the TMZ exposé in the foyer. The Pom galloped down the hall so Sunny could scoop her up. "There's my baby. Mommy missed you."

"Ryan! What are you doing here? You're supposed to be working on the Peterson file." Vince commanded authority even before he descended the stairs. "Did you get those press releases done like I told you?"

"Yeah, Dad. Absolutely. They're being finished as we speak."

Vince ambled down the steps one by one and his attitude plunged with his altitude. "What do you mean they're being finished. You were the one who was supposed to work on them. You don't have time to take off a week."

I tried to jab Ryan's card into his hand, but he evaded me.

"It's no problem. I finished the lion's share and I've got one of the graphic artists in the office dressing the presentation up a bit." Ryan spun Alyce around in front of him. "Alyce wanted to surprise you with a family vacation."

Alyce flung herself into Vince's arms and knocked Sunny's hand off his shoulder in the process. "Oh, Daddy, don't make us leave. This will be our first trip as a family."

Vince softened his eyes on Sunny. She gave him a

tremulous smile. He turned back to Alyce. "How did you find out we were here?"

Alyce opened her mouth to speak, but Ryan cut her off. "Sunny told us. It was her idea that we all be here together."

Sunny looked like she just picked the year's supply of jelly behind door number three on *Let's Make a Deal*. She stared helplessly from Ryan to Alyce to Vince.

Ryan waved his hand and took Vince's arm. "She must have forgotten. You know these women and their flighty imaginations. Hey, what do you say we let the girls get their nails done and we rent a boat for the day tomorrow? We can get caught up on Colinsport Dynamics."

Alyce handed me the guest check-in documents and I gave her Ryan's credit card. I couldn't get away from there fast enough. I still had to show the Finches to the Monarch suite, but I wasn't sure how to break into their argument between the topics of whether or not Alyce should be left at the B&B while her husband went sailing or if Sunny should be allowed to spend time alone with Vince anywhere on their anniversary trip. Vince made that job easier for me when he yelled for them all to shut the bleep up.

"Enough! Alyce! Let this lady show you to your room and Sunny and I will see you for happy hour. Ryan, I don't want to hear any more talk about work while I'm on vacation, but so help me if you don't get ahead of the Peterson press release, you'll be in the unemployment line before you can unpack your bags! Do any of you have a problem with that?"

I did. But I was pretty sure my opinion wasn't being considered. I just wanted to sort out the rooms and guests and get the happy hour mixer over with so they could get on with their vacation and leave me out of their chaos.

Aunt Ginny handed me the key to the Monarch suite. "Maybe the wine will calm everyone down."

"Sure. Because nothing diffuses an argument like alcohol."

Chapter Eight

I took my tray of quarter-sized chocolate mousse tartelettes out of the refrigerator. Just as I'd suspected, half
of them had been pilfered by a little redheaded gremlin in
patent leather pumps. Over the past few weeks I'd learned
to double everything I made so I always had a decoy set
to slow Aunt Ginny down. Checking that she wasn't behind me, I took out the two Styrofoam egg cartons con-
cealing the rest of the tartelettes and added them to the
plate.

"Ooh, I didn't know we had more of those little chocolate thingies."

"Really? How odd."

"You're getting better at hiding stuff."

Figaro slid around the corner followed by Tammy
Faye barking. The two of them hurtled into the kitchen

and Figaro hunkered down. Tammy Faye stood between my feet; her tail was wagging the rest of her body in a little half-moon on the floor. Figaro was covered in something sticky.

I picked Figaro up and sniffed his neck. "How did you get into maple syrup?"

Aunt Ginny recoiled careful to not get syrup on her dress. "Ugh. Someone needs a bath."

Tammy Faye responded to the word "bath" by barking out a series of dog expletives and shot from the kitchen through the dining room doorway.

"Knock knock." Kim came in through the mudroom carrying a case that had *Laughing Gull Winery* printed on it in sloping script turning into the icon of a gull in flight. Her head was shaved over the ear on one side and her natural blond hair was dyed the color of the 2000 Flushes Blue in Aunt Ginny's bathroom. She'd added a few new piercings since high school, and I thought I saw a new hummingbird tattoo peeking out from her sleeve that wasn't there last week. "I brought the happy for the happy hour. Daniel will be along a little later. Ooh, chocolate."

Kim helped herself to a couple of tartelettes while Aunt Ginny showed her the trays of hot hors d'oeuvres warming in the oven. "Those bacon ones are really good."

I wrestled Fig into the mud sink amid much protesting and lathered him up with his fancy cat shampoo to wash the syrup out of his cottony fur knowing that Aunt Ginny and Kim were shotgunning hors d'oeuvres while my back was turned.

Kim called in to me, "Lily said they'll be here in about fifteen minutes. I'm to text Daniel once they've all arrived. He doesn't want you to put any wine out until he gets here to talk about nuances!"

I watched over my shoulder as she wiggled her fingers and popped the rest of a date in her mouth. I came back into the kitchen with Figaro wrapped in a warm towel from the dryer. His eyes had a slight look of alarm to them, probably fear of Tammy Faye seeing me kissing his nose and calling him my babushka. Something he normally loved after a bath. Of course, he might just love that the bath is over.

I handed him to Aunt Ginny. "Can he stay in your room until I can comb him out?"

Aunt Ginny cradled Figaro and crooned to him, "Look at the little babushka."

Tammy Faye made a growling bark that sounded very similar to laughter.

Figaro rumbled a low moan of humiliation and Aunt Ginny took him to her room.

I plated the warm dates while Kim told me about the wines they were serving tonight. "Those chocolate tarts will go great with the jammy Pinot I brought."

Aunt Ginny returned to the kitchen and opened her mouth to speak. The Alexa cut her off and made an announcement: "This is your reminder. Hide the Dove Bars from Poppy." Aunt Ginny blushed and backed out of the kitchen. "I forgot something in my room."

Kim walked over to the nine-inch-tall black cylinder next to the toaster. "What in the world is that?"

"That is Aunt Ginny's new Alexa. I'm not sure what it does, but it does it at the wrong times. And it doesn't listen to me at all."

The doorbell rang, and on the way to answer it I asked Kim if I looked okay. "You look great. I love the violet boots. I'm stuck with boring black and white because I'm working."

"You've never been boring a day in your life."

I brought a tray of cheese, fruit, and crackers into the library where the tour group was assembling. There were two couples in addition to the ones staying with me. And of course, Lily, their tour guide.

Kim had set up a card table behind the couch for her staging area and was covering it with a black tablecloth. She caught me eyeing her presentation and grinned. "The black hides the wine stains."

I set my tray of glasses down and Aunt Ginny tapped me on the arm. "Poppy, this is Lily Snow, from Pink Sandals Boutique Tours."

Lily was about my height. Thin and athletic with skin just a touch this side of leathery from years of living at the shore worshipping the sun and sand. She ran her hand through shoulder-length white hair with a faded pink streak running down one side. She wore the Cape May spring uniform: flowered board shorts and long-sleeved rash guard. She offered me her hand, then produced a business card that had *Pink Sandals Boutique Tours* printed in pink filigree. "It's so nice to finally meet you, Poppy, after all the times we've spoken on the phone."

"We've been looking forward to this event for weeks. I'm so glad you called us. If you need anything tonight just let me know."

"Right now, I think we're all set. I'm still waiting on one guest, but"—she lowered her voice to a hush—"I did want to apologize that we had a last-minute couple join the group just yesterday. I tried to explain to them that the details were all finalized, but they would not be persuaded."

"Would that be Alyce and Ryan Finch? They arrived this afternoon. They've booked a room with us."

Lily's hand flew up to her chest. "Oh no. I hope he wasn't as pushy with you as he was with me. I told them they'd have to get their own lodgings because the rest of the group had already made other arrangements. The Masons are at the Dormer House; my solo traveler is at the Angel of the Sea. I'm not sure where my retired couple is staying."

Aunt Ginny leaned herself into the conversation. "Of course, in the future, you can always book everyone here."

Lily's eyes rolled to the side for a moment and she blanched. "Of course I offered to book them all with you, but sometimes people feel awkward staying with strangers in the tour group. Nowhere to escape if you don't get along."

I gently nudged Aunt Ginny to the side. "Oh, it's no problem at all. I understand. And we had a room available so . . ." Of course, at this point I would have rented them *my* room just to get us some cash flow.

Kim joined us and I asked her if she knew Lily. Kim smiled and gave Lily a fist bump. "Of course I know Lily. She's been hauling her groups around the Cape May tourist trap circuit for years."

Lily grinned and put her hand to the side of her mouth. "Tourists love the whale-watching cruises."

"I didn't realize we had a lot of whales off the coast of Cape May," I said.

Lily shrugged with a cryptic grin. "That's what the brochures say."

Vince and Sunny came down the stairs with Alyce and Ryan nipping at their heels. Ryan was still talking about renting a boat for some bro time. The tension rose like the tide and the room grew awkward and nervous.

Vince turned on the bottom step and held one finger up to Ryan's face. "Zip it!"

Sunny searched the library and her eyes found mine. She had changed her clothes into flowing black palazzo pants and a backless black halter. Her makeup was flawless, but her face was strained. She handed me Tammy Faye and whispered, "Poppy, I have a migraine. Do you happen to have any Excedrin?"

I wasn't sure what I was supposed to do with the Pom who was aggressively licking my hand, but I thought handing her right back might not portray the best customer service, so I took her with me. By the time I'd reached the medicine cabinet I realized that Tammy Faye did not so much adore me, as I'd first suspected, but that I still smelled like bacon.

I deposited Tammy Faye in the kitchen and got a glass of water for Sunny. A still damp Figaro rose up from the back of the kitchen sectional and stretched like Bela Lugosi rising out of Dracula's coffin. "You're supposed to be in Aunt Ginny's room, Fig."

Tammy Faye yipped at Fig and I felt she was issuing some kind of challenge. I moved his dry food to the countertop as a precaution.

By the time I made it back to the library with Sunny's medication, Lily was leading off the introductions: "I'm your tour guide, Lily Snow. I've spoken with all of you before today through phone calls and email, but now we get to meet face-to-face. I'm a New Jersey native who got tired of the rat race in the city and found the emergency exit button. I became a tour guide almost twenty years ago, and I've been showing visitors to all the beautiful gems we have here in South Jersey. I love to surf, boogie board, and lay on the beach soaking up Mother Nature."

Aunt Ginny whispered, "If she soaks up any more of it Gucci will try to turn her into a briefcase when she dies."

I gave Aunt Ginny a sharp look that bounced off her day pearls.

A young couple in their early thirties were obviously expecting. The husband was friendly looking. The sort in high school we called preppy. Blue Dockers and a blue and yellow plaid button-down shirt. His dark hair was neatly trimmed in a bland style that said "average joe." The woman was quiet and shy. The girl who lived next door with wavy brown hair and thick cat-eye glasses. She kept her face turned down and was glancing around the room without making eye contact with anyone for more than a second or two. She held on to the man's hand like a lifeline. "We're the Masons. I'm Willow and this is my husband, Ken. I work at a women's shelter in Rehoboth, and Ken is the assistant manager of the fishing lure department at Sportsmart."

Ryan snorted and Alyce shot him a warning look.

Willow put her other hand on her round belly. "This is our first time in Cape May. We're on a babymoon, as you can see."

Aunt Ginny jabbed me in the side and hissed, "What in the world is a babymoon?"

"I don't know. We'll have to look it up."

Kim leaned in and answered us, because clearly we don't know how to whisper, "It's the last hurrah as a couple before the first baby is born."

"When did that become a thing?" I asked.

Aunt Ginny gave Kim a sharp look below narrowed eyebrows. "You're making that up."

Kim smiled and shook her head no.

Aunt Ginny leaned forward to get a better angle to gawk at Willow's stomach. "Since when is it okay to drink alcohol while you're pregnant? I thought doctors put the kibosh on that about the time your lot came along."

Kim's eyes could have fallen into her lap, but she managed to keep them in her face. She snapped her look to Aunt Ginny. "Shh!"

I yanked Aunt Ginny back. "You can't say stuff like that. It's none of our business."

Aunt Ginny frowned. "Your generation messes everything up."

"All right, well, keep it to yourself."

Kim added, "Or at least until we're alone in the kitchen."

Aunt Ginny crossed her arms in a pout and glared at me. "She shushed me!"

Yes, and I'll give her a medal of bravery for it later.

Everyone congratulated Ken and Willow and all eyes shifted to a retired couple dressed head to toe in western denim like they'd just pulled in from the Cowtown Rodeo.

They were both fluffy with pink smiley faces. They had a matched set of short white hair like they'd used the same salon with a two-for-one special. The woman had a gold ring on every finger and several gold bracelets circled each wrist. Her fingernails were painted bright coral to match her flowered cowboy boots.

"Hi, we're the Smiths. I'm Rosie and this here's Cowboy Bob. We're retired now. We used to own a tack shop in Harrisonburg, but it seems now we're the ones been put out to pasture. Our son Jimmy took over the family business a year ago, so now we travel."

Cowboy Bob interjected, "Got a Winnebago."

Rosie went on. "Our kids surprised us with this trip for a belated anniversary, and since we're in between graduations and grandchild birthdays we thought why not. You only live once. Right, Bob?"

Cowboy Bob knew a good topic when he saw one. "Staying at the campground—in the Winnebago. Sleeps six."

Rosie giggled. "Bob loves his Winnebago."

Everyone greeted Cowboy Bob and Rosie and their heads turned to Ryan and Alyce.

Alyce started to speak, but Ryan cut her off.

"Ryan Finch. My wife." He cocked his head briefly in Alyce's direction. Ryan reached across her and put his hand on Vince's shoulder. "I have the great pleasure of being the right-hand man every day for this guy, my father."

Vince added, "In-law."

Ryan continued unabated. "I'm a senior account executive at BakerCom. I could tell you about some of my famous clients, but then I'd have to kill you." Ryan laughed at his joke, then realized he was the only one laughing and shut it down. "People so famous they would be infamous if I weren't so good at my job. Yeah. I make almost six figures a year. My wife and I are here to spend quality time with Dad and his beautiful wife, Sunny."

Vince's eyebrows slowly migrated north to where his hairline used to be.

Alyce snorted and Ryan leaned into her.

Vince narrowed his eyes and growled low, "Alyce, don't make one of your scenes."

Alyce crossed her arms and started to gently rock back and forth in her seat. She had a red welt growing on her upper arm on the side where Ryan was sitting.

Sunny reached for Vince's hand.

Lily said a little too loudly, "Okay, who's next?" and turned the floor over to Vince and Sunny. Before they could introduce themselves, the doorbell rang.

Kim jumped up. "That will be Daniel. I'll get it."

When Kim threw the door open a very stylishly dressed woman was standing on the other side. She had a short black bob cut at an angle where one side was longer than the other like one of those twirly slides on the playground that I'd seen while walking quickly past. I was pretty sure her one-shouldered red cocktail dress was designer. Sawyer was always poring through fashion Pinterest boards, and I thought I'd seen her dress in some fancy collection. She had on impossibly high heels and apple-red lipstick that I'd never be able to get out of the cloth napkins.

"I'm with the wine tour. I'm so sorry that I'm late. It's not easy to get an Uber around here." Kim hung up her beaded wrap and I welcomed the newcomer.

"You're not late; everyone is just introducing themselves."

Lily offered her hand. "We've been corresponding through email. I'm your tour guide."

"It's nice to finally meet you."

Lily ushered the woman into the library. "This is Zara Pinette. She's joining us from Portland. Zara, we were just making the introductions. Why don't you go next?"

"I'm Zara. I have a lifestyle brand called ZaraLife. You may have heard one of my podcasts on meditation or seen one of my vlogs on going vegan or embracing your own style on every budget. I tell people how to live with simple elegance."

Sunny perked up and leaned toward Zara. "Oh my gosh, I've seen your website, haven't I, Vinny? I just love your throw pillows. And your clothes; you have the best style."

I considered my own style. It was sort of plus-size catalog meets bag lady. I wished I'd worn a nicer blouse. I saw Kim pulling her white dress shirt down over her black trousers self-consciously and knew she was thinking what I was thinking.

Zara wore modesty like an accessory. She gave a demure smile and bowed her head. "I'm just here to do some sketching of the quaint houses and get some ideas for my fall line. And, of course, to drink some wine."

Before the circle could turn their attention back to Vince and Sunny, there was a crash in the kitchen. Aunt Ginny flattened her lips together. "I'll just go see what the ruckus is all about."

She headed for the kitchen, where it sounded like a metal lid was spinning on the floor trying to come in for a landing.

Vince had been mostly quiet, watching the rest of the tour group with concentrated interest. Now it was his turn to introduce himself and Sunny. He leaned toward Zara. "How long have you been in Portland?"

Zara casually crossed her legs. "My whole life."

Vince leaned back in his chair and took Sunny's hand in his. He extolled his virtues of being CEO of BakerCom to the group and introduced Sunny as his hot young wife. Sunny gave a giggle and snuggled into Vince.

It was unfortunate that that was the minute a damp Figaro chased a very wet Tammy Faye down the hall and through the library. After a lap around the sofa, Tammy Faye jumped up into Sunny's lap and shook herself while Figaro disappeared behind the chair.

Alyce took the distraction as an opportunity to shoot a barb aimed for Sunny's confidence. "Tell them what *you* do all day, Sunny."

Sunny looked around at the roomful of expectant eyes. "I'm a stay-at-home wife and mother to Tammy Faye."

Alyce sneered. "Tammy Faye is the dog."

Zara uncrossed her legs and took a deep breath. "That's all you do all day? A pampered housewife?"

Sunny's lip gave a slight quiver and she looked around the room for someone to come to her aid.

Willow looked down at her belly and tried to find somewhere to put her arms.

Rosie said, "Well, what's wrong with that? It takes a lot of work to run a family. It's an important job that too many girls are turning their backs on nowadays."

Zara ignored the older lady and looked down at Sunny. "You're right. I'm sure women fought for generations for gender and pay equality so they could stay home and fold laundry."

Alyce laughed again. "Please. She wouldn't know how to fold laundry if she was streaming a YouTube tutorial on it."

Ryan gave a warning look to Alyce and she flushed deeper yellow.

Sunny squared her shoulders. "I thought women fought for the right to make their own choices in life and not have someone else tell them how they should live."

Zara was caught momentarily on top of her soapbox with nothing to say.

Kim grabbed my arm. "Do something."

I jumped to my feet. "Okay. Now that everyone knows everyone, I've made some delicious treats to pair with the wines Daniel has sent from the Laughing Gull. Why don't we get this party started?"

The doorbell rang. Lily, Kim, and I all let out a whisper of relief.

I opened the door to Daniel Nickson, who immediately started to apologize. "The bridge was up."

Kim grabbed his arm. "No worries. We've made introductions and we're ready to hear about wine."

Daniel correctly interpreted my look as, *For the love of God, get in here and save us*, and he went straight into host mode as Lily turned the group over to him.

I hustled Figaro back into the kitchen where Aunt Ginny was elbow deep in the plate of bacon-wrapped dates. "How did Tammy Faye get so wet?"

Aunt Ginny pointed to Figaro's overturned water bowl. "There may have been an incident."

Aunt Ginny and I brought the food to the library on white platters and Kim followed behind with matching plates and forks.

Daniel was in the middle of describing the first wine, a Sangiovese that only wine club members normally got to try. He was a good-looking man in his early forties. Broad shoulders and slim hips with eyes the color of a Tahitian lagoon. His brown hair was cropped short to make it hard to pick out the flecks of silver. Women loved going to the Laughing Gull Wine Wednesday Book Club. Maybe it was the Chardonnay, or maybe it was the host. He had the tour group eating out of his hand. All except for Ryan, who was fact-checking Daniel's presentation on his iPhone.

By the time they got to the Pinot paired with the

chocolate tarts, the tour group had relaxed into nummy goodness. They discussed their different B&Bs and the weekend itinerary. Vince kept to himself and scanned the group from the back of the library, while Ryan did the rounds and showed himself friendly to the young and single—in other words, Zara. I had to shoosh Figaro from the room when I caught him about to pounce on Tammy Faye, who was eating cheese out of Sunny's hand.

The happy hour crossed over into the dinner hour and Daniel said his goodbyes. "It was so nice meeting you all. As a special thank-you, and an apology for being late, I will show you two more wines from our reserve tomorrow and let you sample them when you come for your tasting."

The tour group was thrilled as the promise of extra wine made amends for everything. Lily and I spent the next thirty minutes making dinner suggestions and carting everyone out the door. Those not staying with me were being dropped off at their restaurant of choice by Lily, who also acted as designated driver, and they were ushered out to her van.

Ryan excused himself to the side porch off the dining room to make a phone call while Alyce said she was going to her room to change.

Vince and Sunny took the absence as their chance to escape.

"Thank God that's over." Kim carried a stack of dishes to the kitchen.

Aunt Ginny snagged the last bacon-wrapped date as Kim passed by. "Who knew there could be so much drama at a wine tasting?"

Tammy Faye was scratching at the back door, whimpering to be let out. The cheese must not have agreed with her. I was just about to attach her leash when I caught movement out of the corner of my eye. I adjusted the curtain to get a better angle. "Tammy Faye, you're going to have to wait a minute."

Aunt Ginny tried to look around me. "Why? What's going on?"

Kim came over to join us at the door. "What's out there?"

"Just Daniel kissing Alyce Finch goodbye behind the garage."

Chapter Nine

Figaro was snuggled into my neck fast asleep when my alarm went off at five. I hit Snooze and immediately faded back to black. The next thing I knew I was getting a vibrating belly massage wake-up call. I rolled onto my side and drifted off again. After Figaro made several more attempts to wake me up, which included walking across my face and knocking various things off the dresser, he unleashed his pièce de résistance and played reveille on his scratching box. I turned over and threw a peacock pillow at him, which he was ready for.

Six twenty-two and I was bone tired. I didn't get to bed before midnight what with the scandal of Kim's boss locked in an embrace with Ryan's wife. Kim and Aunt Ginny and I were so revved up with shock that it took me several levels in my video game to wind down. Then

around two a.m., Sunny decided to loudly air her griev-
ances about the way Ryan and Alyce treat her and Vince
wasn't getting it. He insisted that Sunny was overreact-
ing. He still thought Alyce was stunned from her mother's
death. I was well versed in the intimate details of their argument, as I'm sure were Aunt Ginny, Alyce, Ryan, Mrs.
Pritchard next door, and possibly Mr. Murillo in the house
behind us. This was one time Mr. Winston had dodged a
bullet by not having that hearing aid.

I flopped out of bed and stretched. Figaro sat patiently waiting at the door. *Pest.* I checked my phone to
see if I had any appointments I'd forgotten about. There
were two texts from Gia. One was: **I miss you.** The other
was: **Sierra has a great idea for a muffin.** *Freakin'
Sierra.*

After some deep breaths, a shower, and a dusting of
makeup, I wound my damp hair up in a twist and pinned
it down. There was no time for anything fancy, as I had to
get breakfast on for the guests. I'd have to get my workout in after they left the house for the day's tour.

Tammy Faye was waiting in the kitchen next to a crystal pedestal dessert bowl. There was also a container of
grain-free, gluten-free wild venison dog food with mixed
vegetables. "For the mighty hunter with a warrior spirit."
I looked down at the four-pound pouf with painted toenails. "Do you have a warrior spirit?"

Tammy Faye's ears perked up and her tail started to
wag her in circles around the trash can. I spooned out her
wild venison into the crystal bowl and placed it on the
floor in front of her. Figaro tried to nudge his way forward to inspect what she was getting. Tammy Faye let out

a tiny growl and dove snout-first into her gourmet breakfast. I dumped Figaro's can of chicken goo onto a paper plate and set it in his usual spot. His ears pinned down to his head and he glared at the crystal goblet.

Aunt Ginny breezed into the kitchen, wearing jeggings and a flowy embroidered peasant blouse. She looked at Tammy Faye. "That was for the dog? I almost ate it in the middle of the night. I thought it was your lunch."

"I can't afford that for lunch."

"You don't need to make breakfast for me. I'm meeting Royce for brunch. I'll just have some juice and coffee. Unless you have some of those lemon curd muffins. If you do, I'll have one of those too. Did you hear that ruckus last night?"

"All three hours of it."

"I would never take sides in someone else's argument, but Vince is totally right. Sunny needs to respect that his daughter comes first."

"Are you kidding? The way Alyce treats Sunny? She doesn't deserve that. Alyce is a grown woman with a husband of her own. Don't give me that look. I saw them too. I didn't say happily married. Just married. Sunny is Vince's wife. Vince needs to put his daughter in her place."

"Well, it sounds like Sunny only married Vince to get his money."

"We don't know that. It's no wonder Sunny is worried that Alyce is up to something underhanded. Even you think she's another Anna Nicole Smith."

The front door chimed, and Sawyer came down the hall. "Good morning."

I handed Sawyer a coffee cup. "I'm just saying Alyce

needs to live her own life and stay out of Sunny and Vince's marriage."

Sawyer poured herself some coffee. "Ooh. Is this the Alyce who was making out with Daniel Nickson after last night's happy hour?"

Aunt Ginny and I dropped a look on Sawyer.

"Kim texted me."

I took a long drink of my coffee and remembered the good old days in Waterford, where people minded their own business. Well, at least my neighbors did. But then I never did anything exciting worth gossiping about. "Wasn't it weird how Ryan didn't let Alyce get a word in the entire happy hour?"

Aunt Ginny took the lemon curd out of the refrigerator and set it on the counter in front of me. "He was very rude and controlling. I wouldn't stand for that. I *didn't* stand for that."

Sawyer and I gave questioning looks to Aunt Ginny to see if she'd elaborate.

She looked down at her hands. "I've said too much."

"What's this lemon curd for?" I asked.

Aunt Ginny nudged it toward me. "Just giving you a hand with breakfast."

Sawyer pointed to the floor. "Whose dog is that? And why does Figaro look so angry?"

Figaro was swishing his tail very close to Tammy Faye. She kept one eye on him while she ate.

Aunt Ginny took a martini glass out of the stemware cabinet. "Figaro is angry that Poppy gave him a paper plate. And that is Tammy Faye Baker."

"With the crying?" Sawyer made finger wiggles around her eyes.

Aunt Ginny grinned at me and transferred Figaro's mush to the martini glass. When she placed it back on the floor, we all stood back and watched as Figaro sniffed it, then tucked in with gentlemanly grace.

There was a knock on the back door. I waved our new chambermaid in, and what I saw caused me to wish I could send everyone home and go back to bed. Victory had come to work in pink satin shorts and a white terry-cloth tube top the size of an Ace bandage. It wasn't just me. We were all stunned. Only Aunt Ginny recovered.

"I think I have that same outfit."

Victory smiled and looked down at herself. "Thank you. I like yours too, Mrs. Ginny. Ees that maternity?"

On what planet would an eighty-year-old woman be wearing maternity?

"Yes." Aunt Ginny plucked at her top. "And the pants are too. I like this tummy panel. It'll expand when I get the cheese blintzes this morning."

Victory nodded like this was a solid plan, but Sawyer and I were trying to take in too much too soon. That's when Alexa went off and started playing "Take Me Home, Country Roads."

Aunt Ginny cocked her head. "Huh. I think I dreamed about John Denver last night. Alexa, stop."

I needed more coffee. "Victory, where are your clothes?"

"I get uniform from you, yes? Ees part of job?"

Aunt Ginny shrugged. "Well, they obviously weren't handing out maid uniforms with the visas, were they? Come on, I have something that might work."

Victory followed Aunt Ginny to her bedroom. Sawyer and I took a moment and stared at each other.

Sawyer giggled. "I can't wait to see what comes out of there."

"It's gonna kill me." I took out the rest of the ingredients for the lemon curd muffins and put the cheesy egg and potato casserole in the oven to warm. Sawyer was greasing the muffin pan when we heard a crash from the sunroom followed by Tammy Faye's protests.

Figaro was sitting on an end table; an African violet in a broken pot lay on the floor underneath. Tammy Faye was standing a few feet away looking from me to Figaro, one paw off the ground practically pointing at him.

"Fig! What did you do? You know better than this."

Figaro looked at Tammy Faye through slits for eyes and flicked his tail.

The little Pom moved to stand behind my ankles.

Sawyer picked up the broken pottery. "I'll get this. You go and get those muffins started. I've been thinking about them all the way over here this morning."

I returned to the kitchen wondering what to do about Figaro, who was acting out now that Tammy Faye was here, when a bigger problem presented itself.

Victory emerged from Aunt Ginny's bedroom at the back of the kitchen wearing a sexy low-cut French maid costume with thigh-high stockings.

Sawyer came in just in time to see me choke on my coffee. "Whoa!" Sawyer giggled and had to cover her mouth. "Oh, Poppy. That is so much better than I imagined."

Aunt Ginny emerged behind Victory with a genuine feather duster in her hand. "Look, it fits her. What? Why are you making that face?"

"We can't send Victory in front of guests wearing that. It's no better than what she came in here with."

Aunt Ginny shrugged. "It's just for one day. What can it hurt?"

Sawyer wiped the tears out of her eyes and whispered, "Ask Aunt Ginny where she got the uniform."

Aunt Ginny's eyes widened. "It was 1985 and I was dating the Lieutenant Governor."

I put my hands over my ears. "I don't want to hear this, la la la."

The rest of the morning was one of making and serving breakfast, catching Aunt Ginny sneaking the muffins, and trying to usher Tammy Faye back into Sunny and Vince's room. The only real catastrophe was when Ryan came into the kitchen to request lobster crepes for breakfast tomorrow, as if, and saw Victory sitting on an island barstool eating a muffin.

"Well, hello, gorgeous, who do we have here?"

Victory shot her hand out. "I am Victory. Please to meet you."

"Why are they keeping you in the kitchen, Victory?"

"I am waiting for guest to leave."

Ryan did not seem to have the same need for personal space that the rest of us had, and Aunt Ginny poked him with a wooden spoon and pushed him backward about six inches away from my new chambermaid.

I inserted myself between them. "I'm sorry, but the kitchen is for staff only, Mr. Finch. Perhaps I can bring you some more coffee to the dining room."

Ryan looked Victory up and down. She didn't flinch, but the rest of us felt dirty. "That'd be great. Can Victory bring it to me?"

I wanted to smack him in the face, but Alyce saved me when she poked her head into the kitchen. "Ryan, Daddy and *her* are leaving for a carriage ride before the tour. We have to do it now."

Ryan winked at Victory. "Later."

He left the room and Victory kept on nibbling her breakfast as if nothing had happened. "He ees American peeg, yes?"

We all answered her in unison: "Yes."

Chapter Ten

"Here is a picture of Zara having brunch at Fuel with her stylish friends. I read the Kardashians eat there. I love her shoes."

Sawyer shoved her phone under my nose for the hundredth time since we'd hit Walmart in Rio Grande. It was the best part of my day. Breakfast was finished, the kitchen was clean, and all the guests were out sightseeing. Aunt Ginny was out with Royce, as long as he'd remembered where they were meeting, Victory was cleaning the rooms, and I'd managed to convince Sunny that Tammy Faye would love a carriage ride around Cape May. Sawyer and I were shopping for a proper chambermaid uniform that wouldn't get me a starring role on some South Jersey brothel exposé.

"Oh wow, here's Zara at a nightclub called Tamale. Why don't we ever go clubbing?"

"Because we're in our forties and too tired from working on our feet all day to do anything more than crash in front of the television at night."

Sawyer swiped her screen up and made another gasp. "Bump that! She can't be more than ten years younger than us and she's reading Tolstoy in a rose garden. We need to start living a more exciting life."

I put two pairs of gray yoga pants size two and five white T-shirts Extra Small in my cart. "I just don't know if I can handle more excitement."

Sawyer showed me a picture of Zara in a hiked-up red bandage dress and killer heels straddling a Harley. "She has sixty thousand followers on Twitter. This is living your best life. Don't you ever worry about how much of your life you've wasted and what's passed you by?"

I paused with the extra-large pack of toilet paper halfway to the cart. "Yes. All the time."

She nodded. "Me too. Look at this. She's at the opening of that new restaurant by the chef who won *Chopped* last season."

"Dear God, don't mention *Chopped*. That competition was enough chaos to last me for a lifetime." I grabbed a couple of sports bras in the largest size Walmart had and put them in the cart to wear under my pink chef's coat. Maybe the compression would give me an extra two inches of breathing room.

Sawyer put a pair of size seven shorts in the cart for herself. "You're starting to sound like Aunt Ginny."

I snapped my head in Sawyer's direction. "I am not. Besides, Aunt Ginny has been out clubbing twice this week with that wild pack of rebels that she hangs with."

"Why don't we join them sometime?"

"You don't know what you're asking for. Last week

they convinced me to take them putt-putting. Then they had me take them through the drive-through of every fast-food restaurant on Route Nine from Courthouse to Rio Grande. They called it a progressive dinner. The smell of onion rings almost killed me."

"See, that sounds like fun."

"You weren't the one driving a car full of eighty-year-olds gassed up on Big Macs and Whoppers."

Sawyer grabbed a flowered satin kimono and floppy hat and put them on. "Well, I need to do something. Things went bust with Adrian, and Valentine's Day was a fiasco."

I handed her a pair of silver glitter sunglasses. "I may be in the romance protection program if things go badly with Tim or Gia when I tell them I'm committing to the other one."

Sawyer flopped on a lounge chair in the outdoor furniture display and took a selfie with Chilly Willy from the freeze pop display. "Which one are you going to pick?"

"I don't know. I love them both."

"That figures. I can't get a decent man and you have too many. Why don't you give me one of yours? Not Tim. I'm done with chefs. Present company excluded."

I cocked an eyebrow.

"And not Gia either. His mother scares me half to death. He waved to me across the courtyard a few months ago and she gave me the evil eye. All the plants in my shop were dead by the weekend."

"You could always go back to your ex-husband." Not that I would ever let that happen, but I was looking to shoo the conversation away from my man problems.

"Not if he was the last man on the planet. I'm swearing off men. I'm going on a man cleanse."

"You want me to see if Joanne Junk is available?" I grabbed a couple exercise DVDs and threw them in the cart.

"Ha ha. Very funny. I could do better than Joanne." Sawyer picked up one of the workout DVDs from the cart. "Sixty minutes to great abs. I'd be ten minutes to vomiting. Are you supposed to be doing all this?"

"Not really. But nothing Dr. Melinda suggested is working. I'm getting stronger, but the muscles are still surrounded by a thick padding of fat like they're waiting for a celebrity endorsement to come out. I need some new ideas." I spied a magazine at the register titled *Keto Diet* and put it on the belt.

Sawyer added her Nice'n Easy Chestnut Brown to the pile. Her eyes popped. "I know what we could do." She started waving her hands in front of her.

"Now I'm terrified." I started to unload the rest of the cart with one eye trained on the peanut M&Ms. I could hear them calling to me. I bet I could have been a peanut M&M sniper in another life.

"I'm not going to tell you what it is right now, but it's going to be fabulous! It's just what we need to shake off this gloom."

The cashier held up Victory's pants. "Are you sure you got the right size, hon? They only stretch so much."

I gave her my best South Jersey glare.

She shrugged and popped her gum and rang up the yoga pants.

I turned back to Sawyer. "Just when does this workout take place?"

Sawyer was so excited she was practically doing a shimmy to the register. "I don't know yet, but I'll text you when I see the schedule."

The cashier thumbed through the keto magazine she'd just scanned. "That's a lot of meat. Are you sure this is healthy? I would think lettuce—"

I took the magazine out of her hand and put it in my purse. "Would you just finish please?" I made a face at Sawyer. "As long as it's not one of those boot camp classes where a drill sergeant yells at you or you have to roll tires or carry logs around."

Sawyer grinned. "Oh, it's nothing like that. You'll love it. Trust me."

The cashier held up the DVDs. "Good for you, hon. Going to start working out. Better late than never."

That was all the fat shaming I could take for one day. I considered my options. *Tell the cashier to go pound sand?* No. Judging from her seventy-year-old tan, she's from around here and won't be impressed by my attitude. *Leave all my stuff and walk out?* No, I'd just have to come back later and get it again. *Slap that gum out of her mouth?* Possible winner.

I didn't have time to enact my plan of Jersey girl vengeance because Sawyer pushed me into the rack of Juicy Fruit. "You need to learn some manners, you wrinkled old cow." Sawyer dumped ten boxes of gum all over the conveyor belt and gave the woman a staredown while I swiped my card and grabbed my bags.

The cashier started to ring up the first pack of gum and we took off out of there before the greeter on the scooter woke up from his nap to chase us down.

We ran through the parking lot and hopped into my car like we were skipping school, only much better than that one time I tried it by walking across the football field during morning announcements like I was under a cloak of invisibility. I floored it—you know, in case the scooter guy was after us on his fifteen-mile-an-hour hot wheels—and headed straight for Starbucks.

We were in a fit of giggles when my phone rang Duran Duran's "Union of the Snake."

"Hey, Kim, what's up?"

Kim didn't ask me what was so funny. Her voice was tight and had an echo like she was cupping the mouthpiece with her hand. "You need to get down here right now and help me with this disaster. One of the tour guests is dead. . . ."

Chapter Eleven

We flew down Route 9 and over the West Cape May bridge to the Laughing Gull Winery, where an ambulance and a fire truck were parked out front. Sawyer and I threw open the doors to the gift shop full of wines, wine-themed decor, and T-shirts along with a variety of cheese, olives, crackers, charcuterie, and chocolate to complement any wine-tasting flight. Standing around the shop and looking a little shell-shocked were a couple of patrons who'd had the misfortune of choosing today to visit and the rest of the tour group we had met at the B&B for happy hour.

Lily jumped off a barstool in the corner and jammed her phone in her pocket. "Oh, Poppy, thank God Kim called you. We could use the help. It's been madness here. It's just terrible. Daniel tried CPR, but it didn't work. The paramedics are here now. We've corralled in

here to give them some space. One minute he was fine . . .
a little inebriated . . . kind of fast for a guy that size . . .
but that's why I do all the driving . . . the next thing we
knew, he was gone."

"Who was gone? Which tour member?"

Her pocket buzzed and she fished her phone out. "I
have to take this; it's my lawyer. I've never had anyone
die on a tour before."

I looked around and saw Ken and Willow huddled in
the far corner, Willow with her hand protectively on her
belly. Then over by the T-shirts that said *Wine o'clock*
were the retired couple, Rosie and Bob. Rosie gave me a
sad little wave. A miserable-looking employee whose
name tag had "Jess" written across it stood behind the
cash register biting her nails.

The door to the tasting room opened a crack and Kim
popped her head out just as blue flashing lights pulled up
behind the ambulance. "Oh no. Now the cops have come.
Girls, in here, quick!"

Sawyer and I trampled into the tasting room and let
our eyes adjust to the mood lighting. Even though the entire structure was aboveground and built just a few years
ago, it was made to look like the inside of a natural
cave—a million-dollar natural cave with bistro tables and
throw pillows. Big faux stone walls on all four sides with
high windows and a massive stone fireplace dominated
one end. A small fire was lit more for ambiance than heat.
Set around the fireplace were a leather sofa and two
matching love seats with a slate coffee table in the middle. Scattered around the room were a few more bistro-
style tables and chairs, each set with a candle in a jar and
a menu. And at the back of the room was a long polished
carved maple bar in front of a dramatic backdrop of wine-

soaked barrels. Empty wineglasses and half-eaten plates of food were scattered everywhere.

Ryan and Alyce were off to the side whispering between themselves, and Sunny was kneeling on the floor in front of the sofa, crying, where two paramedics stood over the lifeless body of Vince Baker, flat on his back with his mouth open and eyes open but vacant. Daniel stood a few steps away on his cell phone. His eyes were so white and round they looked like two shiny golf balls.

Kim pulled us back toward the bar. "Daniel is beside himself. He performed CPR until the paramedics arrived, but they weren't able to revive Vince either. He's on the phone with the insurance company now. Nothing like this has ever happened here before today. The paramedics think he had a heart attack."

Sawyer put her hand over Kim's. "Are you okay?"

Kim's eyes welled up with tears and she nodded. "It was so scary. He clearly had too much to drink. He was yelling at everyone; he was slurring his speech. Then his face got all red, he knocked over a glass of wine, then he staggered over to the couch and flopped down. I was taking a tray of glasses to the kitchen when I heard a scream. I ran back out here to see what was wrong and the blond woman he was with was hysterical. She yelled for us to call nine-one-one."

I took a look at Sunny, who was breathing into a paper bag.

Kim snuffled. "I don't even know the man's name."

"It was Vince," I supplied. "Vince Baker. And his wife is Sunny."

Sawyer leaned around me to get another look at Sunny. "That's his wife? I thought she was his daughter."

I nodded at Sawyer with wide eyes and turned back to

Kim. "Do you know what he was so angry about? Why was he yelling?"

Kim let out a breath and rolled her eyes. "The two women he was with did nothing but argue and snipe at each other." Kim nodded her head in the direction of Alyce and Ryan. "That one over there, and the one by the couch. Whenever one of us took a new wine to the table, one of them would be saying something mean to the other. Petty stuff like 'it's not your money' and 'all you do all day is spa treatments.' He finally pounded the table and yelled for everyone to shut up and leave him alone. That's when he went over to the couch. I remember thinking, 'Good for him,' for not letting them walk all over him. Even Daniel was keeping his distance and staying behind the bar, and he loves to schmooze the guests. He says they buy more wine if they feel like they're buying it from a friend.

"Everything happened so fast after that. The paramedics have been waiting for the police. They said it was protocol. But the police only come when the paramedics think something is off. Why would they need the police to report a heart attack?"

"I don't know."

"Most of the tour group are waiting in the other room. They said it was to give the family some space, but I think they were just tired of being around them. I thought I was going to have a riot on my hands when that man collapsed. Everyone was pointing the finger at everyone else and making accusations. Lily was no help—she just fell apart." Kim nudged me. "Your name is listed as one of the emergency contacts in the tour documents."

I groaned. "Why am I an emergency contact? I don't know any of these people."

"Probably because they're staying at your bed and breakfast. Can you help calm everyone down?"

"I'll do my best."

The door opened and a crackle of police radio announced the arrival of Officer Amber and Officer Consuelos. My stomach bottomed out and I braced myself for the accusation my high school nemesis was sure to issue.

Amber and I went all the way back to when instead of a gun and a badge she used to carry pom-poms and three different flavors of Bonne Belle Lip Smackers. She went from being my high school bully to being my middle-aged bully. Frankly, I thought I should get a commendation for all the bad guys I'd stopped since my unfortunate launch back into South Jersey society. But every time I turned around, Amber was trying to arrest me on some crazy exaggerated complaint. She caught my eye and made a look like she just bit the inside of her cheek.

Sawyer groaned. "Oh great."

I sighed. "Why is it never her day off?"

Amber walked over to the paramedic who squatted down and started gesticulating around Vince's face. Amber was nodding along to his debriefing.

Kim put her head down on the bar. "Oh no. What am I going to do if she arrests me?"

Sawyer put an arm around Kim's shoulders. "Why in the world would she arrest you?"

Kim peeked out through her fingers. "Because I served that man his final wine right before he died."

"Honey," I said, "you didn't even know his name. How were you supposed to know he was going to have a heart attack?"

"You hadn't seen Barbie in twenty-five years. That didn't stop Amber from arresting you."

"Fair point."

"And legally we can be held responsible if he was overserved. But we only gave him the routine flight. Five glasses of wine with two ounces in each. That's only equal to two regular glasses of wine. He had to have been hammered when he got here." Kim stood up and rolled her shoulders. "Well, let's get this over with."

I cheered her on and she went to face the uniforms. Daniel shut his cell phone off and joined the officers by Vince's body.

Sawyer and I watched the exchange of information; then Officer Consuelos took Sunny by the arm and led her away from the others to get her statement.

I silently wished her luck. I'd been in her shoes before. I looked over to where Amber interviewed Kim and Daniel. They kept shaking their heads and shrugging like they had no idea what happened. Sawyer leaned over and lifted her chin toward Alyce and Ryan. "Who are they?"

"Vince's daughter and son-in-law." The two of them had their heads together deep in conversation. Their eyes darting toward Sunny and Vince. Ryan was chewing his fingernails to nubs.

"Do they look nervous to you?"

"Maybe they're still in shock."

"Maybe that's what mourning looks like when you're rich and spoiled."

"Speaking of . . . have you seen Zara Pinette anywhere? She's supposed to be here."

Sawyer looked around the room. "She wasn't in the gift shop. Maybe she's sick today. Let's do a slow lap and check outside."

We took a walk around trying to avoid Amber's notice.

On the far side of the room was a set of French double doors that led out to a private patio surrounded on all sides by a vine-covered trellis. Sitting on the patio wearing a flowered white maxidress and oversized red sunglasses was Zara. A glass of red wine was in front of her, and she was taking selfies in various poses with the wine. Every couple of shots she'd check the screen and make adjustments for another round of pictures.

"Zara, are you okay?"

Zara yawned and shrugged. "Sure."

I gestured to the French doors. "Do you know what happened . . . in there?"

Zara made a pouty face and took another selfie. "I know the old man did a lot of yelling. It's why I came out here."

Sawyer mumbled, "I don't think he was that old."

"Do you know what he was yelling about?"

"The little hipster was on him from the time we left the B and B to convince him to go sailing. I think he got fed up. I know I did."

Zara started typing on her phone with two thumbs. "Hashtag vacay . . . hashtag blessed . . . hashtag best life." She put her phone down and took a sip of her wine. "Is it time to go to the next winery yet?"

"Well . . ."

Sawyer cleared her throat.

I glanced at her. "What?"

I felt a tap on my shoulder and turned around to look into the steel-gray eyes of Officer Consuelos.

"Ms. McAllister. Are you and your aunt part of the tour group?"

"No, the deceased and his family were staying at my bed and breakfast."

He looked around the garden for hidden redheads of the four-foot-ten variety. "And Mrs. Frankowski?"

"She's at home as far as I know."

His shoulders and the wrinkles in his forehead relaxed. "All right. And what is your name, ma'am?"

Sawyer giggled and put her hand out in introduction. "Sawyer Montgomery. Do you need to take my statement, Officer?"

Good Lord.

Officer Consuelos smiled at Sawyer and indicated a table and chairs a few feet away. He turned to Zara and said, "I'll be back to get your statement shortly, ma'am. Please stay put."

Sawyer turned her head to wink at me before she followed him.

"What happened to the cleanse?"

"What? It starts tomorrow."

I gave her a look—and she very well knew what it meant too, but she tinkled her fingers at me in return and followed the good-looking police officer. Who, I might add, had been at my house many times when Aunt Ginny was on house arrest and not once did I ever try to flirt with him. Just sayin'.

Zara watched them walk away and wrinkled her nose. "Statement about what?"

"McAllister."

Oh crap. I turned around. "Amber, hello." *God, these two move silently like cats.*

"You're starting to be like a trailer park in a twister. If there's a dead body, I know you're somewhere in the vicinity."

"Well, it's a small island. We're all in the vicinity."

"You know what I mean. Now what in God's name are you doing at another crime scene?"

"I didn't get here until after he died."

"So, you're contaminating my crime scene."

"Why do you keep saying 'crime scene'? I was told he had a heart attack."

She looked at Zara, who was back on her cell phone. "Step inside with me for a minute."

She closed the French doors behind us as the paramedics hoisted Vince onto a stretcher and covered him completely with a sheet. One of them handed a clipboard to a man wearing a jacket that said *CORONER* across the back. Then they strapped the body down and wheeled it through the gift shop out to the ambulance. While the door was open, I could see that a pretty young woman in a police uniform was in the front room taking statements from everyone else.

Amber lowered her voice. "Paramedics reported some questionable findings and called it in. Until there's an autopsy, it's considered a suspicious death."

"Oh, poor Sunny." I looked back to the couch where Sunny had broken down to sobs again.

"Yes, poor little multimillionaire."

"You don't think she had anything to do with this, do you?"

"If I've learned anything in my time on the force it's that killers make the best widows. This time . . . we'll see."

Amber asked me a few questions about the guests and what I'd observed about them last night. She took my statement, then moved on to Alyce while Officer Consuelos came back inside and pulled Ryan aside.

Sawyer was waiting for me at the bar when we were done. "Did Amber ask you about Sunny and Alyce arguing?"

"Lots. She also wanted to know how they acted at the B and B. I told her pretty much the same as how I'd heard they'd acted here."

Sawyer looked at Sunny sitting on the couch looking lost. "Why don't you go talk to her? I'm going to go ask Zara a few questions, since Ben is finished with her."

"Ben?"

Sawyer grinned. "That's what Officer Consuelos told me to call him."

"You need Jesus." We parted and I walked to Sunny and put my hand on her shoulder. "I'm so sorry. What happened?"

Sunny threw herself into my arms sobbing. "I don't know. I just don't know. He didn't feel well this morning and we talked about going home. But he seemed to perk up after breakfast. He wasn't drinking any more than the small samples of wine that were included in the tastings. By the time we arrived here, he was getting more and more stressed and said he was having trouble breathing. I thought it was because of Alyce and Ryan, so I helped him over to the couch. Then he collapsed."

I rubbed Sunny on the back. "I heard there were arguments."

Sunny sniffled and yawned. "Ryan and Alyce were in rare form today. I don't know why Ryan has been so obsessed with getting Vince off alone with him, but today he practically said it was an intervention." She turned bloodshot blue eyes up to mine. "What would Vince need an intervention for?"

"I don't know. Did you and Alyce argue?"

"No more than usual." Sunny buried her face in her hands. "I've tried to be a peacekeeper, but Alyce hates me. She thinks I've stolen her father away from her. She hated me when we were in school and she hates me still."

"You went to school together? As in the same class?"

"Not the same. Alyce was a year ahead of me. To be honest, I don't really remember her much. We ran with different crowds. She was very quiet, you know? I don't remember her ever being at any football games or school dances."

"And you were?"

"Always. I was busy with my friends, the other cheerleaders, and the jocks. We were at all the events and parties like you do in high school. Everyone had their group of friends they hung out with. I was with mine."

I felt a prick of irritation sting me in the back of the shoulder blades. I had not had much success with cheerleaders in the past. "So, you figure she was doing all the same things you and your popular friends were doing, just with different people?"

"I don't think I was popular. I was just hanging out like everyone else. She got much better grades than me. I think she was on that National Honor thing. I could never do that. I was in all the basic classes. But I was still smart enough to go to community college. Plus, I got the internship at BakerCom when I graduated. I was hoping the work experience would get me some credits to be able to transfer to a university. But then I met Vince." The tears started to flow again and Sunny sobbed. "What am I going to do, Poppy?"

I remember being in her shoes the day John was diagnosed with cancer. That was the day the mourning began. "It's going to be hard for a while. And you'll wish you could have gone with him. But it will get better. I promise. You'll get through this and Vince will always be with you."

Amber came up beside us and looked from me to Sunny and back to me. "I need to speak with Mrs. Baker."

I gave them their privacy and the door to the gift shop opened. Sawyer poked her head in. "Psst. Poppy. Com'ere."

I moved toward Sawyer while a team of officers started bagging and tagging all the wineglasses, open bottles of wine, and leftover nibbles. "How'd you get out there?"

"I walked around. There's a gate from the patio that leads out front hidden in the hedges."

"How was Zara?"

Sawyer rolled her eyes. "She said she didn't know who Vince was. When I told her, she said she just found out that he was dead when Ben questioned her. Apparently, she'd been on the patio trying to catch the right breeze to blow her dress out for her Instagram post."

"She'd been out there a long time. She didn't hear the ambulance or the police cars?"

Sawyer shrugged. "She said she gets in the zone when she's working. So, I went back into the gift shop. I've talked to most of the people on the tour. They are all saying the same thing. The ladies argued throughout the wine tasting. Ryan is an insufferable bore who spent the day trying to impress Vince and wear him down to go off alone with him—creepy. And Vince got stressed out and collapsed. No one saw anything. They all think it was a heart attack."

"Well, the paramedics saw something that made them think it was so suspicious that they called the cops."

Amber called the room to attention. "Officer Crabtree,

please bring everyone from the gift shop in here. Officer Consuelos, get the young lady from the patio."

Sawyer snickered under her breath. "Crabtree."

When Amber had everyone's attention, she brought the verdict. "Those of you who are not a part of the Pink Sandals wine tour are free to go. We have your contact information if we need to get ahold of you. We have to request that the rest of you be patient just a little while longer."

Ken Mason raised a hand. "What does that mean exactly?"

"I strongly suggest that you stay close by. I might have to call on you over the next few days with further questions and I know you don't want to impede an open investigation by being hard to reach." There was much grumbling and protest from the tour group, but Amber wasn't fazed. "It should only take a day or two and then I'm sure you'll be able to return to life as usual. Your tour guide says that you're booked at various wineries for the next week, but the Laughing Gull is closed until further notice."

Daniel's face turned the color of a Coppertone Water-BABIES sunburn. "What! That's ridiculous. How can you close my business because someone had a heart attack! How is that my fault? It's the start of the tourist season and I have bookings every day. I'm calling your boss. This is a typical abuse of power." Daniel stormed from the room and disappeared through the door behind the bar.

I almost felt sorry for Amber. And then she pointed at me. "And you need to keep your big nose out of things."

My hand wanted to fly up to my nose, but I willed it to stay down. *My nose is regular size.*

Lily led the rest of the tour group out to her van. They were already trying to get a refund on the rest of the tour.

Sawyer and I were trying to escape out the door with them, but Kim grabbed my arm. Her eyes were ringed with black from crying and there were gray trails down her cheeks. She lowered her voice to a whisper: "Girls, please. You have to help us. My heart goes out to the family of the deceased. It's been an awful, tragic day and I can't imagine what they're going through right now. But we could lose everything if Amber says it was the winery's fault that that man died here. There could be fines, or lawsuits, not to mention that death is only good for business if you're an undertaker."

Sawyer scrunched her face up. "Why would it hurt you? Daniel owns the winery. Couldn't you just go back to your old job at the Tropicana?"

Kim clenched her teeth. "I shouldn't even be thinking about this with his widow sitting right over there, but Jess and I invested thousands into the winery for new vats and varietals of grapes from France. I never even told Rick that I cashed in my 401(K). You do not want to be there for that conversation. If the winery goes under, we have nothing left. There has to be some way we can help the Baker family without destroying all of our lives in the process. Please can you help us?"

Chapter Twelve

"The Bible says: 'With great power comes great responsibility.'" Aunt Ginny folded her arms across her chest and tried to stare me down.

"That's not the Bible. That's Spider-Man."

Aunt Ginny narrowed her eyes. "Are you sure? I think it's in the Bible."

"Not unless there's a chapter written by Stan Lee."

Sawyer giggled, then hid behind her Frappuccino.

Aunt Ginny turned to her new expert fact-checking device on the counter. "Alexa, who said: 'With great power comes great responsibility'?" Alexa answered, "Uncle Ben from *Spider-Man*," and Aunt Ginny unplugged it. "Kim needs you. She called over here to ask me to buck you up about it."

"I know. We just left there."

"What are you going to do?" Aunt Ginny cocked her head to the other side and tried a staredown from a different angle. "You have to admit that on some supernatural level you may owe it to Kim to get involved."

"Say what now?" I glanced at Sawyer and she had to look down at the table to keep from snorting. I couldn't find the words I wanted, so I kept shaking my head hoping they would bounce to the front.

Aunt Ginny placed her hands on the kitchen table where Sawyer and I were sitting with our coffees and Walmart shopping bags. "The curse."

"I am not cursed. That . . . psychic . . . was a charlatan. I'd rather drive to Wildwood and put a dollar in Zoltar. I think his advice would be more accurate. Besides, I was nowhere near Vince when he died."

Aunt Ginny counted on her fingers. "He was staying in this house. You fed him breakfast. You were the last one to tell him to have fun today when the tour group came to pick him up. So, it counts."

Sawyer gave me an evil little grin. "You're the Kevin Bacon of death in Cape May." She laughed through her nose at my glare.

There was the sound of heavy little feet running down the stairs. A few seconds later, Figaro skidded into the kitchen with Tammy Faye hot on his tail. Figaro jumped on the table to escape the tiny Pom and slid to the end on the Walmart bags, and Tammy Faye did a victory trot around the island and drank out of Figaro's water bowl. Figaro crouched down and wiggled his butt, ready to pounce. Tammy Faye realized she'd gone too far and bolted from the kitchen with Figaro loping sideways after her.

"I am not the harbinger of death to this community. And I'm also not legally allowed to get involved. Something Amber reminds me of every time she sees me. That and how much she wants to arrest me for anything that annoys her."

Sawyer plucked a tuft of Figaro's hair off her Eagles jersey and dropped it on the floor. "We should try to help Kim, though, don't you think? She's always been there for us every time someone dies around you." Her words sounded reasonable, but her green eyes sparkled with mischief. "Besides, you said you were looking for a distraction so you could think of something other than Gia and Tim."

"I am looking for a distraction. And I do owe Kim a lot. But I want nothing to do with this."

Sawyer nodded and the side of her mouth caught the straw in her Frappuccino.

Aunt Ginny smacked the table. "That settles it! Tomorrow we start investigating."

"Whoa! Hold on there, Mrs. Pollifax. No one said you were involved in this. And we didn't settle anything. We don't even know if there's anything janky going on. Vince might have had a very ordinary heart attack. He did run a big corporation. That's a lot of stress. Not to mention that whole family dynamic."

Tammy Faye chased Figaro back through the kitchen.

Aunt Ginny's mouth puckered up like she was sucking on a lemon. "You know how I know it was murder?"

"Tell us, Columbo."

"Because you're involved."

Sawyer sucked in her bottom lip to keep her mouth shut.

Aunt Ginny stood up as tall as her four foot ten would allow. "What did that psychic say? Mayhem and murder would follow you?"

"Destruction and misery. She said destruction and misery would follow me all the days of my life." I felt my words stick in my neck and cleared my throat.

Aunt Ginny finally nailed the staredown. "And?"

"And everywhere I go I'll find nerf un derf. . . ." My words petered out at the end, but Aunt Ginny wouldn't let me off the hook.

"Nothing but death!" She raised her arms up in field goal position and rested her case.

Seriously. She can't always remember to put on pants, but every word spoken to me six months ago by some whack job she has with perfect recall.

Sawyer fished her shorts and her Miss Clairol out of the Walmart bag. "Maybe we should go visit that psychic and ask her about removing the curse."

Aunt Ginny dug around the bag to see if there was a prize for her. "While we're at it we can see if anything was shady about Vince's death."

This day has gone all to hell. There was a loud crash in the sitting room followed by a hiss and a yelp. We rushed in there and found Figaro hunched behind an end table by a broken vase. His ears were pinned down and his tail was tucked up underneath him.

"Figaro! Again?"

Tammy Faye pranced into the room and looked around, surprised. She yipped a couple of times to make her point that she was very distressed by what she found. She leveled an accusatory bark at Figaro.

I bent over to pick up the pieces of broken china. We all jumped back in shock, including Tammy Faye, when Victory rose up from the floor behind the couch with a stretch and a yawn. "Ees eet my job to clean vase?"

Chapter Thirteen

Sawyer grabbed her chest and Aunt Ginny grabbed Sawyer. "Sweet mother of Jesus! I thought it was a zombie."

Even Tammy Faye jumped back with a yelp.

Figaro hunched down on the end table, his golden eyes round like two butterscotch candies.

"Victory? What are you doing back there?"

"Sorry. Sometimes I jus' fall asleep or somesing like that."

"You fell asleep? Behind the couch?"

Victory pulled herself upright and smoothed her sexy costume uniform. "Yes. Ees no big deal."

I was too stunned to formulate a follow-up. "I have some items for you in the kitchen."

Victory nodded and followed the procession back through the dining room.

I led her to the Walmart bag and handed her the stack of yoga pants and T-shirts that Sawyer and I had bought hours ago. "You can wear them for your regular uniform, but you'll be responsible to wash them with your own laundry, okay?"

Again, Victory shrugged. "Yes. These ees my first real Amerecan clothes. I cannot wait to try sem on."

Aunt Ginny looked at the tiny stack in Victory's arms. "Knock yourself out."

Victory knitted her eyebrows into a v. "I don't know what dis means, 'knock yourself out'?"

Sawyer gave her a small smile. "It means you can go try them on now if you want to."

Victory's face lit up. "Okay, I am going now. Bye." She walked out of the mudroom door and down the driveway with her arms full of clothes.

Sawyer's eyebrows shot up. "I meant she could try them on in the bathroom."

The front door opened and Tammy Faye let out a series of excited yips. Sunny entered the foyer looking disheveled and weary. Her hair hung limply around her face and she had circles of exhaustion under her eyes. The young woman looked like she'd aged fifteen years since she'd left that morning. She scooped the Pom into her arms, buried her face in Tammy Faye's neck, and started to sob.

I asked Aunt Ginny if she'd go make a pot of tea and led Sunny into the library. Sawyer gave me a sad wave goodbye and let herself out.

The sun goes down early in March, and even though it was just about dinnertime it was already getting dark. There was a chill in the room, so I lit the fireplace. I sat in a wing chair facing Sunny and handed her a box of tissues. We sat in silence until Aunt Ginny brought in the tea and joined us.

Sunny snuggled Tammy Faye, who seemed to sense her heaviness and lay down by her side with her nose on Sunny's leg. "My doctor in New York called me in a prescription for a sedative. I'm going to go to bed in a little while. I don't usually take medicine, so I don't know if I'll be awake for breakfast in the morning."

Aunt Ginny put a hand on Sunny's knee. "Don't worry about that now. Poppy can make you something and bring it up to your room when you're ready."

I gave Sunny an encouraging smile.

Sunny stared into the fire for a few minutes before speaking. "Alyce and Ryan have been awful today. They're always terrible to me, but they were especially ugly today." Sunny looked at Aunt Ginny, who nodded for her to keep going. Through more tears she said, "Vince was lying there dead, and all they cared about was his will, and his life insurance, and where his money would go."

I took a deep breath. "I'm so sorry, Sunny."

"Ryan doesn't know this, but I heard him call his lawyer and say they want to contest Vince's will. How do they even know what's in it? I don't even know what's in it."

Aunt Ginny shook her head. "Wills bring out the worst in families."

"We aren't a family. Not really. Alyce never accepted me. It's not like I stole her dad away from her mom. Her mom had been dead almost seven years when I started working for Vince."

I poured her a cup of tea. It was chamomile. I hated chamomile. It was slimy, like drinking an aloe vera plant.

"You said earlier that you were an intern for BakerCom, didn't you?"

Sunny smiled wistfully while stroking Tammy Faye. "I didn't have any work experience other than waitressing at Hooters to work my way through college. With that on my résumé, all I could get was an unpaid internship. But just a month after starting at BakerCom, Vince hired me to be his personal assistant. His regular admin had gone on maternity leave, so he said I could have the position until I transferred to a university. Then Vince said the pregnant lady decided not to come back after all. So, I was offered to stay on as his assistant permanently." Sunny picked up her tea and sipped it. "He said he saw something special in me and knew I could go far with BakerCom. He even had one of the older, more experienced women train me on some of the specialized software like Excel and PowerPoint."

Aunt Ginny snorted. "And how did that go over?"

Sunny shrugged. "She didn't like me very much. But she was a religious woman. Every time I walked into the room she'd look up to Heaven and cry out, 'Dear Jesus, help me.' Once she finished training me, I think she left to go work for a religious organization called Give Me Grace—at least that's what she said when I asked her. She had a lot of experience, so I'm sure she got a promotion."

Aunt Ginny and I made the briefest of eye contacts, then turned our attention back to Sunny. "I got really good at scheduling Vince's appointments and making appointments for sales meetings." Sunny yawned. "I'm sorry, I'm just so tired." A tear slipped down her cheek and she stood up. "If you don't mind, I think I'm going to go up to bed."

I started to walk her to the foyer when there was a knock at the front door. Call it habit, call it a sixth sense, call it whatever you want. The hairs on my arms started to tingle and I knew it was the police.

Aunt Ginny put a hand on Sunny's arm. "Wait here a minute while Poppy gets the door."

I looked out the side window and had a Cape May County badge shining back at me. I opened the door to find a tall, broad-shouldered cop with sandy blond hair. "Ms. McAllister."

"Officer Birkwell. To what do I owe the pleasure?"

"I just need to check Vince Baker's room."

I put out my hand.

He shook his head. "Don't have the search warrant yet. I was hoping you would be cooperative. We'll have one in the morning and I'll just have to come back during breakfast, so we might as well do it now."

Given Sunny's condition, I thought it would be best not to subject her to anything more tonight. But before I could say so, she poked her head around the door. "I don't mind. Tammy Faye and I have nothing to hide."

I sighed. This was a bad idea. Not to mention it broke my perfect search warrant streak. "I guess you should come in then."

Aunt Ginny gave him that staredown she'd been working on earlier. All that practice with me had warmed her up for the big league. He took a step back and leveled a stare of his own.

When they were done trying to intimidate each other, I led him up to the Purple Emperor suite and he had a thorough look around while Sunny waited with Aunt Ginny. It took longer than usual because Sunny had unpacked their suitcases with a grenade. Clothes, shoes, bags of gourmet dog cookies, boxes of saltwater taffy, pots and compacts of makeup were covering every surface. He used a pointed retractable wand to lift a leopard thong off the lamp and move it aside.

"I'm sure she won't be happy that you're moving her underwear."

Officer Birkwell leveled me a stare. "That's a man's."

"Eww."

He did a very thorough poking through their suitcases and drawers.

"What exactly are you looking for?"

"Can't tell you."

"Can I help?"

"Nope. You can't even come in here."

Forty minutes later he had searched the room and taken pictures of everything. He finally shook his head and left the room empty-handed. He met Sunny at the bottom of the stairs. "Thank you, Mrs. Baker. Do you have a purse or backpack of sorts that isn't in your room?"

"I have my Kate Spade bag here." Sunny retrieved a pink designer bag from the hall table and Officer Birkwell went through it.

He pulled out Sunny's prescription bottle and read it. His eyes flicked up to hers for a moment. "Mrs. Baker, I'm sorry, but I'll have to confiscate this for now."

Sunny burst into tears. "But why? I just got those tonight."

"Do you have a receipt?"

She sobbed. "I never take the receipts. The ink gets on my manicure."

Officer Birkwell placed the bottle in a plastic Baggie he pulled from his pocket and wrote on it in black Sharpie. "Your belongings will be returned to you when they are cleared. It's my duty to inform you that with this being an open investigation we may need to call on you again for further testimony."

Sunny pulled out a tiny pack of tissues from her purse and blew her nose. "I understand."

He gave us a final nod, made *I'm watching you* finger motions from his eyes to Aunt Ginny's, and left us for the night.

I put my hand on Sunny's shoulder. "I'm so sorry. I'm sure nothing will come from it."

Sunny started crying again. "I'm going to bed." She scooped up Tammy Faye and dragged herself up the stairs.

When we heard her close her bedroom door, Aunt Ginny grabbed my arm. "Do you see now why we need to get involved?"

"No. Why?"

"Officer Birkwell wasn't here for a social call. They're looking for something that killed Vince, and they suspect her. Policemen asking questions are being policemen, but little old ladies asking questions are just being little old ladies. That's Miss Marple." Aunt Ginny leveled me a grave look and a slow nod.

"God help us."

Chapter Fourteen

It was five o'clock in the morning and something nearby was rumbling. For a change, it wasn't Figaro sitting on my neck. I reached over to my nightstand to get my cell phone and found the pointy-eared ball of fur. Figaro was in midswipe to knock my cell phone to the floor.

"No. Give me that." I grabbed the phone and checked my messages. Seven texts from Kim since last night. Someone had leaked it to the local news that there was an incident at the Laughing Gull. Kim sent several poop emojis and a meme of a dog in a sweater begging that said *please help me*. She wanted to meet for coffee this morning, so I typed back that I would be at La Dolce Vita to do some baking and could meet her there later.

Figaro swatted my herbal sleeping pills off the nightstand and gave me a self-righteous blink.

"I wouldn't look so smug if I were you. You can't pop the lid off the cat food."

I got dressed in my workout clothes and went downstairs. I made some coffee and fed Figaro and Tammy Faye, who had miraculously escaped Sunny's room after I'd deposited her in there again. After a walk, some yoga, a protein smoothie, taking the dog out for a drag around the yard, and a shower, I was ready to get dressed for the day. I took my time this morning. I blew my hair out and set it in hot rollers while I carefully applied my makeup. I picked out a stretchy green dress that showed my best curves to their full advantage and paired it with chunky tan booties. My back would be killing me before lunch, but I had to fight back against a skinnier, younger opponent with a belly button ring.

Ryan and Alyce had come back around midnight and rung me to request a late breakfast. I thought Ryan was under the misguided notion that I was his private staff instead of him being a guest in my establishment with set serving times. But since Sunny had already told us she'd be sleeping late I prepared a few things and set them on the buffet for Aunt Ginny to supervise. Yogurt and granola parfaits with figs, cherries, flax seeds, and walnuts drizzled with honey. Slices of pecan date bread with orange butter. And a warming tray of crispy bacon for Aunt Ginny to put out with the coffee and juice. There was no sense in putting it out ahead of time or the guests would come down to an empty tray and a bacon-stuffed cat.

With everything under control at home, mostly because everyone was still asleep, it was time to seduce the barista. I mean, time to make the muffins.

The first thing I noticed when I arrived at La Dolce Vita was that for the second time this week no one was waiting for me in the kitchen. No smiling Italian offering me a latte. *What the hickory?* The speakers were pouring out a sexy R&B station instead of the old standards, and muffled voices were struggling through the hiss of the frothing wand to whisper rumors of insecurity to my ears. I put my purse on the desk in the office and walked into the dining room. Sierra was at the espresso machine frothing a pitcher of milk while Gia was sitting at the bar in the place of a customer, watching and instructing her about angles and depths. She lost control of the wand and milk shot out of the pitcher onto her tight white T-shirt. It was stretched so thin I could read the washing instructions on her bra tag.

Gia took a towel and wiped the counter in front of him and told her to try it again. He looked up and caught my eye. "You are more gorgeous every time I see you."

Mission accomplished.

Gia stood and walked toward me with a sly grin. "Why are you so dressed up today? Is this all for me?" He pulled me against him and nuzzled my neck.

I giggled. "You wish. I have a meeting with Tim later to discuss the summer menu."

Gia stopped nuzzling. He dipped his head and narrowed his eyes playfully with a message that said, *Check.* With a knowing grin he leaned in and kissed me.

Behind him, Sierra dropped the frothing pitcher. "Oh no. Giampaolo, I am totes sorry. I'm such a klutz."

Gia gave me one last look under a raised eyebrow that promised we weren't finished yet and went to instruct Sierra on how to—wipe up milk?

Sierra shot me a look that said, *Sorry, not sorry*, and bent down low to swipe at the milk on the floor just in front of where Gia was standing. At least she was wearing pants today. According to the tag, they were made in Taiwan.

Gia turned to the far side of the counter and took a clean towel from a drawer.

I shot my hand out and knocked the frothing pitcher off the espresso grate. *Oops.*

Thunk, splat, clank. Sierra shot upright with milk streaming down her face. Her dramatic eye shadow creating more of a panda look under her eyes. "Uhck, gross! Come on!"

Gia looked from Sierra to me and tipped his head slightly. His lip twitched in amusement, but he kept a straight face.

I handed Sierra the damp towel she had been using to clean the bar and shook my head sympathetically. "It's probably a good idea to use the mop to avoid accidents. That grate is narrow."

She held her shirt out with two fingers. "What am I going to do now? I'm going to smell like a baby bottle. Giampaolo, do you have a T-shirt I can change into?"

Gia quirked an eyebrow at me. I knew he had a gray concert T-shirt in his office. He knew that if he let her wear it the consequences would be dire. I saw his lip twitch again. "Let's finish cleaning this up and you can go home and change. If you have a shirt with buttons, that would be a better uniform."

I returned to the kitchen feeling just a teeny bit victorious. I don't know who was winning, but at least I was able to fire off a shot of my own. I hadn't made up my mind if I was ready to say goodbye to Tim and commit to Gia, but I'd be darned if I'd let him be stolen out from under me by a child who wasn't old enough to serve anything off the evening cocktail menu.

I put my apron on and started getting ingredients together. Kim had left me some wine from happy hour, and I had an idea for two no-bake desserts. I was going to make a strawberry tiramisu with the sparkling sweet red, and some no-bake Moscato cheesecake shooters with macerated blackberries. My phone rang Tim's ring tone and a few pellets of shame over my behavior from the past half an hour speckled my face. I answered right away to shut Van Halen up. "Hey there."

"What are you wearing?"

"Uh . . ." I could see right down the plunging neckline of my dress to my Spanx—the real ones this time. "Just normal baking clothes." *Not something sexy.* "Why?"

"I want to take you to lunch."

"Ooh. Is it someplace fancy?"

"It might be."

"Does Gigi own it?"

Tim laughed. "No. I wouldn't do that to you. Not after that stunt she pulled."

You'll have to narrow the options down. "Okay. Should I call you when I'm done?"

"Just be done before one. I have to stuff the sausage."

The strawberry I was holding shot out of my hand. The line went silent while I tried to decide if I was supposed to read into that last comment or not.

Tim laughed. "No, really. One of my suppliers is bringing me some Iberico pork and I'm making sausage and peppers for the special tonight."

"You've been waiting all day to say that to someone, haven't you?"

I could feel Tim blush through the phone. "Yeah. I have."

"You're impossible. I'll call you by one." I hung up with him and my phone immediately rang Duran Duran.

"It's Kim. Can we meet now?"

"I'm making desserts at Gia's, but come to the back and we'll talk while I work."

I went out front to put in an order for two cappuccinos and caught Gia standing behind Sierra holding her hand on the frothing pitcher moving it up and down. He was instructing her on frothing milk, and her look said that milk was not what was on her mind.

"Since you're practicing your frothing, can you make me two cappuccinos? One with regular milk and one with alternative?"

Sierra threw me some shade like I was interrupting a private moment. Gia let go of the milk pitcher and stepped back. "Good. You need the practice. I won't always be here to help you."

Where is he planning to go?

The front bell jingled, and Gia's mother waddled in like the black death. She was even shorter than Aunt Ginny and wore her silvery steel hair up in a tight bun. Somehow, she always smelled like oregano, like she was bottling it in a dark room in the back of her restaurant. Gia's ancient and lecherous uncle was with her. "Buongiorno, ciao, Giampaolo."

Gia came around the bar and cheek-kissed the older man. "Zio Alfio, ciao." He held his hand out to me. "Zio Alfio, you remember Poppy."

"Hello, Zio Alfio."

Zio Alfio wiggled his eyebrows and said something that made Momma pull his ear until he apologized.

Gia stepped in between us laughing nervously. "Hey, okay, Zio. Va bene, no?"

Gia's uncle Alfio spotted Sierra and threw her a lecherous wink. "Chi è la bambina?"

Momma's face turned up in disgust. "Un altro con morale sciolto."

Phew, for once she isn't mad at me.

Momma looked over at me and spit on the floor.

Oh. Never mind.

Gia hugged his mother, which gave her the chance to mouth an obscenity at me behind his back.

"Well, I'd better get to my kitchen." *Please don't set me on fire.*

Momma followed Gia and Alfio over to one of the tables muttering unpleasantries about me, I'm sure.

I heard the back-door chime to my freedom and Kim called my name. I headed back to the safety of my domain of almond meal and arrowroot flour.

Kim hung a striped hobo bag on the doorknob. "It's too much. I just can't."

"What's going on?"

"It's Daniel. He almost put himself in the hospital last night."

I moved aside my gluten-free ladyfingers. "What? How?"

"He took an overdose of sleeping pills."

"On purpose?"

"He said it was an accident. He said he took two to settle his nerves so he could sleep after yesterday's crapfest. Then he said he was so overcome with worry that he forgot and took two more."

"Is that enough to put you in the hospital?"

"If you combine it with the bottle of wine he had it's enough to be worried about. He called me at three when he was having trouble breathing and realized he took too many. I called him an ambulance."

"I am so sorry. Is he going to be okay?"

Kim ran her hand over the row of studs on her left ear. "Yeah. I think so. The ER doc said it wasn't enough to kill him, but they gave him a shot of something anyway. With a needle. Not a shot glass."

"Sure."

"I mean the guy has had terrible luck. He lost his last business in Hurricane Sandy. His wife left him. He's in debt up to his eyeballs. That's why Jess and I invested with him. We believe the winery could be a great success. If he could just catch a break. And now this poor man has a heart attack in the tasting room."

"How was the business before yesterday?"

"Great. The wine is really good. Sales are solid and it's been mostly locals so far. Jess and I didn't just throw money at Daniel because he's a nice guy. We did our research. We signed up to do wine tours with Lily Snow to grow our tourism all year. She brings her tours through, we get year-round sales, and she gets ten percent of what they buy. Once tourist season officially begins, we expect to rake in a haul and double our profits before Labor Day."

"That sounds awesome. So why are you all freaking out? You've only been closed for one day. For all we know the police could reopen you tomorrow."

"Something weird is going on. The police brought the K9 squad after you left yesterday. They're looking for something. They won't tell us what, but they checked the front and back rooms and all of our cars."

"Drugs?"

"That or explosives, but since the man didn't blow himself up, I think it's probably the first one."

"Okay, so worst-case scenario. The autopsy finds Vince was on drugs. How would they tie that to Daniel?"

"I have no idea. But the skinny kid, Ryan something— Vince's son."

"Son-in-law."

"Okay, whatever. He showed up last night right after the K9 team left and threatened Daniel."

"Threatened him how?"

"With a lawsuit. He said, 'This is your fault. I know what you're up to, and I'm going to sue you for every penny you've got.' And we've already established that Daniel doesn't have a lot of pennies."

"Doesn't Daniel have liability insurance? I thought all businesses had to have it. I had to get a policy in case someone falls at the B and B and wants to sue me." *Considering Ryan is lawsuity I'd better make sure that's paid.*

Kim's eyes changed to flint. "Apparently, Daniel is not current with the insurance premiums. If we're sued, none of us have that kind of money. We'd lose everything."

Chapter Fifteen

I'd been stood up. It was a first for me and I did not care for it. It came with equal parts humiliation and fury. Tim had asked me to meet him at Rosa's at one fifteen and it was now two o'clock. My phone buzzed and I retrieved a text from him: **Sorry, babe. Sausage guy came early. I'll make it up to you.** Kissy emojis.

At first, I thought it was a joke, but when Tim didn't jump out of the alley and yell, *Surprise!* I realized it had finally happened. I had become less appealing than a meat delivery. I got in my car not sure if I should cry, eat, or call Gia and say, *Let's do this.* Am I really that shallow and vindictive? One minute everybody wants a commitment and the next I've been replaced with a future Eagles Cheerleader and the guy who brings the sausage.

I had a lot of emotions from the day, and I dealt with

them in the time-honored tradition of eating my feelings. I'd been so good for weeks and it had resulted in the loss of three pounds. My elbow weighs three pounds. A girl can only take so much. I went across the bridge to North Cape May and hit the first fast-food drive-through I found and ordered the self-pity special. Also known as a vanilla milk shake and super large fries. The fries were for Aunt Ginny and the milk shake was practically a protein smoothie. I rolled the windows down and a few of the fries caught in the breeze and flew into my mouth. It would be rude not to eat them now, so . . .

By the time I pulled in the driveway, I had the first nigglings of remorse. I brought what remained of everything into the kitchen to relinquish to Aunt Ginny. I planned to tell her to eat them, hide them, or destroy them—I didn't care which—just do it fast. Those fries had the stench of regret on them.

Aunt Ginny was bent over double staring into the oven with the door closed and the light on. Tammy Faye was sitting by her feet also staring into the oven. "What are you doing?"

"Making a potpie."

"Why are you watching it?"

"My doohickey should have gone off by now."

I faced the device on the counter. "Alexa. How much time is left on my timer?"

"You have seventeen timers set."

That explains so many things.

There was a thumping sound coming from under the kitchen sink.

"What is that?"

Aunt Ginny stood and shrugged.

I put the fries and milk shake on the island, then went to the sink and opened the cabinet door. Figaro blinked his orange eyes and stuck his head out.

"How long have you been in there?"

He saw Tammy Faye and shot across the kitchen into the hall.

I turned to Aunt Ginny just as she was dipping a french fry into the milk shake.

She popped the fry in her mouth. "Are you done with this?"

"It would appear so. Do you want me to check your potpie?"

Aunt Ginny stuffed another fry in her mouth. "It's been in there a really long time."

I opened the oven door and stuck my hand on the rack. Then I touched the crust. "How long are you supposed to cook it?"

"An hour."

"Well, you forgot to turn the oven on, so I'd say it has about fifty minutes left." I closed the door and set the oven to four hundred. Then I set the oven timer. "I'm going to make some peach pie pancakes for breakfast tomorrow. Do we have any peaches left or do I need to go to the store?"

Aunt Ginny answered through a mouthful of fries, "Check the pantry."

I opened the door to the closet with the hidden steps to the third floor that I used every day when we had guests staying. There was someone on the other side of the door and they lunged at me. I screamed and jumped back. Victory fell into my arms. Her eyes fluttered open and she yawned. "I am feenished with some bedroom."

"What are you doing in there?"

"Mmm. I fell asleep or somesing like that."

"You fell asleep standing at the door?"

"Mmm. I theenk maybe yes."

"And what in God's name are you wearing?" Victory was dressed in a traditional maid's uniform—if this was the 1920s and we were at Downton Abbey. She had on a long black dress with a starched white apron framed in Battenberg lace.

"My friend let me borrow eet for today. She work at the psychic house as hostess."

"You mean the Physick Estate?"

Victory shrugged. "I dunno, maybe."

Aunt Ginny had hit the bottom of the milk shake and her straw was making a hollow empty sound. "I like it."

I shot her a look. "Of course you like it. You're wearing a pink silk kimono."

"I'm going to my Japanese watercolor class this afternoon."

"I think they call that cultural appropriation now."

"I don't care what they call it. I won this at a poker game on Okinawa in '62 and I'm wearing it."

I turned back to Victory. "What happened to all the uniforms I bought you yesterday?"

"Zey are all dirtee."

"How is that possible? I gave you four T-shirts."

"I spill somesing."

I let out a frustrated sigh. "Come out of there. I don't even remember why I was going in there now."

Victory adjusted her poufy white mobcap. "Do you know there ees all thees food in there?"

Peaches. Right. I walked into the pantry and the door shut behind me. I found the string and pulled on the light. I checked the trapdoor—just in case; don't ask. I still have anxiety when I think about it. Then I scanned the shelves for a jar of peaches.

Voices muffled but clear enough to make out were coming from the ceiling. Ryan and Alyce's room was right above me.

Alyce was crying. "What are we going to do? This was our chance to convince him to change it back."

Ryan still had that condescending tone with his wife that made me want to hit him in the head with a bat. "It's your fault he changed it in the first place. If you'd been a better daughter, he would have left things alone."

"You don't know that! She tricked him. You know she refused to sign the prenup."

"Your dad could never refuse the double Ds. She probably held out on him until he wrote you out."

"Ryan, don't be crass."

"I'm sorry, Princess, but I caught them on the conference room table the first week she was on the job. I got promoted to keep my mouth shut."

I could hear Alyce stomping around, her footfalls drowning out her words. All I made out was "disgusting" and "old enough."

"It might not be too late."

"Ryan. We can't. It's too soon after Daddy."

"It might be our only option. You're in line to get everything if she's gone."

Chapter Sixteen

I came out of the pantry and put the peaches by the refrigerator. I tried to digest what I'd overheard before
they left the room. It was too awful to imagine what Ryan
and Alyce were up to. "Has anyone seen Sunny today?"

Aunt Ginny shook her head. "Not a peep."

Victory was slumped over the island playing with the
lace on her starched apron. "Ees Sunny one who look like
movie star or ees one who look like badger?"

Aunt Ginny answered her. "Movie star. The badger is
the daughter."

Victory rolled her eyes up to her forehead. "I not see
her seence I make bed."

"Where was Sunny when you saw her?"

"Een bed."

"In the bed?" Aunt Ginny and I glanced at each other
with mirrored concern. "What do you mean, in the bed?"

Victory shrugged. "Lady was een bed when I clean room. So, I feix bed around her." She made tucking motions with her hands. "She say she does not mind theese."

I tried to swallow, but a lump grabbed on to the sides of my throat and refused to go down. I couldn't catch my breath. *I've developed asthma. I didn't even know stress-induced asthma was a thing, but now I have it.*

Aunt Ginny leaned against the counter to look at Victory. "You can't clean the guests' rooms while the guests are still in them."

When Aunt Ginny is the voice of reason you know something has gone horribly wrong.

Victory looked at me and lifted one shoulder. "You say to have room clean by one. It was half twelve."

I tried to take a couple of deep breaths, but they wouldn't come.

Victory held up both hands. "What is beeg deal?"

Aunt Ginny patted me on the back like I was choking. "Next time, if the guest doesn't leave the room you don't clean it for that day."

Victory nodded like we were negotiating terms. "Okay. What about dog?"

All I could do was shake my head and mutter nonsense.

"Ladee geeve me money to let dog out of room."

Aunt Ginny said to no one in particular, "Well, that explains the Houdini act."

The doorbell rang, followed by Tammy Faye's announcement that the doorbell rang. I rounded the corner from the kitchen in time to see Figaro gallop across the hall from the library to the sitting room and bat Tammy Faye on the head on his way past. Tammy Faye jerked her snout in alarm and left her post at the front door to chase after Fig.

I opened the door to find my very own Guardian of Despair, Officer Amber. *It's been about eighteen hours since I was questioned by the police, so this feels about right.*

"McAllister. Are you just going to stand there or are you going to ask me to come in?" When I didn't answer she let out a melodramatic sigh and came in anyway, which I kind of thought was against the law somehow.

"What do you need?" Tammy Faye came to sit by my feet and growl at Amber in a show of support. Aunt Ginny appeared at my elbow in a show of snoopiness.

"Is Mrs. Baker in?"

"I think so, although I haven't seen her all day. Things have been very quiet here."

Figaro chose that moment to produce another run-by swatting incident, causing Tammy Faye to yelp and scamper after him in a series of ferocious snorts.

Amber pushed her Ray-Bans to the top of her head and raised her eyebrows.

Sunny saved me further embarrassment by coming down the stairs in gray shorty pajamas. The robe from her room hung off her shoulders like a cape. Her hair looked like she'd lost a fight with a woodpecker and her eyes were red from crying and ringed in dark circles. "I saw the police lights; is everything okay?"

Amber gave a slight head nod to Sunny. "I'm sorry to bother you, Mrs. Baker. I had a few more questions to ask you."

Sunny wrapped the robe tight around her. "Of course. What do you need to know?"

Amber motioned across the foyer. "Why don't we have a seat."

Sunny followed Amber into my library and Aunt Ginny followed Sunny. I headed back down the hall wondering when my house because an adjunct police headquarters. A moment later a very disgruntled Aunt Ginny joined me in the kitchen complaining to whoever would be sympathetic.

"Impertinence! Take you over my knee!" Aunt Ginny stomped over to a wall speaker by the banquette and turned the dial on the old intercom system.

"What are you doing?"

"Amber wants her privacy to interrogate that poor girl. I'd like to give her a piece of my mind."

Careful, there are very few pieces left.

"People made fun of me for installing this in the seventies. Who's laughing now?" The speaker crackled to life and Amber's voice came through a bit fuzzy at first, but Aunt Ginny dialed her in clear.

"No medications of any kind?"

Sunny's voice quivered. "No, only vitamins."

Victory came up behind Aunt Ginny and pointed at the intercom. "Is thees for spying?"

Aunt Ginny answered her, "It was when Poppy's high school boyfriend was over."

So many alarming memories flew to my mind. *That's going to keep me awake half the night.* "How'd you turn on the one in the library without Amber seeing you?"

"Threw myself against the wall and said it was my gout acting up. Now, shh!"

Amber had an edge to her voice that said she was in full-on cop mode. "Then where did the Xanax come from?"

"I only got that last night. My doctor prescribed it to

help me sleep. I just lost my husband." Sunny started to sniffle.

"We checked the bottle. Two pills were missing."

"I took them at the pharmacy. Besides, if I could take two pills without dying do you really think it was enough to kill Vince? He outweighed me by eighty pounds."

Aunt Ginny nudged me. "That's a good point. Good for her."

"Tell me about the wasabi peas."

Wasabi peas?

Aunt Ginny yanked my sleeve. "What is that, some kind of street drug?"

"I have no idea. Maybe food?"

Victory leaned against the table on her elbows. "Eet sound like gang."

Sunny sniffled. "What about them?"

"Officer Birkwell found a couple of unopened bags in your room."

"Is there a problem with that? Vince loves . . . loved wasabi peas." Another sob. "They were his favorite snack."

Oh, so you do eat them.

Amber sounded unfazed. "Did you take the wasabi peas to the winery yesterday?"

"No. Of course not. We bought cheese plates. The winery already had some on the table, I think."

"Do you remember who put them out?"

"No, I'm sorry. I wasn't really paying attention."

"It's important that you remember, Mrs. Baker."

"I'm sorry. I don't know."

There was silence for a minute like Amber was thinking or taking notes. "How much wine did Mr. Baker drink?"

"Just what they gave us. I think there was five kinds, but we only got a little bit of each one."

"Did he drink any of yours?"

"No."

"Did you eat anything at the tasting?"

"We had crackers and goat cheese with a chocolate fig spread."

"And you're absolutely sure Mr. Baker only had the five samples at the tasting."

"I'm positive."

"Okay. That's all I have for now."

We could hear Sunny leave the room and run up the stairs. A moment later Amber's voice came through the intercom. "McAllister. Can I talk to you please?"

I gave Aunt Ginny a dirty look, pushed the Talk button, and said, "I'll be right there."

I walked into the library and turned the intercom back off.

Aunt Ginny yelled, "Impertinence!" from the kitchen.

I faced Amber. "What's up?"

Amber's police radio crackled, and she turned it down. "Vince Baker had a physical two months ago. He didn't have a heart problem. He was probably healthier than both you and me. Especially you."

I decided to ignore the jab at my weight. "Well, yeah. I guess so. He had a hot young wife to keep up with."

"Listen, McAllister. I need you to keep this to yourself; the M.E. hasn't found a cause of death."

"What about he passed out and stopped breathing? That seems accurate."

Amber's face pinked. "Are you trying to piss me off?"

"What? No. I'm just saying. Why does the M.E. need a more detailed cause? The man had a heart attack."

"Because the paramedics documented that the victim's eyes were glassy and bloodshot and his face was red, but his blood pressure was very low. He had a trace amount of white powder on his upper lip and two of his fingers, and his tongue and airway were swollen."

"Do you think he had an allergic reaction to something?"

"Postmortem tox screen showed high amounts of alcohol and phenobarbital in his blood."

"Phenobarbital? So, he died of an overdose?"

"No. He clearly had more alcohol in his blood than you would get from five samples of wine over the course of an hour, but the phenobarbital was not at a high enough concentration to kill him."

"Not even when mixed together? Like when you take sleeping pills with a shot of whiskey?"

Amber raised her eyebrows in question.

"I've heard some people do that."

"The victim was a big guy. The M.E. is running more tests, but, in the meantime, we're treating his death as a homicide."

Why is she including me in this?

"We found traces of phenobarbital in a bowl of wasabi peas at the Laughing Gull. Someone clearly had the intention of malice and Mr. Baker found himself on the other end of that intention."

Why do I feel all buttery all of a sudden?

"Here's where you come in. The only people who had access to the victim who could have laced the peas were those on the tour group and the winery staff. Now, the staff are all locals, but every tourist on the tour group is from out of state. I want to keep them under surveillance until the M.E. can determine the cause of death and each person can be cleared."

I was getting a bad feeling about how my particular circumstances could possibly help these people stay in town. "Uh-huh. How do you plan to do that? You can't keep them here against their wishes."

"According to Lily Snow, the wine tour was booked for the whole week. I want to move the entire group to your bed and breakfast for the rest of the tour."

"What? No way. I can't fill up my house with more people. This is my busy season."

"Are you busy? Really?"

"I will be."

"How many guests do you have booked for the next week?"

"None until next weekend, but . . ."

"See? So you can do it."

"Why do you need to keep the whole group? Why not just the people already staying with me? No one else knew Vince before yesterday."

"Because they might have seen something or heard something and didn't realize it was important at the time. I know in my gut that Vince Baker was murdered, and until I figure out who did it I want to keep a close eye on all of them. It's probably only for a few days. A week tops."

"A week?!"

"This isn't fiction, McAllister! It takes longer to get through red tape in real life than on one of your mindless TV shows."

"Well, nuts, Amber! Why do I have to be dragged into this?"

"Because you are either the luckiest person I know when it comes to solving crimes, or the unluckiest to keep getting caught up in them. Either way, you and your aunt are incredibly nosy and have a way of finding things out that my badge prevents people from telling me."

"You want me to spy on them."

"Just like you and Aunt Ginny spied on me tonight."

"I mean, that was really more of Aunt Ginny's doing—"

"And whatever you hear, you call me immediately. I don't want you to get involved! I can't stress that enough. I just want you to keep your ears open and disclose the information to me. The last thing I need is to fill out an incident report on why you were held at gunpoint because you went all Hercule Poirot and sat everyone down so you could monologue about which one of them is a killer. You get into enough trouble without my help."

"No, I . . . yeah, that does happen."

"And one more thing. You can't say a word of this to Mrs. Baker or the daughter and son-in-law. Are we agreed, McAllister?"

If I do this, maybe she'll ease up on the accusations in the future. I put my hand out. "I'll do my best, partner."

Amber looked at my hand and let out a long sigh. "I'm regretting this already."

Chapter Seventeen

Sunny disappeared into her room for the rest of the day. Tammy Faye was making herself at home going back and forth between her suite and the main level whenever she wanted to stir up trouble or push Figaro's buttons. I'd filled Aunt Ginny and Victory in on the extra guests for the week. Victory wasn't fazed since more rooms meant more tips, but Aunt Ginny marched around complaining about police brutality and the problems with the Bush administration. I wasn't sure what year she thought it was or which President Bush she was angry with, but it seemed safer to avoid the topic and let her vent to Figaro, who watched the protest from the back of the chair in the sunroom.

I had to run errands and make a plan for breakfast for another week. I thought that Amber's request might just be an elaborate scheme to send me to bankruptcy in my first year. I was about to go to bed when Ryan asked me for the fourth time for the Wi-Fi code. How hard was it to remember "butterflywings"? It's literally the name of the place. When I asked him where Alyce was he looked at me like I'd sprouted horns. *Okay, sorry I asked.*

I finished work early for a change, so I decided to have a spa night. I did a deep conditioner on my hair and tied it up in rags so I would have loose curls in the morning. Then I smeared an avocado masque on my face and neck and circled my eyes with wrinkle relaxer. I smothered my hands and feet in a softening treatment and covered the lotion with thick socks. I had just lain down around eleven to let the beautifying sink in when there was a pattering on my window. I ignored it, thinking it was a branch or a stinkbug, but when it happened two more times I got up and heel-walked to the window to investigate.

To my horror, Tim was in the front yard holding up a blanket and a picnic basket. I grabbed the curtains and covered my green-caked face and slid the window open. "What are you doing?"

"I'm sorry, Mack. I should have never stood you up like that. Please forgive me."

I peeked through my curtain to see him hold up a bouquet of apology roses.

"Can we have that date now? I brought you a surprise."

I looked at my flannel shirt and sweatpants. "I'm not exactly dressed for a date." *Or anything that requires me to be seen by another human.*

"I don't care. I just want to be with you. Please."

Mrs. Pritchard's light came on and she yelled into the night, "Get out of my trash cans or I'm calling the cops, you hooligans!"

That was quickly followed by a new panic when I heard Ryan talking to Tim from the sun porch: "Hey, man. Do you deliver around here?"

"Naw, dude, this is my girlfriend's house."

"Really? The big redhead or the sexy maid?"

I hollered from the window so Ryan knew I could hear him, "I'll be down in a minute!"

Oh man. Of all the nights. I stumbled around the room trying to peel off socks and unwind my hair. *This is when a wig would really come in handy.* I grabbed a towel and wiped the green off my face and splashed water on myself. I slipped on lotion in the bathroom and banged my knee on the tub. I tried to pull myself up and slipped again pulling the shower curtain down with me. I finally righted myself and wiped my feet off on the bathroom rug. I reached for the sink and spotted both Figaro and Tammy Faye sitting in the doorway watching.

"I can tell you're both laughing at me."

Tammy Faye started wagging her tail.

I pulled off my flannel shirt and threw on a sweater dress and my UGGs. It was roughly thirty-five degrees outside. I didn't know what Tim had in mind, but I wanted my bases covered. I ran my fingers through my damp hair and put on a swipe of mascara. I would need an hour to properly fancy up this presentation, so for now I was just praying for the cover of darkness.

"Hey, there you are." Tim got up from the porch swing he'd been waiting on and pulled me into a kiss. "I thought you might have fallen back to sleep."

"Sorry, I had to get dressed." I could feel my knee swelling, reminding me of the disaster I left in the bathroom.

Tim put his hand on the back of my head. "What's this in your hair?"

I reached up and found I'd missed a rag roller. *Great.* I tried to unwind it and look sexy at the same time. "I had my hair up earlier." I opened the door and tossed the rag back inside the house. "What did you want to talk to me about?"

Tim picked up the bouquet of pink roses and held them out to me. "I'm sorry, Mack. It was stupid of me to break our date for a delivery."

I resisted the urge to reply, *Yeah, it was.* I took the roses and played it cool. "I understand you have to work."

"You know you're more important to me than the meat guy."

"Of course I do." *Do I?*

Tim took my hand and led me to his car. "I thought we'd go down to the Point. Wait till you see what I brought us."

"It's sausage, isn't it?"

He stopped and I felt his shoulders stiffen. "Uh . . . Yeah. Was that dumb?"

"No, don't be silly. I can't wait to see what you made with it."

He grinned and his shoulders relaxed. We talked about his day and upcoming menu ideas he had while we drove down to Cape May Point and parked at the edge of the sand under the moonlight. Tim turned off the car and covered us with the blanket. The car was toasty, but the wind was howling and the surf rumbling off the ocean made the temperature drop fast.

He opened his picnic basket and the smell of fennel and herbs wafted up to meet me. There was a thermos of hot chocolate, little skewers of sausage and peppers with wedges of provolone, and strawberries in a chocolate balsamic glaze.

"I can't believe you put this together after working all day."

"What? I can be romantic." He poured me a cup of hot chocolate and we watched the waves crash against the jetty as the tide was coming in.

I took a bite of the sausage and cheese. "I bet the special was a big hit tonight. These are delicious."

"Right! It's all about the pig." Tim launched into a twenty-minute diatribe about the quality of pasture-raised meats versus mass-produced. "And they're finished with macadamia nuts right before they're harvested."

I took another sip of my hot chocolate and looked down at the sausage on a stick. I'd kind of lost what little appetite I'd started with. I understood the reality of the food chain, but I didn't want to think about it when I ate. Now all I saw was a baby pig eating a macadamia nut thinking life was going to be fun. I swallowed hard. "Well, I guess if you have to go, a last meal of macadamia nuts is the way to do it." Tim was passionate about food and farming and going back to nature. I had lived the past twenty years passionate about Kentucky Fried Chicken and Hostess lemon pies, so I had very little to add to the topic.

"I'm sorry, Mack. Am I geeking out on food again?"

I grinned at Tim. "No, I love how serious you are about your cooking. That's why Maxine's is such a success. People can taste the passion."

Tim glowed with the praise. "I owe a lot of that to you. We were sinking before the *South Jersey Dining Guide* came out. Now I don't have time to turn around. We already have reservations through Labor Day."

"That's amazing! We'll have to do some special desserts to match the theme weekends."

"I have some ideas about that, especially Pirate weekend—" Tim broke off midthought. "But I really want to hear about how things are going with the bed and breakfast." He picked a strawberry and popped it in his mouth.

"Good. We're picking up. I have a few bookings—not as many as you. Of course, it's a good thing that I don't have anyone for next week because Amber has commandeered my rooms."

"Amber Fenton? High school nemesis turned cop? That Amber Fenton?"

I took a small strawberry and nibbled it. Chocolate balsamic dripped down my cleavage. *That figures.* "The same."

"What's she doing to you now?"

"She wants me to help her investigate a potential murder."

Tim stopped with his hot chocolate on the way to his mouth. "Are you serious?"

I filled him in on how Vince Baker had died at the wine tasting and why Amber thought that someone on the tour group had murdered him.

"From what you told me it sounds like the wife."

"The wife? Why would you say that?"

"She obviously only married him for his money. No twenty-year-old hottie wants to marry a dude in his fifties. What do they have in common?"

"I don't know. They seemed happy when they arrived at the B and B." *How much do people need in common to make a relationship work?*

"She must be a good actress then. She's probably playing the long game. And considering all the trouble you get into, please promise me you'll be careful around her. I just got you back in my life and I don't want to lose you."

"I promise not to let Sunny catch me in a dark hallway and stab me."

"Good." Tim leaned over and kissed me. Then he took my hand in his. "I've missed you so much. I never wanted to run Maxine's without you. I wish you would just come on full-time."

"What would I do with Aunt Ginny? She's already a menace to the community."

"She'll be fine. She's gotten along without you there every day for almost thirty years."

"She's a lot feistier now. Someone's been sending me pamphlets in the mail about elder abuse in nursing homes. I think it's the staff of the Sunset Assisted Living Center."

Tim laughed. "I bet it's Aunt Ginny. She's wicked sharp. Don't worry. We'll figure it out when the time comes."

He kissed me again and all my troubles started to melt away.

"So, are you any closer to being ready to make an honest man out of me?"

I tried to measure out a delicate balance of honesty and tact. "A decision like that is so important I want to make sure I can give it my full focus. Right now, I'm so distracted with Sunny's suffering, and Amber pressuring me to be her spy, that my attention has been divided."

Tim drew lines on the back of my hand with his fingers. "I see."

"Could you give me until these people are out of my

house and Amber is finished with me to give you my answer?"

Tim picked up my hand and kissed it. "If that's what you need."

I could have stayed there all night, but Tim yawned and checked the time on his phone. "I don't want to take you home, but I have to be at the restaurant at five to prep Sunday brunch."

I started packing up the food. "Just when I'm feeling sorry for myself that I get up early to work out, you remind me how early the restaurant business starts."

Tim threw the blanket into the back seat and started the car. "Just think, if we owned a bakery, you'd start work at two a.m. to get the breads and viennoiserie made for the day before we open."

"Forget that. I'm going to start a night bakery. One where everything is ready by two a.m. and I go home and sleep until noon."

"You're hilarious. Wait till I tell Dina down at the Cake Box that you said that."

"Who's Dina?"

"She's the chef who supplies all the pastry to the local coffee shops. All except the one you work at, of course. But then you-all don't have pastry—just muffins, which is hardly living up to your abilities. You're capable of so much more."

I was quiet the rest of the way home. Was I letting Gia down by not making La Dolce Vita croissants and Danishes every morning before seven? No way did I want to step up to that. That used to be my heart's desire, but life had gone in other directions. Had I grown in new ways, or had the old dreams just died?

Tim pulled up in front of the house and let the car idle. He walked me to the door and leaned me against the house for a kiss good night. "I have to ask you something that I've been wondering all night."

I caught my breath. "Sure, anything."

"What is this green stuff over your ear?" He ran his finger down the side of my face and produced some leftover avocado face masque.

I felt my cheeks grow hot. "That's face cream."

Tim laughed. "I thought maybe you were going wolverine on a bowl of guacamole when I arrived."

"Somehow that's more embarrassing than the masque."

Tim's eyes grew intense. "Baby, you never have to worry about how you look to me. I know you're gorgeous."

My breath caught in my chest and he leaned in to kiss me again.

The front door flew open and Ryan was standing there holding his tablet. "Oh hey, Poppy. What was that Wi-Fi password again?"

I'm going to kill Amber for making me do this. She'd better be right about it being murder, because if I have to keep Ryan here for long it'll be a double.

Chapter Eighteen

"So, you've gone from no dairy at all to all dairy, all the time?"

I picked at my cheese omelet. "The keto diet is protein and fat. Most of the recipes are loaded with cheese and cream."

I'd spent the early morning hours making desserts for Tim's restaurant and I was exhausted. For the first few months after my husband died, those were the hours I'd be finally falling asleep. Now I was up at five a.m. making chocolate cupcakes with red wine poached pears like a sleep-deprived idiot. *This has to stop. I need to sit my heart down for a serious talk about our feelings and rip the Band-Aid off. I can't love either man if I'm dead.*

Sawyer had come over to help me with the morning's breakfast service since Aunt Ginny was out on a date with

Royce. She took a forkful of my omelet. "Ohmagawd, how is that healthy?"

I wound my fork around a string of melted cheese. "I don't know, but I've done Paleo for six months and I have a net loss that weighs less than this omelet. Everyone is raving about the keto diet and how much weight you can lose, so I thought I'd try it."

"I thought you weren't supposed to worry about your weight. Didn't Dr. Melinda say to get healthy first and the weight loss will come?"

"Bold words from someone eating a cinnamon roll the size of a cantaloupe."

Sawyer pulled another layer off the pastry and popped it in her mouth before I could retaliate and take it away. "The keto flu has made you cranky."

"I've noticed. I think I need more coffee." I picked up the carafe and filled my cup for the third time that morning. Sawyer held up her cup and I topped her off.

"When does the cast of *America's Most Wanted* show up?"

"Lily said sometime after breakfast when they all check out of their B and Bs."

"How'd she convince them to move here?"

"It seems the campground lost power to Rosie and Bob's hookup and there were no other slabs available, and the Pinette and Masons' bed and breakfasts were suddenly overbooked due to a computer error. I was the only one in town with room for everyone and I've generously offered for them to stay here for free."

"That's awfully nice of you."

"Amber can be very persuasive."

Sawyer popped another clump of sweet roll in her

mouth. "Maybe Lifetime should make a show about you and your curse."

Figaro trotted into the kitchen with his nose in the air, sniffing. He zeroed in on Sawyer and headed for the table to beg.

I cut into another bite of egg and cheese. "Why don't we take a ride up to Court House this week to see if we can get an appointment with Madame Fakesalot."

Sawyer held a bit of pastry down to Fig, who sniffed it. "If you think she's a fake psychic then why do you want to see her?"

"Morbid curiosity."

"Uh-huh."

The front door opened, and trouble rumbled down the hall clucking and tittering. Aunt Ginny entered the kitchen, followed by her three lifelong best friends. They'd grown up together, gone to school and fought over boys together. They'd been bridesmaids in each other's weddings, some of them many, many times. Their friendship had been forged in the fires of life's trials. Now here they were limping into my kitchen like they'd just returned from a tour in Afghanistan.

"What in the world happened to you?"

The ladies shook their heads and clamped their mouths shut like they didn't know what I was referring to. Mrs. Dodson, often the leader of the group because of her bold personality, cocked her head and said, "We don't know what you're talking about. What are you eating and is there any left?"

Mrs. Davis, the silliest of the bunch, who seemed to have mood-changing hair colors, pointed to Sawyer's pastry. "I want one of those. Eggs I can do on my own."

Mother Gibson, an African American women who'd spent more than forty years as the superintendent of her Baptist Sunday school, just raised her hand and leaned against the island like she was deep in prayer for my soul. Probably a good idea.

Aunt Ginny slowly walked over to the cabinet and took down four mugs. She winced with the effort and I jumped up to help her.

"Were you in a car accident?"

She swatted my hand. "No. What are you? Some kinda nut?"

Mother Gibson gave a little chuckle. "Yeah. She wasn't driving."

I poured them each a cup of coffee and took the rest of the cinnamon rolls out of the oven where they were resting.

Mrs. Davis put some cream in her coffee. "Ginny, show Poppy what Royce gave you last night."

Aunt Ginny wouldn't look at me, so now I really wanted to know what it was. "Let me see."

"No."

"Oh, come on."

Mrs. Dodson chuckled. "Show her, Ginny. She understands man trouble."

The three biddies all laughed at the private joke and my curiosity was killing me.

Aunt Ginny huffed and pulled her hand out of her pocket and put it in my face.

"A ruby solitaire?"

Sawyer jumped up to see. "Oh, it's so pretty, Aunt Ginny. Does this mean you're engaged?"

The biddies broke out in howls of laughter and Aunt Ginny snapped, "No it does not!"

I glanced at Sawyer to see if she understood what I'd missed, but she looked as confused as I was. "If it's not an engagement ring, then what is it?"

Aunt Ginny shoved her hand back in her pocket and grimaced. "It's a promise ring. Royce said he wants to commit, and this is a step in that direction."

Mrs. Davis tittered. "Royce is taking it slow on account of his mother might not approve."

The biddies broke into another fit of laughter.

I put my hand on Aunt Ginny's shoulder. "Oh. Were you hoping it was an engagement ring?"

Mother Gibson chuckled. "She was hoping it was a bracelet."

Aunt Ginny stuck her tongue out at Mother Gibson. "I'm too old to get married. Or promised. What was that fool thinking?"

Sawyer was a hopeless romantic. It had not served her well thus far, but she kept at it. "Maybe he was thinking he loves you."

"Psssh. Whatever." Aunt Ginny handed me some lunch plates one at a time. "I'm not ready for any kind of commitment. The wedding season of my life is over. I'm in the take me out on a Wednesday for five-ninety-nine prime rib season of life now."

"I see. Well, you don't have to do anything you don't want to do. But that ring is gorgeous, so you should enjoy it."

Aunt Ginny looked down at her ring and rolled her eyes.

Sawyer took her plate to the sink. "Do you-all want to sit down?"

In unison the ladies protested, "No!"

I cocked my head at Aunt Ginny, who wouldn't look

me in the eye. Scandal was in the air and I knew she was the fountainhead.

The ladies stood around the island picking apart the pastries when the house began to vibrate. We all froze in place and Sawyer grabbed my arm. "What is that? Is it an earthquake?"

"It's coming from the front of the house."

We moved through the dining room to the sitting room to look through the bay window. The antique Limoges bird plates hanging on the wall shook as fast as my property values plummeted when an enormous touring Winnebago pulled up in front of the mailbox. I half expected Mick Jagger to fling open the door and ask which way to Madison Square Garden, but the Pink Sandals Boutique Tours van rolled in right behind, followed by a little green Volvo.

Victory materialized next to me, back in her knee-length black serviceable with bib apron, and peered through the window over my shoulder. "Whoa. That ees beigger than every house een my veillage."

"Amber thought it would be more convenient for everyone if they stayed here in case they were needed since my bed and breakfast is not booked up for next week."

Victory scrunched up her nose to look at me. "Why ees our bed and brickfes' not booked up?"

"We've had some . . . complications."

Tammy Faye ran up to the window to get a better look at the action. Figaro shot a paw out from under the couch and tagged her. She yelped and ran from the room.

The doors to the Volvo opened and Ken helped Willow out. Lily started gathering luggage and hauling it up to the house while Zara took a minute to adjust her sunglasses and check her cell phone before leaving the tour van. The Winnebago powered down and the temperature in the yard dropped ten degrees. I could hear Mr. Winston's television again.

Lily put two suitcases on the front porch. "Thank you for doing this. I can't believe the other B and Bs were overbooked for the week. I've never heard of a mistake this big. This whole tour has been a disaster."

Sawyer picked up two suitcases to take inside for me. "Especially for Sunny Baker."

Bob and Rosie emerged from the Ark and joined everyone on the porch. Rosie handed me a small valise. "We're just going to bring our toiletries in. No sense in unloading the Winnebago for just a night or two. We've decided not to stay for the rest of the tour. But tonight will be nice. We've never stayed in a B and B before. It will be a nice change." Bob didn't look so sure. He glanced back at the silver behemoth longingly.

I brought the last of the suitcases into the foyer. Everyone looked uncomfortable and put out by the circumstances. They should have all been enjoying another flight at a new winery right now. "Why don't you come in and make yourselves at home. I'll put on the kettle and we'll have some tea and blueberry scones; then we'll get the rooms sorted."

I went back to the kitchen to ask Aunt Ginny to put the water on and get the teapots ready and found all four biddies with bags of frozen vegetables stuffed down the backs of their pants. "Oh my lord, what have you-all done?"

Aunt Ginny shrugged. "Nothing."

Mrs. Dodson said, "We're old."

Mrs. Davis said, "Bursitis."

And Mother Gibson laid her head in her hands and groaned.

I put the water on and got the teapots ready. I took out the pan of blueberry scones that was supposed to be for breakfast tomorrow and put the sparkly sugared wedges on a decorative plate.

Sawyer came in through the kitchen door carrying Figaro like a baby. "I got the teacups and dessert plates out, but we still need forks and spoons." She put Fig down and went to the silverware drawer while I plated the iced lemon cookies. Aunt Ginny grasped for a lemon cookie, but her arm wouldn't reach and she couldn't lean from her perch at the table.

Sawyer handed me two tins of tea, blueberry cobbler, and Assam. "What's in your-all's pants?"

I poured hot water over the leaves in the pots. "Peas and carrots. They've done something and they won't admit what it is."

I saw a twinkle in Sawyer's eye when she picked up the tray of sweets and headed into the sitting room. I followed her a minute later with the teapots.

Awkward silence was spread around the room. Bob and Rosie were on the couch staring at their hands. Zara was sitting on the piano bench facing the piano. Willow was in a wing chair on her cell phone and Ken stood behind her with his hand on her shoulder. Sunny was standing in the doorframe biting her lip. She wrapped her arms around herself.

I set the tray on the coffee table. "Where's Lily?"

Rosie gave me an apologetic smile. "She said she had to go but to tell you thank you."

"Okay. Well, I think you'll all love your rooms when we get you settled. We have some delicious tea and scones to welcome you." I told them what the offerings were while Sawyer poured tea and tried to pass around the sweets. No one took any.

Ryan and Alyce came in the front door and took a look around the sitting room. Ryan helped himself to a scone. "Hey. What's going on?"

Alyce tried to take the scone that Sawyer offered her, but Ryan smacked her hand and gave her a warning look.

Ryan addressed the room as a whole. "So, I guess you guys are stuck here with us now."

Willow started to cry, and Ken asked if they could be excused. He led them out to the sun porch.

Zara cast a glare at Sunny. "I don't need any dessert. I need to get out of here." She grabbed her wool poncho. "I'll be back in a few hours. You can show me my room then. I'll need you to remove any flowers or air fresheners before I return. I have severe allergies and scented things bother me."

Ryan watched her slam the door. "Geez, is it me or does she have an attitude problem?" Ryan led Alyce out of the sitting room and up the steps to their suite.

Rosie gave me a sad smile. "Don't mind her, honey. She's just angry because she can't get a flight home today. None of us really have the heart to stay on the tour after yesterday. Bob and I are leaving in the afternoon tomorrow after we have our interview with the police."

"I understand." *They were already questioned by the police at the winery. This interview sounds like something Amber made up.*

Sawyer cast a glance at me with the plate of scones still in her hand. She offered it to Rosie, who took one but didn't take a bite.

"So, I hear you and Cowboy Bob like to travel."

Rosie nodded enthusiastically. "It's always been my dream to see all fifty states. Now that Bob is retired, we're finally getting the chance."

Bob nodded.

I sat in the chair Willow had vacated and Sawyer sat on the couch next to Rosie. "Oh, what fun. Where have you been so far?"

Rosie nibbled the scone. "Well, we've done Yosemite, and the Pacific Coast Highway. Of course, I'd always wanted to do the studio tour there in Hollywood. Bob and I tried out for *Let's Make a Deal*. We dressed as a donut and a cup of coffee. We didn't get on."

Bob crossed his arms in front of his chest and shook his head.

"I'm sorry."

"Oh, and last November we went to the Peanut Festival in Dothan, Alabama—that was a hoot."

Bob barked out a laugh that could double for calling the dog in: "Ba-*ha*!"

Tammy Faye peeked around the corner.

"Well, it sounds like you're off to a good start."

"Now that Bob has the Winnebago, he wants to do the East Coast. Most of it doesn't seem as exotic as the Peanut Festival."

"I can see how that would be a challenge. Cape May does have a lima bean festival in October." *Because who doesn't want to celebrate lima beans.*

Rosie put her scone on the napkin Sawyer handed her. "Honey, it's been a trying day. Would you mind terribly if we just waited in the camper until you're ready for us?"

"Oh, of course. Um. Since everyone else is occupied, I could show you to your room now."

"If it's no trouble."

I got Bob and Rosie set up in the Swallowtail suite, and I took Ken and Willow's bags up to the Adonis butterfly suite for when they came in from the porch.

When I returned to the sitting room, Sawyer was crouched down in front of Sunny in the wing chair. Sunny was crying, and Sawyer was covering her hand with her own.

Victory was sprawled on the couch eating a scone and Tammy Faye was next to her begging. Victory gave Tammy a blueberry from her fork.

I stepped into the foyer out of Sunny's eyeline and cleared my throat. Victory looked up at me inquisitively. I jerked my head for her to come to me. She got up and brought her scone with her.

"What ees eet?"

"Victory, you're at work right now. You can't sit in the guest area in your uniform and eat scones."

Victory took another bite. "Ees scone not for servants?"

Oh God, way to make me feel like an oppressive overlord. I lowered my voice to a hiss. "Of course you can have scones; just eat them in the kitchen."

Victory gave me a curtsy for added humiliation and headed back through the sitting room so she could grab her tea on the way to the "servant's quarters."

I joined Sunny just as Sawyer was handing her a box of Kleenex.

"Everybody hates me. Do you think they're angry because Vince died and they have to stay here against their will?"

Sadly, yes. Yes, I do think that. "Oh, I don't know. I'm

sure they realize you are going through a terrible time and they just don't know what to say."

"We should never have joined this tour. Vince didn't want to come back here. He said there were ghosts in Cape May. He said Cape May was cursed for his family, but I was so excited. I won the trip in a sweepstakes and I knew if I pushed him he would give in to me. He couldn't tell me no about anything. I never imagined this. . . . He was right. I should have listened."

Chapter Nineteen

I got the new guests settled and left the biddies to their destructive nature. Sawyer and I made plans to have dinner together later and watch a movie. Sawyer texted Kim and asked her to join us so we could try to cheer her up. I was making the most of the afternoon by going to La Dolce Vita to get some baking done for the coffee shop and the B&B. Maybe tomorrow I could sleep in until six and catch a workout before the breakfast service. *Could I get away with serving Cheerios and Pop-Tarts since I didn't actually book these people as guests?*

I entered through the back door in the alley and caught a snippet of a very interesting conversation coming from Gia's office at the back of the kitchen.

"Can I say bad words?"

"No, you cannot say bad words. Where do you get this?"

"Nonna says bad words."

"Well, I will have a talk with Nonna."

"She says I have to wait till I'm old like her, but I don't know how old is Nonna?"

"Nonna is very, very old. She might be a hundred."

Henry coughed. "But I'm only four."

"So, you have a long time to wait."

There was silence, like Henry was thinking. "I'll just stick with regular words. It's too hard to get that old."

"That sounds like a smart plan."

I peeked around the doorway into the office to see Henry sitting in Gia's lap and they were swiveling back and forth in the office chair.

Henry saw me before Gia did. "Poppy!" Henry launched himself at me, followed by a round of coughing.

"Hey, Sweets. Why are you still in your pajamas?"

Henry rolled his eyes over to his father in a scowl. "He thinks I'm sick." Followed by more coughing.

"Mm-hmm. And I take it you disagree?"

Henry folded his arms across his chest and gave a single firm nod.

I put my lips on his forehead. "You are pretty warm. I wonder if all that heat is making your hair grow."

Henry's hand shot up to his head and Gia and I laughed.

Gia grinned. "Have you come to bake, or did you miss me?"

I yawned. "Both."

"Bella, you are working too much."

"I'm just tired from getting up early."

"Are you sure that is all? Maybe you should take a few days off and get some rest."

"Well, it's that and making the extra desserts for Maxine's several times a week."

Gia gave me a half frown, half smirk. "That would be easy enough to fix."

I chuckled. "I promised Tim I'd be his part-time pastry chef."

"Is it about the money? 'Cause I can give you more money."

"You're already overpaying me as it is."

"I don't need to make a profit. The ladies already flock here to stare at how hunky I am, and the men come to stare at Karla's legs."

Gia's sister called from the other side of the kitchen, "You better believe it!" Karla's waist was impossibly small, her makeup impeccably applied, and her lush mink-brown hair wrapped in a perfect topknot. "Half the people who come here don't even like coffee."

Henry and I laughed; then Henry coughed. "What is 'hunky'?"

Gia made a serious face and flexed his arms in front of his chest. "This is hunky."

Henry and I laughed harder and Gia responded with mock outrage, "What! You do not think Giampaolo is manly enough?!"

Then he started chasing me in a circle and Henry laughed so hard he started a choking fit and we had to calm him. Gia rubbed his back. "Okay, okay. Settle down."

I leaned down to Henry in his father's chair. "When I was very little, if I got sick, my mom used to make me tea with honey and lemon. Do you want me to make you some?"

"Is it yucky?"

"Not the way I make it."

Henry nodded his acceptance of my offer and I left the two of them together. I was putting the water in the kettle and I overheard Henry say, "Poppy would be a nice mommy."

My heart nearly burst out of my chest. I did not hear Gia's response, but I didn't think I could handle it if I had.

My mind was frozen in the moment. I raised a drawbridge in my heart to lock it down. I knew exactly where my thoughts wanted to wander right now, and I couldn't let them go any further. I could not—I would not let my love for Henry influence my feelings for Gia. They were strong enough without getting wrapped up in the longing for a child I could never have on my own.

The teakettle whistled, and I jumped. *Snap out of it, Poppy!* I made Henry's tea and just before taking it in to him added an ice cube and let it melt.

We gave him the tea and had him blow on it. He sipped it and smiled.

"It taste-es like candy."

"Good. Sip it slow and I'll check on you in a little bit, okay?"

Henry nodded, and Gia and I left him to his Minions video and went into the kitchen.

I reached for my apron and Gia pulled me against him. He whispered in my ear, "I love it when you are here." He kissed my cheek and released me.

"Really? How is Sierra today?"

Gia narrowed his eye and his lip twitched to a thought of mischief. "Are you jealous?"

"Don't be ridiculous. She's a child."

Gia gave me a knowing grin that made me want to punch him. "Mmm-hmm."

I tried to change the subject: "How long has Henry been here?"

"A couple of hours. My mother said he wanted to be with me and she cannot say no to him. She can teach him to cuss, but she cannot say no." Gia shook his head and shrugged. "I'm taking him home soon and Karla is working the rest of the day."

"Poor baby."

"Me or Henry?"

I gave Gia a look and he winked. "Do you want . . ."

He didn't have to finish. "Yes."

I checked on the pastry case out front while he made me a dairy-free cappuccino and Karla blew me kissy faces behind his back.

We were low on both breakfast and sweets. I didn't have time to make a bunch of drop cookies, so I decided to make two pans of bars.

I took out ingredients for a couple of simple items that could do double duty here and at the B&B: orange walnut muffins and a savory cheese biscuit with garlic and rosemary. And I decided on my gluten-free shortbread with candied ginger, and mint cheesecake brownies for St. Patrick's Day.

"Here is your cappuccino, Bella."

I cradled it in my hands and inhaled. "Mmm. Like liquid sunshine and happiness rolled up in a blanket of love."

Gia was looking at the ingredients on the counter, but he rolled his eyes up to mine. "There is definitely the love."

My face grew hot. "Ooh, this coffee is very warm." I took a loud sip.

I looked at my workbench, then back to Gia. He grinned and took a step closer. I should be taking a step backward, but my legs had grown roots. One mention of love and my body had decided we were doing things her way from now on.

Gia put his hands on my waist and leaned down to kiss me. I closed my eyes. And then Henry giggled.

Gia and I snapped our heads in his direction. Gia muttered a string of Italian that I couldn't keep up with.

Henry giggled and said, "That's what Nonna says."

Henry ran to my side and I hugged him. "You are supposed to be resting, young man."

"I want to be out here with you and Daddy."

I gave Gia a pouty lip. "Why don't we bring your chair out here, but we have to keep you over there by the office because you're sick and I'm about to make shortbread."

Henry did a little dance followed by a fit of coughing, and Gia wheeled the chair into the room with us.

I washed my hands and spent the next hour making the mint brownies and gluten-free shortbread with finely chopped crystallized ginger dipped in melted white chocolate and telling Henry stories that my mother used to tell me when I was stuck in bed sick. Back in the days before my father died and she dropped me at Aunt Ginny's before checking herself into a mental hospital.

Karla poked her head in to sniff but never touched anything because she didn't want any cellulite showing through her size two leather pants. *I mean, dear God, just buy a size four and eat the brownie.*

When the last of the muffins and biscuits were finished, I cleaned the kitchen and it was time for Gia to take Henry home for a nap. Henry gave me a kiss goodbye and was bundled up and belted in his car seat with a pack of cookies for later.

Gia pulled me close. "Will I see you tomorrow?"

I knew he could feel my heart beating through his shirt. "I don't know yet."

He gave me a quick kiss with one eye on Henry—who had both eyes glued to us.

I gave them a little wave as Gia's Spyder pulled away from the curb.

Chapter Twenty

Figaro was in the bay window sleeping when I got home. Tammy Faye must have been with Sunny, so Fig could finally let his guard down. I entered the house and found Zara, Willow, and Rosie sitting in the library drinking coffee.

"It's such a shame. He was too young to have a heart attack."

"And his poor wife. She's just beside herself with grief."

"I wish there was something we could do to help her. Maybe we should send flowers to the funeral."

"Oh, that is a good idea."

"Hello, ladies. How are you this afternoon?"

Zara didn't look up from typing on her cell phone.

Rosie gave me a smile. "Fine. The B and B is just lovely.

I must have spent an hour on the porch this afternoon in the swing."

Willow rubbed her stomach. "Ken and I are looking to take some home tours this week. Maybe you can recommend some places."

"Of course."

Zara set her phone down on the arm of the chair. "Are there any carriages with designated photographers? Since I'm still here I may as well get some shots for my website."

"I don't know the answer off the top of my head, but I'll make some calls and let you know right away."

I could tell that she appreciated my effort because she made eye contact with me for a solid three seconds before getting back on her phone. I sensed that was her equivalent of sending a muffin basket.

I ran upstairs to put my purse away and heard the television playing in Zara's room. I had just left her in the library, so I gently knocked on the door. When there was no answer, I tried the glass knob. It wasn't locked, so I cracked it open and peeked inside. Victory was sitting on the bed watching *The Price Is Right* and eating a tube of Sour Cream & Onion Pringles.

"Victory!"

Victory turned her head to the door with two Pringles hanging off her lip like a duck bill. "What?"

"Have you lost your mind?"

"No. Ees fine."

"Turn off that television and get out here right now!"

Victory screwed up her face like she was dealing with an unreasonable request, but she did as I said.

When I'd closed the door behind her, I took her up to

the third-floor landing. "What would make you think that it would be okay to hang out in a guest's room and watch TV?"

Victory nodded like she was confident she'd prepared for this quiz. "Because guest ees not ein room."

I had so many things to say about privacy and decency and what I expected from employees—but right now morbid curiosity wanted to follow this line of thinking to see just where it would lead. "And what if the guest were to return?"

"I tell her not to come back for one hour while I turn down bed."

"You told her not to come back?"

"Yes. I tell her room weill be ready after four and she say okay. That geive me one hour to take break."

"Victory, you take your break in the kitchen."

"Keitchen have no TV."

"Then you watch TV when you get home after work."

Victory gave me a look like I was too simple to understand the situation and she had to break it down real slow for me. "*Price Ees Right* ees only on een afternoon." She patted me on the arm. "Do not worry. I weill get it on YouTube later."

Oh, thank God, I was so concerned she would miss it. I called after her, "Don't do it again!"

She waved the Pringles can above her head in dismissal without looking back and trundled down the steps.

I needed another cup of coffee. And a new chambermaid. I wrote an email to myself: Call the service and see if there are any other candidates they can send over. Don't tell Aunt Ginny. *And sent it.*

I stashed my purse in my room and called the tourism

office to ask about the carriage rides. Then I went to the kitchen to get that cup of bourbon. I mean coffee.

Aunt Ginny was sitting at the kitchen table, propped up on a frozen Stouffer's family-sized Salisbury steak that I distinctly remembered throwing away weeks ago when we started the Paleo Diet. A diet that Aunt Ginny currently had amnesia about.

"What is that?"

Aunt Ginny looked up from the crossword puzzle she was doing. "What is what?"

"Under your butt."

"Nothing that concerns you." She looked back at her puzzle book and called me a diet Nazi.

I looked back at Aunt Ginny's family-sized ice block. "Where have you been keeping it all this time?"

"You have your hiding places and I have mine."

The Alexa beeped and announced, "This is a reminder—stop flashing at me and mind your own business."

I leveled a stare at Aunt Ginny.

She gave me a blank look. "What? That could mean anything."

I flopped down on the bench seat across from her. "When are you going to tell me what you did to yourself?"

Aunt Ginny went back to her crossword puzzle. "Are there pigs with wings on the roof?"

"No."

"Then not yet."

The front door bell chimed in the kitchen and Kim and Sawyer came down the hall. "We're here. We brought *The Secret to My Success* and *Ferris Bueller's Day Off*."

Sawyer and I had seen *Ferris Bueller* so many times we could quote it by memory.

Kim was carrying a grocery bag full of snacks and Sawyer had a tray with four iced coffees from La Dolce Vita. She handed me one with a pink straw. "This one is yours and Karla said to tell you that Sierra made them." Sawyer rolled her eyes.

"I'll need to check it for arsenic."

Aunt Ginny peered over the top of the coffees. "Which one is mine? And is Sierra Gia's new little chicky?"

Sawyer handed her an iced mocha. "This one's yours, Aunt Ginny."

I cut in with, "She's not his girlfriend. She's just a new barista." My words faded out by the end and I'd lost some of my indignation to uncertainty.

Kim opened a bag of pretzels. "She really bothers you, huh?"

"No-wah." *I just want to swing her around the room by her belly chain.*

Aunt Ginny snorted. "What a crock. You're so jealous you can't see straight. Look at how you went out of here today."

"What? These are my normal clothes."

"You didn't dress that nice when Royce took us to see *Wicked* for Valentine's Day."

I narrowed my eyes at Aunt Ginny. She was in a button-pushing mood today. "Why don't you show Kim your promise ring."

Aunt Ginny scowled and stuffed her hand under her good butt cheek.

Kim lit up and came over to Aunt Ginny's side. "Ooh, show me."

Aunt Ginny pouted. "No. I donwanna."

Sawyer sniffed. "Something smells good. What's for dinner?"

I leveled my gaze on Aunt Ginny. "Salisbury steak apparently."

Kim pulled her phone out and sighed. "Another text from Daniel. The police have shown up with a search warrant."

Sawyer sat on the other end of the bench seat and scooted to the middle. "Why are the police so focused on the winery?"

I was immediately irritated with Amber. *If she was going to go after Daniel, why make me keep all these people in my house? Daniel lives in West Cape May.* "Can they search someone twice?"

Kim shrugged. "I don't know. The first time he was being cooperative and we were still in shock because someone had died. We didn't know they were going to say it was murder and target us as suspects."

Aunt Ginny grabbed a handful of pretzels. "What are they looking for?"

Kim shrugged and texted while she talked. "They've been checking our food. They already took everything we had that wasn't sealed. We'll have to file an insurance claim to restock."

Sawyer leaned back in her seat and stretched her legs under the table. "If there was something wrong with the food then why did no one else get sick? Everyone ate the same thing."

I had to force myself to keep my mouth shut about the wasabi peas. I loved Kim to death, but she had a lot more faith in her boss than I did. After seeing Daniel kissing Vince's married daughter the night of the mixer, my imagination could concoct a couple of different motives for murder. Especially when you factored in what a charmer Alyce's husband was.

Aunt Ginny snapped her fingers in front of my face. "I said, don't you agree?"

"Agree with what?"

"That the police should be investigating Vince's son-in-law, Ryan. That boy's a real tea bag."

Sawyer cocked her head to the side. "Like Lipton?"

"What does that mean?" I asked.

Aunt Ginny looked at each one of us in turn. "That thing the kids say when a man is an unpleasant know-it-all. A tea bag."

Iced coffee shot out of Sawyer's nose and Kim dropped her phone.

"What?" Aunt Ginny asked. "Am I not saying it right?"

I took a deep swallow of my coconut iced latte. "Oh no, you said it right. Ryan is a class-A tea bag." Sawyer kicked me under the table.

Aunt Ginny stood up muttering to herself, "I don't know why people act like I don't know what I mean half the time." She turned her frozen entrée ninety degrees and carefully sat back down on it. "I still want to know why a pregnant woman would go on a week-long wine tour for her bellymoon."

"Babymoon."

"That's just as dumb. Why don't one of you go ask her while I put my ice pack in the oven?"

Sawyer took a bolstering drink of her cold brew. "It's terribly insensitive, Aunt Ginny."

"I don't care. You're looking for a murderer, aren't you?"

We looked at each other and I spoke. "Yeah, but not the pregnant lady who didn't even know him."

Aunt Ginny sighed like she was dealing with three very slow-witted tea bags. "You can ask her in a way that's subtle. I have to believe that a pregnant woman would not choose a booze-filled vacation to celebrate having a baby without an ulterior motive."

Aunt Ginny's argument made me feel a little queasy. There was no way what she was saying could be true. Was there?

Kim stuck her fist in the middle of us. "Rock, Paper, Scissors for it."

"What? No way—one-two-three." Kim and I had thrown paper and Sawyer threw rock. To be fair, Sawyer always threw rock the first time because she was trying to remember what the other two signals were.

Sawyer pulled her hand back. "Oh man. What am I supposed to say?"

Aunt Ginny hoisted herself up from the banquette and put the half-thawed entrée on the table. "Hold on." She tottered over to a slim cabinet and pulled out the cordial glasses. "There are bottles of sherry and port in the credenza in the library. Tell them it's a little pre-dinner aperitif and see if you can work it into the conversation naturally."

I got up and took a plate down and filled it with cheese and crackers. "I'll take this, so it seems more legit."

Sawyer didn't look convinced, but she took the tray of glasses and whispered to herself as we headed down the hall to the library, "Work it in naturally."

The women had been joined by Rosie's husband, Bob, and they all stopped talking when we came in the room.

Sawyer set the tray on the coffee table in front of Rosie and Willow on the couch. She smiled at the ladies and went over to the credenza, took out the liquors, and brought them back to the table where I had placed the cheese and crackers. Then, very smoothly, Sawyer looked at Willow and said, "Can you have more alcohol since you already had a lot of wine this week?"

I was so glad I'd put those crackers down already.

Rosie's head bobbed like she was thinking, *I told you so*, and she'd been patiently waiting for someone else to say it.

Willow's face pinked and she put a hand on her belly.

I jumped in with, "She means would you rather have some iced tea or seltzer. We're not nosy." *Nice save, Poppy. Just shy of pathetic.*

Willow's eyes softened from their hawk-ready-to-strike sheen and I let myself breathe again. "Nowadays . . ."

Ooh, starting out of the shoot with a jab at our age. Okay.

"The doctors say it's very safe for pregnant women to have a couple glasses of wine a week. But since you seem so concerned about my baby, I only tasted the wine and spit it out. I didn't drink it. I did, however, eat about five pounds of cheese and olives. Since I'm swelled up like a balloon and have elephant ankles, the wine probably would have been a better choice. Do you feel better now?"

I don't know about better. I felt properly chastised. A little annoyed.

Sawyer mumbled, "I'm sorry." And fled the room.

I gave Willow a weak smile. "We just want to make sure you have something you can enjoy so you aren't left out."

Zara sneezed. Twice. She wrinkled her nose and looked around the room distastefully. "Poppy, are you wearing perfume?"

I thought back many hours ago to when I first got dressed for baking. "Yes, I did put some on, but that was very early this morning."

Zara covered her mouth with her hand. "I'm very sensitive to smells. Would you mind?"

"Oh, sorry." I took a step toward the door and considered the intercom. The women and Bob were watching my every move. I just didn't feel like I could pull it off with subtlety, so I had to abandon the espionage. "Let me know if there is anything else I can get for you."

Zara cocked her head. "Did you find out about the photographer?"

"Yes. That is something you have to book in advance say for a wedding or a head shot, but any driver would be willing to take your picture during the tour with your cell phone free of charge."

Zara sighed. "Okay."

And you're welcome. I left the room and hotfooted down the hall to the kitchen, where Sawyer was being comforted by Kim and Aunt Ginny.

I put my arms out and she apologized, "I know; I left you there. I'm sorry. I panicked."

Aunt Ginny patted her on the arm. "Well, you crashed and burned on that one. What did they say to you after Sawyer left?"

"Zara told me my perfume made her sick . . . so there's that."

"Aww." Aunt Ginny shifted in her seat and winced.

Kim stood up and grabbed our movies. "Why don't we

go start girls night and get the mean tourists out of our head?"

Sawyer grabbed the pretzels, and I got the rest of the bag of snacks. "Let's do it. I have a case of something in my room that I think you'll really appreciate."

Sawyer grinned. "Is it what I think it is?"

"You know it. Diet Dr Pepper. Bottled last January."

Kim got three glasses out of the cabinet next to the fridge. "Sweet! My favorite vintage." Before we left the kitchen, she turned to Aunt Ginny. "Be sure to use Vaseline."

Aunt Ginny waved Kim away. "Shu-shussh!"

Kim gave me a cryptic smile on the way up the secret stairway through the pantry.

Chapter Twenty-one

"What do you mean you've been detained?" Kim picked up the remote and paused the DVD.

I looked at Sawyer and she mouthed, *Daniel.*

Figaro was curled up in my lap, but I didn't remember him getting up there. I stroked his head and he stretched out a paw.

"That's insane; how can they think that? Did you check the recording? They're going to find out eventually. They almost saw it the day he died. I'll take care of it."

Sawyer stuffed half a cupcake in her mouth and shook her head. Whatever was happening, we could tell it wasn't going well.

Kim rolled off the bed and started to pace. "Well, we have to do something. I can't just sit here and let them arrest you. . . . Did you call Jess? I'll do what I can."

Kim threw her phone back on my bed and Figaro

opened one eye to glare at her nerve. "You won't believe this."

Sawyer still had a mouth full of cupcake. "Amber took Daniel down to the station."

I added, "Daniel's in trouble and needs your help."

Kim nodded. "Yeah. Can you believe it?"

I took another piece of cheese and Sawyer and I both said, "Yep."

Kim froze in her pacing and squared her shoulders. "What? You don't really think Daniel killed Vince Baker, do you?"

I shrugged. "I don't know either one of them, Kim. But we know Daniel was sneaking around with Alyce, so it's not too farfetched to come up with a motive."

Kim's eyes narrowed to slits. "You of all people should be more sympathetic."

"I am sympathetic. I just can't sit here and say I know he didn't do it like I could if you or Sawyer were being detained."

Sawyer took a drink of her Diet Dr Pepper. "Who are *they* and what are they going to find out eventually?"

Kim blinked a couple of times and her eyes rolled to the left. "Ugh. We may have a security feed that we didn't tell the cops we had."

Sawyer choked and chocolate crumbs flew out of her mouth and onto my Laura Ashley comforter.

I was tossing cheese into my mouth and missed, and a wedge hit me in the eye. "Oh my God, Kim. Why didn't you tell them?"

Kim twisted her hands together. "There's some inflammatory evidence on the tapes—but not about the murder, some wine-related stuff."

"They won't care about that. They're only investigating Vince's death."

"If it gets out it could be very bad for us."

"Well, what is it?" Sawyer brushed the crumbs off her lap and onto a napkin.

Kim jumped on the bed and sat on her knees. "Okay, but can you please promise not to tell anyone?"

I shrugged. "Probably. I don't know what it is."

"I told you we invested in some new varietals of grapes over the winter, right?"

Sawyer and I answered in unison, "Uh-huh."

"Well, they aren't exactly in bottles of wine yet."

"Uh-huh."

"So, to augment our stock, Daniel has been supplementing with . . . store-bought wine. Just until ours is ready for bottling."

Sawyer's eyes popped and she sucked in a breath. "You're stealing someone else's wine and selling it as your own?"

"Oooooh, Kim. You know, I'm pretty sure that is not just unethical—I think it's illegal."

Kim waved her hands in front of our faces. "No no. We're not selling it. The only wine we sell really is our own."

"Then what are you doing?" I asked.

"Daniel buys wine and refills our 'special vintage' bottles for tastings. Those special reserve wines he previews for the wine club; those are boxed wine from Costco. He refilled some of the reserve wines during the tasting last Saturday and it's on the tape."

Sawyer shook her head. "Oh, Kim."

"I know. I know. It's terrible. Our wine is really good

and we're signing up a lot of subscriptions. But no one wants to do a flight of just four wines. So, Daniel had to supplement the tasting room with what he calls our reserve. But we only sell the four wines that are ours. I promise."

I thought about it for a minute. "Is he selling subscriptions based on the box wine tastings?"

"No. Absolutely not. Reserve wines are limited edition. When our new wines are ready, they'll be labeled as completely different reserves than the ones they're tasting this summer." Kim watched me and Sawyer hopefully.

I didn't know what to think. I wasn't exactly versed in wine law. Was it fraud if you weren't selling it? I don't know. Is it fraud if I dial it in one morning and serve Hungry Jack pancakes to the B&B guests? I don't know that either.

I could tell Sawyer was in the same boat as I was. She sat there biting her lip and staring into space.

"Well," I said, "I don't know where to go with what Daniel is doing, but what does he want you to do?"

Kim sucked in a deep breath and let it out. "We need to watch those security tapes. Daniel wants to know if there is any evidence to the murder on them before he turns them over to the police and possibly lets it out that he's serving rogue wine."

"And what do you need us for?" Sawyer asked.

"We can't exactly walk in there like it's a Thursday afternoon. The police have sealed the building. We need to . . . kinda . . . break in."

Sawyer groaned next to me and reached for the Little Debbie Nutty Bars.

I put my hand out. "Hit me."

Sawyer put one cellophane pack in my hand and ripped another open with her teeth.

Kim had the look of a mom who had five minutes to take the kids ten minutes to school. "Do you have any questions?"

I looked at the TV screen. "Yeah. How did we get to Ferris on the parade float? I thought we were just kidnapping Cameron."

Sawyer nudged me and said with a mouthful of nutty bar, "You fell asleep for an hour. We didn't want to wake you."

Kim was bouncing in place now. "Girls!"

"Fine. But I have to get out of this skirt and put on my breaking and entering outfit."

"Just hurry."

Chapter Twenty-two

Ten minutes later—and I think we should all pause there and take that in—I had changed into black leggings, a long-sleeved black T-shirt, and black boots. Six minutes of the time was spent hoisting on a pair of high-waisted Spanx because of the nutty bar inflation protocol. Sawyer helped yank it up over my muffin top and we shaved two minutes' time off my personal best. I put my hair up in a ponytail and grabbed my phone and keys. "Let's go."

Sawyer grabbed the bag of pretzels and two Dr Peppers on the way out of my bedroom. "Emergency rations."

When we hit the bottom, I realized I'd left my cell phone charging by my bed. "I'll meet you in the car." I ran back up the two flights of steps, grabbed my phone, locked my bedroom door, and started back down. On the second landing I paused a moment as the door to the Scarlet Peacock opened and Ryan started to come out. I was startled, but I said, "Good night."

He gave me a wary look, backed into the room, and slowly closed the door again.

It was weird and unsettling, but I pushed it out of my mind for now. I had a winery to break into.

We drove over to West Cape May in silence. Sawyer and I were very invested in helping Kim, but was Kim being duped by her business partner? We'd already established that he was at least two kinds of cheater. Maybe he was a murderer. *Next time Amber asks for my help I want an immunity agreement. She still has Aunt Ginny on the inside, so I know she'd arrest me and my Spanx if the opportunity presented itself.*

We turned at the wine barrel filled with freshly planted pansies silvery in the moonlight and drove down the long driveway to the winery. There was no patrol car in sight, so on a scale of one to ten that dropped my stress level down to a twenty-five.

Sawyer opened the glove box and took out a flashlight. "Do you think they're even watching this place?"

Kim looked around. "Maybe the night shift is on the way."

I had an uneasy feeling in my stomach, and it was dancing the tango with the nutty bars. "Don't be so sure no one is watching. The police are getting very sneaky and doing surveillance with trail cameras and motion detectors. If they're watching, they already know we're here."

Sawyer groaned. "The door is covered with police tape. How do we even get in?"

Kim started walking toward the vine-covered pergola.

"Follow me." She reached in the ivy and found the latch for the hidden gate. Soon we were on the secluded patio. The French doors had police tape crisscrossing them from the inside.

I scanned for a tiny red or green light to indicate any recording equipment. My heart stopped when I saw a blinking red light, but I realized it was the alarm panel inside the winery blinking that it was armed. "Well, I don't know how we're going to get in, Kim. Not without breaking through the police barrier."

"Not here. Around back." Kim pushed against the vine-covered trellis at the back of the pergola and the trellis swung out making a small opening. Kim and Sawyer breezed through, but I felt like a gigantic Alice looking at the tiny door and wondered if there was a cookie to shrink me nearby.

Sawyer motioned with her hands. "Turn sideways. You can make it."

Sawyer was delirious. Little Debbie will do that to a person. I turned sideways to shimmy through the opening. My butt caught on the hidden latch, and my boobs pulled about ten feet of vine with me. "I'm stuck."

Sawyer had to feel around my butt to unhook me so I could clear the apparatus. Once I was through, I left a trail of vines that spelled *breaking the law over here* with a big arrow.

Kim led us to the back of the winery where there was a heavy metal door, a dumpster, and several crates of empty bottles. Behind the winery were a couple of large wooden outbuildings with corrugated metal roofs.

I pointed to the closest structure. "What's in there?"

"The big one holds the vats where we make the wine

and put it into the oak casks, and the smaller one is a bottle-sterilizing room."

Sawyer pulled a vine out of my hair. "Where do you keep the barrels after you put the wine in them?"

Kim motioned to the large building again. "You can't see it from here, but after they're filled, they go in the underground cellar for aging."

I debated on whether or not to ask my next question, but Sawyer took the words out of my mouth.

"Have you ever seen Daniel actually make wine? You know, from grapes?"

Kim crossed her arms in front of her chest in a peeved fashion. "You mean so I know he's not just pouring boxed wine into new bottles?"

I nodded. "It's a fair question."

"Yes. Jess and I even helped harvest the grapes last October."

"All right. Unlock this door and let's do this."

Kim shook her head. "This door doesn't open from this side."

"Say what now?"

"This is a fire door. It only opens from the inside."

Sawyer put her hands on her hips. "So how are we getting in here, Kim?"

Kim pointed to a little window about ten feet off the ground.

"I'll wait in the car." I started walking away and Kim grabbed my arm.

"Poppy, please. We can do this."

"Who is we? I barely got through the lattice of vines."

"You can stand on the dumpster and boost Sawyer into the window. She'd be up in the loft. Then she can come down the stairs and open the fire door to let you in. Easy peasy."

Sawyer and I were clearly dealing with a crazy person. We stared at Kim, neither of us speaking for half a minute. Then both of us speaking at once.

"What fantasy would lead you to believe Sawyer and I are capable of doing that?"

"Poppy and I are terrified of heights, and falling, and falling from heights, and dumpsters."

Kim started to cry. "I know. It's too much. I just don't know what else to do. Rick and I have been happy together for eighteen years. It was a good run. I should remember that when he leaves me for losing all our money and I end up in jail for being an accessory to murder."

I put my hand up to stop the tears. "Oh my God, okay, fine! We'll try. But why are *we* getting on the dumpster to shimmy up the side of the building? Why aren't you?"

"I'm the lookout. If the cops show up, at least I work here. I can say I came to pick up my purse or something. Why would you be here?"

Sawyer mumbled, "Because our friend went insane and forced us."

I tossed Kim my car keys. "In case they want you to leave you'd better be able to make it convincing. But give us a signal, okay?"

Sawyer stacked a couple of crates on top of each other and used them to reach the handle on the top of the dumpster. I gave her a good push and she used the momentum to wiggle herself to the top. "Eww. It's so gross up here."

Kim put her hands together like a stirrup. "Okay, Poppy. Now you."

I laughed.

"Come on. We can do this."

Sawyer lay down on her stomach on top of the dumpster and hooked her foot on the lid hinge. She made a face like she was about to eat a spoonful of beetles.

I stepped one foot in Kim's hands and reached for the handle of the dumpster. "Okay!"

Kim tried to lift me up while Sawyer grabbed my arms and pulled. I didn't move two inches. *This might be the single most humiliating moment of my life. I'll have to write the coach at Curves and apologize for my bad attitude now.*

Sawyer stopped pulling. "Hold on." She disappeared on the other side of the dumpster for a second and came back with several feet of frayed twine. She tied it off and braided it into a rope with a loop on one end. "Grab ahold of this." She tied it around her waist and threw the other end over the edge of the dumpster and lay back down.

"Are you sure about this? I could pull you right off of there."

She made a big motion to hold on to the handle. "If you're not up here in fifteen minutes you can find a new best friend."

I smiled. This was how we were going to do this? Ferris Bueller quotes. "You've been saying that since the fifth grade." I grabbed the rope and put one foot on the side of the dumpster.

Kim got underneath of me and pushed against my butt with all her might. I didn't think I was moving at all; then my chest touched the handle on the dumpster lid. Between my little bit of yoga strength and Sawyer using her entire body as a counterweight I found myself on top of the dumpster.

"How you doin'?" Sawyer asked me.

"I'm dying."

"You're not dying. You just can't think of anything good to do."

Kim was unaware of our state of mind, because she abandoned us. "Oh, I almost forgot. You have thirty seconds to disarm the alarm. The code is nine-four-six-three. It spells 'wine' on a phone keypad." She disappeared back around the side we came in on.

Sawyer grabbed my shoulder. "I'm going to kill her."

"I'm not going to stop you."

Sawyer and I looked up at the small window above us. Neither of us could reach it on our own, and there was no way I'd ever fit into it if I could.

Sawyer untied the rope from around her waist. She accidentally looked down and panic grabbed ahold of her. Her knees started to buckle. "I can't do this. Why did we let her talk us into this?"

I took her hand. "Look at me. We're almost done."

"I'm going to fall."

"No, you're not. Listen, the question isn't what are we going to do. The question is, what *aren't* we going to do. And we aren't going to fall."

A brief flicker of amusement crossed her face. "I'm gonna need some hot fudge after this."

"I'll buy." I spread my feet and balanced myself with my back against the building. Then I squatted down in chair position.

Sawyer climbed onto my legs. "I've got the ledge."

I cupped my hands and she put her right foot in them. Then I straightened myself up. I heard a tinny screech of rusted metal on metal when she opened the window. Then she disappeared and scrambled through. "I'm in. Oh, thank God. I can't believe it."

I looked over the edge of the dumpster. *Crap.* Getting

down was easy. Doing it in one piece was another story. I tied the rope on to the handle and lay on my stomach. I tried to shimmy to the edge of the dumpster and kick my legs over. I heard the distinct sound that every plus-sized girl knows from her nightmares. *Riiip. Crap on a crab, are you kidding me!*

The fire door opened, and Sawyer called out amid a furious beeping, "What was that code again?!"

I hung over the edge too far to go back and too high to jump down. "It spells 'wine'!"

The door slammed shut.

I rappelled down the side of the dumpster. And by "rappelled," I mean wiggled and slid in slow motion over the edge and got rope burn on both hands all the way down, but my feet landed on the ground, so I counted it a win. It was a win with a six-inch gash in the thigh of my leggings. I was almost trendy.

The fire door opened again, and I rushed inside to Sawyer's arms as the door slammed shut with a loud clang. "Only the meek get pinched. The bold survive."

"Poppy?"

"Yeah?"

"I left the flashlight on top of the dumpster."

I started to giggle. Then Sawyer started to giggle. We could see a little because our eyes were preadjusted to the darkness from being outside so long. "There. Is that a computer?"

Sawyer felt around until she found the Power button for the monitor. The screen blazed awake. "It's still logged in."

I started to look around the room for anything that would indicate Daniel was either guilty or innocent—I didn't really care which one at this point. I just wanted to get the heck out of here. Kim could sue him and try to get her money back if he committed any crime at all and a good lawyer could make a case for her innocence. I searched the file cabinet, but all I found were receipts for bottles, office supplies, printing, and assorted vendors and—of course—Costco. Another drawer had payroll records, and another had sales slips. Nothing seemed unreasonable. Depressing maybe. Daniel had more bills than I had and that was saying something.

Sawyer called me over. "Here are the security files from Saturday." We saw the back-room file with a mountain of boxed wine next to empty bottles and a hose and funnel of sorts. At one point Daniel came in and funneled wine from a box of red into a fancy bottle and took it out with him.

I pointed to the screen. "Go to that one that says: 'Tasting room.'" We fast-forwarded to the part when the tour group arrived. It was sad and unsettling to see Vince Baker still alive. Sunny and he walked in hand in hand. She looked so happy. I had to swallow a lump in my throat. I pulled out my cell phone and hit Record to make a grainy copy of the video. First Daniel greeted the group and moved them over to the polished tables where they sat down for their flight. At the first table Bob and Rosie sat with Ken and Willow. Zara chose to sit by herself until Lily joined her. At the last table Vince and Sunny were joined by Ryan and Alyce.

Sawyer paused the video. "Did you see that?"

"Yeah, Daniel rubbed his hand down Alyce's back when he led her to sit down. Ryan is so far up Vince's butt he doesn't even notice."

She hit Play again and Jess brought in three trays of cheese and meats with breadsticks and bowls of green and purple olives. She was about to put a plate of cheese on Zara and Lily's table, but Ryan intercepted it and put it in front of Vince.

Everyone drinks the wine that Jess brought out as they mill about and visit each other's tables. It's clear on the video that Alyce and Sunny are having words and Vince is getting irritated. Ryan keeps touching Vince's arm and Vince clearly doesn't like it.

"Stop." I pointed to the screen. "Stop it there. Back it up."

"What am I looking for?"

"Right there. Daniel's approaching Vince's table with a tray of several glasses of wine. See the cheese and olives?"

"Yeah."

"Now press Play."

Daniel stood there with his back to the camera talking for a few minutes while members of the tour group came over to take their wine off his tray. When Daniel moved on, there was a small bowl of green pellets sitting on the table in front of Vince.

I pointed to the bowl. "See that?"

Sawyer leaned in closer to the screen. "What is it?"

"Wasabi peas."

"How'd it get there?"

"I don't know. Did you see who put it on the table?"

"I only saw Daniel's back."

We rewound and fast-forwarded the tape three times and all we knew for sure was that the bowl was not in the shot when Daniel was approaching the table. Tour members came and went to pick up wine while Daniel talked, and we never saw anyone put the bowl out. We admitted defeat and let the video play on the fourth time. It was clear that Alyce and Ryan and Sunny were making every-one uncomfortable. The group thinned out away from Vince's table. The next wine, a red, was brought over by Lily. She passed around four glasses and left immediately. A few minutes later, Vince was starting to stagger and smack the table. The rest of the tour group had pretty much banded together away from the Baker family. Then Kim brought the last flight of red wine with a tray of truffles. Her face was strained, and she seemed irritated. She left the table and three minutes and twenty-six seconds later Vince stumbled over to the couch with Sunny and collapsed.

I checked the video output on my phone to be sure that I had the whole feed. It wasn't as clear as the original and I moved around too much, but we got it. I saved it and Sawyer put the computer back the way she found it. "What do we do about fingerprints?"

"Good point." I spotted a box of tissues and grabbed a few for her. I was handing them over so she could wipe everything down and I spotted a Polaroid pinned to the corkboard next to a Dragon House Chinese menu. "Sawyer, look at this."

She looked up from wiping down the mouse. "That looks like Daniel. Is that his wife?"

Daniel was on a fishing boat called the *Cape Diem* with a beer in one hand and his arm around a slightly chubby brunette. "I'm pretty sure that's Alyce Finch."

Sawyer shoved the tissues in her pocket and leaned in to see the snapshot. "I think you're right. She must be a teenager. She's a little bit on the heavy side, but she still has the same eyes. They're really close to each other. The eyes, not the people."

I looked around and nothing else jumped out at me as suspicious. I snapped a copy of the Polaroid to show Aunt Ginny. "Let's go. Kim is probably going crazy right about now."

"Good. It's her fault I smell like Cup Noodles."

We ran down the loft stairs to the fire door and pushed it open. It was darker outside than when we went in. The moon was obscured behind some trees. Sawyer led the way around to the secluded patio and held the trellis door for me. We were almost home free. Just through the gate and back to the front of the winery.

We stopped short at the edge of the building just outside the gift shop not believing our eyes. Sawyer ran in a blind panic over to the front door and back. The parking lot was completely empty. Kim and my car were gone.

Chapter Twenty-three

"Oh no she didn't." Sawyer was on the upward swing of a fit and I knew there was no stopping her. "She'd better have a brilliant reason for abandoning us or I will wring her neck."

I took out my cell phone and dialed Kim.

She answered in a frenzy. "You've got to get out of there. They're patrolling the area, and someone comes by every twenty minutes. I'm waiting at the Gray Pelican down the road." Kim clicked off.

I told Sawyer we were in danger and we started bobbing and weaving through the scrub grass down the driveway. Right when we got near the road, we thought we saw headlights coming toward us, so we both hit the ground flat on our stomachs. A Brother's Pizza delivery car drove by and we groaned.

Sawyer stood up and brushed her jeans off. "I think I literally have ants in my pants."

I rubbed my arms with my hands. "I would cry if it wasn't so cold out here. Why didn't we wear coats?"

Sawyer pointed ahead. "That's the road. We've almost made it arrest-free. Come on."

The sky opened like a faucet and dumped sheets of icy rain on our heads. We sludged the rest of the way to the road fueled by ire and outrage. Kim was sitting in the Gray Pelican Café with three tepid hot chocolates and half an Italian hoagie when we arrived. We hit the door side by side and threw it open. Kim jumped as a flash of lightning lit up our dripping silhouettes. A police car drove past the front window followed by a crack of thunder that rattled the silverware in the metal canisters.

Kim watched the cruiser. "Finally. He must have gone on break." Her words were swallowed up by the tension crackling off Sawyer's shoulders.

I put my hand out. "Keys."

Kim handed me my keys and grabbed the hot chocolates. "Wrap up my hoagie, Mario. I'll come back for it in the morning."

Sawyer downed her hot chocolate like it was a shot of tequila. But even then she didn't look like she was ready to forgive Kim for what she'd put us through tonight.

We made Kim sit in the back and I cranked the heat to try to dry us off. On the way back to the B&B we gave her the highlights of our search, leaving out anything about Daniel or the peas. By the time I pulled into the driveway I was asking about the photograph. "Do you know if Daniel and Alyce Finch knew each other before this weekend?"

"I don't think so. Why?"

Sawyer gave Kim a cryptic look. "Ask him."

We said goodbye much deflated and somber compared to the excitement we had when girls night began. I didn't bother taking the back stairs. I stomped up the main staircase to my room and took a long hot shower with two shampoos and an extra-long conditioning. I even broke out the jasmine sugar scrub. Something was bound to cut through the stench of chow mein and lies.

I blow-dried my hair and put on my warmest jammies, then nudged Figaro over to his side of the bed. Before I could turn back the covers my phone said, "Ciao." Gia was texting me. The message said: **I need you.**

I dialed him immediately. "What's wrong?"

His voice was strained, and his words were clipped. "I am sorry to disturb you so late, but Henry is very sick. His fever won't go down. We've just come home from the emergency room with prescriptions, but he won't take them. He is asking for you. Do you think you could come over and see him for just a minute for me?"

"Of course. I'm on my way." *My poor sweet boy.*

I threw on my coat and shoes and flew down the stairs. Gia's address texted through as I was getting in the car. He lived a few blocks from the coffee shop. I recognized the street name and sped over there saying a prayer for Henry all the way. I threw the car into park at one of the meters. It was covered until May and residents would have rioted otherwise.

Gia lived in the upstairs level of a tan and blue gingerbread duplex. The owner had built a flight of steps from the side yard up to a private entrance on the second story.

I took the steps two at a time and Gia flung the door open before I was halfway there. He had dark circles under his eyes and his face was pale. "I'm so sorry to ask you to come all the way over here this late. He's weak from coughing and he's been asking for you for over an hour. I thought maybe if you could get him to take his medicine his cough would settle down."

"You never have to be sorry about calling me." I entered Gia's living room and a little blond head rose up and peeked over the back of a brown suede sofa. "Poppy?"

"Hey, buddy. What's going on?"

Henry broke into a fit of coughing that sounded like a dog barking.

Gia handed me a plastic medicine cup with a pink liquid, and I handed it to Henry, who took it down in one swallow. Gia made a face and shook his head. "Why wouldn't he do that for me?"

I put my hand on Henry's back and hugged him to me. "Okay now. You know what we're going to do?"

Henry shook his head no.

"We're going to go take a steam bath while Daddy boils some water for special tea."

Henry gave me a single nod and led me to the bathroom. I shut the door after us and turned the shower on hot so the small room would get steamy. I sat on the white tile floor on a green rug and Henry sat in my lap. "Now I don't want you to talk for a while. I just want you to breathe in the steamy clouds."

Henry nodded that he understood and then promptly asked me a question: "Will you tell me a story?"

"Let's see. How about a story about a fire-breathing dragon? And we're sitting in his lair on a pile of treasure surrounded by the sulfur smoke coming out of his nostrils as he snores."

Henry's eyes got really big for a second and he coughed.

Then he settled down against me to listen. Somewhere in the middle, when the dragon was trying to find us under a giant golden goblet, Gia joined us and gave Henry his tea. Gia grabbed a homemade salve with eucalyptus and sat on the floor next to us. Henry drank his tea while Gia rubbed the salve on his chest and back and the dragon flew us around the ramparts of the castle over a battlefield covered with gray bun-headed, rolling-pin-wielding trolls.

Gia saw through the symbolism and snorted.

Henry's cough had settled considerably by the time the shower had run out of hot water, and we moved him into his bedroom. "Somebody likes dinosaurs."

Henry gave me a very serious look. "Me."

"Yeah, I kinda figured that." I made a silly face and Henry grinned and hugged me closer. I put him in his little bed, and he scooted over and patted the mattress next to him.

Gia turned on a humidifier and gave me a look. "You really should have seen that coming."

So, I climbed in next to Henry and he moved onto my lap. I scooted over more and Gia climbed in next to us and pulled me against his chest. We were like a set of Russian stacking dolls. I rubbed Henry's back and he settled down to sleep.

Gia whispered in my ear, "This is not exactly how I imagined us in bed together."

I giggled quietly. "You've thought about it a lot?"

He gave me a sly grin. "Endlessly."

My cheeks grew hot and my stomach gave a little quiver. I was really glad he hadn't seen me trying to get up that dumpster. "What did the emergency room doctor say?"

"It will be a few days before he's back to jumping on the couch and asking for tacos for breakfast."

"I think he just needs to rest."

"I tried. He would not settle down. He said he wanted Poppy to give him the yucky medicine because you'd make it tasted better."

"Aww."

"You gave him the exact same cup I did, but he would not take it from me."

I smiled to myself. "He just wants a mom."

Gia's chest tightened against my back. The air hung heavy between us. I tried to swallow, but there was a lump caught in my throat. I felt Gia's cheek rub against my hair. We stayed like that, cuddled into each other, until Henry's breathing changed from raspy to the steady breathing of deep sleep.

Gia and I gently moved out of the bed and laid Henry down to sleep comfortably. We tucked a T rex under his arm, and he hugged it and rolled away from us.

"Would you like something to drink?" Gia offered.

"You need to get some sleep."

"I can sleep when I'm dead. Please stay."

My skin was on fire with the way he was looking at me. "How about one cup of tea?"

His smile lit up the room and that fire worked its way down to my ankles. "Why don't you go sit down and I'll make the tea."

Gia tried not to yawn. "Okay." But he didn't leave my side. His apartment was small. The kitchen had black cabinets with silver handles, stainless-steel appliances, and a white granite countertop with flecks of silver in it. His cabinets were full of signs that a small child lived there. A Teenage Mutant Ninja Turtles dish set was lined up next to a set of square white bowls and plates. Gold-fish crackers, gummy snacks, and animal cookies shared space with kalamata olives and margarita salt. A box of Alpha-Bits cereal sat on the refrigerator next to a box of Raisin Bran.

The red kettle whistled, and I poured hot water over tea in two square mugs. Gia carried them out to the living room and placed them on a cream-colored stone and iron table. His black and tan hardwood floors were both a shade darker and lighter than the leather sofas, and a pair of blue throw pillows matched the paint on the walls. I wondered who helped him decorate. I hoped it wasn't an old girlfriend.

I sat on one end of the sofa and Gia sat on the other end facing me. "I don't know what I would have done if you hadn't come over tonight."

"It was no trouble."

"You're in your pajamas."

Aw crap. I rushed out of the house so fast I didn't think to change.

"I see you like Daffy Duck."

I felt my ears get hot. "I have other pajamas. I mean you know, nighties—night *things*. To wear for bed. To sleep! . . . Soo . . . yeah." *I could not sound less sexy right now.*

Gia's eyebrows were half raised and his lips were parted. He blinked a couple of times and his mouth un-furled into a slow grin. "I think you look sexy right now."

Gulp. "You should have seen me an hour ago."

"Oh?"

I gave him all the gruesome details about the winery and our recon mission. Nothing should diffuse thoughts of romance like climbing on a dumpster. When I got to the part about walking down the road in the freezing rain his eyes lost their mirth.

He said something in Italian that I didn't understand, followed by, "Bella, you should have called me. I don't want you walking down the road in the middle of the night in the rain. You could get sick or hit by a car. What would I do if something happened to you?"

See if Sierra can bake? I smiled to myself. "Nine is hardly the middle of the night. Besides, how were you going to come get me if you were in the emergency room with Henry?"

"I have six sisters and two brothers. Any one of them would have picked you up for me, no questions asked."

"Good Lord! There are nine of you? I only know of Karla and Pierro."

"The others . . . are around. Now, at least tell me about this Vince and why you think Daniel killed him."

I showed Gia the video and told him about my suspicions. "I don't know that Daniel killed him. But he definitely has a motive. He's in heaps of debt, possibly committing wine fraud—if that's a thing—and he's having an affair with Vince's daughter, so if she inherits, his money problems could be over."

Gia nodded and sipped his tea.

"But since motives are going around, Vince's daughter and Ryan also stand to inherit a fortune now that Vince is dead. And Ryan is a nasty piece of work."

"How many daughters did Vince have?"

"Just the one as far as I know."

"So, who is married to Ryan?"

"Alyce."

"And who is having an affair with Daniel?"

"Also Alyce."

Gia did not show surprise. If anything, he showed anger. He let out another string of Italian—maybe this went along with how tired he was—and his knuckles were white from gripping his tea mug. "Why do you not think the wife is a suspect?"

"She just lost her husband and her grief seems very real to me. I don't think she's faking."

"Are you sure you aren't just being sentimental because you lost a husband too?"

"What do you mean?"

"Is she grieving as much as you think she is? Or are you seeing yourself when you look at her?"

Huh. "I don't know. I didn't think about that."

"You have such a tender heart. I think maybe you give people too much benefit of the doubt sometimes. It is one of the things I love about you."

Do not say it, Poppy. Do not ask that question. My voice caught in my chest and my words squeaked out on a raspy whisper: "What else do you love?"

Gia put his mug down. "I love your smile. The way you get nervous and ramble your words." He scooched closer. "I love the way your eyes light up when you get coffee. I love the way you dance around the kitchen when you bake and you don't know I'm watching. I love how gentle you are with Henry, and how you take care of Aunt Ginny." He was on the edge of the cushion now and his hip was touching mine. It was shooting fire up the right side of my body. "I love how you care about making sure no one feels left out, and all the ways you try to make the people in your life feel special." Gia leaned so close I felt his breath on my neck. "I love all of you, Poppy."

When he said my name, it was like lightning ran down my neck, through my spine, and out my fingers. My lips were on his in an instant and he pulled me to him. I wished I could freeze time and stay here forever.

A spasm of coughs behind the couch grabbed our attention and Gia pulled away from me very reluctantly. "Buddy, you should be sleeping." Gia checked his watch. "Well, it has been four hours. It is time for your medicine again."

Henry pointed to me.

"You want Poppy to give it to you?"

Henry nodded a single nod. Gia poured the pink liquid in the plastic cup and I handed it to Henry. He drank it down and barked out another cough.

I looked at Gia a little differently than I'd ever done before. "I'll go start the shower."

Gia gave me a tired smile that spoke so much more than his words. "I'll make the special tea."

We repeated the process from earlier, but this time with a story about a clandestine spy ring made of secret agent garden gnomes and an evil skinny redheaded twenty-year-old gnome who lived in the mountains. We finally got Henry back to bed and he drifted peacefully off to sleep. And apparently . . . so did we.

Chapter Twenty-four

I was having the most delicious dream. I was snuggled into a fluffy black panther and he was purring in Italian against my neck. I ran my hand down his back and he draped a paw around my shoulders.

Henry giggled. "Poppy."

My eyes popped open to see Henry's face about two inches away from mine. Sunlight was streaming in through his bedroom window and a pair of strong arms were wrapped around me. Henry giggled again. "Daa-dee."

I felt Gia stir and realized that I was pressed up against the length of his body. We must have fallen asleep together. I rolled my eyes back to Henry. *This is not good.*

Henry hopped from one foot to the other and back. "Daddy and Poppy. Daddy and Poppy." Then he coughed for a solid minute.

I swallowed a hard lump that had formed in my throat

and twisted my neck to see Gia grinning. "Buongiorno, bella mia."

We were on a foam mattress on the floor next to Henry's bed. I remembered Gia putting it there so he could lie down while Henry slept, but I wasn't sure how I'd gotten there.

Gia must have read my mind. "You tried to leave around four and he woke up and begged you to stay."

I sat up and looked around. "I vaguely recall that; the rest is a blur."

Gia grinned. "You refused to leave him. Then you fell asleep and I didn't want to wake you."

But how did I get down on this mattress snuggled up against you?

Henry was jumping on his bed now. "I feel better."

Gia motioned to Henry. "Come here so I can check your fever."

He came obediently over and presented his forehead.

Gia put his hand over Henry's eyes and muttered something in Italian. "*Bene*, good. Your fever is broke. But I want you to settle down. You are going to take it easy today."

I tried to stand up without too much obvious grunting and cracking. Thank God for the yoga, but even yoga can't erase that you're forty-something.

Henry grabbed me around the thigh. "Poppy, you can sit next to me and have waffles." Then he started to cough.

I checked my phone, but it was completely dead. "Oh, Sweets, I have to go home. I have to make breakfast for some guests." Not to mention I was acutely aware that I hadn't brushed my teeth and my hair looked like I'd been four-wheeling through the Pine Barrens.

Henry's lip jutted out. "Will you come back?"

"If I can, I'll check on you later."

He seemed mollified by that and hopped his way out to the dining room table. Gia pulled me against him and kissed my forehead. "Can you have coffee first?"

Those were definitely the magic words. The only thing to make that offer irresistible would be if it were served in bed. But the clock above the stove said it was eight a.m., and my breakfast service was in an hour. *Aunt Ginny will kill me when I get home.*

Gia gave me a long hug goodbye on the landing outside of his door. I hoped that would give me the strength to face Aunt Ginny when I arrived home.

Why is it that when you need help cleaning something or carrying groceries no one can hear you holler but try to sneak through the front door first thing in the morning and you suddenly have cymbals on your feet?

Figaro gave me a loud whine like he had suffered a grave injustice having no one to pester in the middle of the night. Tammy Faye shot out from the sitting room and joined him in a whine of her own, wanting to know where I'd been until eight in the morning. Figaro greeted her with a hiss. I told them I had an emergency and had to get to the kitchen to get breakfast ready. Only the kitchen was already full of a drama of its own.

Aunt Ginny sat at the island flanked by Biddies number one and two while Biddie number three was getting down coffee cups and Sawyer was plunging the French press. I waited for someone to launch into me, but they just stared. In deafening silence.

"What?"

Aunt Ginny cocked her head. "Well?"

"Well, what?"

Sawyer narrowed her eyes at me, but Mrs. Dodson held her hand up to quell whatever might have been said.

Aunt Ginny licked her lips and took a deep breath. "Where were you?"

"I'm sorry I didn't call, but I was at Gia's with a—"

They weren't listening anymore. As soon as I said "Gia's" they were whooping and jabbing each other.

"What's happening right now?"

Sawyer turned to the cylinder on the counter. "Alexa, un-pause."

The music cranked up and started playing a Meghan Trainor song from the middle.

Oh no. It's about the walk of shame. And now they're dancing to it. They're never going to let me live this down. Thank God Georgina isn't here. Somehow I think a former mother-in-law playing the odds of who you'll sleep with would add a-whole-nother level of humiliation to this nightmare.

Mrs. Davis patted my hand. "I hope you had a wonderful time."

Mrs. Dodson rolled her eyes. "You kids today are a lot looser with your morals than we were. I hope you're being careful."

Careful to what? Not break a hip?

Sawyer handed me a cup of coffee. "Gia is so sweet."

"What are you even doing here?"

"I wanted to help with breakfast." She held up a pan of French toast.

"That seems unlikely."

"Plus, Aunt Ginny called me."

There it is. I looked at Aunt Ginny. "Who else did you call?"

She looked around the room. "This is it. And Royce."

Great. Now we're including Royce in my business. "What do you-all think happened?"

Mother Gibson cocked her head. "You spent the night with a sexy Italian—we don't want to know the details."

Mrs. Davis nudged her. "Speak for yourself. I want to hear everything."

I was beginning to see what was going on. This evil little granny mafia had made bets on whether or not I had spent the night with a man and which man it happened to be.

Aunt Ginny and Mother Gibson seemed a little perturbed with me.

"And why are you two so disappointed?"

Aunt Ginny shrugged. "We're team Tim."

Mother Gibson nodded. "There's nothing like reuniting with your first love." She grinned at Aunt Ginny. "Right?"

Aunt Ginny shoved her hand in her pocket.

Mrs. Dodson gave me a serious eyebrow lift. "You will have to cut one of these men loose soon, you know. Nobody likes a love triangle."

"I'm not in a love triangle," I sputtered. "I've barely dated either one of them."

Aunt Ginny shot me a frown. "Really, Poppy. If you would just make up your mind, we could all move on with our lives. Don't be dragging this thing out any longer. You're not in a romance novel."

Mother Gibson shook her head. "No man's gonna stick around forever."

"I know that when I choose one or the other—to date! Not even to marry, geez—when I pick one there will be no going back to the other if it doesn't work. I want to be sure of my heart before I make such a big decision. Rushing into things hasn't served me well in the past."

Mrs. Davis gave me a sly smile. "Sure. And in the meantime, you can test the temperature, so to speak."

They all howled in laughter but Mother Gibson. She just shook her head and smiled at me.

"Well, I don't want to disappoint everyone, but what you think happened didn't happen."

Sawyer picked up a cup of coffee and took a sip. "Well, I don't see how it couldn't. You wore your sexiest outfit."

I gave Sawyer my most intimidating warning. "I will deal with you later."

I couldn't go into any more detail because we heard voices coming from the dining room. My wine tour guests had come down for breakfast.

Aunt Ginny pointed at me. "What's happening with your hair?"

"If you must know, I slept on a mattress on the floor."

Aunt Ginny blinked twice. "He made you sleep on the floor? Is that an Italian thing?"

The biddies cackled. Even Sawyer had to hide her face behind her coffee.

I smoothed down my Daffy Duck pajama shirt and put on a purple apron covered in butterflies. I grabbed the carafes of orange juice and coffee and started through the kitchen door into the dining room with as much dignity as I could muster.

Sawyer called after me, "You might want to get that plastic dinosaur out of your hair!" The mafia broke into gales of laughter as the door swung shut.

Chapter Twenty-five

Ryan and Alyce were sitting at the table across from each other. They were in mid-argument when I walked into the room, and the tail end of it slithered around my ankles and tried to trip me. Ryan hissed at Alyce, "We're too close to mess this up now." He spotted me and made such an obvious *not now* look to Alyce I almost laughed out loud.

Very subtle, Ryan. "Good morning. I hope you slept well."

Alyce held up her coffee cup. "My room is hot. I think the thermostat is broken. Could you send Maintenance to look at it?"

I filled her cup with Colombian medium roast. "Of course. I'll send someone this afternoon." *I have Bob Vila on speed dial.*

Ryan held up his hand that he didn't want coffee. "Just juice. What are you serving this morning?"

"French Toast Casserole."

"I really expected the food to be fancier in a bed and breakfast. Don't you have a separate menu for when VIPs visit or something?"

"No. We just have the one menu, but the selections change every day."

"Well, what is it tomorrow?"

Hopefully it'll be an Egg McMuffin on your way out of town. I smiled. "I'm still working on it."

Aunt Ginny came through the door with a wooden box in her hands. She walked up to Ryan and opened it. "Tea bag?"

I had to throw my face into my elbow and pretend to cough. The kitchen roared with laughter just on the other side of the door.

Ryan's face was blank. He shook his head no. "Do you think you could get me some fresh papaya for tomorrow?"

Seeing as how it's the middle of March and we're about five thousand miles from Hawaii, doubtful. "I'll see if the market has any."

I entered the kitchen, where the biddies were bent over double in hysterics. Aunt Ginny was getting bags of frozen vegetables for each one of them. Mother Gibson took her bag of lima beans and shoved it down the back of her polyester slacks. "Oooh, that's better."

"You-all are terrible. I can't believe you did that."

Aunt Ginny shook a bag of succotash at me. "I can't believe you let me believe it was 'tea bag.'"

I took trays of Canadian bacon to the dining room and

Sawyer brought out a pan of French Toast Casserole. Bob and Rosie had joined Ryan and Alyce at the table. By the time I'd filled their cups with coffee and juice, Willow and Ken were seated. Everything was unduly strained. Either every couple were fighting with each other or these people really didn't get along. I suggested some museums—which were shot down. I recommended shopping on the Washington Street Mall—which was scoffed at. And finally, I threw out that I had a cabinet full of board games and puzzles in the library—which got me stares so cold I almost caught frostbite.

Aunt Ginny brought in a bowl with three kinds of fresh melon balls with mint, sensed the mood, and quickly retreated back to the kitchen.

Zara entered the dining room in a gorgeous yellow sundress and yellow and white wedge lace-up sandals. She sniffed. "I'll take mine out on the screened porch if you don't mind." She filled up a plate with French toast and went to sit alone with her phone on the swing.

Rosie whispered to Bob, "She isn't very friendly, is she?"

Bob shook his head and shoveled in a forkful of the buttery maple casserole.

I filled a bowl full of melon balls and took it out on the porch to join Zara. "I brought you some fruit in case you'd like to try it."

She pointed her fork to the table in front of her. "Put it there."

I did as she said and sat in the chair next to the swing. "I'm so sorry your tour was cut short."

Zara shrugged. "C'est la vie. Lily said she'd make arrangements with the other wineries if I wanted to still visit them."

"Do you?"

"I would like to go to a couple. I came on this trip mainly for the home tours. I'm planning a Victorian Chic theme for my fall line of home goods."

"Oh, that would be . . ." *Busy.* "Very nice. So, have you always been interested in wine?"

Zara took a dainty bite of French toast. "Not really. I did an Internet search for things to do in Cape May. I had the location planned before any of the activities. When I saw I could save eighty percent on a bed and breakfast with the tour package I jumped on it. It was nice of you to let us stay for free."

Yes, it was, wasn't it? "What's it like traveling with a group of strangers? I don't know if I could ever do something like that."

She tilted her head back and forth while she chewed. "It's fine. I keep to myself. I'm used to being a solo traveler. I don't really need other people to be happy. I like my privacy."

"I guess it's a relief that you didn't know the man on the tour who died then."

"I certainly feel sorry for his wife, less sorry for his daughter and son-in-law, but I didn't know him, so it didn't ruin my holiday. I hope that doesn't make me sound like a terrible person."

"No, of course not. Just curious, why less sorry for the daughter and son-in-law?"

"They seem like horrible people. I tried to stay away from all of them, but if you ask me they caused his heart attack."

I told her to enjoy her breakfast and let me know if she needed anything else and went back to the kitchen.

The biddies were quietly digging into their own French

toast and coffee, and Sawyer handed me a plate of meat. "I believe this is all you can have this morning."

"Shows what you know. I made keto biscuits yesterday and I'm gonna fry me an egg."

I took the carton of eggs out of the refrigerator and Tammy Faye bounded into the kitchen and hopped up on my foot. "What are you doing in here?"

"Poppy?"

I looked up to see Sunny standing in the entryway. She was wrecked. Her eyes and cheeks were hollow, and she needed a shower and some clean clothes. "Hey there. It's good to see you up and about."

"Could I eat in here with you?"

"Of course you can."

The biddies looked at Aunt Ginny, who gave one of her stage whispers: "Widowed."

The biddies slow-rushed Sunny and enveloped her in a bosomy hug. Mother Gibson led her to the table. "Come on, baby, you need some vitamin C and a good dose of butter and syrup. We'll get you fixed right up."

The ladies cooed over Sunny and told her she would get through this. The four of them had lived through it a total of ten times between them. Aunt Ginny was throwing the curve off on that one.

Meanwhile, I fed Figaro what I was sure must be his second breakfast of the day. Then I watched as Tammy Faye nudged him out inch by inch until she had her entire snoot in his martini glass. Fig sat to the side swishing his tail. I felt sorry for him until he threw his paw out and swatted Tammy right on the head. She backed off and he dove in. "Good for you, Fig."

Everyone in the kitchen was occupied, so I snuck into the dining room to check on things. Only Willow and

Ken were left at the table. I overheard the word "divorce"; then Willow was crying and Ken was apologizing. "I can't take it back. Either you forgive me, or you don't." They both straightened up when they saw me.

"Don't mind me. I'm just coming in to check the sideboard."

Ken got up and left the room, and Willow started to cry harder. "I'm so sorry I keep crying. I'm just really emotional right now."

"Of course you are. You're allowed. You're pregnant."

"What?"

I pointed at her stomach with my elbow. "The baby."

"Of course." Tears fell from her eyes again and Willow got up and left the room after Ken.

Maybe I should wait in the kitchen until guests are done from now on.

Zara popped her head in from the screened porch. "Poppy. Can you help me with something?"

"Sure." I joined her by the swing. "What do you need?"

Zara handed me her cell phone. "I'm going to use your swing as a backdrop for my sunburst pillows and crackle vases." She struck a casual pose. "Could you take some pictures of me that I can upload this afternoon?"

"I'll try." I took a few shots. "I don't really know what I'm doing."

Zara changed her facial expression with each pose. "I'm sure you're doing fine. I'm very photogenic, so there will be something I can use."

I kept taking pictures as long as she kept changing positions. "I don't really understand how you're going to use these for your pillows and vases."

Zara sucked her cheeks in and tilted her head at a

forty-five-degree angle. After I took the shot she sat up and reached for her phone. "I'm going to photoshop them in later."

"Won't people be able to tell they weren't really here?"

She was swiping through the pictures. "People believe what they think they see. They don't usually analyze things. These are good. Thanks." She handed me her plate and fork and left through the dining room.

I followed her and began clearing the table. When I returned with full hands to the kitchen, Victory was sitting at the island eating French toast remnants from the baking pan.

"Thees ees very good."

"It's French Toast Casserole. Do you have that where you live?"

"We have toast, but not weith so much butter and cream. I like eet."

"I see you're finally wearing the uniform I bought for you. I was just getting used to the other one. What happened?"

Victory didn't look up from the pan. "I speill somesing."

"Okay. Well, you can probably get started in about an hour. I heard the Swallowtail suite couple mention they were going to walk on the boardwalk."

"Ees good. They need to walk more."

Oh. Okay. I wonder what she thinks about me?

Sawyer put her plate in the sink. "Don't forget we have that exercise class tonight."

"I didn't forget. What do I need to bring? Water bottle? Yoga mat?"

Sawyer grinned and drummed her tented fingers. "Don't

you worry about that. I'm going to go buy our equipment right now. I'll take care of everything."

"I'm more worried now than I was on the dumpster."

"Bwa ha ha." Sawyer backed out of the kitchen.

She's such a weirdo. I giggled to myself.

Over at the banquette, Sunny was being hugged again by each of the biddies. She had Tammy Faye tucked under her arm. "Thank you, Nanas. I'm going to go take a shower now and then I'll go for a long walk with Tammy Faye."

Mother Gibson waved goodbye. "You'll feel much better, honey."

"It'll perk you right up." Mrs. Davis added her own wave.

I faced the seniors who had gotten me into more trouble in six months than I'd found on my own in four years of high school. "What are you-all up to tonight?"

"Oh, nothing."

"Quilting bee."

"I've got my Bible study class."

Even Aunt Ginny shrugged. "I might go to Bingo."

"Okay. Good. Those all sound like safe choices. I'm going to go take a shower and change into clothes. Then I've got some baking to do. I'll see you-all later?"

The biddies all nodded and smiled sweetly. "Have fun, honey." They waved as I left the room.

They're not fooling anyone. They're definitely up to something.

Chapter Twenty-six

My current round of bed and breakfast guests were going to wear me out. Between the moody, the egotistical, and the conniving, I had to get out of there. I went to my happy place made of sugar and chocolate.

Chamber music filled the dining room of Maxine's, setting the ambiance for Monday's candlelight lobster specials, but the kitchen was rocking to Fall Out Boy and flash-fried cheeseburgers. I stood in the doorway taking in the hustle with the smell of peanut oil and caramelized onions. Juan was shaking his butt to "Light 'Em Up" while he toasted buns on the salamander, and Chuck held up a triple-decker cheddar heart attack on a dinner plate. "Poppy! You want a monster burger?"

Hellz yeah!

Tim shut the door of the walk-in and hollered over the music, "She don't want that, Chuck! She's on a diet."

"Oh, sorry, Poppy."

I whimpered to myself. *I switched to keto.* I gave Chuck a smile. "I can take a patty with cheese on a salad when you're done."

Chuck pointed his spatula at me. "You got it!"

Tim came over and gave me a peck before spinning away with a rubber container of fresh crabs that had a Quentin Tarantino kind of night ahead of them.

I took an apron off the hook and got ready to make two giant caramel mousse cakes.

"Hey, gorgeous, where's your chef coat?"

I didn't want to admit that I couldn't button it up after one Diet Dr Pepper and the nutty bar incident from last night, so I gave Tim the first excuse that oddly came to mind: "I spill somesing."

He laughed at me and went back to the walk-in for round two.

I went to the pastry station and set up my recipe. Then I took out my ingredients for the first and fourth layers, a vanilla bean sponge cake. I measured and sifted, whipped, folded, and scraped to the beat of "I Don't Care."

Tim snuck up behind me and grabbed me around the waist. "Can't you hear me calling you?"

"Nope."

He took my hand and spun me around to the music.

I danced with him for a minute. "You know I've got to get this cake in the oven, or it won't rise."

He pulled me close. "I don't care."

I giggled and rolled my eyes. "Aren't you afraid the lunch crowd will hear the bedlam in here?"

"I told Linda to fill the front room first."

The music changed and the lyrics plotted against me. "I'd trade all of my tomorrows for just one yesterday."

The air around me was charged. Tim went in for a kiss and we were interrupted by Chuck.

"Your salad's up, Poppy."

Tim turned to the sous chef. "Chuck. You're fired."

Chuck blew him off and went back to his station. "Sorry, Chef."

I put my pans in the convection oven and set the timer, then reached for the saucier.

Tim intercepted my hand and picked up my salad. "Uh-uh. Let's go to my office. Juan, hand me my monster burger."

I snatched the timer and dropped it in my apron pocket, then followed Tim down the hall. He shut the door behind us with his foot. "Animals."

I laughed and took the seat next to the desk. "They're all housebroken, though."

"I'm not sure about Chuck." Tim picked up his burger with two hands and searched for a good place to get a bite. "How's the investigation coming?"

"Well." I chewed my lettuce and tried for the life of me to imbibe the spirit of the monster burger. "Slow. These people don't like each other, and they don't care who knows it. They spend most of their time at the B and B in their own rooms. So, I have no idea how Amber expects me to eavesdrop on them."

"What does Amber think you're going to overhear?"

"I dunno. She hopes someone heard or saw something that makes one of them look guilty."

Tim snagged a glob of cheese trying to escape by bungee. "Do you really think the wife is grieving?"

"Either that or she's a great actress. One of my other couples is having marriage problems."

Tim's eyes met mine. "How do you know?"

"I overheard them arguing and the woman mentioned divorce. They're expecting a baby soon."

He shrugged. "People get divorced every day. If I'd been married, I'd probably be divorced by now too."

"What makes you say that?"

"Being married to a chef is hard. The business takes eighty hours a week. More in the summer. You have to know what you're getting into."

I chewed a bite of my burger and willed it to go down. It suddenly felt like I was trying to swallow a rock. "Do you know Daniel Nickson? He owns the Laughing Gull Winery."

"Yeah. I know Daniel. Why?"

"He's divorced, isn't he?"

"For a couple of years now."

"Do you know what happened?"

Tim shrugged. "I guess they just fell out of love. I know his ex, Trish. She's pretty cool."

"Kim told me Daniel owned another business that went under from Hurricane Sandy. Do you know what it was?"

Tim thought while he chewed. "He had a little place that did beach rentals down by Congress Hall. Bikes, boogie boards, lockers, umbrellas. That kind of thing."

"What happened? Flood?"

Tim blew out a breath. "Yes. And no. Daniel lost everything, but he had insurance. The problem was, at least according to Trish, he paid fifty thousand dollars to a contractor to rebuild and the guy took the money and disappeared. He'd scammed a dozen businesses and got away with half a million dollars. It was all over the local news."

I felt appreciation grow for my own Itty Bitty Smitty

more than ever. He might be the world's worst handyman, but at least he was honest. "Scumbags."

"Exactly."

"Do you think Daniel could commit fraud?"

"Naw. He wouldn't steal from people."

"What about serving wine that he didn't exactly make himself?"

Tim thought for a minute. "Well, that's not really fraud, is it? I serve pasta I didn't hand roll."

"Yeah, but do you tell people you did?"

"I don't advertise that I didn't. If they asked, we would tell. Thankfully, they don't ask. No restaurant makes absolutely everything from scratch. We'd be too busy churning butter and emulsifying mayonnaise to wrap the scallops in bacon."

"I guess." I took another bite of my burger. "This is really good. What is it?"

"Wagyu. I've been hand-feeding it in the stock room for weeks."

We both laughed and I guess he'd made his point, so I changed the subject slightly. "What would you think if I told you Daniel was having an affair with Vince's daughter, Alyce?"

"While he was married to Trish?"

"No, now. While Alyce is married to Ryan."

Tim wiped his mouth on a napkin. "Daniel's a good guy, but people make bad decisions all the time when it comes to the heart."

You're telling me. "You know the cops detained him last night."

"What? They think Daniel killed that guy?"

"They seem to think he's involved."

"What would he have to gain?"

"Alyce could inherit a fortune if they figure out the will."

"And you think Daniel killed her father so he could get his hands on the money?"

"I don't think anything, but I know they're sneaking around. I think Amber suspects he's involved. Why else would she have detained him?" The timer went off in my pocket. It was time to get the sponge cake out of the oven. I picked up my plate and stood to go.

Tim put his hand on mine. "Listen, Mack, I've known Daniel a long time. He's not the best judge of character, but he's no killer."

"If he's not, then the killer is staying at my house."

Chapter Twenty-seven

Sawyer texted me that she had the afternoon off and it would be the perfect time to take a ride up to Court House. I finished my caramel mousse cakes and gave Tim a kiss goodbye. I waited in the car outside of Sawyer's condo. A beach towel abandoned over the neighbor's railing was whipped into a frenzy in the March wind blowing off the Atlantic. I was wondering who in their right mind would be swimming this time of year when Sawyer flung my car door open and tossed her hobo bag in the back seat. She buckled in and I handed her a coffee. "Are you sure we have to do this?"

She grinned. "Let's just see it as an adventure."

We sped up the parkway to Court House to the blue bungalow where I had my infamous run-in with Madame Zolda and, on a related note, developed my fear of owls. The wooden Psychic sign was no longer in the front yard.

A For Lease poster now occupied the front window under the law offices and next to Hippo Hoagies.

I leaned on the steering wheel and looked out. "Well, that's that. She's gone. Probably run out of town by angry villagers wielding pitchforks."

Sawyer raised her hand. "Not so fast. Let's go ask if anyone knows where she is."

I put the car in park and tried to think of a good reason not to get out. I came up empty. "If you say so."

The hoagie shop smelled like fresh-baked bread and provolone. The Plexiglas sneeze guard covered a plethora of exotic meats. Mortadella with pistachio, plain loaf, Lebanon bologna, capicola, pork roll, and scrapple. It's not that I didn't know what they were; it's that I hadn't seen them in ages. We ate a lot of smoked turkey breast in Waterford.

A middle-aged man in blond dreadlocks sat at a red Formica table with his head down, nursing a coffee. "Hey, dudes. If yooze need a hoagie just let me know, 'kay?"

Sawyer raised an eyebrow at me, and I shook my head. "Maybe later? Right now, we're looking for information about Madame Zolda."

The guy made a lazy stretch backward like a cat doing yoga and revealed a vintage OP T-shirt riding up over a beer gut and board shorts. "Yeah. The weirdo with the haunted car. I remember her."

"Do you know what happened to her?"

He scrunched his eyes together and looked into the recesses of his brain for the answer. "Dude. I think she left. Yeah. Something about her shop flooding . . . and ruining a smoke machine . . . ya know?"

I suspected it was smoky in his mind right now.

He took a pack of Nicorette gum out of his pocket and popped a piece in his mouth. "Yeah. You'd think a psychic woulda known about that ahead of time . . . and moved her stuff out . . . ya know . . . like . . . before the pipe broke?"

I looked at Sawyer. "Yeah. You would think that, wouldn't you?"

Sawyer flattened her lips and half shrugged. "Do you know where she went? Is there a forwarding address?"

He ran his hand through his beard and opened his eyes to the size of half dollars. "Uhhh. Ya know. I think she said she was moving to the Villas on Bayshore."

Well, that's just perfect. "Thanks, man."

He made a fist and put it out to me. "No problem. Take it easy."

I gave him a fist bump. "Sure thing."

Sawyer gave him a fist bump and he ran his eyes over her. "Come back anytime you want a hoagie or anything . . . ya know?"

We got outside and Sawyer giggled. "I don't want to know what 'or anything' is code for."

"Whatever it is, I'm giving it up with my cleanse."

We piled in my car and took off back down the Garden State Parkway for exit 4, Route 47. There was no exit for the Villas because the Villas was a small burg with nothing to see. There was a defunct button factory, and when I was a kid I was sure it was haunted. As an adult I suspect it's a hideout for members of The Family.

The highlight of the Villas is the Milky Way frozen custard stand. They were responsible for at least two inches on my waist, and I was responsible for sending the owner's youngest to space camp in the summer of '86.

Bayshore Road was barely a mile long, so we scoured it from one end to the other in about five minutes looking for a hinky voodoo kind of shop with a weirdo in a turban chanting in the window.

"There! That has to be it." Sawyer pointed to a weathered little storefront in between a consignment shop and The Seashell Bazaar.

The center shop had a moon and stars painted on the door, with assorted crystals dangling from nylon cords in the front display. The door chimed when we entered, and an old woman dressed like Stevie Nicks in a "Rhiannon" video trundled over to welcome us. She was tiny and round and only came up to the top of my rib cage, with her teased-up white mullet marking the last six inches. She had thick round glasses that made her green eyes the size of horse chestnuts and when she smiled a gold tooth challenged you not to stare. "Welcome to The Energy Shop. I'm Stella. Are you looking for charms or talismans today?"

I'm looking for the exit.

Sawyer saw my eyes getting shifty and grabbed my arm. "We're looking for Madame Zolda."

The woman grimaced. "Not here."

"Do you know when she'll be back?"

"Depends on when my restraining order expires."

I gave Sawyer a look to say, *What kind of weirdos are you trying to get us wrapped up with?*

She volleyed back a look that said, *Whatever kind can break this curse and stop the death toll. Besides, this is South Jersey; what do you want from me?*

We'd been friends a long time, so we were well versed in telepathic snark.

I turned to the old woman who smelled like burnt hair and wet dog. "We were told Madame Zolda set up shop here. I take it you've had a falling-out."

Stella waddled behind the counter and started filling a display with pink rocks. The sign said: "Precious and rare rose quartz healing crystal charms in 10 karat gold plate."

I narrowed my eyes at Sawyer. "Look. And you have a birthday coming up."

Sawyer smacked her lips and looked away from me to the woman. "We just need to talk to her. Do you know where we can find her?"

Stella hefted herself up on a low stool. She looked like a cosmetology school practice head submerged in a black shawl inner tube. "My sister was only here for a few weeks. I let her do her readings in the back room. It didn't work out."

Oh, I have to ask. "Oh . . . no . . . what happened?"

She sucked her teeth and rolled her eyes. "Hives. Apparently, she had a bad reaction to my Twiddlebum."

Sawyer choked and I slapped her gently on the back. "And Twiddlebum is . . ."

"Here, kikikiki."

A giant tortoiseshell, what? Persian? Main Coon? I had no idea, but it was huge, and it launched itself gracefully atop the counter and began to swat at the healing charms that ironically did not heal Madame Zolda.

Sawyer caught her breath. "So, Madame Zolda had to move because she had an allergic reaction to Mr. Twiddlebum?"

Stella dangled one of the healing charms in front of the cat. "Miss Twiddlebum. And yes. It was quite a shame, because we had just signed the lease on the shop here. If we'd known she was allergic I would never have agreed to go into business with her. Now I'm stuck for her half of the rent and we aren't speaking."

I opened my mouth—not to gloat but to agree that it was a shame they hadn't foreseen it—and Sawyer stomped on my foot, temporarily rendering me silent. She smiled sweetly at the woman. "Do you happen to know where she is now?"

"I believe she moved to a shack at the foot of the Cape May bridge. It will probably fall down the first hurricane that comes through."

I gave Sawyer a smug look—and she knew why. We thanked Stella and headed back out to the car.

Sawyer strapped herself in and covered her mouth with her coffee cup. "Do not start laughing until we get out of this parking lot. She's watching through the window."

"She probably turned Madame Zolda into Miss Twiddlebum." I put the car in reverse trying to control my breathing, because I really wanted to throw my head back and laugh my butt off. "Do you realize the foot of the Cape May bridge is less than ten minutes away from my house?"

Sawyer started to giggle. "I wonder if Madame Zolda knows we're coming."

"I wonder if she's gotten over those hives yet."

We drove over the bridge and would have missed the little gray shack if it were not for the faded blue sign that advertised Psychic—with a hole punched in the center of the *P*. The legs of the sign were buried in two wooden planters full of sand and the top was covered in bird poop—due to either its proximity to the canal or some kind of owlery strike team enacting paybacks for their fallen comrade.

I parked next to a rusty Toyota that had a crack in the windshield, a dent in the roof, and was missing the back bumper. There was a bumper sticker on the hood that said *Medium—a gift or a curse*. And another that said *Vote Mondale Ferraro*. "This is definitely it."

We tromped up the sidewalk and Sawyer raised her fist to knock on the door.

A wild woman with frizzy copper hair shooting out of an emerald-green turban and giant gold hoop earrings threw the door open. "Come in. I've been expecting you."

"Did you see us in your crystal ball?" I couldn't help myself.

"No. Stella called."

Madame Zolda's front room was full of hanging silks and satins with various fringes and beads—pretty much what I'd always imagined a circus tent to look like on the inside. In the center of the room she had a round table draped with a dark blue tablecloth covered in suns and moons with a crystal ball in the center. Off to the side she had a portable television playing *Days of Our Lives*, and behind it sat a sign advertising payment accepted by Visa and Mastercard through Square.

She wore a green and gold caftan and about fifteen layers of crystal beads that rattled and clacked when she spun around and dropped herself dramatically on a tufted blue velvet chair. "I wondered how long it would take you to come beg me for help." She held out her hands and indicated that we were to sit on the flimsy wooden folding chairs.

I rolled my eyes to Sawyer and gave out the most imperceptible whimper. Sawyer pulled a wooden chair out from under the table and bored her eyes into my soul.

I sighed and started to pray earnestly, *Please, God, don't let me break this chair. And please don't let this charlatan cast an evil spell on me. But mostly the chair thing.*

I sat very gingerly listening for sounds of early splintering.

Sawyer flopped down without a care in the world.

Madame Zolda sat back smugly and drummed her fingers on the tablecloth. "And so, it begins."

Sawyer crossed her arms in her lap and leaned forward. "Thank you for seeing us. Poppy and I wanted to discuss a little matter of some bad luck that she's been experiencing."

Madame Zolda raised her pencil-drawn eyebrows and looked from Sawyer to me with a sparkle in her eye and a tiny half smile.

I was determined not to give anything away. If Madame Zolda was really psychic, she should be able to tell me why I was there.

Madame Zolda cleared her throat and shifted her eyes to a notice next to a hurricane lamp: "Payment before readings. No returns or exchanges. $35 charge for bad checks."

"I'm not looking for a reading. I just want to know if you put a curse on me or not."

Madame Zolda folded her arms across her sparkly bosom and leaned back.

Sawyer opened her hobo bag and took out a wallet. "How much will it take?"

"Put that away!" I snapped.

Madame Zolda reached out a spindly hand covered in costume jewelry. Her nails were painted bright blue with jumping dolphins to match the turquoise stone on her thumb ring. "Fifty and I'll throw in a reading for you while we're at it."

Sawyer pulled out some cash and Madame Zolda snatched it, her hand disappearing into her voluminous sleeve.

"Sawyer," I protested.

"Poppy. This is happening."

I squelched down in my bad attitude and the chair creaked. I held my breath.

Madame Zolda grabbed each of our hands and stared swaying and chanting.

I gave Sawyer another scowl of disdain, but she didn't notice. Her eyes were bright, and her lips were clamped shut. She was giddy with excitement.

After a full minute of gibberish, Madame Zolda screeched out, "Yip yip yip!" She threw her piercing gaze on me. "You are having romance troubles."

"Please. Most of the women who go to psychics are having romance troubles. What else you got?"

Madame Zolda shook her head and her beads rattled. "Your heart is divided. I see two men, but there are secrets."

Sawyer gurgled, "Ooooh."

Madame Zolda ignored her. "You have found an enduring love, but there is another woman in the way."

My mind flashed to Gia. *Freaking Sierra.*

"Your love will be tested. Be sure you make the right decision." She leaned back against her chair.

Well, that was helpful. "How much money do I have to pay to get a positive reading? Like I'm going to meet a tall dark stranger or win the lottery?"

Madame Zolda frowned and shook her hands at me. "You do not believe, but you will see."

"Well, that's just peachy, but I came here to find out why I keep ending up in the middle of murder investigations."

Madame Zolda shrugged. "You're probably just nosy."

I sighed and Sawyer took over. "So, you didn't put a curse on Poppy a few months ago when she came home."

She examined me for a second. "Oh, you are cursed all right, but Madame Zolda did not curse you. That goes back way before you met me and destroyed my sign."

Sawyer's eyes popped like full moons. "Are you saying someone else cursed her? Who? Where?"

Madame Zolda scanned my face probably looking for me to give something away. I wouldn't do it. "I don't know. But until you find the source you will stay in this pattern of death and destruction for the rest of your life."

"Come on, Sawyer. I told you this was all smoke and mirrors."

Madame Zolda's garden gazing ball turned lavender and started to glow. Her eyes flew back in her head and she started to chant again.

"What the crap?"

Sawyer grabbed my hand. "You did it now."

Madame Zolda reached out and grabbed my other hand. "The wolf is masquerading as a lamb. He will attack soon. Someone close to you is in danger. You will not see it coming, but you must act quickly." And just like that everything stopped.

Sawyer and I stared for a minute to see what would happen next.

"It will cost you another twenty to hear more."

I grabbed my purse and stood to go. "No thanks."

Sawyer picked up her hobo bag and stood slowly. "Did you have anything to include for me?"

Madame Zolda turned her palm over and gave her a halfhearted glance. "You will meet someone in a dark alley with icy blue eyes and fall madly in love before the full moon." Then our psychic waved us toward the door.

Sawyer grinned brightly. "Sweet." Of course, when we got outside she changed her tune. "That was fun. What a bunch of garbage—but fuuun."

"Why couldn't I meet someone in an alley? I got cursed twice."

"Probably because you didn't pay."

We discussed our readings all the way back to Sawyer's condo and agreed that the next time we went to see a fake Gypsy in a shack at the bottom of the bridge we needed to bring Aunt Ginny along. It would make her whole week.

Just as I pulled into the parking lot of Sawyer's condo my cell phone rang with Aunt Ginny. "Here she is now." I clicked on. "Hey. I'm just dropping Sawyer off. . . . You what? . . . Did you try telling it to stop? . . . Okay. Well, don't do that. I'll be home in a few minutes. Just go sit in the library until I get there." I dropped my phone back in my purse and answered Sawyer's unspoken question: "Aunt Ginny needs me to come home right away."

"Uh-oh. What's wrong?"

"Apparently Alexa won't stop playing 'The Devil Went Down to Georgia' and she wants to hit it with the frying pan."

Sawyer giggled. "I'll pick you up at six for our work-out class. You'll need a bottle of water and red lipstick."

"What's the red lipstick for?"

Sawyer closed her eyes and shook herself. "Trust me. It will be fabulous!"

Chapter Twenty-eight

I was determined not to let Madame Zolda get under my skin. I spent a few minutes snuggling Fig, then tried my sixty-minute abs DVD. And by "tried," I mean I did three and a half minutes before I got a side cramp and had to stop. I felt like a new woman after a shower and some Smashbox tinted primer.

I fancied myself up for a couple of hours of snooping and baking. My new life goals checklist apparently. I checked email and future reservations—both of which I had in short supply.

I got a call from Amber asking if I'd learned anything yet. I shaded the truth a bit and said, "Not exactly." I'd learned stuff but didn't know what it meant yet. I'd rather put her off than spout nonsense I couldn't back up and get an innocent person in trouble. She called me useless and hung up on me.

I took the main staircase so I could check on Victory's progress with the rooms. The door to the Swallowtail suite was open a crack, so I knew she was cleaning it while Bob and Rosie were at their police interview. I knocked just to be safe and was met with silence. "Victory?" Nothing. I went in the room and looked around. The bed was made, and the dressers were straightened. The vacuum was still in the middle of the floor plugged in. I opened the bathroom door and found Victory standing in the shower leaning against the glass door. For a second I thought I should call 911; then she snored.

I tapped on the glass. "Victory!"

She opened her eyes to little slits and smacked her lips. "I'm cleaning room."

"No, you're not. You're sleeping in the shower."

Victory stretched and grabbed a clean towel off the bar. "Theese towels are verry soft. Where deid you buy them?"

She had the uncanny ability to infuriate me and confuse me at the same time. "You've got to stop sleeping on the job. And why are you wearing Rosie's cowboy hat?"

Victory reached her hand up to touch the hat. "I want to see eif I look like real Amerecan cowboy."

"Well, just put it away and finish up. They'll be back soon. They're supposed to leave today."

"Okay, okay. Geez Louise."

When I was satisfied that she was cleaning again, I left her to it. I was walking past Alyce's room and I heard her talking to Ryan: "I do love you. I'm so sorry about earlier. I'm sorry about everything. Let's do something alone tonight. It's been too long." They had obviously patched up their argument from earlier.

I don't know what she sees in him, but they say there's a lid for every pot.

I hit the bottom landing and saw the mail truck drive by. I went to get the stack of junk mail and late notices that were doing their effort to keep the paper industry in business and stopped short on the porch. Ryan was sitting in one of the rocking chairs, on his cell phone.

"Let's reschedule for next week. I'm sure I can get you what you need by then. . . ."

I tried to act casual and went to the mailbox while he was talking.

"Absolutely, it won't be a problem. I've already got the money on the way."

I took my time going back up the steps while Ryan ended his call. I gave him a friendly smile. "Beautiful afternoon. It got up to fifty-five today."

"Huh? Yeah, okay."

"I didn't get a chance to tell you how sorry I was for what you and Alyce are going through right now."

"Oh right. Yeah. It's tough. Especially on Alyce."

"Of course, Alyce is heir to the estate. Maybe she can do something in her father's honor with it."

Ryan laughed bitterly. "Yeah, I doubt that. Sunny convinced Vince to change his will right before this trip. Alyce isn't getting anything."

"Are you sure?"

"I heard it from the lawyer myself. Well, I listened to Vince's voicemail when he stepped out to use the men's room."

"The lawyer said the will was changed and Alyce was written out?" *No way would John's old law firm ever leave details in voicemail.*

"Yeah. Well, no. It was the firm's lawyer. But he said

he'd made the requested changes and the new will was ready to go."

"And there was no way he was leaving more money to Alyce and not writing her out?"

"No. Vince was a lot of things, but a good dad to Alyce—never. She reminded him too much of his first wife. If anything, he was better to me. That's why I'm sure he left me in charge of the business."

Dear God, if his head swells any more I could tie a basket on him and give hot-air balloon tours over the wineries. "Sure. After all, you were Vince's right-hand man."

"Yeah. It sucks, that he's gone, you know. But I think I'll be able to steer the ship in his honor. He would have wanted that."

"Every dad wants his kids to follow in his footsteps."

Ryan took my encouragement as praise and warmed to the subject. "Oh yeah. But, I mean, you know I'm going to have to change some things."

"Of course. You'd be in charge. What would you change first?"

"I think I'd fire some people. Then I'd hire some new blood."

"Some people aren't carrying their weight?"

"We just need more diversity in the staff."

"That sounds like a great idea."

Ryan sat forward on the rocker and folded his hands. "Yeah. You're right. We need some young guys who will look up to me."

"Umm. Diversity is more of—"

"Right now, all we have is a bunch of old white dudes. And they shut down all my ideas."

"Well, what about diversity of ethnicity?"

Ryan waved me off. "Naw. We got plenty of foreign chicks. Vince was quite the collector."

I glanced at the ceramic squirrel sitting in the flower-pot next to Ryan and wondered what kind of mark it would leave if I hit him in the head with it. "So, you're saying there is already a diversity of women on staff?"

Ryan shrugged. "Yeah. Well. Boobs. There's a diversity of boobs." He put both of his hands in front of his chest. "If you know what I mean. Well, yeah—you know." He looked at my chest. Then jerked his head toward the house. "That's how Sunny got the job."

I dropped down to the chair next to Ryan and lowered my voice. "Are you telling me that Vince only hired women who look like Sunny?"

Ryan rolled his eyes to the side. "Well, some of the Asian chicks are more—" He moved his hands closer to his chest and I barely resisted the urge to slap him.

"I was passed over for promotion three times because I didn't have the right equipment. When Vince says you're underqualified he means you look like Alyce. Don't tell her I said that."

I shot up to my feet. I was fuming, but I had to level my voice and be polite, so I pretended Ryan was Georgina back in the day when I had to listen to her about how to stuff a spa mask and hand lotion in a swag bag. "And how long have you and Alyce been married?"

Ryan sat back on the rocker. "Not long."

"And you met through Vince, I take it?"

"Actually, we met through Todd Milson. He was Alyce's marketing professor and Sunny's first husband."

I dropped my stack of mail and knocked a ceramic rabbit off its swing when I bent over to pick it up.

The screen door slammed on its hinges and Alyce appeared next to Ryan. "Ryan. We have to go now. This guy charges by the hour."

"All right. I've been out here waiting for you. Yeesh. Relax."

"You know I can't relax until we get this taken care of."

They took off to their appointment and I went inside for a shot or three of espresso.

I passed the library and spotted Ken on the couch paging through a copy of *Golf Digest*. "Would you like me to build you a fire?"

Ken looked up from his reading. "Oh no, that's okay. I'm just waiting in here for Willow to cool off. I'm sorry about earlier."

"It's all right. I was married once. It's hard."

"We came on this trip to work on ours. It doesn't seem to be helping."

"Give it time. Pregnancy fills women full of hormones and they don't always know how they feel right away." *At least that was my one experience with it.*

Ken looked back at his magazine and shook his head ever so slightly. "Right."

Oh dear. "Sometimes it helps to remember why you fell in love in the first place." That's what the counselor told us when John and I hit a rough patch. It helped give me a lot of perspective.

Ken closed the magazine. "Willow is amazing. When I met her, she had just moved to Rehoboth and was involved with this group of homeless people who were living on the public beach. She couldn't get the government to step in and help them, so she came into Sportsmart and bought every tent we had in stock and took them down there and gave them away."

"That's amazing."

He smiled to himself. "She has an Ivy League education, yet she chooses to work in a shelter for women who've made some really bad choices in life. Some of them are running from bad relationships, some from addictions; a lot of them have mental illness. She'd work there twenty-four hours a day if they let her. It's hard to get her to come home sometimes." His smile faded and a flash of sorrow glimmered in his eyes. "She's driven to help the less fortunate, but she has trouble helping herself. And she really needs to right now. She's not well." He shrugged and reopened his magazine, telling me the conversation was over.

"I hope you both figure it out." I left him and carried a new burden with me to the kitchen. Halfway down the hall I heard him say to himself, "So do I. I can't keep playing these games."

Chapter Twenty-nine

I headed to the kitchen to check Fig's food and water, since Tammy Faye had been treating it as her personal Sizzler all you can eat buffet, and I caught Aunt Ginny arguing with her Alexa.

Aunt Ginny stood hands on hips facing the cylinder. "Well, why not?"

"There are some things I can't do yet."

"Then what are you good for?"

"Ask me anything factual and I'll answer if I can."

"That's what I did. You are driving me crazy."

"Here's 'Crazy' by Gnarls Barkley."

Music started to play, and Aunt Ginny reached to unplug the device. "Alexa, I'm going to throw you out in the yard."

"I'm sorry to hear that."

I felt like I should cut in or this would not end well. "What are you doing?"

Aunt Ginny startled like she hadn't heard me come in. "Oh, I . . . uh . . . I just asked Alexa, how many jelly donuts did Elvis eat before he died."

"A jelly donut is a donut filled with jelly filling."

Aunt Ginny threw her hands up and yelled, "Ah! That's it. I'm leaving." She grabbed her Bingo bag for the fire station and left through the back door.

I turned to the cylinder on the counter. "Well, it looks like you will live to see another day."

The houseguests were each scattered to the four winds. Zara spent the day working on her website and social media from the screened porch. Ken holed up in the library waiting for Willow to come out of her room. Willow never came out of her room. We'd taken turns listening in through the intercom system like Amber had asked us. It was fruitless because none of these people ever talked to each other. I made sure no one needed me to help with dinner reservations and waited on the porch for my ride.

I was waiting for Sawyer when Bob and Rosie came in under a black cloud.

"What's wrong?"

"Our Winnebago's been towed."

"Towed?! Why?"

Bob raised his hands. "I didn't know it was a tow-away zone."

Rosie patted him on the shoulder. "We were at the police station giving our interview. When we came out it was gone."

Bob sighed. "How can it be a tow-away zone if there's no sign for it?"

Rosie shook her head. "We have to call around to the different towing companies and see where it ended up."

"Oh dear. I'm so sorry. I do hope you find it soon. I know you wanted to leave today." *Amber knew that too.*

Rosie fluttered her hands in front of her chest. "Oh no. I didn't even think of that. Is it still okay if we stay a couple more nights until we get this worked out?"

"Of course. You have the whole week." *Amber made sure of it.*

I logged them in to the guest laptop in the library so they could look up towing companies. I knew in my heart that they wouldn't find anyone who knew where their Winnebago was, but it would magically appear by the end of the week or when the police were finished with their investigation.

Sawyer called me to say she was on her way, but I was to add mascara to my list. I was fairly certain that I was being punked, but as long as it wasn't for combat paint in the boot camp class, I figured I'd survive.

Sawyer pulled up at the curb and double tapped the horn. I hopped in the passenger seat and a purple feather floated in front of my face. "What have you been doing in here?"

Sawyer grabbed the feather. "Bird watching." She gunned the gas and we shot off the curb.

"Whoa. Okay, what are you up to?"

"Nothing. And you promised."

"Promised what?"

"We'd try something new." She drove with one hand on the steering wheel and with the other tossed me her cell phone. "Look at this. Did you know Zara has twenty-six thousand followers on Instagram?"

I paged through the account Sawyer had open. "Why would twenty-six thousand people want to look at this?"

"Because she's a trendsetter."

"Why? Because she wore this big yellow pom-pom thing?"

"People think it's cool."

"I think she's gonna have trouble sitting down in it."

Sawyer blew through a yellow light doing fifty. "I just want to get more out of my life, and she inspires me. For someone her age to have her act all together . . . is that so bad?"

I looked around to see if we were being followed. "No. Of course not. I just don't know if eating sushi while wearing shoes with goldfish in the heels is the way to improve the quality of your life. It definitely didn't do anything for the goldfish."

I heard paper rattling around the back seat and looked over my shoulder.

"Hey! Eyes front, lady."

"Why? What's back there?"

"Don't you worry about that."

I had a growing knot of unease taking over my stomach. I paged through some more of Zara's Instagram photos. "Sawyer. Did you see this one?" I held the phone up and she glanced at it three times while driving.

"Yeah, it's Zara at the beach in a yellow polka-dot bikini."

"No. She's at Walmart in the outdoor section in a yellow polka-dot bikini."

Sawyer jerked the wheel when she went to look at the phone again. "How do you know?"

"Because it's the same display we took your picture on last Friday. She's just photoshopped the beach behind hers. See, there's the edge of the price drop sticker and that's Chilly Willy's hat in the corner."

We stopped at a red light and Sawyer took the phone from me and peered at it through squinted eyes. "Well . . . monkey butt! That little liar. Her post says '#beachday #yolo #DontHate.'"

The light turned green and Sawyer hit the gas.

I thumbed through a few more of Zara's posts. "Here's one that shows her eating soba noodles with her girlfriends in Manhattan, only it's dated Thursday night and she was at my house for happy hour. Sawyer, I bet a lot of these are fictional. She's not even that friendly."

The bag behind me crinkled again and I started to look.

Sawyer made a sound like a car alarm and I snapped my eyes to the windshield.

We pulled into a West Cape May strip mall parking lot and parked in front of Schneider's Smoothies and a pink cinder block building with a neon marquee over the front door that said *Dance Fever*. Sawyer turned off the car and issued a warning: "Keep an open mind." She grabbed the bag off the back seat and a red feather shot out of the top.

Club music flew at me like a camp of bats breaking out of their cave the moment I opened the door. There was a young girl with purple hair standing behind a podium. She was wearing a white T-shirt with the studio logo over a pair of purple fishnet tights. "Hi, I'm Brittany. Do you have a reservation?"

Sawyer gave her our names and she handed us a key on a wrist coil and pointed to a red door that said *Backstage*. "You can go change in there. We'll start in ten minutes."

I followed Sawyer into a locker room full of women in

various stages of dressing in stripper costumes. "What have you brought me to?"

"You're going to love it."

We plopped down in the corner and Sawyer pulled out our "workout wear" from the bag. She handed me a stretchy black satin teddy with a ruffled skirt and thigh-high stockings. I examined her for signs of concussion.

"Please."

I snatched the costume and went into a private stall to change. My first attempt left me with a wedgie and the knowledge that I hadn't worn sexy underwear in so long I'd lost the ability to tell the front from the back anymore. I thought these things used to have two leg holes and straps for the arms. Now it was like wrestling a spider-web into submission. I wished I'd brought a flare gun with me.

When I finally emerged, Sawyer was wearing purple satin booty shorts and a sequined bra; she held up two feather boas. One purple and one red. "Which one do you want?"

"I'll take the red one."

Sawyer giggled and handed me the boa. "This is going to be awesome."

We left the staging area and found the dance floor. The back wall was one long mirror. The other three walls were covered in black velvet and there was a giant disco ball hanging from the ceiling. Brittany had removed her T-shirt and was wearing a lavender bustier with a tulle skirt. She was on a low platform stage warming up. But the most disturbing image was the three old ladies in lace showgirl dresses and fishnets trying to support a fourth old lady in a crimson corset with black tail feathers while she tried to clamp her knees around a stripper pole.

"How's Bingo?"

Aunt Ginny jumped a mile, then slid down the pole to the floor. "Poppy, oh. Good heavens! What are you doing here?"

"I think the question is what are you doing here?"

Aunt Ginny looked to her fellow rabble-rousers for help.

Mrs. Davis was rolling her eyes around her head trying to come up with a plausible answer. "Uh, isn't this Sweatin' to the Oldies night?"

Aunt Ginny blew out a nervous laugh. "We had no idea a place like this even existed."

Brittany called from the stage, "Ginny. Did you get the satin gloves with the finger grips I told you about last week? I really think you'll be able to nail that fireman spin soon!"

"Oh, uh . . . thank you, young lady."

I shook my head at the four of them, looking as stern as possible.

Mrs. Dodson pointed at my right boob with her cane. "I think that strap goes over your arm."

My face got hot and I cringed at myself as I slipped my arm through what I thought was the boob strap. "Oh, that does feel a lot better. Thank you."

"Sure thing, honey."

Women of all shapes, sizes, and ages poured into the room and greeted Aunt Ginny and the biddies like old friends. More than once Aunt Ginny gave me a sheepish look.

The music started playing a lot of drums and slide horn, and Brittany slid a wireless mic over her head. "Okay, sexy ladies. It's time to get empowered."

We took our places around the room. Sawyer and I

fought our way to the back in front of the wall of mirrors. No need to display all this awesomeness to the room on our first visit. The first move was a hundred-and-eighty-degree pivot to face the mirrors, where we stayed in the front for the rest of the class. I caught Sawyer's eye in our reflection, and she felt as ridiculous as I did about it.

The warm-up was a lot of hip shaking and head whipping around. I think I cracked my spine in a place that had been fused stiff for years. Then we moved into slow hip and shoulder figure eights. *At least now I know what that boob strap was supposed to hold still.*

Brittany called out that it was time to strut and grind. I noticed the biddies had no trouble following along. "Now arch your back and stick your booty out. Snap up and swivel that leg. Yeeeah."

Sawyer did a head snap my way and hissed in my ear, "Do you see who I see in the back of the room?"

I threw my knees out and dropped it like it was hot, then rolled up to see a slim brunette in the back of the room in a normal black T-shirt and yoga pants. "Hey! You said we had to wear these stripper costumes."

Sawyer whipped her head around and threw her hip to the side. She dropped her head down to her feet and she shimmied back up. "No. Look who it is. It's Jess. From the winery."

Why is it every time I take an embarrassing exercise class I run into someone I know? Don't these people go on walks? There was so much bouncing and shimmying over the course of forty minutes that my teeth were loose. I thought I would never get over the sight of Aunt Ginny and the biddies rolling on the floor doing scissor kicks until I saw myself in the mirror. *Never mind, they look great.*

Just when I thought the class was over, it was time for props. We got out the chairs so we could practice sitting fan kicks and throwing our knees open while arching our backs.

We finished the final body roll and butt slap, and I made my way to the front to intercept Jess. "Hey, girl. Funny running into you here."

Jess looked at me blankly.

"It's Poppy. Kim's friend."

Jess bit her lip.

"From the winery last Friday."

Recognition shone on her face.

"Sawyer is here too. How are you?"

Jess wiped her face on a towel that had a silhouette of a fan dancer. "I'm okay. I just wish this was all over so we could get back to business, you know?"

"I can imagine. Kim said the police have searched the place twice."

Sawyer popped into the conversation. "That was so much fun. I signed us up for the next twelve weeks of classes."

"Okay, but only if we get matching lace-up corsets like that lady next to us had on."

Sawyer was so excited she shook both of her fists in the air and squealed. She ran off to talk to the corset lady and I turned my attention back to Jess.

Jess gave me a small smile like you give another mom when her kid is being naughty in the grocery store. "It's surreal having a stranger die at the winery where I work every day. Of course, everyone is a stranger for the most part. When it's not our locals it's mostly tourists. Except for Alyce of course."

"Of course. Wait. Alyce is there a lot?"

Jess made eye contact with another lady and gave her a chin nod. "Not a lot. A couple Sundays a month, I'd say. To visit Daniel. I'm sorry, could you excuse me? My sister is ready to go, and she drove me. She only has the babysitter until eight thirty."

"Oh sure. I understand." *I mean in theory . . . I guess.* I watched Jess join a petite brunette who had a family resemblance. She had her purse in one hand and two coats draped over her arm.

Sawyer handed me the class schedule she'd just picked up from Brittany. "What'd Jess say?"

"It seems Alyce visits Daniel on a regular basis."

"Why didn't Kim tell us that?"

"Good question."

The biddies wandered over and Mrs. Davis adjusted her bustier. "So . . . what'd you think?"

"It was fun. I'm still embarrassed, but Sawyer is over the moon."

Sawyer pulled out another class schedule. "I signed us up for the Gypsy Rose package."

Aunt Ginny pointed to the flyer. "Make sure you catch the Thursday night striptease class with Raoul."

Mother Gibson shook her head to the side. "Ooooh, child."

I cut my eyes to Aunt Ginny and she blushed. "I mean . . . I overheard that in the locker room."

"Uh-huh."

The biddies tittered and said they were going to get changed and go to Late Bingo, so we all said good night.

Sawyer put her schedule away. "I have a great idea. Let's go home in our workout clothes and watch *Burlesque* on DVD."

"I can't promise that feather boa will survive Figaro. Aunt Ginny, do you need a ride home?"

"No, I have a date." Aunt Ginny started walking to the exit.

"Aren't you going to change first?"

She tossed me a look over her shoulder. "Nope." She pushed through the crash bar and into the night.

I looked at Sawyer. "I lost control of her a long time ago."

Sawyer laughed. "When have you ever had control of her?"

"I think there was fifteen minutes the summer after I graduated."

We got our things from the locker room and checked out. We were in such a heated discussion over whether the fishnets looked better than the thigh-highs that I walked right out of the Dance Fever door and into Tim and Gigi.

Tim, who wanted to be in a committed relationship with me, and the little blond chef he mentored who threw herself at him and tried to destroy my life as punishment. They were standing motionless on the sidewalk, wide-eyed, with pink smoothies.

Madame Zolda's words punched me in the gut: *There is another woman in the way.*

We stared at each other for a moment. Then I stuttered, "Wh-what are you doing here, and why is she with you?"

Gigi made a show of being horrified over our burlesque outfits like we were the dancing hippos from *Fantasia*.

Tim looked slightly panicked. "Poppy, this is not what it looks like."

I didn't want to hear an explanation. I pushed past him and went straight to the car.

Sawyer jumped in before I had the door shut and revved the engine. She threw the car in reverse and got us out of there with lightning speed. "Oh, Tim, you stupid fool."

Chapter Thirty

I had a fury rolling off me that was so hot it was fogging the windows. I would rather have seen Tim making out with a stranger than drinking a pink smoothie with Gigi. She made me feel like I was back in the eighth grade again. Fat, awkward, and foolish. Gigi even made my baking, the only talent I had in life, sound like I was adding water to boxed cake mix and cooking with a high-wattage lightbulb.

Sawyer didn't speak again until we pulled up behind the Masons' Volvo. "I guess this makes your decision easier."

"What?"

"Tim being out with another woman."

"I'd be a huge hypocrite if I held that against him. Last night I slept next to another man."

"Then what's wrong?"

"Of all the women at the Jersey Shore, why did it have to be her?"

"Do you think he's trying to send you a message? 'Be mine or someone else will snap me up'?"

"I don't know what he's trying to do." My cell phone rang Van Halen and I hit Ignore. "He's been pushing me for a commitment for weeks."

"Yeah, but has he been pushing you to commit to him, or to commit not to be with Gia?"

"I don't know anymore. I don't understand either of these men. Gia has women throwing themselves at him day after day and he doesn't show the slightest bit of interest. He waits until he tells me he loves me and then hires a sexy little twenty-year-old with a twenty-four-inch waist. I caught her trying to give him a lap dance when he was training her on the espresso machine. I'm working on my confidence, but no way I can hold up under that pressure every day."

Sawyer crossed her arms and shook her head. "Unh."

My phone rang Van Halen and I hit Ignore again. "Then Tim tells me he loves me and he wants us to have a relationship do-over. He wants us to run the restaurant together and live the chef life twenty-four-seven just like we'd planned in high school."

"Don't you want that too?"

"I dunno. Maybe? A lot has changed in twenty-five years. I'm not the same person I was."

"Is he?"

"He still loves to cook." I laugh-sighed. "He still plays air guitar. He's more driven than he used to be. When we were seventeen, we liked the same things. AC/DC, *The Goonies*, hanging out on the boardwalk, going to concerts . . . Now the time and space he has in his life for those things is very small."

A few texts came in from Tim and my phone rang again, so I turned it off.

"Do you still love him?"

"I do. I always have. And I can't imagine being with anyone else while Tim still has a piece of my heart. But I sure don't want to deal with Chef Gigi routinely flaring up like a yeast infection."

"What about Gia?"

A torrent of emotions hit me. "Gia is dangerous. I can't breathe when I think about Gia."

Sawyer shook her head. "Men make everything complicated. Women are so much simpler to understand. You know what you need?"

"What?"

"A cleanse. You should go on a man cleanse with me!"

"You barely made it three hours before you were flirting with the cops!"

Sawyer held her hands up. "Hey, flirt on the outside of a cell and you won't ever have to flirt from the inside of one."

"Good Lord, you're a mess." I opened the car door. "I think you're spending too much time with Aunt Ginny."

"Aunt Ginny could teach us both a thing or two about living our best lives." Sawyer stopped on the front porch. "Look at what we're wearing right now. And she's the one out on a date. I'm just sayin'."

"Well, you've got me there." I threw the front door open and we were smacked in the face with a three-way catfight.

Sunny and Alyce were hissing and spitting in the front parlor, and Figaro was sitting on the end table swatting at

Tammy Faye, who was jumping and barking in defense of her mom.

I kept myself safely out of striking distance. "Whoa! Ladies. What is going on?"

Alyce's face was red and blotchy from crying. She pointed a finger in Sunny's face. "She did it. She killed my dad."

Sunny was seething. Her fists were balled at her sides and she looked like a featherweight boxer waiting for the bell to ring. "You have been the most ungrateful child. Always whining and moaning that you don't have enough. Everything is unfair. If your father could see you now, he'd have a heart attack just to get away from you."

Willow came down the stairs, did a pivot at the bottom, and went right back up again.

Alyce threw a claw out and scraped Sunny's arm. "I know what you did. I saw the video."

"I don't know what you're talking about, Alyce. And I didn't kill my husband. I loved him."

Blue lights bounced off the windows and mirrors, and a single *whoop* shot through the air. *I should just rename the B&B the Perp Walk and get it over with.*

Amber came to the door with the beautiful raven-haired lady cop we saw at the winery. "McAllister. This is Officer Crabtree. I need to see Sunny Baker." I opened the door and Sunny slid behind a wing chair.

"Why do you want to see me?"

Amber took her handcuffs off a clip on her belt. "Sunny Baker, I'm arresting you for the murder of Vince Baker." She put the cuffs on Sunny's wrists in front of her and the other officer started reciting the Miranda rights.

Tammy Faye whimpered and tried to bite the officer on the ankle.

Sunny broke down in sobs as Officer Crabtree led her out of the house. "Poppy. I didn't kill him. What do I do?"

"Don't say anything until you talk to your lawyer!" I could have added, *Don't make eye contact with Big Shirley*, but I didn't want to scare her more than she already was.

Sawyer sniffled next to me and dug around her purse for some Kleenex.

Alyce flew up the stairs to her room and slammed the door.

After all was quiet again, Amber turned to me. "What the hell are you wearing?"

I had forgotten I was in my "workout" clothes.

Sawyer sniffled again. "We took a burlesque class tonight. You should try it. Maybe you'd get that stick out of your—"

I quickly cut her off. Amber had room in the back of that squad car for two. "Holy Moley! What happened, Amber? I thought you were arresting Daniel Nickson."

"We found evidence at the scene that would implicate Nickson, but we can't find a connection to the murder weapon. An eyewitness came forward tonight. They captured this and posted it on social media." She pulled out a cell phone and swiped the screen. It was a video taken from one of the winery patrons not with the tour.

The screen filled with a good-looking couple in matching sweaters. "Vacation day five. We're at the Laughing Gull Winery, and we're trying to enjoy our reserve flight, but this basic family is ruining the moment with their drama llamas." The phone panned to Vince's table, where Alyce was facing the camera saying something nasty about Sunny, and Ryan was next to her rolling his eyes. While Vince was yelling at Alyce to knock it off and telling her that she was ruining the trip for everyone, Sunny picked up Vince's wineglass, moved it behind his back, and sprinkled a powder into the wine. She stirred it with her finger and placed it back on the table in front of him. The camera panned back around to the videographer, who sighed dramatically. "There isn't enough wine in three flights to put up with this." And the video ended.

I handed the phone back to Amber. "I don't know what to say. That's pretty damning."

"We got the postliminary toxicology report this afternoon. Vince Baker had moderate amounts of a hypnotic called propofol in his blood. It's not something that's checked on a routine tox screen."

"So, he died from a hypnotic drug?"

"No."

"So, what killed him?"

"We don't know yet. But we found traces of propofol in Cerignola olives on Vince's plate. It was the only appearance of Cerignola olives in the winery and Daniel Nickson has passed a polygraph saying that he did not buy, nor does the winery carry, Cerignola olives."

Sawyer pulled her cell phone out. "I've never even heard of them. How do you spell it?"

Amber ignored Sawyer's question. It was just as well; Sawyer was ignoring Amber's answers. "So, you tell me, McAllister. How does a two-hundred-pound man get that much alcohol in his system after a ten-ounces tasting, eats wasabi peas that mysteriously appeared laced with phenobarbital, and rare Italian olives dosed in propofol, and no one sees anything except his wife jacking up his wine behind his back?"

"Yeah, I can't explain that."

"I'll tell you how. She has an accomplice. One of these people is working with her. My gut says it's Daniel. He may have passed the question about the olives, but he failed the polygraph when we asked about the winery. He's hiding something. And I also want you to keep a close eye on Alyce and Ryan Finch. No one is that obnoxious all the time. Even you have moments, I'm sure, where you're a normal person." She looked at my outfit again. "Not necessarily right now, but other times, I'm sure. Call me if you hear anything."

Amber shut the door behind her, and Sawyer and I watched the cruiser pull away from the curb and disappear down the block with Sunny behind the cage.

Tammy Faye scratched the front door, looked back at me, and whimpered. I felt sorry for the little pest. She already lost her dad; now she may have just lost her mom too.

Chapter Thirty-one

Tammy Faye twitches and grunts in her sleep more than Aunt Ginny. She'd nosed her way into my room around two a.m. and started a scuffle with Figaro. Fig could tell Tammy was in no mood for sport, so he curled up on top of my head and glared at her from a distance. At one point the Pom was running in place while lying on her side on the bed. She was yipping and growling so much we couldn't tell if she was running after or away from something in her sleep. I could tell Figaro was concerned that she'd gone insane, since there was no prey in the bed with us. He monitored the situation from the headboard. For the rest of the night, no matter where I put my legs, Tammy Faye managed to find them.

I jumped out of bed at five, too restless and distracted to sleep. My mind whirred all night like one of those battery-operated spinning squirrels that almost gave Figaro a stroke one Christmas. I dressed in my workout wear—the yoga pants and T-shirt variety. Not the wrong part of Camden at two a.m. variety. Grabbed a hoodie and took off down the block. It was too cold to walk on the boardwalk this morning and the murky sky matched my mood of unrest.

Tim had texted me twelve times last night and left four messages. He went from apologetic to sincere to sarcastic, then furious, back to sorry, and finally discouraged that he'd ruined everything. I was waiting to see which emotion we landed on before I decided how I felt about it. Until I made up my mind about committing, he could do whatever he wanted. But if he wanted a relationship with me, going out with Gigi was equal to getting the housekeeper pregnant in the governor's mansion.

I was also disturbed by Sunny's arrest last night. That video looked like a smoking gun if I ever saw one, but there had to be more to it. Either Sunny was the Meryl Streep of the Upper East Side or Gia was right and I was giving her way too much benefit of the doubt. She sure seemed like a woman in mourning. And I've been there. So, if Amber was right, and I mean *if*, who was Sunny's accomplice? Maybe Alyce and Ryan were just the distraction so no one would be watching while Sunny drugged her husband. Then again, maybe Ryan has no idea what's going on and he's just a pawn. Maybe it's Alyce and Daniel Amber needs to put a tail on. Daniel was the only one of the lot who needed money to stay out of the poorhouse. I was sick of all of it.

I walked past La Dolce Vita. The lights were still off. *I wonder how Henry is feeling today. Maybe I should check on him.* Across the courtyard was Sawyer's darling bookstore, Through the Looking Glass. There was a light on in the very back. I peered through the front window, but I didn't see anyone. She must have left the office light on or something. I'd mention it to her later. Down at the end of the block was Gia's momma's restaurant, Mia Famiglia. I felt my ovaries shrivel up just walking past it. Momma hated me and called me a tramp even though I'd never done anything to provoke her.

The sky opened up and unleashed a monsoon down on my head. I stood looking at Mia Famiglia in the deluge. Maybe Momma could put a counter curse on whoever jinxed me. Battle of the evil juju. I slogged my way home not trying to rush. At some point you have to just accept that this is happening and you're powerless to change it. I was going to be soaked and miserable no matter what I did—just own it and keep moving.

Tim was waiting for me on the front porch. "I snuck up to your room, but there was a little dog in the bed."

"That would be Tammy Faye Baker."

Tim narrowed his eyes. "The televangelist's wife?"

"Yes, that's his wife. She's had work done."

"Come on, Mack. I know you're mad, but you don't even know what you saw."

"I know you and Gigi looked awfully cozy last night."

A flash of anger shot through Tim's eyes. "You of all people have no right to accuse me of cheating."

Zam! *There it is.* "Are you talking about Gia? Or are you talking about John?"

Tim's jaw muscles were working hard to keep his temper in check.

"And I'm not accusing you of cheating on me. I'm angry that you're still buddy-buddy with the woman who has attacked me since the first day we met. I still haven't recovered from the damage she did to the B and B."

Tim took my dripping hand and led me to the porch glider. "Mack, that's what we were talking about. Gigi reached out to me and apologized for everything. She admitted all of it. The slander, the sabotage, the lies. She's removed all the accounts and reviews and she's willing to post positive reviews under her real name everywhere."

"Apologizing to *you* is crap. I'm the one she attacked. Not to mention La Dolce Vita and Maxine's—of course *only the desserts* at Maxine's were bad. Can't you see that even then she was trying to drive us apart? This is personal."

Tim held my hand in his and pulled me closer. "Your lawyer has her running scared. I told her we wouldn't pursue legal action if she undid the damage."

It was forty-six degrees at quarter to seven in the morning and I was soaking wet. But I was so angry in that moment that I didn't know if my shivering was coming from inside or out. I shot up off the bench. "You had no right to say that. It was my decision whether or not to pursue legal action. And she can't undo all the damage. I lost business. Travel agents still recommend guests stay somewhere else. I'm the only B and B not already booked up for the preseason through Memorial Day. People around here have long memories, Tim."

"I understand. But I've lived here my whole life. This is a small town and you don't want a lawsuit attached to your name; trust me on this. Tourists come and go, but the year-round locals are the only ones to keep you in business October through April. I'm trying to protect you."

"Really, 'cause it seems like you're trying to protect Gigi."

Tim stood across from me breathing heavy. Puffs of gray vapor swirling from his mouth.

A little blue pickup truck pulled into the driveway and a short, bald man with deep-set eyes hopped out. He grabbed a toolbox from the passenger seat and hotfooted it up the porch humming along with the brass section playing in his head. "Huhhh huh huhhh huhn huhh hunnn huh, morning, boss. Huh huhhh huhn huhh hum da hum . . . psshh."

Itty Bitty Smitty, my handyman, opened the front door and disappeared into the house, probably to text my former mother-in-law that "Poppy and Tim are having a fight."

"Look, Tim, I have to go change before I catch pneumonia, and I have to get breakfast ready for the guests."

"So, we're just going to leave this right here?"

"I don't want to fight with you. But I want you to see that what you did isn't okay with me. I'm hurt and angry."

Tim pulled me close. "I'm sorry. I should have talked to you first. I should never have told Gigi you would drop the lawsuit. It's your call anyway."

I started to push him away, but I was tired, and cold, and I really did love him. This was the guy who put his life on hold for a year waiting for me to go to college with him. My betrayal of Tim was a lot bigger than forgiving some malicious reviews behind his back. I derailed us for twenty-five years. The fight drained out of me and left me with aftershocks of frustration. "Okay. I'll think about what you said."

Tim kissed me. "Thank you. Will I see you later?"

My cell phone buzzed. I knew who it was. "I have something to do today for Amber, but you'll see me tomorrow."

"I can't wait." Tim kissed me again. He started to say

something, then changed his mind. "I'll see you tomorrow, Mack." My cell phone buzzed again. I waited until he got in his car to leave; then I pulled it out of my pocket and checked the message. Yep. Georgina: **Did you and Tim break up? Are you with Gia now?**

"Smitty!"

Chapter Thirty-two

"Gia would never do something like that."

Sawyer took the tray of bacon out of the top oven. "I thought you said Gia hired a little hussy with implants."

"Birthday Boobs didn't try to drive me into foreclosure." I set a timer for the quiches in the bottom. "Plus, Gia and I never fight."

Sawyer poured herself another cup of coffee. "You and Gia haven't broken through that first fight barrier yet. You're still trying to impress each other. You and Tim crossed that line thirty years ago. In high school, you broke up at least once a month."

"No, that can't be right."

"I gained ten pounds over the summer of '86 from all the ice cream I had to eat with you. Don't you remember the Melissa Bradley scandal?"

A memory of Tim talking too close to a girl with caked blue eye shadow after gym class fluttered through my mind. "Oh yeah. I forgot about her."

Smitty was stretching a measuring tape across the kitchen entryway from the hall. He'd make some notes on a little notepad and grunt every few minutes. "Every couple fights. It's part of being in a relationship."

I stirred the saucepan of stewed plum compote for the plum crisp parfaits. "Are you saying that you and Georgina fight?"

Smitty cocked his head to look directly at me. "Arguing with Georgina is like cage fighting with Tinker Bell on diet pills. She'll call and yell at me any minute now just in case I've done something she'd like to be angry about later."

Aunt Ginny clacked into the kitchen wearing a flared short black skirt over black stockings and a tight black turtleneck. We all turned to see why she was making so much noise. "Haven't you seen tap shoes before?" She was wearing shiny black Mary Janes with silver plates on the toes and heels. She did a little shuffle step on the stone floor and finished with a hamstring stretch and jazz hands.

I took the footed glass dessert bowls out of the cabinet for the parfaits. "Do you have tap lessons today?"

"No." Aunt Ginny grabbed a mug and poured herself some coffee.

Smitty, Sawyer, and I passed a familiar look among ourselves and went back to work.

Aunt Ginny grabbed a piece of bacon off the paper towels where it was draining. "Smitty. I have some light-bulbs for you to change when you're done measuring for the door."

Sawyer also took a piece of bacon. "Why are you putting in a swinging door?"

Ryan walked around Smitty into the kitchen. "Hey, Poppy, I'm going to have a business meeting here today with my lawyer to discuss that situation I told you about. Could we have someplace private to talk? And maybe a coffee service for three?"

"Why don't you take your meeting in the library and we can close the double doors?"

"Perfect." Ryan winked at Sawyer before leaving the room.

I held my potholder out to the side. "That's why. I'm getting a sign that says Employees Only."

I heard Victory giggling all the way down the hall. She came around the corner carrying Tammy Faye. Victory's T-shirt was damp around the neck, and Tammy Faye was licking her throat. Victory giggled again. "No, doggie. No teickles."

I looked over my shoulder at her. "What is Tammy Faye doing?"

Victory stopped and slid her eyes to the side. "Umm. I speill somesing."

"Yes, I see that. But what is it?"

Victory put Tammy on the floor. "Um, I try on lady perfume, but um . . . ees broken and eet speill on me. Doggie likes eet."

Tammy Faye sat on the floor looking at Victory and wagged her tail.

I massaged my temple with my fingers. "Oh my God. Victory, you can't mess around with the guests' personal things. Even if they aren't here."

"Guest ees steill here."

Sawyer breathed out, "Whaaaaat?"

Victory nodded. "I thought I would clean empty room while lady ees ein preison. But I open wrong door and dog run ein room. So, I go ein to get dog, and see beauty-ful perfume bottle. I want to try eet on because eis my first Amereecan perfume. But eet not have smell. Then lady snore and scare me so I speill it."

Aunt Ginny had to sit down. I was just going to die standing up to save the time. "What room were you in?"

"Umm. Scarlet Peascock."

Of course you were.

Aunt Ginny asked, "Isn't that Zara?"

"Yep. The one with sixty thousand followers on Twitter to complain to."

Sawyer sniffed. "I don't smell anything."

Aunt Ginny gave the air a sniff. "Neither do I. Come here, Victory." Aunt Ginny sniffed all around Victory and shook her head. "Nothing."

Smitty sniffed around his workspace. "Maybe it's them Pharaoh moans. Only men and dogs can smell them."

I checked the time and ladled the plum compote over granola in the dessert dishes. "Are you sure about that?"

Smitty nodded. "I saw it on the Discovery Channel."

Aunt Ginny asked him, "Do you smell anything?"

Smitty sniffed again. "Ah . . . no. But then maybe Georgina's Bvlgari Blue is clouding my judgment."

I looked down at Tammy Faye. She was lying on her back next to her water bowl with her tongue hanging out. Figaro was tentatively approaching her to get a sniff. He poked her with his paw, and she wagged her tail. "Do you think she's okay?"

Sawyer reached down and touched her. "She seems

fine. Extremely relaxed. Didn't Zara tell you she was allergic to smells?"

"She made me remove the air fresheners and flowers from her room and complained that my perfume was bothering her."

Aunt Ginny plated the bacon in a veiled attempt to sneak some more. "We need to go check that perfume out for ourselves."

I took the parfaits into the dining room where Ken and Willow were sitting at the table drinking coffee. Zara was in the next room with hers by herself. Bob and Rosie were just arriving when Sawyer brought in the quiches and Aunt Ginny set the platter of bacon on the table. I said good morning to everyone and waited to see how Zara would greet me. She was cold and distant, so . . . business as usual. I went back through the kitchen and grabbed Smitty and Victory. "Come with me."

The three of us went up the stairs and I confirmed that it was indeed Zara's room that Victory had been wandering around in. I whispered to Smitty, "You're my lookout. I need you to check Alyce's thermostat, anyway, so just hang out in the hall, look busy, and let me know if anyone is coming."

Smitty saluted. "You got it, boss. If anyone comes, I'll say, 'CaCaw!' like a crow."

Very subtle. "Or you could just say 'good morning.'"

Smitty grunted. "Good idea."

I knocked on Zara's door just in case. Victory spoke to me like I was slow: "Guest ees ein parloor. We just see her there."

I opened the door and looked around. "Come show me which perfume it was."

Victory led me to the lowboy where in the midst of all the unscented beauty creams and lotions there sat an ornate blue and gold blown-glass perfume bottle. All around the perfume bottle, the finish was stripped from my antique dresser. Victory pointed to the bare wood. "See. I speill."

"Yes, I see that." *And I just lost a year of my life, because this dresser is over a hundred years old.* I bent over the perfume and smelled it. It was like water and air in the mountains with a hint of chemicals.

Aunt Ginny snuck up behind me and jabbed me in the ribs. "Let me see it."

"Smitty," I stage-whispered.

"CaCaw!"

Aunt Ginny picked up the bottle, sniffed it, and poured it in her mouth.

"Don't touch it. What are you doing?"

She smacked her lips. "It's moonshine."

"Moonshine? Are you sure?"

"I'd bet my life on it."

"What are you doing in my room?"

My heart leaped out of my chest the moment I heard Zara standing in the doorway. I stared at her blankly, but Aunt Ginny was quick to recover.

Aunt Ginny held up the bottle. "We're so sorry, Zara dear. But it seems the chambermaid spilled your perfume. She just came downstairs to tell us how upset she is while you were eating breakfast and we came right up to investigate. Of course we'll pay to replace it. It looks custom-made."

Zara looked at the bottle in Aunt Ginny's hand and shook her head. "That isn't mine."

Victory pointed to the dresser. "Of course eet ees. Eet was right here on your dresser."

I nudged Victory. "Uh-uh." I pointed to the perfume bottle. "Has this been in your room all week?"

Zara shook her head. "I don't think I've ever seen it before. And you should remember that I don't wear perfume. I'm allergic. It's a beautiful bottle, though."

Something about this was setting off a silent scream in the back of my mind, but it was like I couldn't dial in the frequency strong enough to hear it.

Smitty came into the room talking. "I checked the thermostat in the Monarch suite and it's working perfectly." He saw Zara. "Oh. Good mor-ning."

I narrowed my eyes at him. *Too little too late, Smitty.* Then I said to Aunt Ginny, "Since you already have the bottle in your hands." *And your fingerprints are all over it.* "Why don't you take it to the kitchen. Maybe the last guest left it in the room and they'll be looking for it."

Aunt Ginny's eyebrows rose as she deciphered my meaning. "Good idea. I'll put it in a Baggie to keep it safe."

We apologized to Zara and left her room. She waited until we were at the bottom of the steps before she shut the door.

I grabbed Smitty's arm. "What happened to the signal?"

"I was caught off guard. A skinny kid came out of the Monarch and asked me to check the heat for his wife. What was I supposed to do?"

"Give me some kind of heads-up so I know you didn't desert me."

"I'll do that next time. By the way, she wasn't in the room. When I asked the kid if she wanted to approve the new setting, he said he doesn't know where she is. I asked him, 'Is she down at breakfast?' And he gave me a look like I was the crazy one. He said he hadn't seen her since yesterday afternoon."

Chapter Thirty-three

Aunt Ginny was threatening to search all the guest rooms for clues to Vince's murder while I was at La Dolce Vita doing today's baking. I knew we'd have a riot on our hands if she was left home alone, so I sent her and the biddies on a reconnaissance mission. I convinced them that they needed to go to every grocery and specialty store in the area in search of Cerignola olives.

"Why do you want these olives so bad?"

"They were found at the winery laced with one of the drugs found in Vince's system when he died."

"How do you know that?"

"Amber told me."

"Are you sure she's not just feeding us red herrings to keep us from investigating on our own?"

"Not now I'm not. I hadn't even thought of that until you said it. If she is, I'm gonna be furious."

"You know what you need to do?"

I shook my head.

"You need to ask Sunny about that powder she put in Vince's wine."

"That's a good idea. And I think we need to know more about Alyce's relationship with Daniel."

Lily called my cell just as I was heading out of the house for La Dolce Vita to set up a tour next month. "I promise this one won't end with a murder."

"Maybe that should be your tag line on the Pink Sandals website."

Lily laughed. "Yeah, that'll bring some business in. *Murder-free since March.* I heard the cops arrested Sunny Baker. I thought she and *Vinnyboo* were so in love too."

"It was a surprise to us all. I'll be glad when the rest of the tour group checks out and we can get back to paying customers as usual." *Or in my case, paying customers as an entirely new concept.*

Lily groaned into the phone. "Oh no. They're still there?"

"Yep. The Winnebago was impounded, Zara can't get an early flight home, and the Masons seem to be resigned to stay the length of their original booking."

"I'm so sorry, Poppy. I promise I'll make it up to you. Let's talk soon about an exclusive tour with the Butterfly Wings."

"That would be fabulous. Thank you." We made plans to get together to discuss partnering and I clicked off. Business was finally looking promising.

The sky was threatening to rain again, so I drove the

two and a half blocks to the coffee shop. There was a little pink Camaro parked in my spot in the alley. *Welcome to tourist season.* I parked at a meter and went through the back door. Gia was trying to read my handwriting on the shortbread recipe.

His face broke into a smile. "There you are. I was about to call you. What is the price point on the shortbread fingers?"

I pointed to the figure on the corner of the sheet. "You have to charge at least fifty-two cents apiece."

He snuck a kiss while I was so close. "Sierra sold a dozen to some college boys on spring break for three dollars each."

"Whoa." I shook my head. "Why would they pay that much?"

"Go see for yourself."

I went around the corner to the dining room and saw Sierra wearing a plaid miniskirt and a white button-down dress shirt tied at the waist. "Well, you did tell her to wear a shirt with buttons."

"Business is up two hundred percent with the after three p.m. crowd since she started."

"Is that why you hired her? To bring in teenage boys?"

He gave me a cryptic grin. "Not exactly."

"What are you up to?"

Gia ran a finger down the side of my face. "I can't tell you yet."

I narrowed my eyes at him, and he narrowed his eyes right back.

"I thought you'd be home with Henry."

"My sister Teresa is with Henry." He pronounced it "Teraaasa." He nodded to an iPad standing up on the counter. "And we are doing the Skyping."

Henry's face came into view and filled the screen. "Hi, Poppy!"

A beautiful brunette with hazel eyes nudged Henry out of the way to look through the screen. I waved and she replied, "This is the Poppy who spends the night?"

Gia replied with a slow, "Yeees."

She screwed up her face and walked away.

Geez, it's like being judged by Figaro. Who knew Karla would turn out to be the nice one?

Gia promised Henry he would call later and instructed Teresa to put him down for a nap. The screen went dark and he wrapped me in a blanket hug and gave me a kiss. "Thank you again for the other night. It meant the world to us. I hope you aren't sore after sleeping on the floor."

"I've slept in worse." *What the heck am I talking about? I sound like I've slept around.* "Like . . . summer camp . . . maybe in a tent . . . I don't know." I tried to slow my racing heart. "How is Henry today?"

"Better. He was laying on the couch watching a movie when I left."

Sierra's nasal voice ran through me like fingernails down a chalkboard: "Gi-aaa. Your uncle is here."

"I had better get out there before Zio Alfio does something inappropriate."

We heard a smack and Zio Alfio laughed. "Eh, va bene!"

"Uh-oh."

I was cutting up berries to soak in sangria for cocktails and cupcakes when Gia's iPad flickered on and Henry's face came back into view. "Hi, Poppy," he whispered. "Zia Teresa won't let me watch TV."

I couldn't stop myself from smiling. "Aren't you supposed to be taking a nap?"

Henry coughed. "I don't want a nap. I'm not a baby."

"Yeah, but you are pretty sick. All those bad germs that make you cough get attacked when you're sleeping."

His eyes were as big as half dollars in the iPad screen. "They do?"

I nodded. "That's why you need to rest."

In the background I heard Teresa yell, "Henry! Are you back on that iPad!"

Henry looked to the side, then back at me. "I have to go," he whispered. Then the screen went black.

Gia returned. "Did I hear Henry?"

I giggled. "He may not be seeing eye to eye with Teresa's plan for his recovery."

Gia chuckled. "That boy. He's getting so big and so stubborn. I remember when he was tiny bambino in my arms."

"That must have been hard having to raise him by yourself."

"When you have a big family, it is sometimes easier to be alone."

I put some butter and sugar in the KitchenAid stand mixer. "I would have loved to have a big family."

Gia pulled me close against his chest and looked in my eyes. "Be careful what you wish for." He tickled my neck with his stubble. "Mmm-hmm. Why don't you come out here and keep me company while I make you a latte?"

Don't have to ask me twice. "Okay." I let him take my hand and lead me to the front. I turned the corner and spied Cowboy Bob and Rosie sitting at the table next to the bar. I dropped down to a squat—oddly similar to the *drop it while it's hot* move from last night. My thighs thought so too, judging from the instant burn I felt.

Gia dropped down with me. "What's the matter?"

"That couple over there. They're staying at my place."

Gia grinned. "So?"

"So, they can't see me here. They'll think I don't take the B and B seriously."

Gia tilted his head and raised one eyebrow with half a smile on his lips.

"I'm serious. It's like seeing your teacher in the grocery store. It's weird." My attention splintered when I heard Bob shush Rosie. I held my hand up to silence Gia and leaned in.

"Keep your voice down, Ro."

"But there's no one else here. We're safe."

"We won't be safe until we get out of New Jersey."

Sierra started moving a bunch of bags back and forth drowning out their voices. I gave Gia a pleading look and he shot to his feet.

"Sierra, can I speak to you in the back, please?"

Sierra practically tripped over her feet running to Gia. They disappeared into the kitchen and I nudged forward behind the bar.

Bob was saying, "He got exactly what was coming to him. I'm not sorry at all."

"I still think we should have left the moment we saw him."

"I wanted to see if he'd face me like a man and apologize."

"Fat chance of that. He was too busy ogling the women."

"Nothing changed there. I don't think he even recognized me."

"Bob, we have to get out of here, even if we have to leave the Winnebago and come back for it later."

"No. It's too dangerous. The minute we make a fuss they'll get suspicious and look into our past. We need to keep our mouths shut and fly under the radar."

"If they figure it out, we'll go to jail."

"I'll go to jail. You'll be fine."

"I won't let that happen, Bob. I won't let them take you. Not after all we've been through."

"Rosie, just shhh! I feel like we're being watched everywhere we go. Just lay low. They aren't even on to us; they're after the daughter. This will all be over soon. Just keep it together."

Now they suspect Alyce? Amber doesn't tell me anything.

"Where did that girl go?"

"We're never getting that coffee. Let's just get out of here."

I heard the sound of chairs scraping on the floor and a few seconds later the front doorbell jingled.

Gia came out of the back to the espresso machine. I tried to stand, but my knees protested. He put a hand down and helped pull me up. "I sent Sierra to move her Camaro. So? What was that all about?"

Her Camaro? Grrr. Freakin' Sierra. "Apparently, Bob and Rosie know more about the Baker family than they've admitted. And I don't think they're gonna find that Winnebago anytime soon."

Chapter Thirty-four

I finished the baking and had cleaned my workspace when Gia came back to say goodbye. He was giving me a very long kiss that was saying something very different from goodbye when Henry popped on the screen.

"Daddy. My bronkites is all better."

Gia pulled away from me reluctantly and squared off with Henry.

"It is not all better, Polpetto."

Henry jutted his chin out and gave a short whimper. His eyes rolled up to his forehead. "Okay, but you know what would make it all better?"

"What?"

"A toy."

"No, you do not need a new toy. You need medicine, and rest, and Nonna's chicken soup."

We waited while Henry thought about his answer. "No, I'm pretty sure a new toy would do it."

I had to send myself offscreen to laugh while Gia convinced Henry to go lie down and play with dinosaurs.

I gave Gia a wave goodbye and he blew me a kiss in return. Then I went across the courtyard to get Sawyer. She was showing a customer to the self-help section. I once told her I'd give her ten dollars to tell them "that would defeat the purpose," but she wouldn't do it. So, while I waited, I browsed my favorite section—the pop-up books. I found one on dinosaurs I thought Henry would love and was about to take it to the register when something caught my eye down the hall. I could have sworn someone just walked from the bathroom to the office and shut the door.

I was about to go investigate, but Sawyer called me up front: "Poppy, come on, I'm ready!" Her assistant manager rang me up while my eyes kept venturing down the hall. Sawyer grabbed my arm and pulled me to the door. "We told Amber we'd be there in ten minutes."

"Is someone in your office?"

"Did you buy that book for Henry because you love Gia?"

"Fine. We don't have to talk about it right now." ·

I drove the few blocks to the police station to visit Sunny. We checked in with the front desk sergeant and she took our IDs and cell phones. I handed her the perfume bottle Baggie and told her it was potential evidence in the Vince Baker case and to give it to Officer Fenton. She eyed us both apprehensively after typing our names in the database. Then she hit a buzzer and the metal door clicked open. "Go through."

Amber met us in the hallway on the other side.

"McAllister, tell me you've overheard something."

"Nothing I can prove yet. I do have a perfume bottle that Aunt Ginny thinks has moonshine in it. It's probably covered in her fingerprints now, but maybe you can test it for traces of something that was in Vince's system."

"Good. We're running out of time here. I need to charge Mrs. Baker or release her. There's no way I'm letting a killer slip through my fingers. I know she isn't working alone, so you need to step it up. We don't allow just anyone to visit here, you know. You're an informant, so make the most of your time and get me a lead."

I made a face at Sawyer and she rolled her eyes.

Amber led us to an interrogation room painted the color of pond scum. There was one solid wooden desk with no drawers, a metal bench that was bolted to the floor, and a pair of metal handcuffs that was hooked around the leg of the bench. There was nothing else in the room so that nothing could be used as a weapon. But very high on the wall was a security camera, and the light was green.

Sawyer looked around with a frown. "Is this the room where you beat the prisoners with a rubber hose?"

Amber blew us both off. "Sit tight. I'll bring her down."

Officer Crabtree dropped off a folding chair and left without a word.

Five minutes later, Amber brought in a very bedraggled and handcuffed Sunny and sat her on the metal bench. The girl clearly wasn't used to life without weekly spa treatments. "You have fifteen minutes."

Sunny started to weep as soon as the door was closed.

We were alone and Sawyer moved to the bench. She put her arm around Sunny. "Okay now, calm down. We have some questions we need to ask you."

Sunny nodded.

I moved the folding chair over to sit in front of her. "First of all, Tammy Faye is fine. She misses her mommy, but she's been busy terrorizing Figaro, so that keeps her distracted."

Sunny sniffled. "Oh good."

"Sunny, I saw the video where you put something in Vince's drink."

Sunny clasped her hands together in prayer position. "It was Splenda."

"Splenda? Why?"

"Vince didn't like dry wine, so he'd have me put a packet of Splenda in his glass when no one was looking. He was the CEO of a Madison Avenue Public Relations corporation and most of his clients are very influential. He didn't want anyone to know that he wasn't sophisticated. He was afraid it would ruin his reputation."

Sawyer snickered. "Rich people street cred."

Sunny's eyes lit up. "Yes, exactly!"

"Where'd you get the Splenda?"

"Citarella, on the Upper East."

"No, I mean, the day you put it in Vince's wine."

"Oh, in my purse. I carry a little Ziploc bag of it in case I'm somewhere that doesn't have any."

"I see. What can you tell me about Vince's will?"

Sunny tried to cross her arms, but her wrists were cuffed, so she just put her hands back in her lap. "What do you want to know?"

"Ryan knows that Vince changed his will before coming here."

I watched Sunny's face for signs of surprise. All I saw was sadness. "Oh no. That's going to cause problems. I told Vince it was a bad idea to remove Alyce from his will. She would never understand."

"So, you do know what's in it?"

"Not exactly. I don't know how much money Vince has."

Sawyer asked, "Do you know why he changed it?"

"To keep Ryan from bleeding Alyce dry. He changed his will a week before we left to say that if something happened to him, I inherit everything. But he left me instructions for what to give Alyce and when, and how to protect her assets. The beach house in Key West is supposed to go to Alyce, but Vince put it in my name because Ryan would sell it out from under her. If Ryan and Alyce ever split up I'm to turn what's hers over to her."

"Does Alyce know about all of this?"

Sunny shook her head firmly. "No, Alyce can't know about any of this. Once she knows, then Ryan knows. Then it's all over. He'll find a way to get what he wants."

Sawyer sat back against the concrete wall behind the bench. "Couldn't Vince just put a rider on the will to keep Ryan from touching the money?"

"Nothing would keep Ryan from hounding Alyce until she's given him every dime. He has some unnatural hold on her. He's been after her inheritance for ages. I told Vince it was the only reason he married her. Vince tried to convince Alyce that marrying Ryan would be a mistake, but that only made her want to do it more. He tried to promote him to the Sacramento branch to get rid of him, but Ryan said he hated California and missed Alyce too much, so he came home after three months."

I thought about that for a minute. "What about a pre-nup?"

"Vince tried a prenup when they got engaged, but Alyce wouldn't sign it. She said Ryan felt like it wasn't a real marriage if they didn't trust each other."

My mind flashed to the image of Alyce kissing Daniel. *She should have signed the prenup.* "How long has Alyce known Daniel?"

Sunny's expression went blank. "Who's Daniel?"

Sawyer explained. "The good-looking guy who owns the winery."

"Oh." Sunny's head gave a tiny shake. "I don't think she does know him. I think we all just met him at the happy hour."

Well then, that was the most successful happy hour in the history of time. "Okay, so how did Ryan and Alyce meet?"

"College. Alyce was taking some business classes at the university and Ryan was auditing the class as a professor's assistant."

Sawyer shook her head. "What is a professor's assistant?"

Sunny's face remained blank. "Some professors will let you sit in on their classes in exchange for personal services."

I leaned in. "Like . . . sex?"

Sunny's face turned scarlet. "No! Like paperwork and bringing them coffee and their dry cleaning. You don't get credit for the class, but you get to learn the material. A lot of students who don't have money or scholarships go to the community college and audit classes at the university to get ahead after they transfer."

"So, Ryan audited the class and met Alyce. Do you happen to know who the professor was?"

Sunny fidgeted with the handcuffs. "Todd Milson. He teaches Marketing and Advertising classes at NYU."

I watched Sunny for signs of surprise. "Did you ever audit Todd Milson's class?"

Sunny wouldn't look me in the eye. "No. But I met Professor Milson when I toured NYU my senior year of high school."

"How well did you know him?" *Come on, Sunny, don't lie to me.*

"We started dating shortly after we met."

Sawyer scrunched up her face. "While you were in high school? How old was this guy?"

"I was a few weeks away from turning eighteen and Todd was thirty-two. We had to keep the relationship a secret because he could have been fired."

Or arrested. "So, how'd you end up at community college and BakerCom?"

"I went to community college because I didn't have the money for university. Then Todd and I got married in my second year and I was going to transfer, but it didn't work out."

"Why not?"

Tears welled up in Sunny's eyes and she tried to blink them away. "Todd had a rare heart condition that we didn't know about, and he died in the middle of a pickup game with some of the basketball players. We'd only been married for six weeks."

Sawyer and I each leaned back in our chairs trying to subconsciously distance ourselves from her pain.

Sunny soldiered on. "So, I stayed at community college to work toward my associate's degree, and a few months later I ran into Ryan on campus. He told me about the internship at BakerCom. He said I would fit right in there."

"How did Ryan get the job?"

"Alyce. Although it was probably Ryan's idea for her to pull some strings for him."

"If he'd only been there a few weeks he must have been promoted really fast."

Sunny's neck and chest turned scarlet. "Ryan can be very persuasive."

I looked at Sawyer. She shook her head just the tiniest bit. So, we silently agreed not to tell Sunny we knew Ryan had caught her and Vince . . . you know.

Sawyer's eyes narrowed and she looked at Sunny. "What about this wine tour? Are you sure you didn't know anyone else before it started?"

"No. Except for Alyce and Ryan of course. I had never even heard of Pink Sandals Boutique Tours before I got the email that I'd won the contest."

"You heard of them when you entered, though."

Sunny pushed her lips together and gave me a slow headshake. "I don't actually remember entering. But I do enter a lot of contests. I guess I just forgot about this one. But it came to my BakerCom email and I hadn't worked there since Vince and I got married. Vince never deactivated my account or removed it from my phone. I don't use it for online shopping and no one else has it, so I must have entered at some point and forgot. When I called the number in the email, I spoke with Lily. She said she received two thousand entries and used some random selection software to pick the winners. It sounded for real."

Sawyer crossed and uncrossed her legs. Then leaned forward. "If you don't mind me asking, why would someone with your money enter a bunch of contests? It sounds like you could have come to Cape May whenever you wanted. In fact, forget Cape May! You could have gone to Paris."

Sunny smiled. "I know. Vince teased me about my contests all the time. I didn't always have money. I grew up an only child with a single mom on welfare. I used to dream about my fairy godmother showing up one day. Then I met Vince and it kind of came true. I found a stack of old postcards from Cape May in a box when I cleaned out the closet in his room and I've been in love with the Victorian houses ever since. It felt like a place princesses would go to vacation. I guess the contests are still a part of my dreaming."

Amber pushed the door open. "Time's up."

Sunny stood slowly, resigned to return to her hopelessness.

I put my hand on her arm. "Sunny, one more thing. Are you sure that Vince didn't recognize anyone on the tour? Daniel . . . Bob and Rosie . . . Ken and Willow?" *Bob and Rosie.*

"No. . . ." Sunny shook her head. "He'd never met any of them."

Officer Crabtree came and collected Sunny and led her down the hall to the holding cells. I felt totally paralyzed watching her go.

Sawyer stood toe-to-toe with Amber and bent her head down to look the little officer in the eye. "How can you possibly think that's your killer?"

"Well, she's the sole heir to a fortune, she was seen

spiking the victim's drink, she was in possession of wasabi peas, and we found a jar of olives in the dumpster behind the winery with her fingerprints on them."

Sawyer took a step and threw her head back. "Uhhh."

Well, I did not see that twist. What about some quid pro quo, Amber? I rubbed my forehead. I could feel a migraine coming on. "Why didn't you tell me about the olives sooner?"

"Because you're not involved in investigating, McAllister. You're just an informant." She pulled out her phone and showed me the evidence photo of the jar of olives. They had a sticker on them from Stater Bros. Markets.

"I've never heard of the place."

"You wouldn't. It's a West Coast chain."

Sawyer jutted her chin out. "See, there's no way Sunny could have bought those olives. She lives in New York."

Amber leveled a look at Sawyer. "Why? Because she can't get on a plane and fly there? Or because she can't order them online and have them delivered?"

Sawyer pursed her lips and her shoulders drooped. She dropped to the folding chair.

Something about this felt like a setup. "Did you know that Ryan spent three months in Sacramento?"

Amber put her phone away and took out a little notebook. She nodded at the security camera over the bench. "I haven't watched the footage yet. What was he doing there?"

"Vince had sent him out there before he married Alyce. He could have bought the olives while he was there. And he would certainly know that wasabi peas were Vince's favorite snack since he worked with him every day."

Sawyer sat up a little taller. "And he is getting a big promotion now that Vince is out of the way. At least he thinks he is."

Amber nodded slowly. "So, you're thinking Ryan could be our accomplice."

That doesn't feel right. "I think it's more likely Ryan would be trying to frame Sunny. I don't see them working together. Can you give me a couple of days to ask some questions?"

"A couple of days may as well be a lifetime, McAllister. I have twenty-four hours to charge Sunny or I have to let her go. She's already lawyered up and he's making threats. The clock is ticking."

Chapter Thirty-five

"When exactly did the Cape May County police put me on the payroll to where they could tell me what to do?" We were on our way back to the bed and breakfast, and to say I was in a little snit would be insulting to bad attitudes everywhere. Reality TV show producers built entire seasons around the kind of tantrum I was having.

Sawyer slurped her Wawa smoothie. "Amber's always thought she could tell people what to do. It goes with the territory of being a cheerleader. The first thing they learn is how to make demands. 'Give me an A!' Also, you're not getting paid squat."

I pulled into the driveway and threw the car in park. "She's got a lot of nerve putting Sunny's freedom off on me—like it's my job to prove her innocence and find other suspects."

Sawyer nudged the car door shut with her hip. "The least she could do is give us one of those lights for the hood of the car so we can go through traffic and park anywhere."

"Right?! Why are all these packages on the front porch?" There was a stack of boxes and mailing envelopes lined up by the front door along with a rubber-banded packet of mail.

Sawyer picked up the largest box. "Someone's discovered online shopping."

"Aunt Ginny is the only person I know who can watch *Hoarders* and be inspired to a challenge." I gathered the rest of the loot and took it inside.

Willow was curled up in front of the fireplace reading a book on the couch. I loaded Sawyer's arms with the packages to take to the kitchen and went into the library to say hello. "You look cozy."

Willow looked up and smiled. "I am. I never get to read at home. I'm always working."

"Will you get to take some time off before the baby comes?"

She put her hand on her belly. "I hope so. This little one will be here before you know it."

"Do you know if you're having a boy or girl?"

"Girl. Ken wanted to name her Jessica after his mother, but we're going with Ella."

"Ella's pretty." I sat in the chair next to the couch. "It's nice that you two got away together before she arrives."

A dark shadow crossed Willow's eyes. "Well. It was as much to work on our marriage as it was to have a babymoon. I'm sure you heard our little fight yesterday."

"Not really. Besides, I was married once too."

"Divorced?"

I purposefully tried to keep my voice light and breezy. It freaked people out when they learned your husband had died. "No. Widowed."

She sat up and leaned in toward me. "Oh, I'm so, so sorry."

And then they ask how it happened.

"What happened?"

"He was sick for a while. Cancer. How have you been feeling? Ken said you haven't been well."

She looked momentarily panicked. "What?" She waved her hand in front of her face. "No. I'm . . . fine. Ken just worries."

"That's because he loves you."

She blurted out, "Ken cheated on me. He had an affair with the woman who works in ladies' golf supplies."

I put my hand on her arm. "Oh, Willow. I don't know what to say."

"This whole wine tour was his idea to work on our marriage. He booked it on the Internet without asking me. I can't drink; I'm pregnant." She started to cry harder.

"Do you still love him?"

"Yes."

"Then I'm sure you can work it out together. Don't give up because of one mistake." I felt my anxiety rising. I didn't know what to do to comfort a pregnant woman. "Would you like some cake?"

She stopped crying immediately. "Oh yes, that would be lovely."

I went to the kitchen and took out a chocolate cupcake with poached pears. I dusted the top with some powdered sugar and got a fork.

Sawyer looked up from her tablet. "What are you doing?"

"I made her cry."

Sawyer bobbed her head. "Okay."

I took the cake out to Willow and she accepted it with a huge smile. "I've been so emotional lately, what with the baby coming and all."

"It's perfectly understandable. Any woman in your condition would be. Maybe a vacation was just what you needed."

"That's what Ken said when he found the wine tour. He's always looking for a good deal." She shoveled the cake in her mouth. "I know the stress is not good for the baby." The fork froze in midair. Willow was looking past me.

I looked over my shoulder and saw Ken standing in the library doorway. His jaw muscles were working overtime and there was a steely glint to his eyes. I felt my stomach bottom out. *What am I afraid of? He's not my husband.*

Ken turned and left. Willow put her plate down, her cake unfinished, and followed after him. "Ken, wait."

If he's trying to get back in her good graces that's a really weird way to go about it.

I joined Sawyer in the kitchen and took out a pint of low-carb ice cream and two spoons.

Sawyer took the lid off the ice cream and set it aside. "Did you ask her if she knew Vince or bought those olives?"

"No."

"Why not?"

"She started crying and I forgot. She said her husband cheated on her."

Sawyer swiped the screen of her tablet. "Oof. Been there. Well, I haven't found proof on Facebook or Instagram that anyone in the Baker family has been to California recently, but I found this." Sawyer tilted her tablet to show me a picture of Ryan posing with a Belgian waffle. "I guess it's too much to ask for him to be holding the jar of olives, isn't it?"

The Alexa chimed. "This is your reminder to . . . oh stuff it, Alexa."

Sawyer and I looked at each other, then went back to what we were doing.

I showed her the BakerCom website I'd found. "All the email addresses follow a pattern. VBaker@Bakercom.com, RFinch@Bakercom.com; if you knew someone worked there it would be easy to figure out their email address."

The front door chimed, and the biddies tittered their way down the hall, Aunt Ginny's tap shoes rat-a-tat-tatting with her steps. Only they weren't alone today. They had a good-looking young man with them who could have been the next star on *The Bachelor*. He was in his early twenties, with dark hair and blue eyes. He was dressed in jeans, a faded T-shirt, tan work boots, and a tan suede jacket. He came in carrying about fifteen shopping bags from various stores.

Aunt Ginny pointed to the table where Sawyer and I had our spoons knuckle deep in sugar-free Rocky Road. "Just put everything over there, Paul."

We grabbed our stuff out of the way. Sawyer moved the ice cream under the table to the seat next to her. Paul gave us an apologetic look and loaded the table with the bags.

Aunt Ginny took off a pair of leather gloves and slapped them on the island. "Well, it was the darndest thing. We went to the mall to look for those olives you sent us after."

Mrs. Davis interjected, "A wild-goose chase if you ask me."

Aunt Ginny grabbed some glasses out of the cabinet. "We hit every store—even the shoe store."

Mother Gibson pulled out a pair of red sling-back heels. "See what I got for church on Sunday."

Aunt Ginny went to the fridge and grabbed the pitcher of tea. "And when we came out, we couldn't find my car."

Mrs. Dodson hefted herself onto a barstool and propped her cane. "I think someone stole it; we should call it in before it gets too late."

Aunt Ginny waved her hand like it was the smallest of inconveniences. "Anyway, we had to get a Yuber to come home. Could you pay him, Poppy?" Aunt Ginny nodded her head toward Paul.

"Sure." I led Paul out to the front porch and grabbed my purse on the way. "How much do I owe you?"

Paul looked a little sheepish. "You don't owe me anything, ma'am. I'm not an Uber driver. I tried to tell the ladies I was just at the Walmart to pick up some bread and diapers, but they didn't seem to understand me. Once they were in the car, I couldn't get them out. So, in the end it was just easier to drive them home and drop them off."

The hamster in my brain fell off his wheel. *Carjacked by the elderly.* "I am so sorry. Can I give you some money for your trouble? Or a loaf of bread?"

"No, ma'am, it's fine. I'm gonna stop at the Wawa." Paul started heading for his car.

*How about I give you a hundred dollars not to call me
ma'am again.*

Paul waved goodbye.

"Thank you." I put my purse on the table in the hall
and made my way back to the kitchen. The biddies were
showing Sawyer all their new treasures.

Aunt Ginny was holding up a bag of potato chips. "I
went looking for a new girdle and found these instead. I
thought we'd try them." She ripped into the bag of mocha
latte chips and they all took one. They all made horrible
faces when they tasted the chips and each one of them
spit them out. Then Aunt Ginny balled up the bag and
threw it in the trash. "Well, that was disgusting."

Mrs. Dodson shook her shopping bag out in front of
her. "I got some circus peanuts, a twenty-four-hour Cross
Your Heart bra—although when I'd wear a bra for twenty-
four hours straight is beyond me—and a can of spray-on
pink hair glitter."

Mrs. Davis reached over to Mrs. Dodson's bag. "Can I
borrow the hair glitter?"

Mrs. Dodson snatched it away. "No."

The doorbell rang and I went to answer it. UPS had arrived with several boxes from Amazon. I carted them
down to the kitchen where the biddies were comparing
their purchases.

Aunt Ginny looked up from her set at the banquette.
"What in the world is all that?"

I set the boxes down on the floor next to her. "You tell
me. They're all addressed to Virginia Frankowski."

She looked at the stack of boxes, confused. "What? I
didn't order anything." She picked up the first box and
cut into it with a steak knife. It was a Lovepat girdle in
her size and the receipt had her name and address on it.

"Well, look at that. I needed this, but I couldn't find my size at J. C. Penney today."

We tore into the rest of the packages, including the ones the mailman delivered. There was a frying pan, some Max Factor ruby-red lipstick, a pack of stick and peel ducks for the tub, a can of kettle corn, a two pack of catnip-filled mice dressed as Darth Vader and Luke Sky-walker, *The Best of The Andy Griffith Show* on DVD, a ten-pound bag of dog food, a tin of Dutch butter cookies, and a box of Turtles.

I gave Aunt Ginny a hard look. "You want to explain all this?"

She shook her head. "I didn't order any of this. Maybe we've been hacked."

Mother Gibson opened the catnip mice and threw one on the floor. Figaro shot out from under the table and swatted it out and down the hall. "Ooh, girl, he is vigilant."

The doorbell rang again, and Aunt Ginny jumped. She gave me a nervous smile. "Maybe that's Avon."

I answered the door and found a package from FedEx addressed to Aunt Ginny on the side of the porch. I also noticed something else.

I took it to the kitchen and held up the package. "Apparently you're enrolled in a cheese of the month club now."

Mrs. Davis's mouth popped into an oval. "Ginny. You told us this morning you dreamed about cheese. Maybe your dreams are coming true."

Aunt Ginny quirked an eyebrow. "Then tonight I'm going to try to dream about John Travolta."

I handed her a cheese knife from the drawer. "You said you couldn't find your car at the shopping center?"

Aunt Ginny blew out a breath like she was preparing for a scolding. "Well, yes, but . . ."

"Aunt Ginny, your car is in the garage."

The ladies stared at me while searching their brains.

Mrs. Dodson slapped Mrs. Davis on the leg. "Oh crap! Thelma, you drove today."

Mother Gibson shook her head. "I wasn't even looking for your raggedy blue trap. I was too busy trying to find Ginny's red boat."

Mrs. Dodson shrugged it off. "Ginny, did you get that Yuber driver's number? We'll just have to call him to take us back."

Aunt Ginny took off her tap shoes and put on a pair of Zsa Zsa feathered slippers. "I asked him to give me his card before he left. He must have forgot. Sometimes these young people can't find their butt with both hands."

I was used to the blatant hypocrisy by now. Sawyer was still wearing hypocrisy training wheels and had to choke back her mocha potato chips.

I looked in a few bags. "You've got a lot of snacks."

Mrs. Davis started unbagging dips and spreads and pretzels and all manner of goodies. "We were undercover looking for your olives."

"Which we never found," Mother Gibson added.

"We had to make it look convincing." Mrs. Davis gave me a look like I should have known this on my own.

Aunt Ginny opened a bag of pretzels. "We went to the gourmet store on the mall and did a wine tasting."

Sawyer eyebrows shot up. "I didn't know they had wine tasting at The Sauce Depot."

"They don't," I said.

Aunt Ginny twisted the top off some raspberry mustard dip. "They do if you open the bottle and tell them you won't buy it unless you know you're gonna like it first."

Mrs. Davis grabbed a handful of pretzels. "So anyway, we couldn't find your cigar-nola olives anywhere."

I wasn't about to tell the ladies I didn't need them to find the olives anymore. We'd discovered the offending jar came from a store on the West Coast. I was just impressed that they remembered they were looking for olives in the first place. They even had the name almost right. But it didn't matter, because another disaster was about to present itself.

Victory came into the kitchen, back in her sexy maid costume I distinctly banned her from ever wearing again, and this time her chest was covered in powder. "Victory!"

She stopped short. "I know. I am sorry. I have to geive other uniform back to my friend. She has psychic tours."

"It's Physick, and where are the uniforms I bought for you? Don't say you spilled something."

Victory stood still, her eyes roving around the room. "Well?"

"I think you know, but you say not to tell you."

The biddies were not helping. They were all giggling behind their hands. Victory could hear them. She slid her eyes to Aunt Ginny and gave a curtsy and giggled.

"What did you need, Victory?"

She pulled her hand out from behind her skirt. She was holding an antique milk glass jar of loose powder in the scent Midnight in Paris. The lid was broken. "I was dusting Ahdonees room and eet roll off table and speill on my boobs."

Aunt Ginny had tears streaming down her face from laughing. I thought Mrs. Davis would pass out from holding her breath. Mother Gibson was biting her lip and shaking her head. Sawyer was sitting at the table covering her face and watching through her spread fingers. I looked to Mrs. Dodson for strength and she let me down the hardest. She laughed so hard she had to grab her cane and run to the bathroom.

Victory looked around at all the packages. "Ees eet someone birthdays or somesing?"

I took the jar of powder from Victory and set it on the counter. "Go get cleaned up." I did a quick search on my tablet for Midnight in Paris perfume powder. It hadn't been made since the 1950s. *This is going to be a nightmare to replace.*

The front door chimed, and I looked at Sawyer. "Is it more packages?"

She peeked her head though the dining room door and waved her hand. "It's Alyce. What should we do?"

"We need to talk to her. Now."

Chapter Thirty-six

Sawyer took the dining to sitting room route, and I went from the kitchen down the hall to head Alyce off in the foyer. Tammy Faye charged ahead like the flag bearer. She cornered Alyce at the bottom of the steps and looked back at me proudly with one foot tucked under her chest in a triumphant pose.

I gave Alyce a big smile and pretended I didn't just see her try to kick the tiny Pom and miss. "Hey there. You are just the person I was looking for."

Sawyer slid around the corner. "Oh, hi, Alyce. How's it goin'?"

Alyce looked from me to Sawyer to Tammy Faye. "Fine. I was just out running some errands."

Sawyer looked Alyce up and down. "Uh-huh. Were you dress shopping?"

"No, why?"

"Your pants are on inside out."

Alyce got red in the face. "Oh, I guess I've been so distracted lately. I must have walked around like this all day. Is there a bathroom on this level so I can fix them before I go up to my room?"

I took her arm and led her to the library. "There is, just down the hall, but before you change, I wanted to see how you were holding up. I know things must be very hard for you right now."

Alyce's eyes softened and her shoulders dragged. She let us lead her to the couch in front of the fireplace. "It's been a devastating week. First my dad"—she choked back a sob—"then to find out Sunny poisoned him."

A parade appeared in the library, with Aunt Ginny carrying a tray of teacups and spoons, followed by Mrs. Davis carrying the sugar bowl and cream, Mrs. Dodson on her cane with a plate of cookies, and Mother Gibson with a stack of dessert plates and napkins. Victory brought up the rear with the pot of tea. All we were missing was Lumière singing "Be Our Guest." I shook my head at each one of them and their shameless fear of missing out on a little gossip.

The ladies set their Trojan horses down and cooed over Alyce, then left the room. Aunt Ginny stopping at the intercom on the wall to "dust it." She gave me a thumbs-up while Alyce's back was turned.

Alyce commented, "Wow, the service here is really good."

Sawyer poured the tea. "I'm so glad you're enjoying it. Now, tell me, why do you think Sunny would poison her husband?"

Alyce's eye twitched and she picked up her tea and blew on it. "I think she poisoned my father to get his money. It's been her plan from the start. She killed her first husband and moved on to Daddy before the man's headstone was placed."

Sawyer spilled the tea out of my cup all over the tray and started mopping it up with some Kleenex. "I thought her first husband died of a heart attack."

Alyce puckered her lips like a duck. It wasn't a good look on her. "Women who look like Sunny have an easier time of getting one over on the law."

Wow, I thought I had self-esteem issues.

"Todd may have died on the basketball court, but Sunny brought him his Gatorade right before he went out there. I don't think it was a coincidence. And the police wouldn't investigate."

I was torn. There was truth to what Alyce was saying. Sometimes the world did look more favorably on the physically beautiful. I know I had never been able to talk my way out of a single speeding ticket, yet Sawyer got pulled over more than anyone I knew and to date she's gotten zero tickets and two phone numbers. I put two cookies on a plate and passed it to Alyce. "Did Sunny's first husband have money?"

"More than she deserved. Professors aren't exactly rich, but considering Sunny grew up with nothing he may as well have been a millionaire. She made out okay with his insurance policy, but she's set for life with Daddy's."

Sawyer and I took sips of our tea and tried to absorb what Alyce was saying. Somehow Sunny always managed to tell the truth but left out just enough details to twist the story to her benefit. I couldn't tell if it was malicious misleading or genuine oversight. "Alyce, how did you learn about the wine tour?"

"Ryan came home and said Daddy had cleared his schedule for a long weekend away and he was stuck with some PR nightmare case for a local politician whose wife embezzled thousands of dollars in cookie money from her daughter's Girl Scout troop. I told him, 'So what, Ryan. I couldn't care less what Daddy does with that money-grubbing tramp.' But when I heard they were coming to Cape May I was furious. I'd been asking Daddy to bring me to Cape May for years and he always refused. He said he was too busy to come here." Alyce took a big gulp from her cup and poured herself some more tea.

I held up the sugar bowl and Alyce dolloped a spoonful into her cup. "How did Ryan find out where Vince and Sunny were going?"

Alyce took a sip. "He saw the reservation in an email. He's Daddy's assistant, so he has access to all of Daddy's accounts."

Sawyer held up the cream. "He was your father's assistant? As in . . . assistant CEO?"

Alyce snorted. "No. Personal assistant. It's like head secretary. Daddy usually has a woman, but Ryan was recently promoted after we got married. Of course Daddy tells him he's a sales executive, but he only works on small in-house clients the other guys land but don't have time to manage."

Sawyer made a face at me and tried to hide it with her teacup.

"So, Alyce, tell us more about Cape May. Why had you been wanting to come here?"

"My mom talked about Cape May her whole life. Her family used to come down-the-shore every summer when she was a kid. She and Daddy even honeymooned at the Mainstay. I always wanted to see it. That's why Ryan and I joined the tour. We almost didn't get in, but Ryan was able to track the tour guide down through Sunny's email and he insisted that we be allowed to join the group. So . . . here we are."

"So, this is your very first time in Cape May?"

Alyce gave me a tiny nod.

Sawyer asked her, "You've never been to South Jersey before this week?"

Alyce gave Sawyer a self-righteous smile and shook her head. "Uh-uh."

Sawyer and I nodded at Alyce. Then looked at each other like this was the most interesting, believable story we'd ever heard.

Alyce placed her cup and saucer on the table in front of her and stood to go. "Where was that bathroom where I could change?"

"Right down the hall. The door is built into the wall under the steps. Look for the disguised handle."

Alyce started to leave and Sawyer cleared her throat. "Oh, Alyce. One more thing. There must be so many perks working for such a successful corporation with offices all over the country. Do you and Ryan get to travel together a lot?"

Alyce snorted. "No. Ryan can't leave New York. He hates flying and he never learned to drive. I just came home from a sales conference in San Francisco last month, but that wasn't exactly a romantic getaway if you know what I mean."

I nodded. "Yes, I think we know exactly what you mean."

Soon we heard the bathroom door close and the fan come on.

Sawyer practically dropped her teacup back on the tray. "Did you hear that? Ryan tracked the tour guide down from Sunny's email. He has access somehow."

Aunt Ginny clicked through the intercom. "Psst. Poppy. Sawyer. Come to the kitchen." She clicked off.

Sawyer's shoulders shook and she gave me a grin. "What was the 'psst' for?"

The intercom clicked back on. "Just get in here."

We joined the eavesdrop squadron in the kitchen. They were huddled around the intercom, working their way through the hodgepodge of high-end snacks. Tammy Faye was dancing on her back feet begging, and they were taking turns giving her little scraps of cheese and pretzels. Figaro watched from the doorway too dignified to beg. He would wait until Tammy Faye was away from the kitchen to pat Aunt Ginny delicately on the arm to pass him a bite the way a gentleman should.

Aunt Ginny met me with hands on hips. "Well, what do you think?"

I knew exactly what she meant. "She told several lies, but some things line up with what Ryan and Sunny have said."

Sawyer grabbed a handful of caramel corn when Victory offered her the bag. "I think we need to talk to Daniel and find out just what he's been up to with Alyce."

"Can you call him?" I removed a piece of cheese from a cracker and bit into it. "He might agree to talk to you.

We've been hoping to prove Daniel's innocence for Kim's sake, but I think we need to face the fact that he's a lot more involved in this mess than a totally innocent man would be."

Sawyer pulled out her phone and tapped a message on it.

The Alexa started to beep when one of Aunt Ginny's timers went off.

I looked her in the eye. "Do you have any idea what that's for?"

"Nope." Aunt Ginny dunked a potato chip into a jar of chocolate sauce.

Victory watched Aunt Ginny with interest, then took a potato chip and dipped it in the chocolate. "Oooh. That ees verry yummy. I leike the choklate; eet ees . . ."

I glanced at Victory. She was standing next to the banquette with half a potato chip in her hand and her eyes were closed. She swayed on her feet a little.

"Victory? Hello?"

Mrs. Dodson blew out her cheeks. "Does she do that a lot?"

Aunt Ginny snapped her fingers in front of Victory's face and Victory's eyes popped open.

Victory looked at Aunt Ginny. Then to Sawyer, then me. Then she looked at her potato chip and dunked it in the chocolate sauce and ate it. "Oooh. That ees verry yummy."

Mother Gibson sat back on the banquette and examined the chambermaid. "Child, what's wrong wi' you?"

Victory shrugged. "I sink I fall asleep or somesing."

I stared at her hard. "In the middle of a sentence?"

Victory nodded with a mouth full of chocolate. "Eet happen to me somes of days."

Great. My chambermaid has narcolepsy.

Aunt Ginny slid her eyes to me with apology. "I did not ask that question in the interview." She sat on the banquette and winced, leaning to her right side.

Mrs. Dodson leaned her head toward her. "Did you use the cream they gave us?"

"Yes, I used the cream. It isn't working."

"Okay, enough already. What did you-all do?"

The four biddies looked at me with wide eyes and mouths screwed shut.

Aunt Ginny finally broke. "Fine! If you must know." She stood up and yanked one side of her black tap skirt down to her thigh. "There! Are you happy?"

Emblazoned on Aunt Ginny's wrinkly left butt cheek was a tattoo that said *Ride or Die* in pretty scrollwork winding through two roses. I blinked twice and rubbed my eyes to be sure I wasn't imagining it.

Sawyer had to snap her mouth shut.

Victory kept nonchalantly eating chips like she saw wrinkly butt tattoos every day.

I looked at each of the biddies in turn.

They stood without saying a word and pulled down the left sides of their polyester day slacks to reveal matching tattoos.

Aunt Ginny looked over her shoulder and gave me a pointed look. "Well?"

"I think yours is a little bit infected."

The other biddies leaned back and looked at Aunt Ginny's butt.

Mother Gibson nodded. "That must be why it still hurts."

Mrs. Dodson added, "You probably shouldn't have worn the fishnets so soon."

I sighed. "What exactly brought on this new rebellion? It wasn't Royce hinting at a future commitment, was it?"

Mrs. Davis shook her head. "That wasn't the *only* reason."

Aunt Ginny gave me a weak smile. "We also had a Groupon."

Sawyer's phone dinged and she checked the screen. "That was fast."

Aunt Ginny and the biddies perked up like a mob of meerkats. They yanked their clothes up and spun around on Sawyer. Their eyes dilated and their ears twitched.

"What's going on?"

"Did something happen?"

I gave Sawyer a warning with my eyes. *For the love of God, don't say a word.*

She took a step back. "I got a match on my eHarmony profile."

The biddies' excitement drained faster than I could suck the jelly out of a donut. They were well acquainted with Sawyer's romantic ventures and considered this a nonstarter. They went back to their snacks with a murmur of "tenth time's the charm."

Sawyer looked at me and jerked her head toward the door. She mouthed, *Now!*

Victory took a long swig of a bottled lemonade. "Ees there peicture?"

I grabbed my purse and made to head out through the hall while Sawyer backed toward the dining room. "I'm not much into their looks."

Mrs. Davis looked at the other ladies and shook her head. "She's not much into their personalities either."

We cleared the kitchen and ran for it.

I hissed, "Tell me this is something good."

Sawyer hissed back, "How does a secret meeting with Daniel sound?"

"Like Kim may have redeemed herself for ditching us at the winery."

"Don't get carried away."

Chapter Thirty-seven

We jumped into Sawyer's car because mine was in the driveway being blocked by Ken and Willow's Volvo. Sawyer tossed me her phone. "They're meeting us in Wildwood. Kim is sending the address now."

I waited for the text to come through and plugged it into the GPS. Twenty minutes and two U-turns later we were facing the boardwalk. We easily found a parking meter—Tuesday night in March was not exactly prime boardwalk season. Funnel cake can only do so much to attract a person to the ocean in forty degrees. People do have their standards.

Sawyer slammed her car door. "I wonder if there's a funnel cake stand open."

Okay, not us. But other people. "Kim says there's a lemon-yellow arcade up here next to a T-shirt shop."

We hiked up the ramp and were on the boards—a combination of weathered planks and concrete. The air was salty and smelled of fried food and rain. The wind was fierce and wanted to pull my hair out by the roots and beat me in the face with it. I turned into it, gathered my hair, and twisted it into a bun so I could look around. "There it is, next to the ring toss."

Sawyer shoved her hands into her pockets and pushed into the wind in the direction of Fat Louie's Arcade. We followed the sounds of electric bells and *chingarings* from games running demo mode to attract teenagers—or grown men with nostalgia and pockets of quarters. The metal gate was up, and lights were dancing and flashing to draw you into neon wonderland. Whoever was in charge was nowhere to be seen, but there was one lone teenager in an Adele sweatshirt playing a vintage Donkey Kong. She had shoulder-length stringy brown hair and a smattering of pimples. Her super Big Gulp sat on the Frogger panel next to her. She never knew we were there.

"Psst. Back here." Kim was in the back corner with the Skee-Ball machines and the basketball toss waving her arms.

We wound our way through rows of video poker and coin pushers. "Where's Daniel?"

The winery owner stepped out of the shadow in the back corner. He was dressed in camo pants and a hooded sweatshirt drawn around his face. "I'm here."

Sawyer sat on the edge of a Skee-Ball ramp and crossed her legs. "Why are we meeting in secret?"

Daniel cast his eyes around the arcade. "Someone's been following me. I think I'm in danger."

I smashed in next to Sawyer and the coin return button jabbed me in the butt, so I had to slide down. "Danger from who?"

"I dunno. Maybe whoever killed Vince Baker."

Well, that seems improbable. "And who do you think that is?"

"I think it's obvious. Vince's wife killed him for the money."

"Okay, but Sunny's in police custody right now. So who would be following you?"

Daniel looked around nervously. He whispered, "Alyce's husband, Ryan. You know he threatened me."

"What about?"

"He thinks he's going to sue me for stealing Alyce away from him. Like she's a business and I'm a corporate spy." Daniel ran his hands through his hair and paced in front of the change machine. "That's what he said. Not beat me up, not kill me—sue me. Oh, Alyce, why did you marry him, baby? Your dad tried to stop you. You should have listened."

"Did you and Vince know each other well?"

"I met him for the first time at the wine tasting."

"I heard you performed CPR for nearly twenty minutes until the paramedics took over. Was that just because he died in your winery? Or because you had a personal connection to him?"

Daniel shifted his eyes briefly to Kim. "I'd like to think I'd try to save anyone's life who had a heart attack in my winery. . . ."

Kim gave Daniel a slow headshake. "But?"

"Well . . . he was Alyce's father and even though he

treated her horribly I couldn't just let him die in front of her. No matter how strained their relationship was, she still loved him."

Kim's eyes snapped to Daniel's. "Just how well do you know Alyce?"

Daniel was fighting an inner war for self-respect and it crept up his neck and spread across his face. "I've known her since she was fifteen."

"What!"

I knew Kim had a fit brewing, and I didn't blame her, but she seemed to idolize her boss and we had to pull the Band-Aid off now. "Daniel, how did you and Alyce meet?"

"She used to come down-the-shore every summer with her parents before her mom died. They stayed around the corner from my beach rentals and she'd come in every day to rent something she was never going to use just to have someone to talk to. She had a little bit of a crush on me." He grinned. "Her father was busy building an empire and her mother was . . . sick."

Sawyer asked, "Sick how?"

Daniel leaned against one of the basketball toss games and shoved his hands in the pouch of his hoodie. "Alyce's mother suffered from bipolar disorder. She wouldn't come out of her bedroom for days, and when she did she'd be crazy fun at first. But that fun would turn into obsessive behaviors like binge shopping, and cleaning until her hands bled, and eventually to paranoia. Then she'd crash and the cycle would start all over again."

Sawyer sniffled. "That's just horrible."

I thought about Vince telling Sunny there were ghosts in Cape May. "Alyce's mother died when Alyce was a teenager, didn't she?"

Daniel nodded slowly. His eyes reflected the sadness from his bitter memories. "The third summer I spent with Alyce, her mother hit a low point. One night she disappeared. Her body washed ashore a couple miles down the beach a couple days later. She was wearing a white cotton nightgown that Alyce had bought her a week before for her birthday. It was like she'd finally had enough pain, so she got out of bed, walked into the ocean, and killed herself."

We were speechless. The intrusive *waka waka waka* sounds from the Pacman games were suddenly jarring and offensive, flaunting their lack of respect for the tragedies of life.

Sawyer dropped her face in her hands.

I put my hand on her back. Neither Sawyer nor I grew up with moms in the house. It's one of the things that bonded us as kids. I knew she was feeling the same grief that I was. I turned my attention back to Daniel. "Are you and Alyce more than friends?" *As if we didn't already know.*

Daniel shifted on his feet. "No, of course not."

Kim clicked her tongue. "We saw you kissing after the happy hour."

Daniel closed his eyes like the moment he was dreading was finally out of the bag. "Fine, yes."

Kim blew a gasket. "You're like twenty years older than her."

Daniel's shoulders cringed north toward his ears. "Nothing happened until she was eighteen. It was a summer fling and it was over when she left for college. Years later after Trish and I married and separated, I got an invitation for Alyce and Ryan's wedding. I showed up and made a fool of myself telling Alyce I loved her and asked her to run away with me. She said no. She was trying to beat her father down the aisle with his new wife before they could steal her thunder. She had to prove to Vince and all his business associates that she was worthy of being loved even if he couldn't see it."

Kim was not as mollified by this as Daniel may have hoped. "Then when did you start fooling around with her?"

"About six months after she married that dip wad husband of hers. She knew it was a mistake right from the start. She came up here one weekend when she was supposed to be on a business trip and we . . . reconnected. We've been seeing each other twice a month."

The blood drained from Kim's face. "I've been working with you for two years. How have I never seen her?"

Daniel looked at his feet. "She comes on Sunday, your day off. I didn't want you to know and think less of me."

I put a hand on Kim's arm to calm her and addressed Daniel again. "She spent the night last night, didn't she?"

Daniel gave me a slow nod. "How did you know about that?"

"Because Ryan told my handyman that she never came home and he didn't know where she was."

There was that weird feeling again. I got it every time I thought about Ryan asking Smitty to check the heat in the Monarch suite. Something was wrong, but what was it?

Daniel sneered. "I'm surprised he even noticed. Alyce found pictures on his cell phone sent from another woman." He gave us a look to punctuate the unsaid. "She knows he's been sleeping around."

Oh my God. That's it. The night we broke into the win-

ery I caught Ryan sneaking out of Zara's room. I didn't realize what was happening at the time because I was focused on helping Kim. And it's not like I sit around and think about what room everyone is in. Two days later Victory spilled moonshine on the dresser and Zara said it wasn't hers. What if I caught Ryan planting evidence?

Kim's voice grew a little shrill and snapped me out of my thoughts: "Yeah, but why keep sneaking around? If she knows he's cheating, why not leave him and be with you?"

"Because of the prenup."

Sawyer head jerked up. "What prenup? We were told she refused to sign it."

Daniel's face reddened and his eyes narrowed. "No, her husband refused to sign the prenup her father set up for her. He brought his own prenup to the table the night before the wedding. Said he'd been thinking about it and it was only fair to protect her assets. I've read it. It doesn't. It gives him half of everything that was hers before they were married. Alyce knew it was a bad idea, but she was too ashamed to call off the wedding. Her father had tried to warn her about marrying Ryan, and she didn't want him to know he was right. Her father's an arrogant bastard, and she married a guy just like him."

That's a terrifying thought. "Did she tell you anything about Vince's will?"

Daniel took his hands out of his pockets and kicked the ball toss. He let out a few colorful expletives that made it clear what he thought about Alyce's father. "Who does that? Just writes their daughter out of the will. Alyce doesn't care about the money, but he may as well have spit in her face. It would have been kinder."

Sawyer and I looked at each other, and I felt we were having the same problem: *Why would Daniel or Alyce kill Vince if they thought Alyce had nothing to gain from his death? Just to get rid of him?* "Did you know she and Ryan are talking to a lawyer to get it changed back?" I watched Daniel's expression. "If they succeed Alyce will be a very rich woman."

Daniel shook his head sadly. "It will never make her happy. All she ever wanted was her father's love. Not his money. The only one who'll be happy with that outcome is Dip Wad, and he'll blow through it in no time."

"Yeah," I said, "but that money could really come in handy for you. Especially after you lost your insurance claim to a bogus contractor after Sandy."

Daniel narrowed his eyes and peered at me down on the Skee-Ball ramp like I was something he'd stepped in. "I lost a dinky little shop that rented rusty bikes. So what? If it weren't a business that my father started in the sixties, I'd have been relieved. That guy did me a favor. Now I can build something that has meaning. And making the winery a success means a lot to me, but I'd rather lose everything all over again than hurt Alyce."

Daniel did seem to really care for Alyce. It was touching and sad at the same time. "So, let me ask you about the afternoon Vince died."

Daniel's shoulders relaxed and he stopped grinding his teeth. "Okay. Shoot."

"What was your impression of the tour group?"

"I was stunned when Alyce told me she was coming here with her husband. And to join her father and his new trophy wife. Her father had sworn never to return to Cape

May after Alyce's mother died, so Alyce never told any-one she'd been coming on her own. And then Ryan . . . It nearly drove me mad seeing her with him. And the way he talks to her. Smug little—"

Sawyer cut him off. "Yeah, we've met him."

"After the first couple of rounds were served, I couldn't go back to their table. I wanted to punch him dead in his smug little face."

We'd all felt the same way since meeting Ryan, so that tracked. "We saw the video of you serving one of the wines. Where did the bowl of wasabi peas come from?"

Daniel's eyes widened in surprise. "How do you know about the peas? I didn't even know about the peas until the cops made me take a polygraph. I'll tell you the same thing I told them: I never saw those peas. My eyes were on Ryan and Alyce, and everyone rushed me to get the glasses of wine I'd brought over. I didn't even have a chance to go to the other table before they were on me too. Only the chick with the short black hair made me come to her. I've never even heard of wasabi peas, let alone bought them. They'd be terrible to pair with wine."

I held up my hand. "Okay, I get it. You didn't serve the peas and you didn't see where they came from."

Daniel unclenched his fists. "Right."

"Did you at any time see anything weird? Anyone putting anything in the wine or on the food?"

"No, no, and no. You're asking all the questions I've already answered. Alyce's family argued the entire time. Sunny kept pushing Alyce's buttons playing the good wife card. Ryan kept shoving Alyce to the side like she didn't matter. Her father told her to shut up every time she opened her mouth to say anything. Everyone else kept their distance. I received two complaints from people not with the tour and had to issue free tasting vouchers for their next visit."

Sawyer tapped me on the leg. She had the next question. "We saw on the video that you, Kim, Jess, and Lily served five rounds. Did anyone else ever serve wine?"

"No."

"Maybe someone the camera didn't pick up?"

"No."

Kim cocked her head to the side. "Well . . . a couple of them didn't care for the reserve wines and wanted something else."

Daniel made a face like he was chewing his tongue.

"What did you give them?" Sawyer asked.

"We don't have a lot to choose from yet, so I think they both took the only wine we don't usually serve to tours."

Daniel nodded. "The port."

Kim nodded back. "But I don't know who they were because the request came through Lily."

Daniel shook his head. "Lily had to pitch in with the flight because everyone on the winery staff had been accosted or insulted one way or another and didn't want to serve them anymore. Kim served the last round and we were ready for them to move on."

"How was the staff accosted?" I asked.

Daniel gave me a look under raised eyebrows. "When Jess pitched in to serve a round, she was groped."

"By who?"

Daniel and Kim exchanged a look. "Ryan."

I closed my eyes and rubbed my temples. "Why are you just telling us this now, Kim?"

"I didn't think it was important. Ryan isn't the one who was murdered."

Sawyer groaned. "He was still involved. Heck, he might have groped Jess by accident while trying to slip something into Vince's wine."

Kim blushed and the hummingbird tattoo on her arm turned purple. "I didn't think of that."

I gave Kim a pointed look. "Is there anything else you haven't told us?"

She and Daniel both shook their heads. "No, nothing."

My knees cracked as I tried to stand up. I put my hand down to help hoist Sawyer off her low ledge. "If you think of anything, call me immediately, Kim."

Kim held up two fingers. "I will. I promise. Daniel does too, don't you, Daniel?" Kim jabbed Daniel in the side.

"Absolutely. You have my word."

Sawyer gritted her teeth and let out a low rumble as we passed the girl playing Donkey Kong. "Like that's worth anything now."

We huddled together to take the ramp down to the car. Sawyer stopped short at the bottom and jerked her head around. "Did you hear that?"

"Hear what?"

"It sounded like a baby."

"Why would a baby be out here?"

"There it is again." She crept over to the area under the boardwalk ramp and squatted down to her knees.

"What are you doing?"

Sawyer gasped. "Oh, you poor baby." She came out with something small and wiggly buried in her arms.

"What is it?"

She came closer to me and two little icy blue eyes blinked from a dark brown face twitching long white whiskers. "It's a sweet little kitten. Are you lost, baby?"

A chill ran up my arms and goose bumps prickled my flesh. I looked to the sky just as a cloud lazily moved past an almost full moon. I spoke just above a whisper, afraid to admit what I knew was true: "You just met your stranger in a dark alley with icy blue eyes and fell in love."

Chapter Thirty-eight

I can neither confirm nor deny that we may have found an open frozen custard stand on the way home. I will also not comment on whether or not they had crunch coat available. What I can admit to is that I was still shaken up about the pseudopsychic's prediction about Sawyer finding new love. A new love who was currently curled up in a shoe box until Sawyer could get him home and give him a bath.

Sawyer turned the car down my street and pulled over to the curb. "I've been thinking, Daniel's and Sunny's stories about the will agree that Ryan was after Vince's money."

"Yeah. And even though both he and Alyce were on the West Coast and could have bought those olives, I don't see Alyce having a motive to kill her father, do you?"

Sawyer leaned her head on the steering wheel. "People who have been hurt very deeply can do terrible things."

"Well, I don't see either Ryan or Alyce being Sunny's accomplice like Amber seems to think." I yawned and opened the car door. It had been a long day and my skin was starting to itch from the vanilla custard that I may or may not have had. "Amber has to charge Sunny in the morning or release her. Her time is up. I think I'll go call her tonight and let her know what we found out and suggest that she let Sunny go and bring Ryan in instead."

Sawyer gave me a slow nod. "I'll call you in the morning and you can tell me how she blew you off."

We said good night and I headed up the front path to the porch, pulling my cell phone out on the way. Tammy Faye scrambled across the hall being chased by Figaro. They did a lap over the furniture in the library; then Tammy Faye chased Figaro back into the sitting room. Figaro gave a loud moan that only cats make; then there was a crash.

I closed my eyes and let a couple of seconds tick by before I went into the sitting room to inspect the damage. Someone had left a china teacup and saucer on an end table and it lay in the floor in pieces. Figaro peered at me from behind a picture frame only showing one side of his face. Tammy Faye had fled the scene of the crime.

I scolded Fig and picked up the pieces of my now eleven-piece dessert set and took it to the kitchen to throw it away.

Aunt Ginny was sitting at the banquette with her head on the table. The Midnight in Paris powder open next to her and my laptop opened to the side. "What are you doing in here . . . Aunt Ginny?" I walked over to her and lightly touched her back to wake her up without startling her. "Aunt Ginny?"

My mouth went dry and my heart began a slow, building pound through my chest and into my ears. "Aunt Ginny." I shook her this time a bit roughly and her head lolled to the side. I tried to take her pulse, but my hands were shaking. I grabbed my cell phone and dialed 911. "My aunt isn't breathing. She's in her eighties. Something's wrong." The dispatcher asked me my address and I went blank. Then she read my address to me and asked if that was right. "Yes, I think so, yes. She was fine this afternoon." That wasn't asked, but I was spiraling and offered it.

"Ma'am, help is on the way. Stay on the line."

Tears spilled from my eyes as I went down the hall to open the front door. I had trouble with the latch; my fingers didn't want to work right. Fig and Tammy sat quietly at the foot of the steps sensing my mood. I went back to the kitchen hoping it was all my imagination. Maybe Aunt Ginny was playing a trick on me. My blood ran like ice through my veins; she was unmoved from how I'd left her.

Amber was the first to arrive. She ran in the house dressed in jeans and a heavy blue parka. "Where is she?"

My voice caught in my throat and all I could do was step aside and point.

Amber dropped her coat on the floor, kicked it to the side, and began to check Aunt Ginny's vitals. "She's breathing. Her pulse is very slow, but it's there." Amber reported the status on her radio and was informed that paramedics were en route with an ETA of two minutes.

The 911 dispatcher came back on my cell phone and

told me she would end the call now—I'd forgotten she was there.

Amber put her hand on my back. "It will be all right. They're almost here."

That was all I needed to completely break down. My lips started to shake and then the silent sobs shook my chest.

I heard the siren in the distance, and a minute or so later the screen door squeaked on its hinge and footsteps clomped into the foyer. Amber left my side to wave the paramedics in and lead them to Aunt Ginny. One of them carried a toolbox of equipment and two more brought in a stretcher.

I stepped aside not knowing what to do with my hands or my arms. All my problems suddenly felt so stupid and hollow. Which man to commit to, dieting, and how much weight I'd lost. I didn't care if I ever ate again; I just wanted Aunt Ginny to be okay.

The EMTs worked on her and asked me questions about her health, was she on medication, and how and when I found her.

I gave them the list of prescriptions and they lifted Aunt Ginny to the stretcher. A spasm wracked my chest. One of the paramedics started an IV while another monitored Aunt Ginny's vitals. The third pointed to the milk glass jar on the table. "Ma'am, what is that?"

"Just some perfumed powder one of my guests had."

The paramedic lifted the container and smelled it. He handed Amber a pair of rubber gloves. "Ma'am, I don't believe this is perfume, but your aunt has evidence of it all over her chest and face. I think she may have ingested it."

I took a close look at Aunt Ginny and saw what he was talking about. I cast worried eyes to Amber. "That was in

Willow's room. I caught Ryan sneaking out of Zara's a couple days ago. What if he put this in Willow's room while he was at it?"

Amber's face remained impassive, but her lips pinched tight and lost some of their color. She turned to the paramedics. "The patient may have been exposed to propofol or phenobarbital or a similar drug."

They made notes on Aunt Ginny's chart and one of them called it in on his radio. They strapped Aunt Ginny's body to the stretcher and started to wheel her to the ambulance. "We're taking her to Cape Regional."

I looked at him confused. "Where is that?"

Amber gathered her parka. "It's Burdette Tomlin. They changed the name."

"Okay. I'm right behind you."

"You're not driving anywhere, McAllister."

I was about to give Amber what for, but she gave me my second shock of the night.

"Get in my car. We can put the lights on. I don't want to scare you, but you need to get there quickly."

Chapter Thirty-nine

I fell asleep around four in the morning when Aunt Ginny was admitted. I dozed in a vinyl chair that was made from a solid block of ice. Every twenty minutes someone new came in the room to check Aunt Ginny's vitals, take blood, or turn off an alarm. Aunt Ginny woke up a couple of times throughout the night, but she was very groggy and kept asking for her cotillion sash. I told her I didn't know what she was talking about and she called me a communist. Around five thirty Aunt Ginny mumbled, "Alexa, set a timer for thirty-six hours and twenty-seven seconds."

I wasn't sure I'd heard her right, so I asked, "What?"

She muttered again. "And get me a scooter."

I stared at the heart monitor blipping in jagged lines and realized Aunt Ginny was programming Alexa in her sleep. I giggled to myself. *Oh my gosh. Is this where all the packages are coming from?*

Sunlight was streaming in through the edges of the four-foot-wide blinds hanging in the four-foot-six window and hit me like a laser beam to the eye. I was about to pull the scratchy pillowcase over my head when I heard the soft crackle of a police radio.

"McAllister. Are you awake?"

I opened my eyes to see Amber standing before me, back in uniform and looking fresh and rested. "I'm awake."

"You look terrible. Why didn't you go home last night?"

I stretched my neck side to side, and it popped like a champagne cork. "I wanted to be here in case Aunt Ginny woke up."

"Did Aunt Ginny's tests come back yet?"

"Her doctor was here about an hour ago." I glanced at Aunt Ginny in her hospital bed, making sure I could still see the sheets rising and falling. "Her blood showed she'd been exposed to enough phenobarbital to knock her out. She must have been inhaling that powder all night to pick up a scent. The ER doctor said her advanced age and other prescriptions she's on made her more sensitive to it, so it didn't take a lot to slow her heart down dangerously low. She's lucky to be alive."

Amber looked at Aunt Ginny and shook her head. "The lab results on the powder should come in this afternoon so we can prove that was the substance the M.E. found in Vince's postmortem. Birkwell and Crabtree are picking up Ryan this morning and bringing him in for questioning."

"Poppy?" Aunt Ginny was waving her hand over her head, her IV dangling off the tape on her arm. I was at her side in two steps.

"I'm right here."

"This hotel is terrible. It's way too noisy. Call the front desk and tell them I'm coming down there."

Amber snickered behind me. "She's going to be fine."

Chapter Forty

When Aunt Ginny finally came to herself, she demanded waffles. I'd explained to her that she was in the hospital from exposure to sedatives. She admitted that she'd been doing research on "the Google" trying to find a replacement for the Midnight in Paris powder so that I wouldn't get in trouble for the B&B breaking the antique jar.

"When I couldn't smell anything, I may have tasted it just a little to see if maybe it was cocaine like they do on *CSI*."

"Have you ever tasted cocaine?"

"No."

"Then how would you know what it tastes like?"

"The cops always know. I think your gums are supposed to get numb. Anyway, my gums didn't get numb the first time, so I tried it again."

I considered a follow-up response about not wanting to find her high any more than I wanted to find her unconscious but discarded it. I was just glad she was going to be okay. The hospital was keeping her today for observation just to be safe and that was a relief on so many levels. All I could think about was choking Ryan.

"So, what about those waffles?"

"Where am I gonna get waffles?"

"Go to the diner. They have waffles. Oh, I know. Call Royce. Did anyone tell him I'm in the hospital?"

"No. The only person I called was Sawyer. She's home making breakfast for the B and B guests."

Aunt Ginny handed me my cell phone from the tray beside her bed. "Tell Royce to bring me waffles."

"And that's how I left her a while later, happily eating waffles drenched in syrup with Royce by her side. His sister Fiona had dropped him off at the front door and he'd forgotten why he was there at first. Fortunately, one of Aunt Ginny's nurses was on break down at the coffee cart in the lobby. She heard him telling the front desk that he'd brought the waffles and figured out who he was and brought him up."

Sawyer poured me another cup of coffee. "I'm so relieved she'll be okay. You should have called me sooner."

"I didn't have time to call anyone. Amber drove me to the hospital. I had to have Connie come pick me up and drive me home after she got the girls off to school."

The dining room door swung open and Ryan poked his head in. He held up his coffee cup to Sawyer. "You think I could get some coffee, beautiful?"

What the . . . I was so stunned to see him back home

from the police station the fried egg slid right off my keto biscuit and landed on my chest. "I thought the police took you in for questioning." I grabbed a napkin and dabbed at the yolk disappearing down my cleavage.

"They did. I'm back already. I didn't kill Vince. I lost a quarter of a million dollars in stock options when Vince died. I'm the last person who would have wanted him dead."

Sawyer took the coffeepot over and filled Ryan's cup. "How's that exactly?"

"Vince was so angry when Alyce and I got married. He said we wouldn't last five years. So, I made him a bet we would."

"And this bet was for . . . ?"

"Stock in BakerCom. Vince drew up a contract saying if we weren't divorced by our fifth anniversary, he'd gift me and Alyce two-hundred-and-fifty-large of his own stocks. But now that he's dead, his stocks transfer to Sunny. Our contract was void the moment the coroner signed the death certificate."

"Ryan!" We heard Alyce's voice coming from the dining room.

Ryan rolled his eyes. "That's the ball and chain." He gave a long, lustful look at Sawyer, then left the kitchen.

She turned to me. "I don't think he was going to get those stocks in a million years. I'd be surprised if those two make it to July."

"No, kitty, no!" Figaro scrambled into the kitchen with something furry and brown in his mouth. He was being chased by Tammy Faye, who was trying to take it from him, and Victory, who was trying to get it back.

Sawyer jumped on top of the banquette bench. "Eww. What is that?"

I grabbed a broom and prepared to whack it. "Figaro! Drop it!"

Fig opened his mouth and let the object fall to the floor. Then he gave it a swat for good measure.

Victory put her hands up and shook them. "No. Do not sweep eet. Eis only weig."

Sawyer and I froze in what we were doing. "It's what?"

Victory bent over and picked up the lifeless brown animal and shook it out. She held it up for us to get a better look at it. "See. Eis weig. For the head."

Sure enough, on closer inspection, that was a brown wig. And it was looking rough. "Oh, this is not good. What room were you in?"

"Um, Adonees suite. Kitty follow me when I do cleaning and he attack it. Doggie try to protect me."

Tammy Faye sat at Victory's feet and wagged her tail at superspeed. Figaro was trying to catch her tail from around the corner of the island.

I took a long look at Victory. She had obviously borrowed another dress from her friend at the Physick Estate, only this one had a floor-length blue skirt, a long-sleeved white blouse with lace trim and poufy sleeves and a cameo brooch at the neck, and she was wearing a black teardrop hat with giant blue ostrich feathers cascading over one side. "You spilled something on the other one?"

Victory nodded. "Yes. Theis eis fancy lady dress."

"Yeah, I got that."

Sawyer pointed to Victory's neck. "The cameo gives it away."

I held up the wig. "We have to sneak this back into Willow's room before she finds out it's missing. Her husband said she'd been sick. I thought he meant pregnancy sick, but maybe she's been through chemotherapy."

"Can you do that when you're pregnant?" Sawyer asked.

I shrugged. "I don't know." I peered down the hall for signs of Willow or Ken. I didn't see either of them, so we made a procession up the stairs to the Adonis suite. I knocked on the door and there was no answer.

Victory turned the knob and whispered, "Housekeeping."

I could hear the shower running and steam wafting out from under the bathroom door. Victory pointed. "Eis steill ein shower. Eis verry long time."

Realization dawned that Willow had been in the shower while Victory had been cleaning the room when the wig was snagged. *I've got to call that agency.*

Victory took the wig and draped it on a round pillow with long Velcroed straps on the bed. "Eet was here before naughty kitty."

Sawyer whispered, "What is that? It looks like a spider with four legs."

I nudged it with my hand. "I dunno. Some kind of back brace? There's a pocket for a heating pad or ice pack."

We heard giggling come from the bathroom and realized Willow was not in there alone. Then the familiar squeak of the taps being turned off and the water stopped.

I hissed at everyone, "Get out! Get out!" I pushed Victory and Sawyer into the hall and pulled the door to. We heard scratching on the wood from inside the room.

Sawyer pointed to the bottom of the door. "The dog is still in there!"

I held my breath and opened the door a crack. A little

yellow snout pushed its way through the crack and Tammy Faye emerged triumphant. I shut the door with a quiet click. "Go go go!" I hustled everyone down the steps and into the sitting room.

Victory grinned. "Ees fun working in bed and brick-fes'." Then her eyes went blank. It was like someone had unplugged her. She dropped to her knees, then face planted on the floor sound asleep.

Chapter Forty-one

I wasn't trained for what to do in the event that your chambermaid falls to the floor dead asleep in a post-break-in narcoleptic episode. *Do I call someone or leave her on the floor?*

Figaro came over and sniffed Victory. Then he swatted at the ostrich feathers on her hat. They swung back at him, freaked him out, and he galloped from the room with his ears flattened to his head.

Sawyer tried to examine Victory with the toe of her sneaker. "Is it dangerous to wake her up?"

"I don't know. I think that's just for sleepwalkers."

My phone rang Duran Duran and I answered it. "Hey."

"What are you doing?"

"Watching my chambermaid sleep in the middle of the floor."

Kim laughed. "Okay. Hey, can I meet with you and Sawyer? I need to talk to you both about something important. You guys won't believe what I found out."

"Sure. Let's meet at La Dolce Vita. I could stand some coffee, and some baking therapy after the night I've had." Plus, I haven't seen Gia since yesterday. *I wonder if Sierra has stolen him from me yet.* I hung up and shoved my phone in my back pocket. "We're going to Gia's." I covered Victory with the chenille throw from off the back of the couch. I stared at her from a couple of angles. "She'll be fine." I was saying it more to reassure myself than Sawyer.

Tammy Faye came into the sitting room, sniffed Victory, and lay down next to her. Sawyer and I took one last look at the world's worst chambermaid and left for the coffee shop.

I parked in the alley at the back door. The pink Camaro wasn't here. Maybe Sierra had the day off.

And if wishes were horses beggars would ride. Sierra was in the front of the pastry case stocking it with the last of the muffins and cupcakes. "People seem to really like these gluten-free things. They sell better than Momma's cannoli."

Oh, you're calling her Momma now. Good luck with that.

"I think Gia would like it if you could make more soon."

I got a shiver up the back of my neck. Sierra giving me instructions on behalf of Gia rankled my attitude like Georgina telling me I had to paint my kitchen beige. "Where is Gia?"

Sierra closed the pastry case with an air of superiority. "He had an errand to run. He told me he'd be back later and left me in charge."

Sawyer blew air through her nose like a bull. "Great, then you must know how to work the espresso machine."

A flicker of unease passed over Sierra's eyes. "Of course I do. Gia says I have a gift."

Sawyer stepped up to the register and rattled off, "Then I'll have a medium extra-hot half-caf quad-shot four-pump raspberry soy white mocha macchiato with micro-foam and caramel drizzle. With two Splendas."

I lost all my available points for coolness when I laughed out loud.

Sierra's mouth hung slack and she blinked like a hummingbird drying its wings.

"Do you need me to repeat that, or you got it?"

Sierra took out a pen and a napkin. "Uh . . . maybe just one more time."

Sawyer repeated the order even faster.

I wanted to giggle like I'd just won first place in the Miss Firecracker Pageant, but I covered my mouth like I was deep in thought over world politics and celebrity breakups and held it together.

Sawyer turned to me and said, "I'm gonna run across the street and check on the bookstore. I'll be back by the time my drink is ready."

"I wouldn't count on that."

Sawyer winked and went out the front door while Sierra checked all the bottles for "macchiato syrup." I could have told her that macchiato wasn't a syrup, but I didn't want to interfere with her "gift." So, I sent myself to the kitchen to whip up another batch of lemon curd muffins while I waited for Kim to arrive.

I had measured and mixed everything and was just topping the muffins with the lemon curd when I sensed an electric sexy crackle around me.

"Bella, you are here. I thought I smelled something delicious." Gia came up behind me and pulled my back against his chest.

"I'm not even baking yet."

"I'm not talking about the baking." He spun me around and kissed me. His skin was warm, and his aftershave smelled of sage and pine. He gazed into my eyes and grinned. "If you keep looking at me like that, I won't be able to go up front and fix whatever mess Sierra has made."

I felt my cheeks get warm, but I made no move to pull away. "Did she figure out what a quad shot was yet?"

He shook his head slightly. "I cannot tell if she's making a latte or a sundae."

I touched the buttons on his dress shirt. "I can't help but wonder—why exactly did you hire someone with her specific qualifications?"

Gia's eyes teased me. "To make you jealous. Some people need a little push to see how they really feel."

Checkmate. He knew it, and I knew it. I wouldn't give him the satisfaction of admitting Sierra had gotten to me.

I put the tin of muffins in the oven and set the timer for twenty minutes. "Hm. So, where'd you go when you left Booty Shorts in charge?"

He grinned and moved the KitchenAid bowl to the sink. "Across the courtyard talking with Zio Alfio. He's been trying to find something for me. Did you ever find out what the cowboy couple was up to?"

"No, I forgot all about them. When I got home yesterday there was a whole new crisis waiting." I filled him in on our boardwalk interview, and Ryan slipping out of police custody, and finally about Aunt Ginny's night in the hospital.

Gia was very upset that I didn't call him when Aunt Ginny was taken in. "I am here for you, no matter what happens; do you not know that?"

A lump caught in my throat and all I could do was nod.

"You mean so much more to me than someone who makes muffins for the café. I can get Momma to make muffins. She will complain, but she will do it. I want to be a part of your life."

I want that too. But . . .

Gia changed the subject back to Aunt Ginny. "Is she home now?"

"No. They're keeping her overnight for observation. Royce is with her. I was surprised she called Royce."

"Why?"

I took the rest of the dirty dishes to the sink and filled it with warm water and dish soap. "Royce gave her a promise ruby and it's got her all wound up. They were supposed to get married out of high school and it didn't work out. Now she's not sure if she wants to commit to him or not." As soon as the words were out of my mouth, I regretted them. *How did I not see that connection before?*

I grabbed a sponge and attacked the mixing bowl like I was teaching it who was boss. I wished I had time to bake some cookies. Baking was my defense mechanism the way a cat takes a bath when it falls off the table or a hockey goalie grabs his water bottle when the other team scores. Without baking I was awkwardly looking for something to do with my hands. *Maybe Gia won't notice.*

Gia started the water in the sanitizing sink. "What is it

with you two not wanting to commit to a man who loves you?"

I could feel my heart pounding through my chest. I scrubbed the mixing bowl like the muffins had baked and burned inside it. "I don't know. Maybe we're afraid of making a mistake and losing him forever."

"Love is built on friendship and respect. A man who truly loves you would not let that part of the relationship die just because the romance did not work out."

"True, but I think Aunt Ginny is just confused as to what her feelings really are."

Gia took the bowl from me, rinsed it, and dropped it in the sanitizer. "Maybe she needs to stop overthinking it and follow her heart."

I grabbed my measuring cups and scoured them in case any sugar bits had worked their way inside the metal. "I guess. But she may have spent most of her married life thinking about what it would have been like to be married to the other guy. She doesn't want to take that into another relationship. It isn't fair to anyone."

"Maybe the next time she needs to give all of her heart away to one man instead of holding a piece back."

I whacked the cups into the sanitizer and grabbed my whisk. "What if she doesn't know how? What if she's stuck in the past and doesn't know how to break free? People were hurt very badly before. She doesn't want to do it again."

"I think she needs to trust herself and take a leap of faith."

"But what if she leaps the wrong way?" I looked at Gia, my heart pleading with him to understand.

He leaned down and kissed the tip of my nose. "I will catch you. Even if you break my heart in two."

"I'm ba-ack. I knew that girl wouldn't—" Sawyer froze in the doorway. She turned around and retreated to the front.

Gia kissed me again, then turned and left the kitchen.

I waited a minute for my hands to stop shaking; then I tossed the whisk into the sanitizer.

Sawyer snuck back into the kitchen and sidled up to me. "Whoa. What was that all about? The hair on my arms is standing straight up. Did you just tell Gia you were choosing Tim?"

"Not exactly. We were talking about Aunt Ginny and then-" I didn't get to finish my story because Kim opened the back door. She was dressed in ripped pink tights and black shorts over combat boots, and she had on a Rage Against the Machine graffiti T-shirt that matched her bright pink spiky hair.

"Knock knock. Is it safe to come in?"

Sawyer took over the talking to give me a minute to get myself together. "Wow. Look at you. You're so pink."

"I've had too much time on my hands this week." Kim looked at me hard. "What's the matter?"

I started taking dishes out of the sanitizer to dry on the rack. "What? Nothing. I was up all night with Aunt Ginny in the hospital." *Well, that story came in handy.*

"What happened? Is she all right?"

Sawyer took Kim's elbow. "Come on. Let's go get a table and I'll tell you all about it. My coffee might almost be done. It's been at least thirty minutes since I ordered it."

My timer went off and I took the muffins out of the oven and set them aside to cool. Then I went to join the girls and try to hide that my heart was breaking.

Kim had set up her laptop and was typing furiously.

I joined them and a latte miraculously appeared at my

elbow. There was a heart of cocoa sprinkled into the foam. I looked up at Gia and his smile melted me down to the knees.

He placed a giant frothy drink covered in foam and dripping caramel in front of Sawyer. "What is that monstrosity?"

Sawyer gave him an evil grin.

He shook his head. "I can see I can't leave you two alone in here with the help yet." Gia took a towel and started working his way through the dining room wiping down tables.

I smiled to myself. *The help. Message received.*

Kim was looking back and forth from one of us to the other. Her forehead was scrunched so tight her eyebrow ring was saluting. "What is going on in here today?"

Sawyer tapped Kim's hand. "Nothing. What did you want to show us?"

"I've been at this for hours. Prepare yourselves. What I'm about to show you is shocking." Kim turned her laptop around to display the LinkedIn website. "I was updating my profile because . . . you know . . . I might be out of a job soon, and I got a connection suggestion for Robert Hinkle."

I sipped my latte. "Who is Robert Hinkle?"

"Guys . . . It's Cowboy Bob from the wine tour. He signed up for our newsletter. Once someone is in your contacts, LinkedIn will suggest them as people in your network. Anyway. I checked out his profile."

She clicked on a link and we were looking at a younger, fitter Cowboy Bob sans the ten-gallon hat, wearing a suit and tie with his arms crossed. He was standing in front of a window overlooking the New York City skyline.

I started reading his profile: "'CEO of Hinkle and Associates. Robert Hinkle is widely known in the industry as the Master of Spin.' Huh."

Sawyer turned the laptop to face her. "I don't suppose it's a coincidence that Hinkle and Associates is a Public Relations firm just like BakerCom?"

Kim moved the mouse and clicked on a link to open the company. "Not only is it not a coincidence, but look at who else has Hinkle on their profile."

The screen loaded and Sawyer gasped. "Vince Baker used to work for Cowboy Bob?"

Kim shook her head. "Oh, not just work for him. Vince was Bob's Vice President of Business Development. Until he staged a coup and took half the company with him." Kim pulled up a twenty-year-old press release from when Vince Baker launched BakerCom. It listed several clients, among whom were included four big celebrity names formerly with Hinkle and Associates.

Bob and Rosie's conversation from yesterday was starting to fill in a lot of gaps for me. "What happened to Hinkle and Associates?"

Kim pulled up another press release dated two years later. "Filed for bankruptcy and liquidated their assets. That must have been when Robert became Cowboy Bob and opened a tack shop. There is no mention of Robert Hinkle running or working for another PR firm after Hinkle and Associates closed their doors."

Sawyer took a sip of her drink and made a sound like the garbage disposal choking on a corncob. She pushed the Frankenlatte away from her. "Well, if that isn't a motive for murder . . . Vince Baker stole Cowboy Bob's empire." Sawyer turned to me. "Why aren't you more excited?"

I shook my head. "Bob and Rosie came in here yesterday morning and I overheard them talking. They didn't sound like they'd planned on running into Vince on the wine tour. I think they were surprised that he was here."

Kim lowered the laptop screen to talk over it. "Maybe they saw this as their opportunity to get revenge."

"I know they aren't sorry that he's dead, but if they killed him it had to be a last-minute crime of passion."

Sawyer drummed her fingers on the table. "So. That happens all the time, doesn't it? And Rosie did tell us they'd done that Pacific Coast Highway trip. They could easily have picked up the olives while they were out there."

Kim swiveled her head between us. "What olives? Why is that important?"

Sawyer ignored her question. "I think we need to tell Amber before she charges Sunny."

"I guess." I wasn't comfortable with this plan. I wanted to get Sunny released, but I didn't believe Bob and Rosie killed Vince. Maybe I should just tell Amber what we found. Like she said, I'm only an informant. "I think—"

The front door chimed and a little redhead in a hospital gown waltzed into the coffee shop. "Poppy? Oh good, I found you."

No one moved an inch.

"What are you doing here? You're supposed to be in the hospital until tomorrow."

"I broke out."

I was too bewildered to speak.

"I'm fed up with their poking and prodding and checking my vitals every few minutes. Who can get any rest with that poodunkery? I had Royce and Fiona drop me off."

"Why didn't you have her take you home?"

Aunt Ginny gave me a look like I was missing the whole point. "I wanted a cupcake." She called Sierra over and pointed to the last sangria cupcake in the case, then turned back to us. "What you-all doing here?"

After a beat, Kim said, "I was showing them that Vince stole Cowboy Bob's PR company."

"Well, how about that." Aunt Ginny shoved half the cupcake in her mouth just as Gia came out from the back office.

He froze in his steps and looked at me.

"She broke out."

Gia shook his head and laughed under his breath. "Dio mio."

Aunt Ginny swallowed her mouthful. "Do you think Bob and Rosie might have killed Vince for revenge?"

"Yes, that thought has crossed our minds. Why?"

Aunt Ginny shoved another bite of cupcake into her mouth and held up a finger. We waited for her to stop chewing and swallow again. "Because I just saw them at the house a minute ago loading their suitcases into the Winnebago."

Chapter Forty-two

Sawyer and I rushed Aunt Ginny to the car and sped home. I pulled up behind the Winnebago just as Rosie came out of the house with a bag of Douglass fudge. "Oh, Poppy. I'm so glad we caught you. It's over. We're going home."

Kim pulled down the street and parked her little VW Bug in front of the Winnebago much like one would use a butterfly net to trap a whale.

I took Rosie by the arm and tried to lead her up to the porch. "What's all over?"

"The investigation. The police have charged the daughter."

Aunt Ginny was still licking her fingers from the frosting. "Alyce? Why'd they charge her?"

The Winnebago honked like a goose with a cold.

Rosie looked around us and held up her hand to Bob, who was raring to go. "No, Sunny. The pretty one."

Oh no. Geez, Amber. "Sunny was Vince's wife."

"Well, that figures. They've just released the Winnebago this morning, so Bob and I are back on the road. Thank you for everything."

Across the yard I saw Sawyer open the passenger door to the goliath camper and climb in. She was going to question Bob to buy us some time.

"Rosie, before you head out, I need to ask you something."

Rosie huffed and looked around me. "Can you make it quick?"

"I was wondering how you found out about the wine tour?"

"The kids sent us on it for our anniversary."

"Oh." I felt a little deflated. I was so hoping she would say she won it in a sweepstakes. *There goes that theory.*

Rosie shifted her bag in her hand and looked at the Winnebago like she was planning to make a run for it. "Of course, neither of them will admit it. They've been playing this game that they had nothing to do with it. They even tried to trick us that they were worried it was a scam. They're two jokesters. It would have been very nice if Vince Baker hadn't been here."

Nope, the theory's alive. "I came across some information today that Cowboy Bob is Robert Hinkle of Hinkle and Associates."

Rosie's face drained of its color.

"And Vince Baker was responsible for sending you into bankruptcy."

Rosie took a step back. "Oh my. How did you ever find that out?"

"News articles. Plus, Bob has the connection on his LinkedIn profile."

Rosie shook her head. "Of all the idiotic—I knew that would come back to bite us. About fifteen years ago he thought he could get back in the game and started working with a headhunter to get another job on Wall Street. He updated his résumé on some website called Monster, and I guess that's when he made that ridiculous account. There aren't a lot of positions open for CEOs, especially for one who has already declared bankruptcy once and disappeared to the country for six years. I told him no good would come from it. We should just enjoy the farm and the tack shop and our daughter's horses and leave the business world behind. But nooo."

Aunt Ginny was leaning over hard, trying to peer into Rosie's bag of fudge.

Rosie clutched it tighter to herself.

I pulled Aunt Ginny back a few inches. "Did you know Vince Baker would be on the wine tour?"

Rosie's eyes went wild. "Absolutely not. When I saw him I nearly fainted. I wasn't sure if he recognized us since it had been so long. So, we kept our hats low and introduced ourselves as the Smiths and hoped he wouldn't look too closely at Bob. Of course, he was looking kinda green around the gills whenever he looked Bob's way, so maybe he was getting an inkling."

The Winnebago horn belched again, and the door opened and spit Sawyer out.

Aunt Ginny put her hands on her hips. "So, you think it was a coincidence that Bob and Vince ended up on the same tiny wine tour in the small town of Cape May?"

Rosie started to duck around me. For a large woman she was surprisingly light on her feet. "What else could it be?"

"But you just happened to be on the same tour where Vince was murdered."

Rosie faked me out and got around me. "Either that or someone is setting us up. Why do you think we're trying to get out of here? If the cops find out about our history with Vince, they'll suspect us. Sure, we had a motive to kill Vince Baker, a lot of people do, but my God, why would we wait twenty years? We have too much to lose now. We just got the Winnebago and had a grandbaby."

Aunt Ginny nudged me. "I hope she means that in the other order."

Sawyer arrived by my side and Rosie waddle-ran the rest of the way to the open passenger door.

I cupped my hands around my mouth and hollered after her, "Did you know anyone else from the tour before this week?"

Rosie hopped up in the camper and slammed the door. Bob released the air brakes and started the Winnebago rolling. They pulled away from the curb and had just cleared Kim's Bug when Rosie rolled her window down and stuck her head out. "The secretary!" They disappeared down the street out of view.

Kim ran across the lawn to join us. "Who is the secretary?"

"I don't know, but we need to find out fast. If Sunny's been charged that means everyone will be leaving soon."

My cell phone rang Van Halen and I answered it.

"Hey, gorgeous. What are you doing today?"

"I'm about to do some Internet research with the girls; why?"

"I just missed you. I don't like the way we left things yesterday. Why don't you bring the girls to Maxine's and I'll get you on the Wi-Fi. Then we can talk when you're done."

"I'd have to bring my laptop and everything."

"That's no problem. I'll make everyone coffee and dessert on the house."

Kim grabbed the phone from my hand. "We'll be right there!"

"I guess we're coming. Also, I need to turn my sound down."

Tim laughed. "I'll see you in ten."

Aunt Ginny grabbed my arm. "I'm going to change while you get your laptop. Do not leave without me."

I promised I would wait and ran in the house to get my laptop and charger. I had to grab seven new Amazon packages off the porch. *We so don't have time for this.*

Ken and Willow were in the library having an argument.

Ken was on his knees in front of Willow. "Why can't we just put it behind us?"

Willow was curled up in a ball like a pill bug. "You will never understand what it was like for me."

I passed Ryan and Alyce's room on the first landing and overheard argument number two. "Alyce, get it together. We are so close. Don't screw this up now by doing something stupid."

Tammy Faye thought we were playing a game and raced me up the steps. I grabbed my stuff from my office and on the way back down heard Zara in the dining room. She had Chinese takeout from around the corner and was laying a feast with the table set for three guests. "Are you expecting company?"

She looked at me questioningly. "No."

"Okay. Enjoy."

Aunt Ginny lapped me and was waiting by the swing. "I'm starving. Do you think Tim could make me a sandwich?"

"I don't know. We can ask him."

"I'd like having a chef in the family. I need someone on call twenty-four-seven who can bring me dinner."

"I thought that's what I was for."

"Yeah, but I don't always want salad."

Sawyer beeped her horn and Aunt Ginny and I piled into her car and Kim followed us over to the marina in her Bug. I was turning out to be a terrible informant. I was too late to stop the Hinkles. I was too late to keep Sunny from being charged. And I didn't know who the secretary was. But I was determined not to rest until I found out who murdered Vince Baker.

Chapter Forty-three

We arrived a few minutes later at Maxine's. We pulled into the empty pre-dinner parking lot and Sawyer yelled, "Eww! Who hung up that creepy Gigi crab?"

It was like my eyes were taking in colors I had never seen before. I had looked right at those perky curls the day Tim proudly displayed Maxine. I knew it was familiar in an unsettling way, but now that Sawyer called it the Gigi crab it was so obvious. *If this restaurant is going to be half-mine, he's going to have to take that down. Then I'm going to set it on fire.*

Tim set us up in a corner booth with curtains. "This is the most private table I have. Guys usually reserve it when they want to propose or cheat on their wives."

I raised my eyebrows at him, and he countered, "Which I would never condone the second one."

He kissed me and the girls teased me about it. He pulled me around the corner away from their eyes and kissed me again. "You know I will always love you, Mack. Gigi will never get between us again."

Maybe now is not the best time to bring up the crab. He was being so sweet, but I still couldn't shake Madame Zolda's words about another woman being in the way. Would I ever be able to trust Tim with Gigi? *What's wrong with me? I've loved Tim my whole life and Madame Zolda is a crackpot.*

"I believe you."

Tim pulled me close. "Good. How about I make you some of those pork roll sandwiches you like."

"Uhh, I hate to tell you this, but I haven't had pork roll in twenty years."

"Really?"

"Yeah, I think it's disgusting."

"How do you just stop liking pork roll?"

"I don't know. I guess I just grew out of it."

"Okay. How about some cheesecake shooters?"

I gave a nod. "There ya go."

"Okay, good. You go do your research."

I rejoined the girls who were all deep in their social media accounts trying to find out which tour member was the secretary Rosie had recognized. Kim was searching for any mention of BakerCom in old news articles, they'd set Aunt Ginny up with Facebook and a list of names to check, and Sawyer was all over Zara's website and Instagram.

"I think you'll really like the Chinese restaurant picture that's coming up. I hear she's eating with Taylor Swift tonight."

Sawyer snickered.

I turned my laptop to LinkedIn and went back to Hinkle and Associates. I'd already searched for Zara and Willow and found nothing. Now I was scanning faces and titles. There wasn't a single person I recognized. But then maybe the secretary didn't have a LinkedIn account. Someone who didn't want to be found would stay off the grid.

I nudged Sawyer. "What did you and Cowboy Bob talk about when you trapped him in the Winnebago?"

Sawyer gave me a droll look. "What it was like working with Vinny the pincher."

Aunt Ginny didn't look up from her screen. "Oh, he was one of those."

"One of what?" I asked.

"The kind of man who can't keep his hands to himself."

Sawyer nodded. "Apparently, Bob had to discipline Vince when he worked for him because one of the *gals* had accused him of being *handsy*."

Kim looked over her laptop screen. "Sexual harassment?"

Sawyer shook her head. "Bob didn't call it that. He said the secretaries wore tight skirts and it riled the men up sometimes."

What a difference a couple generations make. "So, what happened to Vinny?"

Sawyer shook her head. "Nothing. He told Vince to keep his hands to himself and a few months later Vince stole the company from him."

Kim asked, "What happened to the woman?"

Sawyer rolled her eyes. "He said he didn't remember."

Tim brought out shooters of my strawberry wine tiramisu and Moscato cheesecake.

Aunt Ginny grabbed three cups and put one in her purse. "What? It's for later."

I let Sawyer's news roll around my brain for a minute. "Maybe we've been looking at this all wrong. Maybe it was never about Vince's money. We've been so focused on his will and who would inherit that we missed other motives. What if this whole time it's been someone with a score to settle with . . . Vinny the pincher. Kim, you said Jess was groped by Ryan, right?"

Kim nodded. "That's what Jess said."

I continued. "But on the security video, Ryan was standing next to Vince all night."

Kim nodded again. "He was stuck to him like the IRS on a small business."

"Well, what if Ryan didn't grope Jess? What if it was Vince using Ryan as a shield?"

Kim nodded slowly. "I see where you're going with this, but surely Vince would have recognized a woman who'd worked for him?"

"Would he? What if she changed her appearance?" Images flashed in my mind of the brown wig that Tammy Faye mauled. Ken had said Willow was sick and I'd assumed cancer and marriage problems. But what if it was something else? Something dark. "We need to find out which woman used to work with Vince."

I switched from Hinkle to BakerCom and started following links until I found an article in *PR Review* written by Vince Baker in 2010. He had the entire team of BakerCom in a group photo. I scanned it to confirm my suspicions, and then I saw someone familiar standing at the end of the row.

Before I could show the girls what I'd discovered, Sawyer slapped the table with both hands. "Found ya!" She turned her tablet over to show us a picture of Zara Pinette in grade school. She had long straight brown hair and giant rimmed glasses. "I've been looking for this for days. She posted it on Facebook two years ago for Throwback Thursday."

I examined the picture closely and compared it to current Instagram posts. "She's dyed her hair dark and had some work done, because that is not her current nose."

Aunt Ginny glanced at the screen and went back to her Facebook account. "She's had a facelift too."

I looked at the picture. "Why do you say that?"

"Unless she was in a play that was set a decade earlier, that picture is from the seventies. You can tell by the hairstyle, the glasses, and the collar on her dress. If she's really in her early thirties, like we assumed, she'd have been born in the middle of the eighties and all of that would be entirely different."

I looked at Aunt Ginny in admiration. Sometimes that crazy old lady was the sharpest one in the room.

Kim took another look at the photo. "What's that at the bottom?"

Sawyer leaned in closer. "I think it's her name, but that is not a *Z*."

Kim put her hand out to Sawyer. "Here, let me see it."

Sawyer handed Kim the tablet.

She did some clicking and typing, then hit Enter. Then Kim leaned back in her chair. "Whoa."

I held my breath. "What is it?"

Kim flipped the tablet over. "Meet Jane Anderson, first-grade class of 1979." It was the exact same picture, only expanded to show the entire page and the caption.

"How'd you do that?" I asked.

"Reverse image search."

We were all stunned, but Sawyer was hit the hardest. "She's forty-two!"

Aunt Ginny shrugged. "I told you she's had work done."

Sawyer took back the tablet and started tapping again. "But did she ever work for Vince?" After a minute, she took a deep breath and blew it out. "Jane Anderson was a publicist with BakerCom from '96 to '99." She showed us Jane's LinkedIn account. "It hasn't been updated since BakerCom."

Aunt Ginny calmly scrolled through her Facebook pages. "That's probably when she changed her name to Zara Pinette, moved away, and gave herself a makeover."

Kim clapped her hands. "That's her. That's Zara with the old nose and old name. And she worked for Vince. Oh, thank God, Daniel didn't do it."

Sawyer shook her hands out. "I can't believe we found it. She has to be our killer."

"Well, I don't know if she is or not." I turned my computer around so they could see the group photo in *PR Review.*

Kim covered her mouth and pointed.

Sawyer's mouth dropped open and she gasped.

I nodded at both of them. "Picture her with a brown wig and remove the glasses. It's Willow. Only, if the caption is to be believed, she's Susan Wright, Public Relations Specialist."

Aunt Ginny scrunched her face up. "So, they both worked at BakerCom?"

I looked at the group shot. "And not at the same time either. Zara—er, Jane—was only there from '96 to '99. This picture of Willow, aka Susan Wright, is from 2010."

Sawyer shook her head. "So, which one of them killed Vince?"

Aunt Ginny looked up from her Facebook search. "We need some coffee. This tour wasn't a group of strangers. They were all connected through Vince Baker. It's obvious that one of them planned his murder and filled the room with viable suspects to hide themselves in plain sight." Then Aunt Ginny clicked her cheek twice. "Miss Marple."

I left our little snug. Maxine's was about to start their dinner service in about an hour. Normally the bar would make the coffee, but it was still a little early for anyone to be there, so I went to the kitchen. Tim was busy with some giant fish he was cutting into steaks, so I asked Chuck to make us some coffee when he had the chance.

I took the coffee cups and cream and sugar back to the table with me. When I arrived, everyone was huddled around Aunt Ginny's laptop.

Sawyer looked up. "You won't believe what she found."

"What?"

Aunt Ginny grinned at me. "I found Zara's movie."

I cast a questioning glance at Sawyer.

"We all Googled Vince Baker, and Zara, and sexual harassment, and stuff like that—and Aunt Ginny found a link to the ZaraLife vlog from last August titled 'Bad Bosses and Sexual Harassment—My Time with Pervert Vince.'"

I unloaded my tray and set the table. "Well, go on. Let's hear it."

Kim showed me the tablet. "We can't find it. When we follow the link, it's got this four-oh-four error and says it's been removed. She must have taken it down so it wouldn't incriminate her."

Chuck set the French press on the table. "Did you try searching the Google cache?"

I took my seat. "Search the what?"

Chuck pointed at the laptop. "Search the Google cache."

I spun the laptop to face me. "How do I do that, Chuck?"

"It's very easy. Open a browser and go to Google dot-com and type cache colon less than web address greater than in the search box, along with the URL you're looking for, and hit Enter. Or we can use the Wayback Machine."

"I don't know what any of that means."

Chuck took out a pair of glasses and put them on. "Sure you do. Colon is the two dots and less than looks like an alligator coming toward you—"

I spun the laptop toward him. "Don't teach me to fish, Chuck—just hand me the sushi."

Chuck squatted down and started typing. "What are you looking for?"

We told him, "The ZaraLife vlog on bad bosses and sexual harassment from her website."

He seemed slightly mortified and a little uneasy, but after a few more taps he smiled. "Nothing is really ever removed from the Internet. Here it is."

"Chuck, you're my hero."

He blushed and pushed his glasses up on the bridge of his nose. "It was nothing."

"Good Lord. The video has had two million views." Zara was frozen on-screen making a face. I clicked Play and she came to life.

We poured the coffee and watched Zara talk about a terrible boss who she had in her twenties: "Let's just call him Pervert Vince. Vince loved to promote women within the organization as long as they'd give a little something to him after hours. You know what I'm talking about, ladies. Vince made my life hell. I was just out of college and so excited to be doing something with my communications degree, but then my boss asked me out. I knew that was a bad idea, plus I was so not interested. So, I turned him down. Then he blocked my advancement and shut down all my ideas. And he said he'd keep doing it until I made him feel like I really appreciated my position in the company. And in case you're still confused, here's how he wanted me to show him my appreciation."

Zara went on to describe the sexual intimidation and lewd acts that Pervert Vince considered acceptable compensation for the pleasure of working for him. At one point she broke down. "I was utterly humiliated. I vomited in the parking lot; then I went home and scalded myself in the shower. I scrubbed myself with Ajax and still didn't feel clean. I never went back to work. I didn't resign; I just stopped going in. The horrifying thing is, women were being promoted there all the time. They weren't in positions of real power, but they were advanced. Were they all doing what I wouldn't? I was never going to go anywhere, because I refused to play his game.

But when he started to take from me what I wasn't giving, and wouldn't take no for an answer, I had to get out."

The video ended and we sat in silence. We had all had a Pervert Vince in our lives. Every one of us had a scar of shame permanently fused in our memory. The stain of humiliation that robbed us of our innocence and soured our joy into loathing and then rage. We had each risen above it, but in our silence we had failed to keep our sisters safe.

If Zara killed Vince I understood why. I had the urge to go in the kitchen and hug Tim or call Gia and curl up into his arms. Anything to be with a man who was good and kind and didn't hurt women just because he could.

My heart was torn for Sunny. I didn't want to see her go to prison for something she didn't do. Justice can't turn a blind eye because the victim is a monster. But how in the world could she have married him? Maybe she really was only in it for the money.

Sawyer scrolled down. Her voice was a little shaky. "There's a chat log under the video."

There were hundreds of comments from both men and women who shared their own wounds of harassment and assault. They each were carrying the burden of shame that was forced upon them. Men apologized on behalf of their entire sex, and Internet trolls alleged that Zara might have done something to lead her boss on or she should have handled it a myriad of other ways.

Aunt Ginny read one of the comments. "This woman says she worked with Vinny and tried to report him to HR. She got fired because she had no proof."

Kim read another one. "Someone left a response to that. This woman says she also worked for Vinny. She reported him for sexual harassment, and they settled out of court. She's never been able to forgive herself for taking the settlement. These two go on and talk to each other for a couple of days."

Sawyer asked, "Does Zara ever comment?"

Kim scrolled down to the bottom. "No. The last comment was left two months after the vlog aired: 'We should stop talking about it and do something.'"

My phone rang and showed Cape May County on the caller ID. "Hello?"

"McAllister, I have the official toxicology report. I thought you'd like to hear it considering what happened to Aunt Ginny."

I turned the laptop around to face me and opened a browser. "Absolutely." I had a suspicion that wouldn't let me go. I listened to Amber as I searched.

"Vince Baker was killed by a lethal cocktail of alcohol, propofol—a hypnotic—and phenobarbital—a sedative. Each item alone was not administered in high enough concentrations to kill him, but all three combined become toxic. His blood alcohol level was point-one-one. Much higher than it should be after just ten ounces of wine, especially given his weight and the amount of food in his system."

"Sure." I found an old Public Relations Awards Banquet that mentioned Hinkle and Associates and clicked the link.

"We know there was grain alcohol in the perfume bottle. The crime lab has confirmed traces of grain alcohol in one of the glasses of wine that has Vince's DNA on it, and the results came in today to confirm that the powder Aunt Ginny was exposed to was in fact the phenobarbital that was in the peas."

My screen loaded the archives of the Public Relations Society of America annual banquet where Hinkle and Associates won the award for PR firm of the year before they went bankrupt. I scrolled through the photographs until I saw her.

"Are you listening to me, McAllister?"

"I found the secretary."

Chapter Forty-four

I stood in the dining room in front of Zara, Willow, Ken, and an empty chair. The guests were not shy about telling me they didn't appreciate being delayed for their departures. Zara was waiting for her ride to take her to the airport. Her suitcases sat by the front door waiting for an Uber that I never called in. Ken and Willow were waiting for AAA to come change the tire on their car that had a chef knife sunk eight inches deep into the side. And I was waiting for my last guest.

The doorbell rang and I opened it to let in Lily Snow from the Pink Sandals Boutique Tours. "Did they all get off okay? I thought I saw the Masons' car out front."

I ushered Lily into the dining room to join the others. She stopped short when she saw the lineup. "What's going on? I hope no one gave you any trouble staying at the B and B. I have two more tours I want to bring to you next month."

"That will have to wait. Have a seat please."

Lily looked nervously at the others and took the empty seat on the end.

"So, here's the thing. I know what you did. And I understand why you did it. And I'm pretty sure I know how you pulled it off."

Willow started to rock silently in her seat.

The blood drained from Ken's face. He didn't move.

Zara's eyes hardened to steel. "I have no idea what you're talking about."

Lily stood up. "I can see you're having a guest dispute. I'll just get out of your way—"

"Sit down, Lily. I know you're the mastermind behind Vince Baker's murder."

Lily shifted her eyes around the room. "What? Of course I'm not."

I stood up and slowly turned around. "I'm not wired. You can check if you want."

Lily dropped down to her chair and casually crossed her legs. "Why don't you tell me what you think happened and I'll see if I can help you."

"I know the three of you have worked either with or for Vince Baker, and I know he sexually harassed each one of you."

The women scoffed and shook their heads. Willow put her hands on her belly and rolled her eyes. Only Ken gave away that he was surprised when his eyes widened and he made a sharp intake of breath.

Zara coolly folded her hands in her lap. "Don't you

think he would have recognized us when we all met for happy hour if we'd worked for him?"

"I think he did recognize you. Despite the fact that you've had a nose job, you're wearing a wig and glasses, and you've aged twenty years and lost about fifty pounds. I think he was very nervous that he was being set up for a confrontation and he was trying to get out of the tour before his wife found out."

Lily held her arms out. "Don't you see how ridiculous this is? None of us have met before this week, let alone worked together. I've been a tour guide in South Jersey for the past twenty years. How in the world could I mastermind this fanciful plot you've imagined and bring people from all over the United States?"

"You all found each other after Zara . . . Jane . . . posted her vlog about Pervert Vince and told the world she'd been sexually assaulted. You have quite the following, Zara, and your video about sexual harassment went viral in no time."

Zara snorted. "I've never heard of this vlog you're talking about. Where is it?"

"Oh, I know you think you deleted it, but nothing is ever really gone from the Internet. The shortcuts may be removed, and you might be redirected to an error page, but your video is still very much there. I watched it an hour ago."

Zara's eyes lost their hardness and sweat was starting to bead on her upper lip. "You're lying."

"Then how do I know you all met each other through the comment log? When you discovered you were connected through Vince it didn't take long before you were chatting offline."

I looked at Willow. "Susan, you gave in to Vince's

pressure to get the promotion. And after, when the regret settled in, you told HR about the harassment and they paid you off to keep quiet. Am I right?"

Willow had tears streaming down her face.

I handed her a box of tissues. "You've never been able to get past the disgust you feel, so you fill your life with good works and helping people, hoping it will be enough to eventually forgive yourself. I'm also guessing that your husband's affair came about in part because of the strain from the lack of intimacy. It's common to have trouble making a physical and emotional connection after what you've been through, and yours is still pretty recent."

Ken wouldn't look at me, but the pain in his eyes gave him away.

I turned to Lily. "You told Robert Hinkle about the harassment. When Vince denied it, he fired you. Women aren't always taken seriously or treated fairly, and the company took Vince's side. You blamed Bob for not having your back with the allegations, so you set him and Rosie up with a free vacation package and hoped the police would find out about the coup and the bankruptcy. Bob was supposed to be your fall guy on the tour. A tour that you set up with a phony sweepstakes sent to Sunny at her old email address—easily obtained off the Internet or by anyone who had worked for BakerCom since they're all the same."

Lily's jaw tightened and the lines around her eyes deepened. "What does any of this have to do with Vince Baker's death? Everyone in that winery will testify that none of us attacked Vince in any way. We may have detested the man, but that doesn't mean that we killed him."

"The evidence says that you did."

"What evidence? The police haven't questioned me since we left the wine tasting. They don't even know what killed him."

Willow turned from weepy to defiant. "I think you're crazy. I don't even know these other women, and I'd certainly never met the guy who died before. Isn't that right, baby?"

Ken flexed his jaw and wouldn't look at his wife.

I squatted in front of Willow. "So, what if I told you that the police know exactly what killed Vince? And that I know you were responsible for dosing the wasabi peas? You knew he loved them from working with him, and you could have easily stolen the phenobarbital from the women's shelter where you volunteer."

Willow shifted in her seat and her pupils dilated. "I'd say you don't know what you're talking about. If I was carrying around a bowl of wasabi peas covered in drugs someone would have noticed."

"No one would have thought to look in the niche you carved inside your fake pregnancy pillow. My chambermaid found it with your wig. You could have sidled up to the table when the wine arrived and everyone was getting their glass and reached under your maternity blouse to extract the bowl and place it before Vince."

Willow started to cry, and Ken snapped at her. "Oh my God, Susan. You could have killed everyone in the place. Is that why we're here? Why I have to pretend your name's Willow and you're pregnant? I thought it was so you'd forgive me for Barbara. But you needed to commit murder to get over what happened to you five years ago?"

Willow pleaded with Ken, "I didn't use that much. Even if everyone had some, they wouldn't have died from it. I made sure."

I stood up and my knees cracked. "That's true. Because they planned the ingredients to work together. Lily's job was to add the grain alcohol from the perfume bottle to Vince's port, and serve it to him when he sent back a dry wine. Zara was in charge of bringing the olives spiked with propofol with her from Portland and getting them on the table."

Zara gave me a tiny nod.

"What I want to know is how did you get Sunny's fingerprints on the jar?"

Zara's smile didn't reach her eyes. "All their fingerprints are on the jar. I put it on the table next to Alyce when Lily made a fuss serving one of the wines and had everyone distracted. Then I moved to the other side of the table and asked them to pass it down. I even ate one."

"Yeah, you were yawning when we talked. And I gather that you snuck out of the patio enclosure to throw the jar in the dumpster after Vince collapsed?"

She tipped her chin to her chest.

"You were all so clever. You diluted everything so that no one drug was enough to kill Vince by itself; they only became lethal when combined. So why did you take the evidence up to your rooms? Willow, why didn't you get rid of the powdered phenobarbital?"

Willow turned pleading eyes on me. "I was going to do it when Ken went to play golf, but then it disappeared from my room. I thought maybe the maid stole it and I was free."

I turned to Zara. "And why keep the bottle with grain alcohol on your dresser? Why not ditch it at the winery with the olive jar?"

Zara turned a withering glance on Lily. "She didn't give it back to me until we got to Angel of the Sea. I tried to get rid of it when I came to your house. I put it in Sunny Baker's suite when she was downstairs. I figured since she was the prime suspect, I could help the police along, but it showed back up in my room the next day. I was going to move it again when I came up from breakfast, but you lot were standing in my room holding the bottle."

"How did you even get your hands on grain alcohol and anesthesia drugs?"

Zara shrugged one shoulder. "I live in Portland."

Lily let out a dramatic lingering sigh that ended with a groan. "Uhh. This is all very cathartic and all, but what's the point, Poppy? Are you doing research for a book or something? What difference is it to you that we knocked off one more predator? Think of all the young women he can't hurt now."

I held my hands up to calm her down. "Like I said, I get it. And you were real smart about it too. My problem is that Sunny Baker has been charged with murder and she's on her way to Edna Mahan women's prison to await her trial. You didn't just take Vince's life. You took Sunny's too."

Lily shook it off. "I can't help if she's collateral damage. She was Vince's secretary for two years. She had to know what he was like. As far as I'm concerned, she's just as guilty as he is if she knew what he was doing and didn't try to stop him from hurting anyone else. What would you do if it were you who was assaulted? Or your daughter? Or your best friend? Would you turn away and say nothing?"

I looked Lily in the eyes. There was crazy there, but I understood how it was born. "I do know what I would do. And I know I wouldn't commit murder to seek revenge."

"Well, that's too bad." Lily unzipped her down vest and pulled out a small semi-automatic. She pointed it at my chest, and I felt my breathing slow down. I could hear my every heartbeat and the space in between.

Zara dove on the floor. Willow squeaked like a mouse and Ken pulled her behind him.

Zara's wobbly voice came from under the table: "We agreed that the only one to get hurt would be Vince Baker."

Lily kept the gun trained on me. "We also agreed to wait for the last day of the wine tour to kill him and genius here pulled out the wasabi peas on day one."

Willow's voice was muffled through Ken's chest: "I had to. His daughter and son-in-law weren't supposed to be part of the tour and their arguing was driving Ken crazy. He was threatening to call off the trip and go home."

Ken yelled at Willow, "If I'd known you were going to kill someone, I'd have never agreed to the trip in the first place. You need counseling!"

I watched in slow motion as Lily waved the gun over her head. "Everybody just shut up before one of the neighbors calls the cops. I've already lost the last eighteen years of my life because of what Vince did to me! I'm not going to go to prison for the rest."

Time sped up by the end of her speech and I shook myself. "*Gun. Gun.* Lily! Put *the gun* down! Do not *shoot* me!"

Lily's eyes popped whiter and she ducked down. "Who are you talking to? Is someone here?"

Oh my God, Amber. Now! I picked up Tammy Faye's crystal water ashtray from the end table and hurled it at the side of Lily's head. The gun went off and chunks of plaster fell from around my chandelier. Willow and Ken dove under the dining room table with Zara. Lily dropped to her knees like Victory having an episode.

The dining room door swung open and Tammy Faye galloped into the room and launched herself through the air at Lily, latching on to her calf with her tiny jaws.

Lily cried out in pain and Amber—finally—busted through the dining room door with her gun drawn, followed by Aunt Ginny, Sawyer, Kim, and all the biddies armed with various kitchen tools.

Aunt Ginny's Alexa beeped and started to play Neil Diamond's "Sweet Caroline."

"Everyone stay where you are." Amber spoke into her radio clipped to her shoulder, "Bravo Team, move in."

Officers Birkwell and Crabtree kicked in the front door, which was a lot of overkill because it wasn't even locked, and Officer Consuelos ran in from the side porch. They held their guns on Lily and Ken.

Amber held her gun on the group under the table. "Lily Snow, Jane Anderson, and Susan Wright. You're under arrest for the murder of Vince Baker."

The music was building to the crescendo. Amber looked around the room. "What is that? What's going on?"

Nobody moved.

When we finally got to the chorus and the "*bah bah bah*" Aunt Ginny gave a sheepish grin. "Oh. I forgot. That's the alarm for my mac 'n' cheese. . . . I'll just go get that." She backed out of the room and Amber cut her eyes to me.

"Crabtree. Read them their rights."

Amber holstered her gun while the other officers zip-tied the women's wrists and hauled them out to the waiting cruisers.

"Amber. What the crap took you so long to come in here?"

"Good Lord, McAllister. How do you get anything done around here? Aunt Ginny has every old lady in town crammed into that kitchen setting up a sting asking me if they can hold my gun and try on my body armor. And that cat of yours kept doing this god-awful moaning thing. I think something's wrong with it. I didn't hear you say the go word."

I took off my top blouse to get at the tactical vest I had on underneath. "I must have said 'gun' five or six times."

Amber helped me unlatch it. "I don't think you did. I only saw you making finger guns through the monitor in the kitchen right before I came in here." She pulled the vest over my head and I fluffed out my T-shirt.

"Yeah, well, we'll have to watch it again. 'Cause I'm pretty sure I almost died just now waiting for you to make the arrest."

Amber handed me my ponytail holder. "Now you're just being dramatic. But I have to admit, you did a halfway decent job of not screwing it up. And that nanny cam was a good idea."

Aunt Ginny called from the kitchen, "Come 'n' get it!" and we started toward the kitchen.

I dropped my head to look down to Amber. "Are you kidding me? I did great. I think you're gonna want to ask for my help all the time."

Amber shut her eyes and scoffed, "That is never going to happen. This was a onetime thing and only because I was desperate."

"Yeah. We'll see."

Chapter Forty-five

"Isn't it funny how six months ago you were accused of killing a cheerleader, by a cheerleader, and now you're fighting tooth and nail to prove a third cheerleader's innocence?" Aunt Ginny came out of her bedroom dressed in a long black Victorian gown with a veil and gloves. She was carrying the Alexa device.

"It's not like I have something against all cheerleaders everywhere. Have you been taking that thing to bed with you?"

She walked over to the counter and plugged the device in. "I like to listen to music as I fall asleep."

"You also talk to it in your sleep. And apparently order cotton candy sugar." I held up the newly arrived package.

Aunt Ginny raised her eyebrows and paused. "Oh, I do not. But while we're on the subject, I have two more Alexas I want you to set up for me."

Alexa responded, "Sorry, I don't know that one."

Oh no. No way. "The last thing you need is a new Alexa. You've created chaos having just one."

Alexa responded, "'Agent of Chaos' by Hans Zimmer, starting now."

Music began to play, and I had to tell Alexa to stop. *Note to self: change the ordering permissions on Amazon.* "What are you dressed up as?"

Aunt Ginny attached a cameo brooch at her throat. "Victory and I are going over to Cold Spring Village this afternoon to charge people ten dollars to take our picture."

Of all the illegal ideas Aunt Ginny had this one was probably the safest. "Have fun with that."

I heard Ryan and Alyce argue their way down the steps to checkout. I met them in the foyer. "Well, you're off then."

Alyce opened her mouth to say something and Ryan cut her off. "We have an appointment with the lawyer at one to officially begin proceedings to contest the will; then we have to meet with Sunny and the funeral director tonight to make the burial arrangements. So, we have a busy day."

I now understood why Alyce's face was so pinched. "I wish you both the best of luck."

Ryan cuffed me on the shoulder. "Girl, we're coming back next month. Alyce has convinced me that she wants to come to the shore a lot more often, so we'll see you again."

Alyce gave me a sly grin.

"Ryan, I've been meaning to ask you. I caught you coming out of Zara Pinette's room at the beginning of the week. I thought you might be planting evidence, but you were actually returning something, weren't you?"

Ryan took his hat off and squeezed it into shape. "I saw that Zara lady breaking into Vince and Sunny's room with that glass bottle. I didn't know for sure what she was doing, but I knew she couldn't be trusted. I know a fake Instagram post when I see it. Nobody who is friends with Khloé Kardashian would be staying here. No offense."

How is that no offense?

"So, I thought I'd mess with her and put the bottle back in her room to see what she'd do about it."

How are these people getting into each other's rooms? Second note to self: call security company to add dead bolts.

Alyce made a face at Ryan. "We have to go now."

"When is your-all's five-year anniversary?"

Alyce answered, "Four and a half years."

I give you six months. "Best of luck." I waved goodbye as they went out the door.

I heard the sound of porcelain scraping across my cherrywood table and poked my head into the library. Figaro was on the arm of the couch hissing at Tammy Faye, who had her snoot on one of Aunt Ginny's figurines and was pushing it toward the edge. "Tammy Faye! Bad girl!"

The little Pom jumped, and when she realized she'd been caught she whimpered and covered her snoot with her paws.

I rubbed Figaro's head. "She's been framing you all week, hasn't she, baby?" Fig pushed against my hand. "I'm sorry I ever believed you had anything to do with these transgressions."

Tammy whimpered again.

Figaro sat up extra tall and wrapped his tail delicately around his feet. He deserved a little gloating time and I let him have it.

Sunny came down the stairs with a *thump thump thump*, dragging a rolling suitcase behind her. I met her at the bottom of the steps, and she threw her arms around my neck and hugged me. "This is the last of it. I've called for a car to take me to the airport and they should be here soon. Thank you so much for everything. I owe my freedom to you."

"I am so sorry for your loss. I know you have some tough days ahead, but in time it will start to get better."

"I really loved Vince. I know Alyce and Ryan think I only married him for his money, but he was wonderful to me. I just can't believe he ever did those things to the other women. I don't believe it and I don't know if I ever will."

"Was there ever a time when you turned Vince down?"

Sunny smiled and shook her head. "No. It was love at first sight. He was always a gentleman. The first date we went on I just knew. I was never unsure of how I felt a day of my life with Vince. I don't know what I'm going to do without him." A tear slid down her cheek. She wiped it off and gave a little laugh. "I'm not going to start that again. I have to make funeral arrangements this afternoon."

"I thought Alyce and Ryan said they had to meet you at the funeral home this evening."

Sunny grinned. "I may have given them the wrong time." A sedan pulled into the driveway and a driver got out and stood by the car. Sunny whistled for Tammy Faye, who came running. She packed the tiny Pom in her carrying bag.

I put my hand in for a lick. "Bye, Tammy Faye. Thank you for biting Lily for me."

Tammy gave a little bark.

Figaro came over to stand in the foyer with me to say goodbye.

Sunny gave me one last hug and went out the door. As soon as the car pulled out of the driveway, Figaro flopped over.

"Oh, baby. You're going to miss her, aren't you?" I picked Fig up and snuggled him.

Victory rose up from the floor behind the couch in the library. She was in the Victorian maid uniform again and a Post-it note was stuck to her forehead. "Ees doggie gone?"

I jumped. *Geez, Victory!* "I'm afraid so. Aren't you supposed to be cleaning the bedrooms?"

Aunt Ginny came down the hall. "Did everybody leave?"

I nodded. "That was the last one."

Victory pulled the Post-it note off her forehead and read it. "'Do not tell Poppy I speill somesing on couch.' Oops."

I shook my head at the walking disaster who was my chambermaid. "You know you're a mess, don't you?"

Victory looked at Aunt Ginny and giggled. "Yes. I'm sorry. I'm only here to earn money for university. In Ukraine I study to be nuclear fission expert."

Well, that can't be right.

Aunt Ginny leaned into me. "Thank God the US is not in the fallout zone."

The front door opened, and Sawyer walked in. She stared me down and my stomach bottomed out.

Aunt Ginny took my hand. "It's time. Are you ready for this?"

Chapter Forty-six

"I'm freaking out a little bit." My hands were shaking, and I couldn't catch my breath.

The biddies were sitting around the island watching me like birds on a bare branch. Kim and Connie were sitting at the banquette with tissues and ice cream at the ready.

Sawyer put her hand on my arm. "Just calm down. This isn't life-or-death."

"It feels like it is. It's the death of a relationship. Probably a friendship."

Aunt Ginny set a cup of tea down in front of me. "You have been letting fear stop you from falling in love for far too long."

"What if I make the wrong decision? My track record is not so good."

Sawyer shook her head. "Honey, you were eighteen years old and away from home for the first time."

Aunt Ginny rolled her eyes. "You didn't even really make a decision, you made a mistake, and let Georgina bully you for the next twenty years."

I had to will my stomach to calm down. I was always prone to nervous nausea. This was no time to throw up. "I loved John. With all my heart. But I spent the first few years of our marriage wondering what might have been. I don't want to be in that agony again."

Connie folded her hands in front of her. "I've been married to Mike for eighteen years, most of them happy, and I still wonder what it would have been like to marry Jason Seymore, who took me to Senior Prom. I think it's just part of life."

Kim nodded at Connie. "I love Rick and I know we'll be together for the rest of our lives, but some days I wish I'd moved to Florence right after high school and studied art."

Aunt Ginny waved her hand. "You need to stop being scared to be wrong and take a chance to be happy."

My lip trembled. "I just want to be loved."

Sawyer cocked her head and took my hand. "Honey, look around. You are loved."

I looked around the room at all the kindness pouring from each woman and the encouragement in their smiles. They'd all embraced me as one of their own from the moment I'd returned home in a funk from the high school reunion. Every lady in here would walk to the ends of the earth for me. They were all my ride or die girls and they inspired me to live my life to the fullest with them. Figaro wound himself around my ankles and purred. All the love I ever needed was right in this room.

Aunt Ginny stood up. "I've made a decision."

Uh-oh.

"Somebody give me a quarter."

Oh God, where is this going?

Everyone started digging through their pockets and bags for loose change. Mrs. Davis had her hand down in her bra. I couldn't process that right now.

"Do I have a say in this?"

Aunt Ginny looked at me. "No."

Connie fished a quarter out of her purse and held it up. It may as well have been the hangman's noose.

Aunt Ginny took the quarter and stood over me. "We decide now. Everyone in this room agrees that you need to make a decision about a man before you lose them both."

I saw nods all around. *Traitors.*

"This decision is not for our sakes. It's for yours."

Oh, I do not have a good feeling about this.

"Consider this your intervention."

Do I really need an intervention?

"I'm going to flip this coin, and whoever it lands on, you're going to be with him officially."

Mmm, I don't know. . . .

"Heads it's Gia; tails it's Tim."

"Wait!"

"We're doing this."

"No."

Aunt Ginny flipped the coin high in the air.

Oh my God. No no no.

It spun so slowly I could see George Washington's face grinning at me with every turn. Everything else faded away and all I could see was the glint of the silver with each rotation. My heart rose up to my throat.

Aunt Ginny caught it and slapped it on her wrist. She lifted her hand and peeked at it.

I held my breath.

Aunt Ginny looked me in the eye. "That moment, right there. From the time I let the quarter go until I caught it again. In that moment when you thought it was being decided for you . . . your heart knew who you hoped it would be, didn't it?"

My heart started to race, and my voice trembled. "Y-yes."

"Then go tell him."

I raced to the car and put it in drive. I was really doing this. I didn't know how it would work out, but I knew I had to take a leap now or I would never be happy. All the way there I tried to calm my nerves. I was going to be choked by my own emotion before I could tell him how I felt. How I'd felt from the first time we'd met.

I threw the car to a stop, ran into the kitchen and into Gia's arms. "I love you. It's always been you. I'm sorry it took me so long."

Gia's lips met mine with all the passion we hadn't acted on for the last six months. His arms tightened around me and his hands ran through my hair and pulled my head closer. I could feel his heart beating in my own skin. Nothing else mattered. I was finally home.

"Ah-hem. And who is this?"

I was startled by hearing a woman's voice in the kitchen and followed it to the entry to the bar. Henry was holding the hand of a gorgeous blonde. She looked like she had stepped through the pages of a Victoria's Secret catalog.

Henry looked up at the goddess. "That's Poppy."

Gia's arms tensed. "Bella, do you trust me?"

The smoke of confusion started swirling around me. "Is this another sister?"

Gia tipped my chin up to look into his eyes. "Just remember I love you, with all my heart."

The woman practically purred. "A sister? No, honey. I'm Alexandra, Gia's wife."

Recipes

Paleo Blueberry Scones

Makes 6–8 scones

Ingredients

2½ cups blanched almond meal
1 cup tapioca starch
¼ cup coconut flour
½ cup coconut sugar
1 teaspoon baking powder
½ teaspoon pink salt
½ cup coconut cream (the solid top half of canned coconut milk)
¼ cup coconut oil (melted)
2 large eggs, room temperature
2 teaspoons vanilla extract
1½ cups blueberries
Cut sanding sugar (not Paleo but pretty)

Directions

Preheat oven to 350 degrees. Line a sheet pan with parchment.

In a medium bowl, combine almond meal, tapioca starch, coconut flour, coconut sugar, baking powder, and pink salt.

In a small bowl, whisk together coconut cream, coconut oil, eggs, and vanilla extract. Add to the dry ingredients and combine to make a workable dough, like biscuits. Fold the blueberries into the dough.

Form dough into a ball on the lined pan, then pat down to about one inch thick to make a disk. Sprinkle with sanding sugar if you want them sparkly and crunchy. Cut into 6–8 wedges and wiggle the pieces apart. Bake for 18–22 minutes, until golden. Let cool on the pan until ready to handle.

Gluten-Free Lemon Curd Muffins

Makes 12 muffins

Ingredients

2½ cups gluten-free flour
1½ teaspoons baking powder
½ teaspoon baking soda
1 teaspoon pink salt
¾ cup sugar
Zest of 2 large lemons
¼ cup juice from the 2 lemons you zested
1 cup sour cream
½ cup butter, melted
2 large eggs
1 teaspoon vanilla extract
1 jar lemon curd

Directions

Preheat oven to 375 degrees and grease a 12-cup muffin tin or line with cupcake papers.

Place the gluten-free flour, baking powder, baking soda, and salt in a large bowl and whisk until combined.

Add sugar, lemon zest, lemon juice, sour cream, butter, eggs, and vanilla to a mixing bowl and beat until fluffy.

Add the dry ingredients into the mixing bowl and mix on low just until combined. Be sure not to overmix your batter or you'll have rubbery muffins. The batter will be slightly stiff.

Fill each muffin cup halfway with the batter. Make a little well in the center with a spoon. Add 1 tablespoon of lemon curd into each muffin well hole. Top with the remaining batter to cover the lemon curd. Smooth out the tops if you want rounded muffins out of the oven. Mine didn't change shape at all as they baked.

Bake 15–20 minutes until lightly golden brown and a toothpick inserted in the center comes out clean.

Leave to cool in the pan for at least 10 minutes. I brushed the tops of the warm muffins with a pastry brush dipped in the remaining lemon curd, but that's optional.

Gluten-Free Strawberry Tiramisu with Sweet Red Wine

Makes 8–10 servings

Make at least 12 hours before serving.

Use a 13 x 9 x 2-inch glass baking dish, or thereabouts.

The wine I used was a sparkling sweet red with notes of strawberry, blackberry, and rosé. You could substitute with sparkling grape juice, but I'd use a low-sugar strawberry preserve in that case.

Ingredients

1½ pounds strawberries
1¼ cups strawberry jam
½ cup sweet red wine
¼ cup orange juice
16 ounces mascarpone cheese, room temperature
¼ cup sweet red wine
1½ cups chilled whipping cream
⅓ cup sugar
2 tablespoons sweet red wine
1 tablespoon vanilla extract
2 packs gluten-free ladyfingers—about 30

Directions

Rinse, hull, and slice strawberries.

Combine the jam, ½ cup wine, and ¼ cup orange juice. Whisk together.

In a separate bowl, combine the mascarpone cheese and ¼ cup wine. Mix together until smooth.

In your mixing bowl, combine the whipping cream, sugar, the remaining 2 tablespoons wine, and vanilla extract. Whip on high until soft peaks form.

You're going to layer your tiramisu like you're making a lasagna. Start with enough of the preserves mixture to cover the bottom of the baking dish. Cover with 1 layer of the ladyfingers. Spoon about half of the preserve mixture over the ladyfinger layer. Cover each ladyfinger, but you don't have to drown them. You need to reserve half the mixture for the next layer. On top of that, spread about half of the whipped cream/mascarpone mixture. Add a layer with about half of the strawberries. Now repeat the first three layers.

Ladyfingers . . . preserves . . . whipped cream. Don't add the rest of the strawberries just yet. Put them in a bowl and cover with plastic until it's time to serve. Cover your tiramisu with plastic and refrigerate at least 12 hours or overnight.

Just before serving, top with the rest of the strawberries. If you want to toss those strawberries in a ¼ cup of additional sweet red wine at the last minute, I won't stop you.

Gluten-Free Moscato Cheesecake Shooters with Drunken Blackberries

Inspired by Cooper's Hawk Restaurant's Ice Wine Cheesecake

I used a Moscato that had notes of white grape, nectarine, orange blossom, and honeysuckle.

Ingredients

For the crust

2 cups gluten-free vanilla crème sandwich cookies
3 ounces melted butter

For the topping

2 cups fresh blackberries
2 tablespoons sugar
2 tablespoons Moscato

For the filling

¼ cup Moscato—warm
1 packet (5 grams) unflavored gelatin powder
3 8-ounce packages cream cheese
1 cup orange blossom honey
½ cup Moscato
Pinch salt
½ cup melted white chocolate
½ cup heavy whipping cream

You will also need small clear cups—whether you use real glass or plastic doesn't matter, but make sure they are clear so you can see the layers.

Directions

Preheat oven to 350 degrees. Crush gluten-free cookies in food processor. Mix in melted butter. Spread on a cookie sheet and bake for 8 minutes. Set these aside to cool.

Toss blackberries in sugar and Moscato. Cover and place in refrigerator for several hours or overnight until you are ready to serve the shooters.

Warm $\frac{1}{4}$ cup of Moscato—don't boil it. Sprinkle on the gelatin and lightly mix it. Sit it aside and let it bloom. Heat the gelatin in the microwave for 20–30 seconds or until its dissolved and clear. Set it aside and let it cool to room temperature—but not so much that it gels.

Place cream cheese in the bowl of your stand mixer, or use a hand mixer, and beat it on medium to fluff it up. Now add your honey, $\frac{1}{2}$ cup Moscato, and pinch of salt. Beat until light and fluffy. Add in your gelatin wine mixture and beat until smooth.

Melt your white chocolate either in the microwave or in a bowl over a saucepan of simmering water. Add your melted white chocolate to the cheese mixture. Set this aside.

In a deep bowl, beat $\frac{1}{2}$ cup of heavy cream on high until stiff peaks form. When your cheesecake mixture is cool, fold in your whipped cream.

Assembly

Put 1–2 tablespoons cookie crumbs in the bottom of your glasses. Just enough to cover the bottom. Fill glasses with cooled—but not set—cheesecake. Chill for at least 3 hours. Top with drunken blackberries before serving.

Gluten-Free Sangria Cupcakes

Makes 12 cupcakes

Ingredients

For the sangria fruits

½ cup chopped strawberries
½ cup chopped blackberries
2 tablespoons sugar
½ cup sangria for macerating
Segments from the orange you zested

For the sangria syrup

1 cup sangria
½ cup sugar

For the cupcakes

1½ cups gluten-free flour
1 teaspoon baking powder
½ teaspoon baking soda
¼ teaspoon salt
¾ cup sugar
2 eggs
½ cup butter, melted
1 teaspoon vanilla
½ cup full-fat Greek yogurt
1 orange, zested
¼ cup sangria

For the sangria buttercream

> 2 sticks of butter, softened
> 1 cup palm or vegetable shortening
> 4½–5 cups powdered sugar
> ½ cup sangria syrup
> 1 orange, lemon, or lime used for garnish

Directions

For the sangria fruits—this step can be done first or a day ahead

Chop strawberries and blackberries. Place in a Mason jar or nonreactive bowl. Add 2 tablespoons sugar and ½ cup sangria. Set aside. Overnight would be even better because it would really infuse the fruits with sangria flavor. After you zest your orange, cut off the rind and the pith and cut into segments. Then chop the segments into 2 or 3 pieces. Add to the sangria fruits.

For the sangria syrup

Put 1 cup sangria and ½ cup sugar in a saucepan over medium heat. Once the mixture comes to a boil, turn the heat down and let simmer on low for 30 minutes. Set aside to cool.

For the cupcakes

Preheat the oven to 350 degrees.
In a small bowl combine the gluten-free flour, baking powder, baking soda, and salt. Set aside.
In a mixing bowl combine the sugar, eggs, melted but-

ter, vanilla, Greek yogurt, and orange zest. Mix until well combined.

Slowly add half of the dry ingredients to the wet, stirring to combine. Then add the remaining ¼ cup sangria to the bowl. Mix just to combine. Add the remaining dry ingredients and combine well, but don't overmix. You don't want the cupcakes to be rubbery. Add the sangria fruits with the liquid into the batter and fold together.

Divide batter into cupcake tin either greased or lined with cupcake liners. Fill cups to ⅔ full.

Bake for 15–20 minutes until lightly browned and a toothpick inserted in the center comes out clean.

When cool, brush the tops with the reduced sangria syrup. Let dry. Then frost with sangria buttercream and top with an orange, lime, or lemon wedge.

For the sangria buttercream

In a mixing bowl, combine the room temperature butter and shortening; beat using an electric mixer for 2 minutes, until light and fluffy. Add ½ cup sangria syrup. Mix well.

Begin to add in the powdered sugar, about 1 cup at a time. Mix on low until combined. Beat on high for a few seconds to fluff the frosting up after every cup. Add enough powdered sugar to make a light and fluffy frosting. If the frosting won't hold its shape it's too runny.

Frost cupcakes or fill a piping bag with the tip of your choice and pipe frosting according to your style preference. I used a star tip and piped the frosting in a spiral. Top each cupcake with a fruit wedge or a curl from the rind.

Gluten-Free Dark Chocolate Cupcakes with Red Wine Poached Pears

The wine I used was a sweet red wine from Cooper's Hawk Winery called Romance Red. It has strong notes of Concord grape with light notes of maraschino cherry. You could always substitute Port or, for a nonalcoholic version, a Concord grape juice.

For the pears

8 ripe but firm Bosc pears
2 cups sweet red wine
½ cup sugar

For the cake

7 ounces dark chocolate, chopped
½ cup (1 stick) butter cut into tablespoons
2 cups gluten-free flour
2¼ teaspoons baking powder
1½ teaspoons baking soda
½ teaspoon kosher salt
1 cup almond meal
¾ cup cocoa powder
¾ cup (1½ sticks) butter, softened
1⅓ cups sugar
3 large eggs
½ cup poaching wine leftover from poaching the
   pears or ½ cup red wine still in the bottle if you
   didn't drink it yet. You probably should have read
   down to here first.

Powdered sugar for dusting (optional)

Directions

To poach the pears

Peel pears. Cut in half. Using a teaspoon, scoop out the core and seeds; discard. Chop pears into dice-sized pieces. Combine pears, 2 cups of wine, and ½ cup sugar in a heavy pot. Bring to a boil, then reduce heat and simmer, stirring occasionally, 20 minutes. Drain pears in a colander over a bowl to reserve the liquid.

To melt the chocolate

Either in a microwave or in a bowl over a double boiler, melt the 7 ounces chocolate with ½ cup butter cut into tablespoons. Stir until smooth. Set aside.

To make the cake

Preheat oven to 350 degrees. Grease 2 cupcake pans or line with cupcake papers.

Combine gluten-free flour, baking powder, baking soda, salt, almond meal, and cocoa powder in a bowl. Whisk together and set aside.

Measure out 1½ cups of poached pears. Set aside. In a food processor (or a blender) add the rest of the poached pears and pulse until smooth like applesauce (pear-sauce?).

In a mixing bowl, beat ¾ cup butter and 1¼ cups sugar until light and fluffy. Add eggs one at a time. Now add in the melted chocolate.

Be sure to scrape the sides of the mixing bowl between additions to be sure everything is being incorporated evenly.

Add ½ the dry ingredients to the butter and chocolate mixture and mix until combined.

Then add the pureed pears to the bowl and mix until combined.

Add the rest of the dry ingredients to the bowl and mix until combined. Now add ½ cup of the reserved poaching liquid. (If for some reason you don't have ½ cup reserved you'll want to add new wine to the batter. If you already drank that wine we'll just do without.)

Final step

Fold in the 1½ cups poached pears to the chocolate batter. These are the best part of the cupcake.

Scoop batter into cupcake wells ⅔ full. Bake 18–20 minutes or until the top springs back and a toothpick comes out of the center clean. You want to make sure to bake these long enough because there is a lot of moisture from the pears. You also need to let them cool entirely before frosting and serving them. I tried to eat one that was still warm and it completely fell apart. I mean, I ate it anyway, but still.

Dust with powdered sugar to finish—or don't. These are great as muffins and the poached pear bits make them very special.

Gluten-Free Sparkling Raspberry Cake Balls

The wine I used was a Cooper's Hawk sparkling raspberry dessert wine that had notes of raspberry candy and vanilla.

Ingredients

For the cake

1 cup gluten-free flour
1 teaspoon baking powder
1 stick butter, softened
⅔ cup sugar
1 egg
1 teaspoon vanilla extract
½ cup sparkling raspberry wine

For the frosting

1 stick butter
½ cup palm or vegetable shortening
¼ cup raspberry jam, stirred smooth
3–4 cups gluten-free powdered sugar
2 tablespoons sparkling raspberry wine

For the white chocolate shells

24 ounces white chocolate melting wafers or chocolate chips
2 tablespoons vegetable oil

Directions

To make the cake

Preheat the oven to 350 degrees. Either grease or line an 8 x 9-inch cake pan with parchment paper.

Combine the gluten-free flour and baking powder in a medium bowl. Whisk to combine. Set aside.

Combine butter and sugar in a mixing bowl and beat on medium speed until light and fluffy. Scrape down the sides of the bowl. Add the egg and vanilla and beat until well combined.

Add about half of the flour mixture to the batter and beat on medium speed until incorporated.

Add half the wine and beat on medium speed until incorporated.

Add remaining flour and beat until smooth.

Finish with the remaining wine. Beat until smooth.

Spread batter evenly into the prepared cake pan. Place in the center of the oven and bake for 18–20 minutes or until lightly browned and a toothpick comes out of the center clean. Remove cake from oven to cool completely. Make the frosting.

To make the sparkling raspberry buttercream

Combine butter and shortening and mix until smooth. Add the raspberry jam and mix until combined. Add half of the powdered sugar and mix on low until smooth. Add remaining powdered sugar a little at a time and beat until fluffy. You may not need all the sugar to get the right consistency. Slowly add the wine. When well combined, add more powdered sugar as needed to get to the right consistency. You want this to be about the consistency of canned frosting. Don't let it be too runny or the cake balls won't hold their shape.

To assemble the cake balls

Crumble the cake into a large bowl with your hands. When the frosting is ready, add the cake crumbs to the mixer bowl with a whisk attachment and beat on low until well combined. Cover and place the bowl in the refrigerator for at least 2 hours or overnight.

Line a baking tray with parchment or wax paper. Form small round balls by using a cookie scoop or rolling a rounded tablespoon's worth of mixture between your palms. Place the balls on the prepared wax paper–lined baking sheet. When balls are complete, place the baking tray in the refrigerator for 1 to 2 hours.

Melt the white chocolate in a microwave-safe bowl in the microwave on 30-second intervals, stirring between each, until smooth. Stir in the vegetable oil.

Remove the balls from the freezer. Drop balls one at a time into the melted chocolate; use a fork to scoop them out, wiping any excess chocolate on the rim of the bowl before transferring back to the wax lined–baking sheet. Let them harden completely.

Acknowledgments

A special thank-you goes to Harry A. Milman, Ph.D., and John Griffin, lab director and forensic scientist, for their assistance in developing the lethal cocktail that would be used as the murder weapon in *Wine Tastings Are Murder*.

Also, thank you for not reporting me to the authorities as a suspected murderer. See, it really was for a book.

Connect with

Visit us online at
KensingtonBooks.com
to read more from your favorite authors, see books
by series, view reading group guides, and more.

Join us on social media

for sneak peeks, chances to win books and prize packs,
and to share your thoughts with other readers.

facebook.com/kensingtonpublishing
twitter.com/kensingtonbooks

Tell us what you think!

To share your thoughts, submit a review,
or sign up for our eNewsletters, please visit:
KensingtonBooks.com/TellUs.